The novels of
Kate Quinn are...

"ADDICTIVE... A riveting
plunge into an ancient world that is both
utterly foreign and strikingly familiar."
—C. W. Gortner, author of *The Queen's Vow*

"EPIC... Engrossing and dramatic relationships... drive this
entertaining story."—*Publishers Weekly* (starred review)

"GRIPPING... So vivid it burns itself into your mind's
eye and stays with you long after you turn the final page."
—Diana Gabaldon, #1 *New York Times*
bestselling author of the Outlander series

"SHEER ENTERTAINMENT,
drama, and page-turning storytelling...
Well worth reading."
—*Library Journal*

PRAISE FOR

Empress of the Seven Hills

"Power and betrayal were never so addictive than in this gorgeously wrought tale of star-crossed lovers caught in the turbulent currents of Imperial Rome. Kate Quinn deftly contrasts the awesome splendor of torch-lit banquets with the thunder of the battlefield. *Empress of the Seven Hills* is a riveting plunge into an ancient world that is both utterly foreign and strikingly familiar—where you can feel the silken caress of an empress and the cold steel of a blade at your back."

—C. W. Gortner, author of *The Queen's Vow*

"[An] epic, sexy romp—the long-awaited sequel to *Daughters of Rome* . . . Readers will delight in the depictions of historical figures like Hadrian and Trajan, as well as the engrossing and dramatic relationships that drive this entertaining story." —*Publishers Weekly* (starred review)

"Kate Quinn outdoes herself with a story so compelling that the only complaint readers will have is that it ends. From the moment Vix and Sabina appear on the page, readers are taken on an epic adventure through Emperor Trajan's Rome. No other author brings the ancient world alive like Quinn—if there's one book you read this year, let it be this one!"

—Michelle Moran, national bestselling author of *The Second Empress*

"Quinn handles Imperial Rome with panache." —*Kirkus Reviews*

continued . . .

The
LION
and the ROSE

A NOVEL OF THE BORGIAS

Kate Quinn

BERKLEY BOOKS, NEW YORK

THE BERKLEY PUBLISHING GROUP
Published by the Penguin Group
Penguin Group (USA) LLC
375 Hudson Street, New York, New York 10014, USA

USA • Canada • UK • Ireland • Australia • New Zealand • India • South Africa • China

penguin.com

A Penguin Random House Company

This book is an original publication of The Berkley Publishing Group.

Copyright © 2014 by Kate Quinn.
Excerpt from *Lady of the Eternal City* copyright © 2014 by Kate Quinn.
"Readers Guide" copyright © 2014 by Penguin Group (USA) LLC.

Berkley trade paperback ISBN: 978-0-425-26876-6

Library of Congress Cataloging-in-Publication Data

Quinn, Kate.
The Lion and the Rose / Kate Quinn.—Berkley trade paperback edition.
p. cm.—(A novel of the Borgias)
ISBN 978-0-425-26876-6 (pbk.)
1. Borgia family—Fiction.   2. Rome (Italy)—History—1420–1798—Fiction.   3. Nobility—Papal
states—Fiction.   4. Political fiction.   I. Title.
PS3617.U578Q56 2014
813'.6—dc23
2013032104

PUBLISHING HISTORY
Berkley trade paperback edition / January 2014

PRINTED IN THE UNITED STATES OF AMERICA

10 9 8 7 6 5 4 3 2 1

Cover design by Danielle Abbiate.
Interior text design by Tiffany Estreicher.

For another remarkable grandmother
Virginia Quinn
reader, critic, and cheerleader extraordinaire

Special acknowledgments to my wonderful team at Berkley Books for being so willing to think outside the box in publishing Giulia Farnese's ever-sprawling story. Further acknowledgments, thanks, and hugs to all my hardworking beta readers: Stephanie Dray, Eliza Knight, Christi Barth, and Kristen Stappenbeck-Baker, some of the smartest and most insightful readers ever to burn the midnight oil, reading this book's rough draft pages and helping me make them better.

PROLOGUE

December 1494

Leonello

"This is all terribly anticlimactic," I complained to my mistress. "Captured by enemy forces, and where are the dungeons? The torturers? The chains? At the very least, you should have been sold into the harem of a Moorish merchant prince. That would be a story worth telling." I hurt too badly to laugh at my own joke, so I gave a shallow sigh instead. "There is no literary scope in spending a few nights drinking French wine with French generals, listening to French compliments, then being escorted back to Rome in luxury."

"I think it was a trifle more harrowing than that." Giulia Farnese looked across the carriage at the bandages wrapping my chest and shoulder and hip, the splints a French surgeon had strapped to my broken fingers, the black bruises that covered nearly every visible inch of my flesh like splotches of pitch. "How is the pain, Leonello? And don't just grit your teeth at me stoically, please."

"Why, it's a very splendid pain," I said airily. "We've gotten to know each other very well, really—perhaps I shall give it a name and keep it for a pet when this is all over." I had been beaten to a pulp by French pike-men, for daring to defend my mistress when French scouts descended like wolves on her traveling party as she made her way toward the Holy City. More precisely, I'd been beaten to a pulp because I'd killed three of those French pike-men and wounded two more before they brought me down, and such men do not like to be humiliated by a man like me.

I am a dwarf, you see. The kind you see in motley at fairs, juggling wooden balls, only I do not juggle and never have. I have the short bowed legs and the oversized head and the broad torso of my kind, but I also have uncommon skill at throwing knives. I can core a man's throat like an apple at ten paces, and it was for that skill I was hired as bodyguard to Giulia Farnese, the Pope's golden mistress. If she'd had a strapping youth for a guard, the French would have killed him at once—enemies fasten first on strapping youths when they look for those who might prove a threat. No one bothers to notice the dwarf. Not until I kill them, and then it's too late.

Though in the end, I suppose it didn't matter that I'd sprung to her defense. Giulia Farnese hadn't escaped the French because of my knives. She was going home because His Holiness the Borgia Pope had paid three thousand *scudi* for her release. The purse had arrived last night, delivered by a messenger who had flogged his horse at a gallop every stride from the Vatican. Just two days in captivity and now we were rumbling back to Rome, a carriage and two wagons escorted through the barren winter countryside by four hundred suddenly gallant French soldiers.

"Are you sure you're comfortable?" Madonna Giulia was studying me, her dark eyes uncommonly serious. She was the most beautiful woman in all Italy, or so they said: Giulia la Bella, the Venus of the Vatican, the Bride of Christ (when people were feeling rude). Reams of bad poetry had been written to her white breasts, her rose of a mouth, her famous golden hair that cascaded all the way to her little feet when loosed. Men from the Holy Father on down trembled at the sight of her—but I had dogged her footsteps day and night for the past two years; I had seen her squint-eyed with sleep and sneezing from sickness; whimpering in childbirth and cream-faced under her cosmetic face masks of bean flour and egg white, and I rarely noticed her beauty anymore.

"We should have delayed longer, Leonello," she was fretting. "You aren't fit to travel yet, no matter what the surgeon said!"

"Two days of that swill the French call food was quite bad enough, Madonna Giulia. More would have killed me." It took every ounce of concentration I had to speak coherently around the sluggish, pain-filled exhaustion. My tongue might as well have been made of stone.

"Was it really only two days?" Giulia stroked her daughter's golden head where it slumbered against her shoulder. Little Laura wasn't two years old yet, but even she had felt the tension of the past few days, clinging to her mother like a limpet. "It felt like a year."

"Thanks be to the Virgin, I spent most of it unconscious." Or perhaps it was Santo Giuliano the Hospitaller I should thank in my prayers; he had a soft spot in his heart for killers like me. I've killed more than Frenchmen in my day, and for darker reasons than the defense of the Pope's mistress.

The carriage felt stuffy, and I reached out my splinted fingers to nudge open the shuttered window. A wave of pain flashed through my hand, and I had to bite down savagely on the inside of my cheek. French boots had stamped on that hand, trying to get my knife away—every finger was broken, and the littlest finger gone altogether. The French surgeon had made a clean, cauterized stump of the mangled thing at the same time he had splinted my other fingers, probed and cleaned my wounds, drained blood and excised bone splinters, purged and bandaged and did whatever else surgeons did to keep their victims alive. It must have worked, whatever he did while I was unconscious, because I was no longer bleeding from every orifice. Most of my hurts had faded into a dull roar of pain limping along below the surface—all except the hand. It was the chest wound that nearly killed me, but somehow it was my mangled hand that hurt the worst, a bright white-hot flash of agony every time I moved.

It doesn't matter, I reminded myself whenever I looked at my remaining splinted fingers. *You don't need a little finger to throw your knives.* My knives had been returned to me—with elaborate French compliments, of course, for my bravery. May God rot them all.

My mistress caught the flash of pain across my face. Of course she did—she was a whore, after all, even if she did have only the one illustrious patron, and she could read men as easily as I read the pages of my favorite books. "Your hand—"

"Leave your fussing, *madonna*," I said irritably, pushing back the blackness that threatened to swamp my vision. "I assure you, I haven't traveled in such comfort in all my life. I feel like a sultan." Madonna Giulia had her carriage back; the French general had tactfully returned the stolen horses and even added a wicker-bound flask of his own wine should La Bella find herself thirsty on the day's ride to Rome. My mistress had displaced her sister and mother-in-law to ride with her maidservants, and insisted I take the whole second seat for myself so I could make the journey lying down in comfort. But my pride demanded that I sit upright, and La Bella scolded me for being a stiff-necked fool, and pride and pain and scolding together had me half-lying and half-sitting, and altogether half-comfortable. It was still better than being crammed into the wagons with all the rest of the servants, and for that I had to thank her.

"I wasn't going to have you bumping all the way back to Rome in that jolting wagon," she returned. "Not after what you did for me."

"It doesn't matter." I drank in the cold air from the open window, the wind coming in to slap at my unshaven cheeks. The dry brown hills were empty of passersby—one look at the mass of swaggering soldiers and the French lilies on their rippling flags, and every villager within eye or earshot went to ground. We might as well have been riding through a land of ghosts. "Though it was quite an impressive tantrum you pitched this morning until they moved me," I conceded. "All that shrieking and stamping of feet."

"Yes, I've gotten very good at tantrums, haven't I? It may only have been two days, but I think the French are quite glad to see the back of me." My mistress had a temper sweet as honey and a nature as easy-flowing as a running stream; in ordinary days her servants doted on her and took shameless advantage of her—but for the French, she played an entirely different role. She had put on a splendid performance as the Pope's pampered mistress: throwing fits, hurling insults, and exploding into tears at the slightest provocation. She looked very grand in her sumptuous traveling furs, and when she moved to wrap Laura more soundly in her own cloak, I saw the gleam of a huge pearl at her throat.

I tilted my head. "They let you keep that?"

"Yes." Madonna Giulia looked down at the enormous teardrop pearl that had been her Borgia Pope's first gift. "I spread a good many of my other jewels among the French officers—goodwill gifts, you know. But I did keep my pearl." She patted it like a pet.

I kept my voice neutral. "What else did you have to give the French, besides your jewels?"

She wrinkled her nose, wry. "Why, surely you know they were all perfect gentlemen. So I intend to tell everyone, should I be asked."

"Including the Holy Father?"

She looked out the window. "Especially the Holy Father."

"I don't remember much," I said, and fumbled the words. I hate fumbling. "That first night. You went to dine with General d'Allegre . . ." And returned very late, her gown creased, two spots of color burning high in her cheeks, with a surgeon in her wake to tend my wounds, and food and blankets and lamps for her cold and shivering servants. "They refused to send me a surgeon until then. The French general, did he—"

She looked at me calmly. "He was a perfect gentleman."

The creak of wheels and shuffle of marching feet came to me through the window, and the ever-present French smell of onions and stale sweat. I suddenly couldn't bear the stench and struggled to close the shutter again. Giulia reached over to latch it for me. "Leave it!" I snapped. "I may be nine-fingered, *madonna*, but do you think I am too feeble to manage a bolt?"

She sat back, lashes veiling her eyes as she stroked Laura's head again, and I bit my lip. I had a viper's tongue that liked nothing better than to sting people when it was in the mood, and my mistress was easy prey for my temper, having none of her own. I could say it was the pain in my hand and my bandaged chest that made me sharp, but in truth I was always sharp. In the old days when I made a precarious living in the Borgo district fleecing sailors out of their money over card games, I'd thought it was poverty made me ill-humored. Surely steady money and a safe place in the world would make my tongue lose its edge. But for over two years now, I'd had steady money and as secure a place as could be wished as Giulia Farnese's bodyguard; I had good food to eat and all the fine books in the world to read while I hung about waiting as my mistress went to confession or got her dresses fitted—and none of it made any difference. Kindness, apparently, had been left out of my makeup along with that extra foot of height that would have put my mistress's eyes level with my throat instead of my eyes level with her collarbone.

"Do excuse my rudeness, *madonna*," I said, my voice still sharp. *Dio*, but I wanted a drink.

Giulia shifted her sleeping daughter aside on the cushioned bench, uncorking the wicker-bound flask of wine. She poured me a cup, not spilling a drop in the jolting carriage, and I sipped.

"Thank you," I said, and managed to mean it this time.

She smiled, deftly adjusting the cushions under my bandaged side. "I won't forget it, Leonello," she said. "That you defended me, and Laura. I'm so sorry you were hurt—"

"I'd take another broken rib right now if you'd just cease thanking me," I complained. I'd only done what I was paid for, after all, so I didn't see the need for all this fussing and fawning and gratitude. I'd done my job, and there was an end to it. "I want more wine, dammit."

"Done." She leaned forward with the flask. "And I'll stop thanking you. But I won't forget."

We passed the rest of the journey in companionable silence.

Night had fallen by the time we reached the gates of Rome. Torches waited, papal guards in impassive ranks mixed with Borgia guards in their colors of mulberry and yellow; churchmen on horseback in a throng behind. The procession halted, and I saw a cloaked horseman ride toward the French captain with one hand raised.

"Cesare." Giulia peered out the carriage window, making a face at the sight of Cardinal Borgia, her Pope's saturnine eldest son. "No doubt he'll hold me in utter contempt for getting myself captured."

"I've rather missed him," I said. "He makes life interesting. I wonder if he's killed anyone lately."

"I can never tell if you're joking or not, Leonello."

"It's generally a safe assumption." I had my suspicions about Cesare Borgia and the things he did for his dark amusement—but such things were not even to be whispered of.

Torchlight flickered over the lean planes of the young Cardinal's face as he and the French captain traded a series of flowery courtesies. Bows were exchanged, compliments, protestations of gratitude, and then a bull-like figure shoved through the lines of papal guards toward the French. "Out of my way, you whoresons," snarled His Holiness Pope Alexander VI, born Rodrigo Borgia of Spain. He raised a fist in warning to a French sergeant who did not move fast enough, and my mistress barely had the chance to ease little Laura off her lap and rise from her seat before her papal lover wrenched the carriage door open.

"Giulia," he said thickly, and swung her down before her feet could even touch the steps. His broad arms wrapped her tight, and I saw his lips move in what might be a genuine prayer of thanks, this most wordly of pontiffs. The French looked amused and the papal guards were grinning by the time the Pope finally set his mistress of the past two years on her feet. He was tall, swarthy, heavy-shouldered; still a bull of a man at sixty-three. A fitting match for his family emblem of the Borgia bull. "You're unharmed?" he demanded, cupping her face in his big hands.

"Quite unharmed, Your Holiness." La Bella's tired face creased in a smile. "Overjoyed to see my Pope again."

He lifted her up and kissed her, and the French captain covered his grin with his hand. I saw that the Holy Father had discarded his papal robes for a black velvet cloak trimmed with gold, grandly spurred Valencian boots, a sword and dagger at his belt, and a cap with a dashing feather. Trying to look the cavalier for a mistress who had spent the past two days being complimented by young French gallants? What fools men make of themselves for beautiful women. Even popes.

More courtesies between Cesare Borgia and the French captain, as the Pope ignored them all and continued kissing Giulia, and at last the thing was done and the French escort retreated. Cesare Borgia gave a faint shake of his head, sauntering past his father, and leaned his auburn head idly through the carriage window.

"Little lion man," he greeted me, as he always did. His lean handsome face was cut sharply across by shadows. "The French didn't kill you?"

I gestured at my bandages. "They tried, Your Eminence."

"Never count on the French to do anything right." Cesare Borgia was no bull like his father; he had all the languid grace of a serpent as he lounged against the carriage. "How many did you kill, during this adventure?"

"Three."

"And wounded?"

"The wounded don't count." I studied him. "How many did *you* kill, during my adventure?"

"What, how many Frenchmen?"

"How many anything."

"What a thing to be curious about." He had dark eyes, quite without bottom, and they never held anything warmer than amusement. They were amused now, looking through the shadows at me. "My man Michelotto told me you were asking questions."

"Did he, now." I tilted my head at Michelotto, Cesare Borgia's stone-faced shadow—a fellow with no expression whatsoever whose stare could make a saint twitch. "It's no crime to ask questions, surely."

"That depends who you ask the questions about." The young Cardinal smiled. I smiled. We'd been playing this game a long time, Cesare and I. It involved a woman, and how I thought she might have died, but I was hurting too badly tonight to indulge in any more games of cat and mouse.

Cesare Borgia strolled away, raising a hand in reply to the French captain who had trotted off with a final languid wave. The Pope sent a baleful look after the French party, muttering, "I'll see them all in graves!" But Giulia Farnese smiled and tugged the Holy Father up into the carriage, and with a lurch it swung into motion again and rolled through the gates of Rome. I gave His Holiness the best bow I could manage from my litter, but he was kissing Giulia again and I looked out the window. It was too dark to see more than the shadows of buildings and passersby, the occasional lantern or torch or spill of light from an open door, so I took in a deep lungful of night air instead, banishing both Cesare's games and the twist of agony from my hand. I smelled night soil and mud and smoke; river rot and dead cats and blood. It smelled like home.

"You'll stay with me at the papal apartments tonight," the Pope decided, finally sparing a kiss for Laura's sleeping head before wrapping Giulia more firmly within the circle of his arms and his black velvet cloak. "Damn the cardinals if they complain. You can see the progress Pinturicchio has made on the frescoes—"

"After I see all my people safely home and settled," Giulia interrupted him. "I want to put Laura to bed, and I intend to see that Leonello is made comfortable. Then I'll come along to the papal apartments."

The Holy Father waved a dismissive hand. "Let the servants tend to them."

"I will tend to them, Your Holiness. They are my responsibility."

I saw the Pope's startled glance as he looked at his mistress. She'd never contradicted him in anything before, at least in my hearing. I turned my face away to cover a smile as she gazed back at the Holy Father with calm assurance. This was the woman who had faced down French pike-men unflinching. Not the starry-eyed, easygoing little beauty he had plucked from her husband and taken for his own.

I wondered if His Holiness realized just what a change there had been.

"I'll leave you at the Palazzo Santa Maria, then," the Pope finally conceded in his sonorous Spanish-accented bass. "As long as you come along to the papal apartments afterward! I want you with me tonight, minx—I've not seen you for six months, with all your journeying." Before her capture by the French, my mistress had left her papal lover for a long jaunt to the countryside, first helping to settle his daughter Lucrezia in her new marital home in Pesaro, and then returning to the Farnese family seat in Capodimonte for another extended visit. "Six months," the Holy Father grumbled, wrapping her tighter. "Six *weeks* is too long!"

"You wouldn't have me back at all if not for Leonello." Giulia turned her smile on me, still stretched out in my seat opposite. "You've heard how he defended me?"

The Pope's fierce dark eyes found me through the carriage's shadows. "You'll be tended by Our own physician, little man—you'll want for nothing. You'll be well rewarded, We promise in the name of God."

I gave the best half bow I could manage lying down. "Your Holiness."

He had already forgotten me, looking back to Giulia. "Now that We have you back and safe, We deal with the French. If they so much as laid a finger on you—"

"They were all perfect gentlemen," Giulia said smoothly. "Though I must admit I found those cannons of theirs rather fearsome."

"They may have cannons, but their king is a fool."

Perhaps, I thought, but a fool with a claim to the kingdom of Naples in the south. When old King Ferrente died, King Charles of France had declared he would press his claim, and he'd come to do so with an army of near twenty-five thousand. Twenty-five thousand French pike-men would be enough to make any man nervous if he faced them, but the Pope looked merely contemptuous. "Little Charles wants Naples?" he snorted. "Let him come through Rome first, and I'll make him beg for it."

"Will you?" Giulia laced her pale fingers with his swarthy ones. "That I would like to see."

"Well, you won't, because I'm sending you to safety first, *mi perla*. One stint of captivity is enough!" He dropped a kiss on her forehead. "I'll let Charles think I mean to grant his claim of title to Naples—he'll make his troops behave themselves, if he thinks he'll get that out of me. I'll promise him this and that, and when he marches on Naples I'll let him strand himself there while his army gets sick and his supply lines fail."

"Will they start failing?"

"Cesare will make sure of it. I'll give him to the French for a good-faith hostage; he'll plant a few seeds of discord, then he'll escape. Meanwhile, I'll hook us an ally or two against the French. Milan must be feeling rather nervous by this time. Perhaps Venice too." The Pope did not give any more details of his plans before an audience, even an insignificant audience like me, but his chuckle was wicked as a stream of good sins as he wrapped Giulia more tightly in his arms. "Bah! Now I have you back, *mi perla*, I'm full of plans. And you"—giving her ear a fierce tweak—"had better be full of remorse for causing me all this worry! Next time I tell you to cut your visit to your family short and come home to me, maybe you'll listen!"

"Yes, Your Holiness," she said demurely.

The Pope cleared his throat, and I wondered if he had forgotten I was there. "It *was* only your family you went to visit, wasn't it?"

"I saw my husband." Giulia's voice was direct. "If that is what you mean."

Rodrigo Borgia's heavy hand tensed on his knee, fingers drumming. "And?"

A graceful shrug. "And nothing."

The Holy Father still looked anxious. The most powerful man in Christendom, a force of nature in ecclesiastical robes, and he still felt the prick of anxiety over Giulia's young husband. The absurdly named Orsino Orsini, blue-eyed and handsome and straight as a lance—but I had seen more spine in an oyster. He'd known from the beginning that his marriage was merely a polite fiction, a legality pasted over the private trade of financial patronage for use of his wife—but he'd taken one look at his innocent and beautiful bride when they traded their wedding vows and regretted the bargain. He'd pouted in the country for the loss of his wife ever since, not that it stopped him from accepting Rodrigo Borgia's patronage. The young Orsino had come to visit his wife in Capodimonte when she had come for a stay with her family; I'd wondered if he meant to woo her back from her papal lover, but he had lost his nerve. He'd barely mustered up enough courage to tell Giulia that he would be happy to take her back when the Pope was done with her, and that was not the kind of passionate declaration to light a fire in a woman's heart.

"Your Holiness." Giulia drew the Pope's chin toward her with a fingertip. "Orsino did not rescue me from the French. *You* did."

"And would have if they'd carried you to the ninth ring of hell." His hand stole under her furred cloak to her breast. "Come here, *mi perla . . .*" His private name for her. She nestled closer, lifting her face, and I looked out the carriage window and counted the rotations of the wheels. I'd never been more relieved when the horses finally halted at the Palazzo Santa Maria. I was surprised the passion igniting in the seat opposite me wasn't streaming out through the shutters like the pale plume of smoke that had announced Rodrigo Borgia's election as Pope.

"Leonello, let me fetch the guards to carry you down—" My mistress disentangled herself from the Holy Father, her mouth swollen from kissing, and began to fuss over me. I was tempted to bite her head off again, but there was no stopping her when she began to fuss, and anyway I was still too weak to walk under my own power. The wound at my shoulder had broken open, as I could feel even through the bandages, and my hand was throbbing as though some patient sharp-toothed beast were chewing it off. I closed my eyes and concentrated on the blackness behind my eyelids, blackness thick enough to swallow pain. Any pain, even the pain when my litter was awkwardly trundled out of the carriage and carried into the pretty little *palazzo* beside the Vatican where the Holy Father had installed his mistress in her papal seraglio.

"Madonna Giulia—" Another woman's voice sounded in my ears, brusque, accented with the crisp tang that belonged to Venice. Though it had been a long time since Carmelina Mangano had seen Venice, and I knew all the reasons why. No wonder she sounded hopeful as she asked, "Messer Leonello—is he dead?"

"No," I answered in place of my mistress, and opened my eyes. The girl with the Venetian voice hovered beside my litter as it was carried through the *palazzo* toward my little chamber. A girl of perhaps twenty-two in a plain wool gown with the sleeves rolled up, tall as many men and thin as a kitchen ladle, with a cloud of wiry black curls bundled at the base of a long neck. Tired-looking, because she too had been part of our captured party, and she must have made a dash from the wagon bearing the other servants to catch up with my litter. She was no beauty like Madonna Giulia, but she had a pair of eyes like black fire and she smelled like cloves and cinnamon, and she carried herself tall and proud as a queen. Maybe I stood only a hand-span over four feet, but I had a liking for tall women.

Not this one, though.

"I'm not dying," I said from my litter, and gave our household cook a grin because I knew it would frighten her. Good. It was her fault I was in this litter to begin with, and I had no mind to be forgiving. "In fact, I'm determined to make a full recovery. I know how that must disappoint you."

Her face darkened and she stamped off in the other direction. "Bring him a hot posset, Carmelina," Madonna Giulia called after her, and I closed my eyes again as the guardsmen brought my litter into my chamber and laid it down on my narrow bed. The pain in my hand no longer seemed quite so acute. Perhaps it had been no lie, what I told Carmelina. Perhaps I *would* make a full recovery.

Pray I don't, I thought at her. *Or I'll ruin your life.*

Carmelina

When I first came to Rome, I'd had nothing to my name but a tattered bundle of recipes and a mummified hand in a bag—and on that shaky foundation, I'd built myself a future. Cook to Madonna Giulia Farnese, feeding an entire *palazzo* that housed not just the Pope's mistress but the Pope himself when he came for intimate little suppers at La Bella's table. Well, to be fair it was my cousin Marco Santini who held the title of *maestro di cucina*, but Marco was a card-playing fool who would rather sweat over a *zara* board than an oven, and everyone in the household knew who really ran the kitchens. Me, Carmelina Mangano, the best cook in Rome even if I was a woman, and I'd *earned* that. I'd earned all of it, with nothing more than a little luck and the skill in my hands—and now here I was returning to Rome once again, and everything I'd built was about to crash on my head.

All because of one horrid, overobservant dwarf.

I had to stop twice and press myself against walls as the other servants in Madonna Giulia's traveling party streamed back to their old quarters in chattering packs. Some were laughing, some bragging of the dangers they'd seen; some were still white-faced and worn from those dangers, and others declared they meant to get drunk at once. I felt numb and cold all over. All I wanted was to crawl off to the tiny chamber that used to hold spare jars of olive oil and now held my pallet and little chest of clothes. But I wouldn't sleep, not yet. "Make him a posset," Madonna Giulia had told me, settling her odious little bodyguard in his own chamber. And whatever happened to me tomorrow, tonight I was still the cook, and the cook stayed awake until everyone in the household was fed.

"*Signorina?*" A boy's voice sounded behind me, and a hand touched my elbow. "You should sleep, *signorina*. I'll make Messer Leonello's posset for him. Make one for you too—"

"You're the one who's going to bed, Bartolomeo." I summoned all the briskness I had in me, which wasn't much after two nights in the middle of the French army, Santa Marta save me. "Off with you, now."

Bartolomeo looked dubious: fifteen years old, freckled and red-haired, long and lanky as a basting needle, with a near-miraculous nose for cooking. My favorite apprentice, not that I'd ever tell him that. "Begging your pardon, *signorina*, but you haven't slept since all this began, or eaten more than a squirrel either. I could make you a nice filling rice *zuppa* with some good *provatura* cheese—"

I scowled. Bartolomeo had been with me in this whole ordeal with the French, and really he'd comported himself very well—helped me parcel out the food we were given, heated up mugs of wine over a brazier to keep everyone warmed on the inside, and kept his voice cheerful and steady through it all, too. But he'd gotten used to seeing me worn and frightened, and that was no good at all. The mistress of the kitchens must be Law Itself: eagle-eyed, all-seeing, fierce, and steely, not a weakness to be seen anywhere. Let your apprentices see you're only human, and it's the beginning of the end as far as discipline is concerned. "To *bed*, Bartolomeo!" I ordered. "Or I'll toast your gizzard in a little good butter and have *that* for a midnight snack!" I must have had some steel left under all the exhaustion, because he bolted off at once.

Though he did stop at the door and give me a smile over his bony shoulder. "We're home, *signorina*," he said. "That's a prayer answered, isn't it? I don't think I had a thought for days that wasn't a prayer to get home. Or," he added practically, "a prayer that the French wouldn't split our heads open with those nasty pikes. Or start raping anybody—mostly I worried about that on your account, and the maids, but with the things you hear about the French . . ." He rumpled a hand through his red hair. "Well, I got a little perturbed for myself, too."

"Bartolomeo—"

"But nobody's head got split, and nobody got buggered either, and here we are." He kissed his fist up to the ceiling. "Thank you, Heavenly Father!"

"To bed!" I thundered.

"You too, *signorina*," he advised. "You look ready to drop." And off he went.

I looked around my empty kitchens. Bartolomeo was right; there had been a great many prayers the last few days. The maids, gabbling hasty Acts of Contrition and whimpering that some unconfessed sin of theirs had brought the French down upon us all as a punishment from God. Giulia's mother-in-law and *duenna* Adriana da Mila, lips moving silently as her fingers twitched over her ivory rosary beads. Bartolomeo, his hands clasped around the wooden cross he always wore about his neck, knuckles white and eyes shut as he sent a simpler kind of plea skyward. I didn't have my apprentice's easy faith, or his untroubled conscience. I just closed my eyes and prayed to see my kitchens again.

My kitchens—sweet Santa Marta save me, I hadn't realized how much I'd missed them over the past six months when I'd been traveling the countryside with Madonna Giulia's household. Now quite empty for the night, my cousin Marco doubtless having gone to play *primiera* with sailors and thieves in the Borgo, and even the last of the scullions having long trailed off to bed. Everything was empty and clean, welcoming me home. The chief kitchen with its enormous hearth and revolving spit, fire banked to a soft glow for the night . . . the scullery next door, all silvery with fish scales and why hadn't the pot-boys been scrubbing down the floors better in my absence . . . the cold room after that, where

I'd stood so many hours whipping up cream tops for milk-snow, or sort-
ing game for plucking and storing . . . the courtyard outside, silent and
black now, but in a few hours it would be full of dawn bustle when the
daily procession of wagons began to arrive with wood for my ovens and
carcasses for my spits and herbs fresh-plucked and dew-wet for my sauces.
Even the kitchen cat with his tattered ear, useless greedy beast that he
was, looked up at me with an insolent *mrow*. "No one's turned you into
sausage yet, you useless thing?" I asked, and he stalked off with contempt
across my kitchen. *My* kitchen, and I felt a great thrum of peace just
looking around me. Most looked for that thrum in the recitations of
Mass or the velvet enclosed spaces of the confessional, but a kitchen was
my church. I was probably hell-bound for thinking anything so blasphemous, but I had greater sins than blasphemy on my conscience, sins
like theft and fornication and altar desecration, so I was undoubtedly
hell-bound anyway. Easy, quiet faith like Bartolomeo's wasn't for me.

"Home indeed," I said, and took a certain small pouch from under
my overskirt. "Aren't you glad?"

She looked happy, if a shriveled and mummified hand enclosed in
a bag could be said to have any expression. A rather dried-up and wrinkled thing, the fingers ancient and curled in on themselves, a single
filigreed gold ring gleaming from one finger, the shrunken flesh over
the ancient knuckles bearing the marks of old knife nicks and burn
scars. The same kind of marks I had all over my hands, the same kind
any cook had—and the severed hand I carried about with me for good
luck was supposedly the hand of Santa Marta herself, patron saint of
cooks everywhere. A most holy relic, and really she should not have been
in the possession of someone as sinful as me, but there was that little
incident of altar desecration in my past, and, well, accidents happen.
And I must say, she seemed to enjoy getting out of a reliquary and into
a kitchen again, because I'd never gotten actually *caught*, had I? Surely
that was a sign of my patron saint's approval.

Of course, someone finally had caught me now. That dwarf with his
sharp knives and his even sharper eyes, threatening to ruin me. Unless—

"He wants a posset?" I told Santa Marta grimly, hanging her little pouch up on the drying rack alongside some sprigs of rosemary. "I'll give him a posset."

She didn't approve, I could tell from the way her ring glinted at me in the banked glow of the fires, but I tied on an apron resolutely and began mulling some wine . . . and an hour or so later, long after Madonna Giulia would have settled her daughter and her bodyguard and gone rustling off through her private passage to the Vatican to see her Pope, I was tiptoeing up the stairs with a steaming cup in hand.

Leonello's chamber was a tiny high-ceilinged nook wedged in at the very top of the *palazzo*. Madonna Giulia had seen him well settled on his narrow bed, his wounds rebandaged, the covers drawn up, his collection of books in easy reach and a branch of fine wax tapers lit and glowing if he felt like reading. The shadows danced over his face—a rather handsome face, despite the deep-set eyes and prominent forehead. His lids were closed, his dark hair rumpled and one arm pressed close against his bandaged side. I thought of leaving the mulled wine and skulking away like a coward. But then his eyes opened soundlessly, hazel eyes full of their usual bitter amusement, and he did not look one whit surprised to see me.

"Well, well," he drawled, and managed to raise himself to one elbow even though a hiss of pain escaped through his teeth. "Come to ravish me, *Signorina Cuoca*? Pardon me, make that *Suora Carmelina*."

Hearing my proper title in that smug voice made my teeth hurt. I thumped the cup down beside his books, so hard it splashed. "Mulled wine. Madonna Giulia's orders."

He reached for it. "Our lord Jesus Christ is the only man to be served by nuns. Maybe I've died and been resurrected, to earn such a privilege?"

I glowered. "Drink."

"Something I've been wondering." He swirled the wine, ruminating. "I know you cut your hair and traveled as a man, when you escaped your convent and made the journey to Rome. You're tall enough, and flat as a marble slab in the bargain—you'd pass. But I've always wondered how you got over the convent wall in the first place. Bribery? Ladder? Grappling hook?"

I hesitated, but I wanted him complacent, and feeding his curiosity seemed the best way to accomplish that. "Bribery," I said shortly. "I paid a fisherman to pick me up in the night with his boat. Now drink."

Leonello chuckled, taking a long sniff of his mulled wine. "Smells cloying. Are you trying to sweeten me up?"

"I assure you, it's delicious. Wine, honey, cloves, a pinch of pepper—" I watched him take a sip. "And a dash of hemlock."

He froze, and I lunged. He was strong for a dwarf but the French had left him weak and blood-spent, and I slammed him flat to the pillows with my hand across his mouth. "Don't swallow," I said. "Just hold that wine in your mouth and listen."

His hazel eyes regarded me calmly over my hand.

"You know what I am," I said. "Mostly, anyway. I took the name Suora Serafina when I took my vows at the Convent of Santa Marta in Venice. *Serafina*," I couldn't help saying with a certain exasperation, "so you can stop all this Suora Carmelina business!" And I still couldn't understand how he'd found out in the first place. Only my cousin Marco Santini knew where I'd fled from, and he was sworn to secrecy. To the rest of the household, I was just Marco's orphaned cousin from Venice come to help in his kitchens now that she had no other place in the world. But somehow Leonello had put one fact with another, and then another—my hair, which had been chopped short when I first came to the household; my avoidance of churches and my knowledge of Latin prayers—who knows how many details he'd managed to sniff out? He was far too clever for his own good, or mine.

"You think you can ruin me, by telling the world who I am?" I went on. "Well, you can. Even worse, because I won't just be hauled back to my convent if I'm found. I'll have my hands and my tongue chopped off for desecration, because I stole a reliquary from my convent to get money to travel south."

His eyes widened thoughtfully over my hand at that. God rot him, he had no right to look so cool, not when my whole inside was bubbling panic. I'd been nothing but a whirl of fear since he confronted me, just after the French attack. Throwing my secret in my face, just to make me cringe. Because according to him, his wounds were all my doing.

"You've no cause to blame me," I hissed. "I don't care what you say, it was not my fault the French found us. It wasn't my fault you had to go throwing yourself into some useless fight and nearly get killed, either. None of it was my fault, Leonello, and you've got no right to destroy me just because you want someone to blame—"

I heard myself babbling and clamped my teeth on my tongue. For a second I could taste splinters, wood splinters and old blood—that would be the last thing I tasted, if an executioner ever drew my tongue out on the block to slice it off, with my hands to follow for the sin of robbing an altar. *Sweet Santa Marta save me.* Because Leonello was looking at me with no pity at all, no pity and no forgiveness either. I hadn't known the French advance would be staking out the road we'd taken, but the only reason we'd taken that road at all was that I was desperate to avoid a fellow traveler in Capodimonte who had recognized me from my girl-hood in Venice. I'd spun a web of lies to persuade Madonna Giulia to change course the next day, and we'd ridden straight into the French advance, and Leonello to his wounds and nearly his death.

Not my fault, I told myself. I'd robbed a convent and broken my vows as a nun; those sins I was entirely guilty of committing—but it was not my fault Leonello was wrapped in all these bloodied bandages.

"So believe me," I snarled, gulping down my fear, "I *know* you can ruin me, little man. You can see to it I lose my hands and my tongue, and I might as well be dead after that because a cook isn't much good without hands and a tongue. But I can ruin you, too."

A gamble. Sweet Santa Marta, it was a gamble, but it was the only one I had.

"Now you know what I am," I went on. "And if you turn me in, I'll tell them you knew from the beginning. Knew that I was a desecrator, knew it for *years*, and didn't do anything—and that makes you as guilty as me. They'll chop your hands and nose off, too, and I don't see you making a living throwing your knives unless you've got hands to throw them with."

His eyes widened over my hand again. Not quite so calmly this time, I thought. I dropped my voice to a whisper, leaning close to him. "Turn me in, Leonello, and I swear in the name of God and the Holy Virgin that I'll drag you down with me. I *swear*." I lifted my hand from his mouth. "So why don't you keep my secrets?"

He spat out the mouthful of wine, making a splash on the floor like blood. Never taking his eyes from mine, he reached for a cup beside the branch of candles. Not the cup I'd brought; a mug of chilled lemon water Madonna Giulia must have placed for him. He drank a deliberate mouthful, rinsing it around his mouth, and spat it out in a neat stream, right onto the front of my apron.

"You know," he said, "I loathe your mulled wine. You always add too much honey."

"Writhe in hell," I spat.

He tilted his head, eyes unreadable as he surveyed the cup I had brought. It sat steaming innocently. "Did you truly poison it?"

"I'll leave you to wonder," I said. "You go right on guessing, every time you take a dish from my hands. Because if I even get a *hint* you might be thinking about turning me in for arrest anyway, I won't wait to find out. I'll just drop a little hemlock in your broth, next midday meal."

He looked at me. "No, you wouldn't."

"I'm a failed nun, Leonello." I stretched my lips over my teeth, but you couldn't call it a smile. "I'm a desecrator and a runaway and an adulteress against God, and I'm already bound for hellfire. What's murder, added on top of all that?"

He regarded me silently.

"Think about it." I turned for the door and added over my shoulder, "Hemlock."

PART ONE

August 1496–February 1497

CHAPTER ONE

❖

You are as wise as you are perfect.

—RODRIGO BORGIA TO GIULIA FARNESE

Giulia

You'd think that the Holy Father would have an all-seeing gaze, wouldn't you? Being God's Vicar here on earth, surely he would be granted divine sight into the hearts and souls of men as soon as that silly papal hat everyone insisted on calling a tiara was lowered onto his brow. The truth is, most popes don't have divine insight into much of anything. If they did, they'd get on with the business of making saints and saving souls rather than pronouncing velvet gowns impious or persecuting the poor Jews. Blasphemy it may be, but most popes have no more insight into the minds of humanity than does any carter or candle maker walking the streets of Rome in wooden clogs.

And my Pope was no exception. He was the cleverest man I knew in some ways—those dark eyes of his had only to pass benignly over his bowing cardinals to know exactly which ones were scheming against him, and certainly that despicable French King had learned not to cross wits *or* swords with Rodrigo Borgia over the past year and a half since I'd been ransomed. But when it came to his family, His Holiness Pope Alexander VI was as dense as a plank.

At least at the moment he was a very happy plank.

"*Mi familia*," he said thickly, and began to raise his goblet but put it down again to dash a heavy hand at the water standing in his eyes. "My children all together again. Cesare, Lucrezia, Joffre—Juan—"

The loathsome young Duke of Gandia preened, sitting at his father's right where Rodrigo could easily reach out to touch his favorite son's shoulder. Juan Borgia, twenty years old now and returned from his lands in Spain. Although he was a duke, a husband, even a *father* (Holy Virgin, fetch me a basin!)—that auburn-haired young lout looked no different to me, lolling in his chair fiddling with his dagger hilt, already halfway through his cup of wine and giving me the occasional leer over the rim. I'd heaved a great sigh that afternoon, watching him strike a pose before the cheering crowd as he disembarked from his Spanish ship. My lover's second son had been wearing silly stockings embroidered in rays and crowns, and I'd realized just how much I'd been hoping never to see Juan or his ridiculous clothes or his leer again. As soon as I heard Rodrigo had summoned Juan from Spain to take command of the papal forces against the French, I prayed so devoutly for a shipwreck. You'd think someone nicknamed the Bride of Christ could get the occasional prayer answered, wouldn't you?

But if I wasn't exactly thrilled to see Juan or his silly stockings again, my Pope was—he had rushed from his elaborate sedan chair across the docks to embrace his son in a great sweep of embroidered papal robes, kissing both his cheeks and uttering a great many ecstatic things in the Catalan tongue, which he saved for moments of high emotion. Nobody else had missed Juan when he departed Rome for Barcelona to take possession of the Spanish duchy and the Spanish bride my Pope had inveigled for his favorite son—but my Pope certainly had. And nothing would do but to gather the whole family together for an intimate evening *cena* in the Holy Father's private apartments at the Vatican.

And what apartments! Just a modest little nest of rooms in the Vatican where the Holy Father could remove his jeweled cope (along with the weight of all Christendom) and relax at the end of the evening like any ordinary man. But Rodrigo Borgia would have nothing ordinary. He had declared he would have the papal apartments new-made, stamped and decorated with a lavishness to surpass anything else in Rome. It had taken two years, but that little painter Maestro Pinturicchio had finally finished the frescoes that had been designed especially for the Holy Father's personal rooms, and the resulting splendor left all Rome gasping. Our small *cena* tonight had been set in the Sala dei Santi: the long table draped with sumptuous brocades and set with solid silver dishes and fragile Murano glass; the ceiling arched overhead painted in double crowns and the Borgia bull; the frescoes framed with geometric Moorish patterns in a blaze of colors, imported straight from Spain.

Pinturicchio had used us all as models for his various scenes— Lucrezia dimpled and tossed her blond head under the beseeching figure of herself on the wall as Santa Caterina; inscrutable Cesare lounged under his own image as inscrutable Emperor Maximilian in a massive throne; fourteen-year-old Joffre pranced in the painted crowd as one of the background figures; and Juan cut a ridiculous figure on the wall in a silly Turkish mantle as a turbaned heathen. I was a Madonna in one of the other chambers, with my Laura on my lap for the Christ child. "Surely it's blasphemous to have a *girl* sit as model for our Lord!" Maestro Pinturicchio had protested.

"Any more blasphemous than to have a harlot sit for the Madonna?" I'd countered, the Holy Virgin's blue veil swinging about my face like a joke. I'd never *asked* to be a notorious woman; I'd been raised for a husband and children like any other girl of noble birth, but here I was. I'd made my own choices, and I made no bones either about what it made me—but I'd been determined to have my Laura in the frescoes along with all the other Borgia children. Maestro Pinturicchio had taken one look at the set of my chin and begun sketching. A nice little man, ugly as the day was long, but skilled. His wife was the most notorious harpy in Rome, and I gave him a rose-quartz and crystal bracelet to give her in the hopes it would sweeten her temper. It hadn't, but he thanked me anyway, and he made Laura look very pretty indeed in our Madonna-and-Child fresco. Though the halo certainly didn't suit her; she was a full three years old now and a proper little imp!

Rodrigo was still looking about the table with misty eyes, and I ceased my musing. "It's not just Our own children here tonight," he continued, beaming like any proud father despite the regal papal We. "Our new children as well. Sancha—"

Young Joffre's Neapolitan wife, Sancha of Aragon, was making doe eyes at Cesare through the candlelight, but she dropped her lashes demurely at her father-in-law.

"—and of course Lucrezia's Giovanni Sforza is here in our thoughts, if not the flesh. A pity he could not join Us—"

Lucrezia giggled behind her hand, not looking very put out about that. My Pope had called her back from her husband's home in Pesaro last winter for a long visit, declaring he could not do without his dear daughter any longer, and certainly I'd been delighted to see Lucrezia again, both of us chattering and gossiping in the Palazzo Santa Maria just like the old days when she'd been a little girl dreaming of marriage— but she had certainly not seemed inclined to go back to her new home now that she *was* married. I suppose Pesaro's provincial pleasures had worn rather thin after two years. Lord Sforza had stamped off home this spring, muttering of duties that could not be put off, and he'd stamped off alone.

"And a pity your beautiful Maria Enriques could not travel with you from Spain," Rodrigo continued, giving Juan's arm another pat. "We would have liked to see Our new daughter."

"She begged to come, but she's breeding again." Juan shrugged, rotating the silver stem of his wine goblet between restless fingers. "I'm happy enough to leave her behind. The cow is always weeping and praying."

"Now, now," Rodrigo chuckled. "She'll be mother to another Borgia prince soon!" He gave an indulgent shake of his head and raised his goblet. "No matter. All of us are together again. As it should be."

His children raised their goblets too, but I couldn't help noticing that not everybody looked entirely pleased to see *la familia Borgia* reunited. Joffre was sulking, squashed in beside Juan and ignored by Sancha, and as for Cesare . . .

"*La familia*," said the Holy Father.

"*La familia*," everyone echoed, and the look Cesare sent his brother across the table could have kindled the napkins.

"So," I said brightly as a stream of papal servants entered with massive silver dishes, "how was the crossing from Spain? Did the waves stay smooth for the Duke of Gandia?"

"Smooth enough," Juan said, eyes flickering to my breasts.

"I suppose your Duchess will be very much distressed to have you gone." Myself, I'd have thrown a great party in celebration.

Juan shrugged again, clearly not interested in his wife. His eyes went to Cesare as the first dishes were laid before us on the *cena* table. "So, brother. Hostage to the French, were you? I hear you ran away."

"Escaped," said Cesare. He was a dark shadow among the candles— in his plain black velvets he seemed to eat the light and refuse to give it back again. "The Holy Father and I arranged it all. I escaped as a groom shortly after we set out from Rome."

"Ran," Juan grinned.

"He was ever so brave," Sancha cooed in her milky-sweet voice. She and Joffre had been recalled from their official seat in Naples to Rome that May, and it hadn't taken me more than a week to start despising that velvety purr of hers. I'd met Sancha only once, at her wedding to little Joffre when he was twelve and Sancha four years older, and that occasion had been quite enough to make me think we weren't destined to be the best of friends. And when Sancha took an idle look at Leonello at her welcoming banquet and told me, "Your dwarf is a fine specimen; have you ever considered breeding him? I have the most cunning little juggling woman—" Well, after that I'd started calling her the Tart of Aragon, and I knew I'd happily watch her choke to death on a fish bone. "Try the carp, Sancha," I suggested, but she was talking over me and toying with the pearl pendant about her neck to draw attention to her breasts.

"Cesare left all his baggage behind, you know." She left off the pendant long enough to hold her wine cup to be refilled again—she certainly could put it away! "And when King Charles went to look, he saw that all those chests that were supposed to be filled with coin and silver plate had nothing but stones under a top layer of ducats! You could hear the scream all the way in Rome."

Juan gave Sancha's breasts an automatic glance, but his attention was all for his brother. "I expect I'll do better than run when I see the French, brother."

Cesare toyed with his table knife.

"You'll send the French packing, boy!" my Pope said warmly. He'd left off his ecclesiastical robes, and in his embroidered doublet and linen shirtsleeves he could have been any merchant father or ducal *paterfamilias*: the proud and swarthy Spaniard surrounded by children who all looked like him. "We taught them a lesson at Fornovo; now you'll finish them off."

Really, after all that fuss the French had made declaring they would annex all of Naples and the papal territories too before they were done, everything had petered out so embarrassingly. Well, embarrassing if you were French. After they got their poxy noses bloodied at Fornovo and had to flee back north, my Pope made me a present straight from the French King's own abandoned baggage: a certain diary in execrable handwriting, detailing the ladies who had shared the royal bed on campaign, with descriptions of their skills. "No, thank you," I'd said, wrinkling my nose.

"Are you sure?" Rodrigo had turned the pages with great interest. "There are a few ideas here. Requiring a bit more flexibility than I'm capable of at my age, to be sure . . ."

"Really, Rodrigo," I'd scolded. "Dirty stories? Whatever happened to giving a woman flowers?"

"Then flowers you shall have." And I'd acquired a pretty little set of diamond roses to clip into my braided hair. Every time the Tart of Aragon looked at them I could see her little nose twitch with lust. Her little nose was usually twitching with lust of one kind or another. For the past two months it had been twitching for Cesare, in whose lap she appeared to be dandling her hand under cover of the damask tablecloth. She didn't have a glance for poor little Joffre—he'd grown to a tall gangly youth, but he still seemed like a child to me, sulking in the shadow of his voluptuous wife and his taller, handsomer brothers. I tried to engage him in the conversation—"You'll be next on the battlefield after your brothers, Joffre!"—but he pushed his lip out in sullen silence and I finally gave up and stabbed at my roast capon, which had been taken off the spit too soon and was now oozing red juice all over my plate like it had been wounded rather than cooked. You'd think the Pope would eat better than anyone else in the Holy City, but you'd be wrong. It wasn't fair, this reputation he'd acquired for dissipation and luxury—my Pope was so indifferent to what he ate, he didn't care if the Vatican cooks fed him or his guests on bread and water. Anyone who wanted a decent meal at the Pope's table had better hope they were eating at the Palazzo Santa Maria, where I presided over the table and my fierce Carmelina Mangano held sway in the kitchens. Carmelina would have taken one look at this half-raw chicken and the burned *focaccia* and the salad with too many capers and gone down to the Vatican kitchens to whack off a few heads.

I pushed my plate away. All this *la familia* tension was giving me a headache, and I always eat when I have a headache, but this food was past enjoying. Besides, I was starting to get just a bit plump again—some women might be able to stay wand-slim no matter what they ate, but my dresses got tight if I even *looked* at a plate of *tourtes*. So very unfair. At least food like this was easy to push away.

"So you're to be *Gonfalonier*?" Sancha was bubbling now at Juan. "Our bold leader against the French! I see bravery in the Borgias isn't limited to just one brother!"

"One might doubt that," Cesare murmured.

"My husband wanted to lead the papal forces, you know." Lucrezia laughed. "Can you imagine? He has trouble enough with those Pesarese captains of his, and now he wants papal soldiers! He thinks he's Alexander the Great, you know; too ridiculous—"

Sancha tittered and Juan guffawed; even Rodrigo had a chuckle at his son-in-law's expense, and I couldn't blame him either because Lord Sforza had gotten very sour this past year and spent most of his last visit pestering my Pope for money. But I couldn't help looking at Lucrezia—sixteen years old now but as poised as a woman of twice as many years, wearing a purple-and-crimson gown cut as low as Sancha's, rubies in her ears and rouge patted on her cheeks and a ring on every finger. She looked eager and glittering, greedy for every eye to be on her, and I thought back to the gently glowing girl who had first blushed at her new husband over my *cena* table.

Well, such girls grew up. And Lucrezia had acted alongside me as her father's hostess this past winter, finally old enough to take her place as the star of the papal court—perhaps it had gone to her head just a little. It certainly would have gone to mine at her age. I had only twenty-two years to my name, but sometimes I felt distinctly world-weary.

They were talking of that mad priest Fra Savonarola now, the one preaching and frothing at the mouth in Florence and getting everyone to give up their cards and their fine clothes and all their other luxuries. "Only in Florence," Juan snickered. "That would never happen in Rome!"

"My Giulia might give up cards," Rodrigo said, giving my cheek an affectionate tweak. "But never her pearls!"

"As if anyone would go about in sackcloth just because one sour old man said puffed sleeves were heretical!" Lucrezia laughed.

"I don't know about heretical," I said, sipping my sour wine. The vintage wasn't up to Carmelina's standards, either. "But puffed sleeves are certainly unflattering. And really, what's more heretical than that?"

Sancha plucked at her puffed sleeves, shooting me a nasty look.

"You'd be the only one safe under Savonarola, eh, brother?" Juan cast an eye over the unadorned black that Cesare usually wore instead of his red cardinal's robes. "Maybe you should have been a Dominican! I'll fight the French and you'll preach hellfire."

"Careful, brother," said Cesare. "Or you might taste it."

Juan just beckoned in invitation, laughing. The two brothers should have looked alike—both tall and lean, both auburn-haired, both handsome—but they didn't. Not at all, and Juan's jittering overbright eyes met Cesare's still, black-steel gaze like a cross of swords. Sancha looked between them with parted lips, and Lucrezia cast her eyes up to the ceiling and said, "Really, you're both such *children*!" But I felt a twinge of disquiet.

"You'll have seen the new frescoes, Juan," I jumped in brightly. "But surely not examined them yet? Perhaps we can take a closer look, before the *biscotti* are brought in. Your figure shows to great advantage . . ."

I took my wine cup in one hand, tucking the other into Rodrigo's broad arm, and we all rose from the *cena* table and flocked to the walls with our painted images . "I *love* me as Santa Caterina," Lucrezia sighed over her own beseeching golden-haired figure. "I still have that dress . . ."

"I don't see why Joffre and I were just figures in the crowd," Sancha pouted. "I could have been a saint too, you know!"

"Or Salome," Juan leered. "The Dance of the Seven Veils—we'd get to see what you look like under the last one, new sister—"

"*Juan!*" Joffre burst out, flushing, but Sancha laughed and struck Juan a playful blow with her fan. One of those tiresome girls who is always doing something flirtatious with her fan. How I longed to smack her with it.

"My likeness is to be in the Resurrection fresco," my Pope was saying, oblivious. "When I have time to sit for it, that is—"

"And you really should *make* the time," I scolded. "Poor Maestro Pinturicchio has already finished everything else!"

"I don't like being painted," Rodrigo complained. "An utter waste of time!"

"But part of a pope's duty is to be preserved for posterity. You'll look magnificent, just wait and see." My pope was sixty-five now, and he had put on weight now that he had no more time for the hunting and riding that had long kept him lean. But his massive shoulders were imposing as ever, his swarthy hawk-nosed profile just as confident, his vigorous dark hair only threaded with gray. The papal bull at the height of his powers.

"This marks the beginning of everything." My Pope beamed all about him: his children painted on the wall, his children clustered around him. "*La familia* reunited! Let's drink to it again."

His eyes were once more full of emotion, but I saw Cesare still glaring at Juan, saw Lucrezia biting her lips to make them redder, saw Sancha aiming hot looks at both her brothers-in-law, and Joffre staring vengefully at Sancha. I saw it all, and all I could think was a horribly, woefully inadequate *Oh, dear*.

But Rodrigo was looking at me expectantly, so I raised my goblet. "*La familia* reunited," I echoed and drank in a prayer along with the wine.

S uch gloom, Giulia!" Rodrigo leaned back on his elbows against the pillows with their papal crest embroidered in gold. "When did you turn doom-cryer?"

"I'm only saying that it's vastly overrated, having all one's family together." I plucked the diamond roses out of my hair and began unlacing my moss-green velvet sleeves. "Holy Virgin knows, it's a disaster whenever my family are all in the same room. In no time my older brother is telling Sandro he's a prancing fool even if he is Cardinal Farnese now, and my sister is telling me I'm a harlot. And your children are even worse! Juan and Cesare looked ready to draw daggers over the *biscotti*."

"Brothers compete. It's what they do." My Pope waved a careless hand, and his massive papal ring glinted in the soft light from the tapers. "It brings out the best in both of them."

"I'll remind you of those words when the blood hits the walls," I said tartly, letting both my sleeves drop. "Why ever did you settle on Cesare for the Church? Anyone can see he's born to lead armies and swing swords—"

"But he's cunning, and one needs that in the Church." Rodrigo poured out a cup of wine for the two of us to share. "To survive in the College of Cardinals, you have to be able to outplot a spider."

"But he's not suited for the priestly life. Not in the slightest!"

Rodrigo laughed, gesturing around him. "Are any of us?" His private chamber was dim and rich, the walls hung in painted canvas that had been laid over in elaborate gilt designs, the bed elaborately curtained in crimson velvet embroidered with the papal crest again, silver brackets everywhere lighting the room with sweet-smelling beeswax tapers. My Pope used to visit me in my official domicile at the Palazzo Santa Maria, by way of a certain passage so very private that all Rome knew about it. But his wave of protectiveness after my return from the French army still hadn't abated, and now I slept more than half my nights at the papal apartments here in the Vatican, where Rodrigo had the sheets scattered with petals from my favorite yellow climbing roses, which he claimed looked like me. I looked around at the silks, the rose petals, the gilt and the glass and the velvet, all overlaid by that somber papal crest, and had to concede that it was not really very priestly at all.

"Is your conscience bothering you?" Rodrigo made the sign of the cross over my forehead with his thumb. "*Ego te absolvo a peccatis tuis in nomine Patris, et Filii, et Spiritus Sancti.* There, you are washed clean of all your sins. Come kiss me."

I smiled and kissed him. The state of my soul had bothered me a great deal when I first became a harlot, a fallen woman, a foul adulteress, take your choice of epithets. But it's difficult to worry about the fires of hell when I get my divine forgiveness expressly from the Holy Father whenever I want it. I kissed him again, and then turned my back so he could unlace my moss-green velvet gown with the gold vines embroidered about the bosom and hem. "So you chose Cesare for the Church—"

Rodrigo groaned, his fingers deft on the laces down my back. "Let it be, Giulia!"

I persisted. "—but why ever did you choose *Juan* for the military life?"

"Because that's how it always is." Rodrigo tickled the back of my neck with one of my golden bodice ribbons, making me squeal. "One son for the Church, one for the battlefield."

"You men!" I couldn't help saying. "Slotting your children into various spaces the moment they're born, as if they were vases to be put into a niche! Just because you have two sons doesn't make them automatically fit for the Church *or* the battlefield, you know."

"Juan's full of fire. He'll make a fine Gonfalonier."

"Juan is interested in nothing but carousing, drinking, and chasing after women. I know how you've missed him while he was in Spain, but I have to say I have *not* missed the way he ogles me."

Or the way Juan teased Lucrezia for the spot on her chin she had tried to cover up with powder, or jeered at Joffre for padding the shoulders of his doublet in an effort to look more the man for Sancha. Or aimed a kick at my little pet goat who trailed me on a gilt leather leash. I loved that goat, had loved him since I'd rescued him from ending up in one of Carmelina's pies when he was just a floppy-eared baby kid, and Juan had put him bleating into the wall with one boot!

"Juan's just a boy," my Pope was saying with all his usual tolerance, unknotting a tangled ribbon at my back. "Perhaps he ogles you, but he ogles every beautiful woman he sees! He doesn't mean anything by it."

He'd cuckold you in a heartbeat, I thought, but didn't say it. To some things Rodrigo was entirely blind, and when it came to his favorite son . . . he hadn't even noticed this evening after *cena* when Juan flung an arm about my waist, looking at my likeness in Pinturicchio's fresco. "Our family harlot as the Madonna," he breathed hotly into my ear, and his fingers stole down to cup my hip. "How's that for irony, eh?"

I'd just smiled, giving his hand a good covert smack. "And this harlot will knock your ears around the back of your head if you touch her again, Juan Borgia."

I'd been able to intimidate him when he was sixteen, but not now. He'd just given me another lingering up-and-down look and swaggered ahead to join Lucrezia and Sancha as they studied the Annunciation fresco with its angels and arabesques.

"Did you see Juan slavering over Sancha?" I said over my shoulder to Rodrigo, feeling the last of my tight laces come loose. "I thought poor Joffre was going to pop with outrage."

"She's a flirt, that one." Rodrigo chuckled, sliding the gown off my shoulders.

"And now all *three* of your sons are competing for her!" I stepped out of the circle of my gown on the floor. "If that's not a recipe for disaster—"

"Bah," Rodrigo said dismissively, and pressed his lips to my shoulder above the edge of my filmy shift. "Take your hair down, *mi perla*. It's a sight I never tire of seeing—one of the great wonders of the world, your hair."

I attacked my pins, and he fell back on his elbows again, happily watching the first of my coiled plaits slither loose over my shoulder. My Pope clearly had no interest in hearing any more about the shortcomings of his sons. He had lost his eldest son, Pedro Luis, many years ago in Spain, a memory that still veiled his eyes in grief whenever he spoke of it, and after that old loss I suppose his indulgence to his surviving children was understandable. "A pity Lord Sforza couldn't join us," I said by way of changing the subject. "I know he misses Lucrezia in Pesaro."

"Let him miss her. He's a waffling fool, and more than that, he's turned out to be a mediocre *condottiere* who does nothing but ask me for money. I wish I'd known *that* when I was considering his offer for her hand!" My Pope reached out to catch a lock of my loosened hair and bring it to his nose, inhaling deeply. I had expensive perfumes by the dozen in glass vials, but part of me was still a country girl, the girl who grew up in a tiny town beside Lake Bolsena and boiled flowers to make perfume, and I still preferred my old homemade scents of honeysuckle and gillyflower to all those expensive mixtures of frankincense and bergamot. "I heard from another mediocre *condottiere* today, you know," my Pope went on, inhaling my hair again.

"Who?"

"Monoculus."

"That's a cruel nickname, Rodrigo. He is not one-eyed; it's just a tiny squint." But I couldn't help a faint smile as I unraveled the last of my plaits. At least my Pope could joke now about my husband. Rodrigo was not jealous when other men looked at me—he just chuckled when envious archbishops ogled my bosom, or florid young lords paid me honeyed compliments. He liked being envied. But Orsino Orsini, he of the tiny squint, still worried my Pope sometimes. Orsino was my wedded husband, a man with the legal right to demand I return to his side, if he ever grew a spine and chose to exercise that right. Even the Holy Father could not really excommunicate a man for demanding that his wife cease committing adultery.

"That chinless little snip can't even scrape up the courage to ask me himself when he wants money," Rodrigo continued with a snort. "Instead he applies to his mother and gets her to ask me. This time, it's to pay his soldiers. They don't listen to him unless their pay is current. Or even when it is current. There's one son who should *not* have been slated for the battlefield!" My husband's family, the Orsini, had been among those to side with the French upon their march south—at least, the more illustrious and prosperous branches of the Orsini. Not Orsino, however, whose mother was cousin and firm friend to Rodrigo Borgia. Where his mother led, Orsino followed.

"We don't need to discuss Orsino, do we?" I shook my hair down, rippling clear to the floor, and Rodrigo clapped a hand to his chest as though pierced through the heart by the sight. I climbed onto the vast bed, sitting cross-legged like a child, and pulled his feet into my lap.

People think it's all jewels and gowns and keeping yourself pretty, being a mistress, but I've found it's a good deal more about peace. Powerful men, whether kings of vast nations or lords of uncounted wealth or fathers of the world's souls, are *tired* men. A thousand voices clamor every moment for their attention, their time, their favors; everyone wants something and they all want it now. When my Pope came to me at the end of the day, he could at least relax with the knowledge that I wanted nothing but him. "Your feet are hurting you again, aren't they?" I scolded softly, rubbing his toes. "Why can't you sit still when you're dictating letters to your secretaries, instead of pacing like a madman?"

He gave a groan of pleasure, but his eyes were serious as they looked at me. "Does Orsino still write to you, Giulia?"

"He does," I said.

"What does he write?"

Still a note of anxiety in my Pope's deep voice. "Nothing very much," I said, kneading my thumbs into the arch of his right foot. "Read the letters any time you wish."

"Oh, I trust *you*. It's Monoculus I don't trust. He wants you back."

"Always," I admitted. It had been a bargain my husband had made, or his mother Adriana da Mila had advised him to make: Take little Giulia Farnese for a wife, let Rodrigo Borgia have her for a concubine, and he will advance your career, my dear boy! Orsino had regretted that bargain since the day he saw me at our wedding, but he still took the rewards, didn't he? A *condotta* to give him soldiers, a hefty annuity, a *castello* in Carbognano and governorship over the town to go with it . . .

My husband had been everything a girl could dream of: handsome, young, and he even said he loved me. I didn't know if I believed that, really—he didn't even know me. But he said he'd loved me since the moment he'd laid eyes on me, and he certainly had his heart in his eyes whenever he looked at me, and that would be enough for most girls. But it *wasn't* enough. What no one bothers to tell dreaming girls is that a handsome and adoring young husband isn't any use if he's gutless.

Still, a gutless husband is better than a brutal one. I'd have to go back to him someday, when either my Pope died or his passion for me did, and I gave a little sigh at the thought. Hopefully the first of those fates wouldn't happen for many, many years—and maybe the second wouldn't happen at all.

"That's enough about Monoculus, eh?" Rodrigo ran a hand over my shoulder, the edge of my shift sliding down my arm. "My children too. It's making you morose."

"That batch of quarreling pups you fathered would make anybody morose!" I said lightly, and Rodrigo brightened just as I'd intended.

"I'll have you know my children are perfect." He pulled me up into his arms. "Shall we make another? A Borgia prince this time, a brother for Laura."

"Juan won't be very happy about that," I murmured between kisses. "He went into such a sulk when I was carrying Laura . . ." Worried any child of mine would supplant him as the Pope's favorite. In truth Rodrigo had always been just a trifle veiled in his affection for Laura. She *was* his daughter, of that I was perfectly certain—you had only to look at the nose (though I did hope she wouldn't grow up with his bull shoulders). But she'd been christened under my husband's name, and in truth when I counted backward from nine months there *had* been a time when I was trying to persuade Orsino to show just a little courage, enough to fight for his wife if he truly wanted to keep her . . .

But I couldn't think of Orsino, not with Rodrigo bending his dark head to plant unhurried kisses across my naked shoulders. "Come to me," he whispered in his Catalan Spanish, and I threaded my arms around his neck and slid myself over him, making my hair into a candlelit curtain shutting out the world.

When I was a foolish virgin girl, I'd prayed very earnestly not to be married off to an old man as so many of my friends were. I dreamed of lean cavaliers and dashing poets, and what girl doesn't? But girls are fools. Poets aren't much good when it comes to love play, when you really think about it—all Dante ever managed to do after years of mooning after Beatrice was fantasize that she might one day give him a guided tour of Paradise. And as for lean cavaliers, well, Orsino was the picture of a dashing young suitor, and our coupling had been awkward, clumsy, embarrassing, and brief. And afterward, he had stood back and given me away.

My Pope *savored* me every time he took me in his arms, tasted my skin and inhaled my hair, kissed me and cradled me and found something new in me every time to caress. "The curve of your spine is like a string of pearls," he would muse, and trace his lips over my back until I was vibrating down to my toes. Or he would drop slow tantalizing kisses over every part of my face from my ears to my chin, everywhere but my lips, until I dragged his mouth down against mine. He liked me bold and never accused me of being wanton; he tossed me and teased me, made me laugh and made me cry out—and my husband might have given me to Rodrigo, but Rodrigo had never forced me. "I've never had a woman by force, and I don't intend to start now," he'd told me, and then stood back in utter confidence to let *me* choose. It's not often a woman has a chance to choose, let me tell you. And I'd considered my options: the handsome young husband with the clumsy hands, or the ecclesiastical lover of more than sixty years who could curl my whole body up in shudders of pleasure?

Well.

"My papal bull," I whispered, and felt the rumble of laughter deep in his chest above me.

He slept afterward, his head heavy on my breast, my arms showing pale about his swarthy shoulders in the flickering candlelight, my hair coiling over us both. "Everything will be perfect now," he murmured, half-asleep. "You at my side, Juan returned, *la familia* reunited . . . the French defeated . . ." A yawn. "God has been kind, *mi perla*."

Unease twinged at me again, and I didn't know why. Not until I rose and dressed and tiptoed out, back to the Palazzo Santa Maria so the Pope would be found alone in his bed in the morning by his entourage, as was proper (even if they all knew I'd been keeping him company there). I yawned as I trailed through the darkened papal apartments, and my feet slowed in the Sala dei Santi as I looked again at the finished frescoes all the Borgia family had admired last night at *cena*. I looked past the frescoes this time, Juan as proud Turk and Cesare as merciless emperor and Lucrezia as pleading saint, to the Borgia bull motif repeated over and over in the floors and the walls. Not the placid grazing ox that had been the family emblem when they were merely the lowly Borja of Spain, but a massive defiant beast gazing about with arrogant eyes. In public appearances Rodrigo displayed his papal emblem of the crossed keys, the keys to the kingdom of heaven. But here there were no keys and no heaven either. There were saints on every wall, but it was the Borgias who dominated—the Borgias and their pagan bull.

"God has been kind," Rodrigo had said. *La familia* united again, as they had not been for years, and the French had been swindled and outplayed by my wily Pope who had played that spotty French King like a harp, vowing eternal friendship and whispering confidential promises, and all the while he had been piecing together a Holy League to oppose them. Rome, Spain, Milan, Venice: all allied against the French, who had found themselves outnumbered and surrounded in Naples. What a victory—and with the French fleeing their shattered campaign, what enemy was there to oppose my Pope and his family?

And last night they had celebrated in these rooms, which might have an Annunciation and a Nativity and a Resurrection painted on the walls . . . but which glorified not God, but Borgia.

Carmelina

Peasant food," I said flatly. "You are joking."

"Would I joke?" Leonello arched an eyebrow at me. "The Duke of Gandia desires a simple repast for midday *pranzo* when he and his party of friends break their fast here in between hunting bouts. How did he put it?" Leonello fingered the hilt of his knife in that despicably suggestive way Juan Borgia did, and cast a leer at the nearest kitchen maid. "'Today we hunt, and we will eat like simple peasants, close to the earth and close to God!'"

"Santa Marta save me," I muttered. "I'll give him peasant food. Barley porridge and boiled goat, *that's* peasant food!"

"Send him that, and you will be out of a job. I assure you that whatever notions he might have about eating like a simple peasant, the Duke of Gandia does not want porridge and goat."

"I know that!" The Duke of Gandia's ways were more than familiar to any female servants in the *palazzo*; he'd come sniffing around all our skirts at one time or another, including mine. He'd been half drunk, and I'd run him off with a cleaver. There are advantages to working in a kitchen.

"I'm sure you know best, *Signorina Cuoca*." Leonello sketched a bow, making sure to flourish his four-fingered hand at me. His eyes were hard and cool, meeting mine with that stare that still twisted in my gut like a fishhook. *I know what you are, Suora Serafina.*

But at least he had not told anyone else—more than a year and a half had passed, and no one had ever come with a rope for my wrists and a writ for my sins. Maybe that demon dwarf really *was* afraid I'd poison him. Or maybe he'd forgiven me, now that his wounds had healed.

Somehow I doubted that.

"One more thing," Leonello added over his shoulder. "Madonna Adriana wants to see you in her *sala*. You and Maestro Marco Santini."

Adriana da Mila, cousin to the Pope and *duenna* of the papal seraglio here. She was also Madonna Giulia's mother-in-law, and I still didn't understand exactly how that worked because most women would object to seeing their son's wife flit off to become the mistress of another man, much less His Holiness the Pope, but Adriana da Mila seemed entirely placid about the whole arrangement. Then again, the only thing that seemed to make Madonna Adriana lose any sleep was the prospect of losing money, and there was no doubt her son had been well compensated for his sacrifice.

Losing money . . . was she going to ask sharp questions about Marco's absences again? The mistress of the household would not be pleased to know just how much of Marco's twenty-five ducats a year went to the dicing tables in riverside taverns while I supervised the kitchens.

"Madonna Adriana will have to wait." I tied on an apron, already marshaling possible excuses as to why the *maestro di cucina* wasn't to be found when it was time to prepare the noonday meal. "My cousin has gone out."

"Cards this time?" Leonello examined one of his sharp little throwing knives, balancing the damascened hilt on the very tip of one stubby finger. He wore his usual livery, which Madonna Giulia had designed especially for him—black doublet and hose and boots—and she had a clever eye because all that stark unadorned black emphasized the green in his hazel eyes, and a miracle of tailoring masked the oddities of his body, making his shoulders look broader and his head less oversized. He didn't look like a figure of ridicule; he looked cool and remote and more than a little frightening, and I wished sometimes that my mistress had left him in the disreputable patched castoffs in which he'd first arrived in this household. "So, is our cook off playing cards again, or *zara*?" Leonello went on. "*Zara*'s a game for idiots, and that cousin of yours is a curly-haired fool."

"Certainly not," I lied. "He's at the fish market, checking a new vendor who promised him a choice load of sturgeon. He is very conscientious." I could almost hear Bartolomeo roll his eyes behind me at the other apprentices. "None of that," I said without turning, and gave Leonello a curt nod. "Please inform Madonna Adriana we will both be along when Marco returns."

He sheathed his throwing knife in his boot top again and sauntered out without a farewell. We never spoke one solitary word to each other beyond the necessary.

"And in the meantime," Bartolomeo snorted, "we've got *peasant food* to make. Santa Marta bung me with a spoon."

"None of that either," I warned, and flapped my apron at the lazy notch-eared kitchen cat who was batting a paw up toward a kettle of chicken bones I'd set to simmering. "Now, for *pranzo*—"

I reeled off dishes, and they stood waiting their orders in serried rows: the undercooks, the apprentices, the carvers, the scullions, the pot-boys; all my obedient soldiers. Well, mostly obedient. Bartolomeo snorted when I gave directions for a dish of lake trout bathed in truffle sauce. "Sweet Santa Marta," he said with a derisive shake of his head. "That is not how peasants eat. Does the Duke of Gandia really think your average Tiber fisherman slathers his trout in truffles?"

"This is how lordlings think peasants eat," I retorted. "Alfonso, you'll take the pork shoulder, I want a red wine glaze and plenty of capers— Giuliano, the capons, a splash of lime and rose vinegar—"

"It should be venison." Bartolomeo interrupted me again.

I glared at him this time. "What?"

"Venison," Bartolomeo repeated, raking an impatient hand through his red hair. "The Duke of Gandia bagged a stag yesterday. I saw when he had me bring out one of my hampers for his guardsmen on the hunt. He'll want to see venison on the table today, not pork shoulder and capons."

"Hmph." I eyed my apprentice, who had passed seventeen and passed me in height as well, and he stared right back instead of dropping his eyes obediently. My gawky eager-to-please apprentice boy had shot up over the past year and a half into a tall young man: standing before me with his freckled arms akimbo in their rolled-up sleeves, and his gaze near as prideful as a Borgia's. Seventeen—a dangerous age for a young cook. It's right about then that most apprentices decide they know better than whoever taught them to boil their first egg. Bartolomeo was showing all the usual signs lately: moving just a touch slowly when I gave him an order, slouching instead of jumping when I called his name, "forgetting" the occasional respectful *signorina* when he addressed me. The last thing you ever want to do is tell an arrogant young cook like Bartolomeo that he's right about anything.

But the Duke of Gandia *had* bagged a stag on his hunt yesterday, and he *would* want to see it on the table.

"Pork shoulder with capers and a red wine glaze, and the capons with lime and rose vinegar," I repeated finally. "*And* the venison, with a sauce of cream and French brandy. I was getting to that, Bartolomeo, if you hadn't interrupted me. Perhaps you'd like to plan the rest of the menu as well, just to save me the trouble? I am all ears for your pearls of wisdom."

"Salad of fennel and blood orange and olives," he said, not turning a hair. "Roasted figs rolled in honey and almonds—"

I gave his shoulder a whack with my ladle. "Enough of that. You can do the chestnut-flour *frittelle*, and not too crisp either. Your *frittelle* are always on the edge of burning."

"They are not."

I waited.

"*Signorina*," he added grudgingly, and began measuring out sweet chestnut flour and sugar. I nodded, clapping my hands and concluding the menu instructions with my usual call to arms—"That's all, now, so I want to see mouths shut and hands moving!"—and I could have sworn I saw Bartolomeo mouthing the words alongside me, but as soon as I whipped my head around at him, he gave me a look of round-eyed innocence. "All right, all right," I called testily, and they all scattered to their tasks.

Butter sizzled as it melted into a pan, olive oil bubbled from the jar with a *glug*, the astringent tang of rosemary and garlic filled the air, and I moved through the bustle like a good general, tasting, sniffing, correcting. "Macerate some raspberries in wine to top those *frittelle*, Giuliano. The good Magnaguerra vintage, and lots of it." This was a meal for Juan Borgia, after all; absolutely everything on the menu would be soaked in wine. "Get that useless cat out of the *way*, Ugo, or so help me I'm drowning it in the cistern!" I ducked under a rack of pots and gave a whack to the spit-boy's shoulder to have him cranking faster on the capons that had just gone over the flames. "A splash more lime for those capons—"

One more sweeping glance over my well-trained team, and I began spooning out sugar and cinnamon myself for sweet *tourtes* of ripe blackberries and toasted walnuts. And I couldn't help a smile, because when I'd fled the Convent of Santa Marta I'd sworn I would never cook sweets again, but somehow I was still the one who always made them. Even after all the training I'd given my apprentices and undercooks, they couldn't equal me when it came to honeyed *crostate* and marzipan *tourtes* and sugared fruits. And no wonder, because *crostate* and *tourtes* and sugared fruits were all I'd made in my two years as a nun. Nuns were all mad for anything sweet, and I suppose it stood to reason. When two hundred women are forced to give up silk gowns and the pleasures of the flesh, marzipan was all they had to make life special.

But it was Giulia Farnese who ate my cakes and *tourtes* now, not my spiteful pinch-faced prioress, and I didn't mind making them for her. At least she said thank you. Though I wondered sometimes if the woman they called the Bride of Christ would laugh if she found out she had a *real* bride of Christ making her meals.

"More sugar, Bartolomeo," I called over my shoulder as my apprentice began tossing *frittelle* ingredients into a mortar.

"There's enough sugar already," he said without looking up.

"No, there is not. A large pinch more."

He added a very small pinch more. I sniffed to let him know I hadn't missed a thing, but let him continue. I needed all my attention to roll out the *tourte* dough; I'd done some tweaking to my father's original recipe, and it resulted in a thinner, flakier texture, but the dough tore very easily. My father was a very great cook in Venice, but I'd begun modifying his recipes lately, something I would have once considered as unthinkable as making a few improving tweaks to the stone tablets of Moses. "You ran away from a convent, girl," I could hear my father roar at me, "and now you're *changing my recipes*?" My father had already cast my name out of the family for good when I ran away from the convent where he'd placed me. He probably cast me out all over again when he realized I'd taken his recipe book with me, and then one more time for good measure when we'd encountered each other by plain chance on the road, and I'd left him unconscious and trussed up in a cellar rather than let him drag me by the hair back to Venice . . . I wasn't proud of any of it, believe me, but if you've already been cast out of a family once, what difference does it make?

Sweet Santa Marta, but I wasn't a good daughter. I was, however, a better cook than my father.

"Bartolomeo," I snapped over my shoulder, "why have you got the saffron out? *Frittelle* do not need saffron."

"Just a pinch. It will complement the flavor of the raspberries."

"It will fight the flavor of the raspberries," I said firmly. "Put it away at once."

Bartolomeo muttered something under his breath, and I wished I were a man. If I were a man, no apprentice would dream of arguing with me, and if they did I could simply beat them until they realized their opinions were not required, as my father used to beat his apprentices, and me as well. Not that I blamed him. Now that I had apprentices of my own to manage, I understood just how much they needed to be smacked for *anything* to sink through their thick skulls.

"I know I'm late!" a man's voice called from the courtyard, and boots sounded through the scullery and then the cold room. "Carmelina—"

"All in hand, Marco," I called back without looking. My cousin would pause in the doorway, looking sheepish and running a hand through his black curls, and then there would be the excuses.

"Sorry," he cajoled me. "I found that, ah, new butcher I was telling you about—beautiful prosciutto on offer, it'll do for the *credenza* tomorrow—"

"That's lovely, Marco." I cut him off before the lie could get any more elaborate; the apprentices were already nudging each other and stifling snickers. "Madonna Adriana wants to see both of us."

"Better give me an apron, then." Marco's dark eyes twinkled. "An artistic splatter of flour, do you think?"

"Never mind the apron," I said, but my cousin in a good mood was infectious. When he'd been the star apprentice of my father's kitchens and I'd been twelve, I'd fallen madly in love with him—and who wouldn't? Tall, muscled, dimpled, and handsome; that was Marco Santini. Of course, shortly after that I'd discovered that he had no sense and no ambition either, and nothing between the ears but dice games and bullfighting bets, and I'd fallen right back out of love again. Still, my reproving smack to his shoulder was a good deal gentler than the ones I gave the scullions. "Bartolomeo, see my blackberry *tourtes* get into the oven—" And my cousin and I trooped upstairs to see the mistress of the house.

"I won four ducats on a single round of *primiera*," Marco said in a jubilant whisper. "Four! I had a *fluxus* hand, see, and no one else had anything higher than a *numerus*—"

"You said you wouldn't go gaming during the week anymore!" I scolded. "On free afternoons only—"

"I felt Lady Fortune sitting on my shoulder, little cousin. Who says no to that?" He kissed his fingertips, and then he looked around to make sure we were alone on the stairwell, and leaned down and smacked my mouth with a kiss too. "Maybe I can pay you a visit tonight?"

"Maybe." I scowled, but gave a half smile. My cousin was a fool, and I certainly wasn't in love with him anymore—but he was handsome. And just occasionally, when his mood flew high from a win and he felt the urge for a bedmate, well, better his little cousin who would at least never pressure him for marriage the way any of the maidservants would have done.

Not that anyone in the household could ever know that Marco occasionally shared my bed. I wasn't afraid of getting caught with a swollen belly—I'd surrendered my virtue at seventeen to another apprentice of my father's, and he'd addled my wits for a week or two, but not so badly I hadn't taken care to safeguard myself with a few discreet tricks involving a halved lime and a tincture of pennyroyal. No, strict chastity wasn't really practiced by the *palazzo*'s maids, no matter what stringent standards Madonna Adriana tried to impose on her servants.

But I had to command obedience from a kitchen full of insolent boys who had to respect me as the inviolable Madonna of the kitchens, a woman far too iron-willed ever to be wheedled by a handsome face or a honeyed word. Marco had no such difficulties, of course, but men didn't. If I'd been born a man, I could forge a career as a cook *and* marry, without needing to choose one or the other. If I'd been born a man, I'd have simply followed in my father's footsteps as *maestro di cucina* in my own right, without anybody trying to stick me in a convent because what else is to be done with an extra daughter when you don't have the money for her to marry.

But it was the way of the world, and I saw no point howling over the unfairness of it all. Even if my bed felt lonely most nights, since Marco really had more fire for the cards than he did for me or any other woman . . . well, a little loneliness in this life I'd made was worth it. Far better than making watery communal stews in a habit that choked under the chin. Because I'd been lonely then too, but I'd also been weeping actual tears at the quality of the olive oil I'd been forced to work with, and saying endless Acts of Contrition because I could never keep my sleeves out of the kettles.

"Ah." Madonna Adriana da Mila greeted us as we were ushered into her private *sala*. A square, handsome woman of middle years, graying hair pressed into perfect ringlets, jeweled and capable hands hovering as usual over the slates and calculations of her household accounts. "Maestro Santini. And Carmelina. You are aware, of course, that the Duke of Gandia has returned from Spain. This has required a rearrangement of our resources here, now that he is establishing a household staff for his own *palazzo* . . ."

When we were released from the *sala* back downstairs, my cousin was no longer smiling. Nor did I think he'd be knocking on my door that night after everyone else had gone to bed.

"You're not being dismissed, you know," I ventured. "Just reassigned within the family. Cook to the Duke of Gandia, that's far more prestigious than cook for the Pope's mistress and cousin!"

"The Duke of Gandia won't have any need of me for months, not when he's leaving soon on this campaign of his against the French and the Orsini! And even when he's at home, he doesn't entertain. He goes out, and he takes his whole household with him!" Marco's long legs ate up the stairs. "Whether he's off campaigning or not, I'll be left sitting about on my thumbs doing *nothing*!"

I was tempted to point out that Marco had done a very good job of sitting about on his thumbs and doing nothing here. "I'm sure it's just a temporary change—"

He rounded on me in the same stairwell where he'd kissed me on the way up. "Someone told that tight-fisted bitch Adriana da Mila I was gone this afternoon! One hour off for a game of cards, just *one*, and she thinks I'm shirking!"

"One hour?" I tried to keep my voice gentle. I owed my cousin a great deal, after all. "What about the *pallone* match two days ago, and the bear baiting last week? The dice games and the *zara* games and the *primiera* games?" All of which I'd covered for him . . .

"You're the one who told her! Don't even deny it!" Marco's voice rose, and I saw a pair of maidservants at the head of the stairs take a peek at us over their heaping laundry baskets. "Everything I've done for you—I took you in, and now this?"

"I didn't tell her anything. But really, Marco," I couldn't help adding, "what did you expect? The whole household knows you don't bother putting in a full day's work anymore!" I flapped the curious maids away with a wave of my hand, and lowered my voice. "How many times did I warn you to be more cautious? Probably one of the stewards dropped a word in her ear!"

The kitchens had been running on my orders for months. Sheer, blind foolishness to think that someone as thrifty and sharp-eyed as Adriana da Mila wouldn't eventually take notice.

Of course, sheer blind foolishness was another gift of my cousin's.

"This is all your doing," he said bitterly. "This is the thanks I get for taking you in—"

I had to sit on my temper at that. Marco *had* taken me in, given me a place in the *palazzo* when I fled Venice and turned up on his doorstep begging for help. But his generosity hadn't exactly gone unpaid, had it? My hands had worked in his kitchens for four years now, freeing him up for all those long afternoons of dice, and I'd covered for him every time!

But that wasn't the way to coax Marco into a better mood.

"Come now." I tried a cajoling smile. "Madonna Adriana only gave me your position because she can pay me less! She's stingier than a vendor hawking secondhand clothes, you know that. And you're getting a better position, really—"

"That's not the point! You still stole *my* position here!" He jabbed a furious finger at me. "I gave you a home, little cousin, I gave you a place in the world when no one else would have you, and you steal *my* position as *maestro di cucina!*"

"*Maestra,*" I couldn't help saying. I'd never heard of such a title before—I'd never heard of any woman taking such a position before—and I felt a queer little flutter in my stomach. Sweet Santa Marta, had I really heard correctly up there in Madonna Adriana's *sala,* all laid out in her unctuous voice? Carmelina Mangano in command over the kitchens of the Palazzo Santa Maria, not as unofficial unpaid second cook, but as *maestra di cucina* at a salary of fifteen ducats per year?

My father would have said it was impossible.

Some involuntary hint of a smile must have broken over my face despite myself, because Marco's cheeks darkened. "Ungrateful," he muttered, "that's what you are. Ungrateful *traitor*—" and he went slamming down the rest of the stairs.

"Marco—" But by the time I'd gathered my skirts and raced to the kitchens, he was already banging through the cold room toward the courtyard with his cloak over his arm.

"*Maestro* Santini?" one of the undercooks ventured, but my cousin was gone without a word, pushing past Bartolomeo, who was simultaneously checking a fresh arrival of dead hens and giving the scullions a brisk tongue-lashing for leaving water spots on the silver. Bartolomeo glanced after him, then looked at me and raised his eyebrows.

"*Signorina?*"

I took a deep breath but let it out again in silence. Marco should decide when and how to tell the kitchens of his departure—he should be able to make his exit with some grace. Even if that wasn't his right, I'd still have done it that way. I didn't want my cousin angry with me. Not out of any fear that he'd inform on me, the way Leonello could—if Marco told the world I was a runaway nun, he'd be in just as much trouble for harboring me. No, I didn't want my cousin leaving angry because—well, he was the only family I had that was still speaking to me, after my flight from the convent.

If he was still speaking to me after today.

"*Signorina*, your *tourtes* are out of the ovens, and the *frittelle*—"

"The venison—"

"The pork shoulder, more salt?"

I shook myself into motion. "Yes, more salt . . . that sauce for the venison, it needs a dash more cream . . . Giuliano, my blackberry walnut *tourtes*, just a Credo's worth more time in the oven to crisp the crust . . . Bartolomeo, is that the first of your *frittelle*?"

"You want a bite, *signorina*?" He flipped one in the air, reaching behind his back with the griddle to catch it again.

"No showing off," I warned, and broke off a flaky corner. At once I could feel my brows rush together over my nose. I tasted sweet flaky goodness, I tasted the usual hints of candied citron and honey—and I tasted mutiny. Delicious mutiny, but still mutiny. "What's this?" I said ominously.

"Sweet chestnut flour *frittelle*," he answered with no shame at all. "With a dash of saffron. Improves the flavor, *signorina*."

"It does not. Saffron is for *sauces*, why would you—"

"Because it works," Bartolomeo said. "You just tasted it. You know it works."

"That is immaterial." I folded my arms across my breasts. "You disobeyed me."

His brows rushed over his nose, too. "The recipe needed it."

"That is my recipe. It is perfect the way it is."

"And I just made it better."

Not just mutiny, then, but blasphemy. I let the silence stretch, waiting until I had the attention of every apprentice, pot-boy, spit-boy, and undercook in sight. If you're going to step on a bigheaded apprentice, then it's best to have an audience. "Bartolomeo," I said at last in the silky whisper reserved for only the greatest of culinary sins. "You are an apprentice. That means you do not give orders, you obey them. You do not change recipes, you follow them. You have no thoughts that I don't approve of, no innovations that don't come from me, and you certainly are not qualified to make changes to *my* recipes."

"Someone should." He folded his arms across his chest, too. "You rely on cinnamon too much. Cinnamon in everything; it's boring."

My voice scaled up. *"Boring?"*

"And orange—why does every blasted recipe in your quiver need a squeeze of orange juice? And as for saffron, it's not just good for sauces. I could tell you a hundred other ideas—"

"Indeed you can," I said icily. "When you are a master cook yourself, and not an apprentice. Then you may muck up your *frittelle* with all the saffron you like, and may Santa Marta help whoever hires you. But until then—" So much for letting Marco announce things his way; the first real test of my authority was already here. "My kitchens, Bartolomeo," I said, and tossed the *frittella* I'd tasted to that useless, notch-eared tomcat. "My kitchens, my way. Because *I* am *maestra di cucina* here now."

"Maestra?" Bartolomeo blinked. "There's no such thing."

"As of today there is."

The apprentices goggled. Bartolomeo looked as if he were trying to decide whether to keep arguing with me or congratulate me, but I wasn't having either. He shouldn't be arguing with me *or* congratulating me;

he shouldn't dare say anything to me at all except "Yes, *signorina*" or "No, *signorina*." After our frightening time with the French army when he'd seen me with all my defenses down, he'd forgotten that. So I shredded him and his pretensions and his recipes up and down with my tongue until he was sputtering and all the other apprentices were hooting, and then he shouted back at me, or tried to because I just shouted right over him, and in the end I'm sorry to say we ended up slinging ladles at each other. It was not dignified to fight with one's own apprentices, especially before the others, and I probably should have demonstrated my new authority by sacking Bartolomeo altogether. But he really was quite a gifted young cook, or he would be as soon as his head deflated. So in the end I put him on pot duty, docked his free afternoons for the next two months, and stripped his wine ration for three, adding a new punishment every time he tried to argue. He should count himself lucky. My father would have taken him into the courtyard and beaten him bloody.

Bartolomeo was scarlet with humiliation by the time I was done, and part of me disliked doing it. Because it had been *good*, that touch of saffron in the *frittelle*. But public mutiny in any kitchens must be nipped just as publicly. And that goes double in any kitchens run by a woman.

"Well?" I glowered, hands on hips.

"Yes, *signorina*," Bartolomeo mumbled, and whirling about, he plunged his hands with a tremendous splash into the nearest sink full of pots. "I mean, *maestra*."

Maestra. I liked the sound of that!

CHAPTER TWO

✦

People tend to believe the bad rather than the good.

—BOCCACCIO

Leonello

"Do try not to fall on me," I told her without lifting my eyes from my book.

"Oh!" Sancha of Aragon brought herself up short in a billow of blue Spanish brocade as she rounded the pew, looking down at me with black brows drawn. "You're the dwarf, aren't you?"

"Your perspicacity is as astounding as your beauty, *madonna*."

"Are you insulting me?"

"Well, you are beautiful." She had startling blue eyes, olive-skinned breasts on generous display, and a supple little mouth that, according to rumor, had sucked half the papal guards.

She tapped her foot at me, but I kept reading. I sat in the chapel's rearmost pew, boots propped impiously on the pew ahead, reading Suetonius's *De Vita Caesarum* through the colored reflections of the stained-glass window overhead. The Palazzo Santa Maria had its own tiny chapel complete with marble-carved altar and rosewood crucifix and an Annunciation all in panes of blue and crimson glass in the window— but no one ever prayed here, considering that the *palazzo* stood adjacent to the Basilica San Pietro itself. I sometimes came here to read, if the *palazzo* rang a little too noisily with female voices to find quiet elsewhere.

"You're La Bella's dwarf," the lovely brunette above me persisted. "That stunted little shadow who follows her about everywhere. Don't you juggle or tumble or tell jokes?"

"No. And what is the Princess of Squillace doing here without so much as a maid in attendance?"

"I left them outside at the door." Sancha of Aragon lifted her little Neapolitan nose. "I am here to pray. Aren't you?"

"Yes," I said, surprising myself. My eyes had not really taken in my book for the past hour. For once, the chapel's hush had made me think of more somber things than my latest reading, and I had been seeing a face superimposed over my book. A woman's face, plain and tired and not so very pretty. Made less pretty by the slash in her throat below. A woman now four years dead, and I had not remembered what she looked like in a long time, but I was remembering now.

Mourning? Not really. She hadn't been a great love of mine; just someone I could call a friend. Not even a close friend. Just a garrulous tavern girl with a sweet voice, who had been kind to me. But I had few enough friends of any variety, and when this one died I'd thought to avenge her. Dwarves have foolish notions.

Anna. That was her name. Worth remembering, even if I couldn't avenge it.

But I had no desire to voice any such thoughts to hard-eyed Sancha of Aragon, who would not care anyway, so I just made an airy gesture. "I may be here to pray, Madonna Sancha, but you're not. What man are you meeting?"

"Get out," she snapped.

"No," I said. "If I leave here I'll have to go back to La Bella, and she's having her hair dressed, which not only takes an eon, but she's reading those wretched Avernus sonnets aloud to the maids and everybody's sighing. All in all, I'd rather be dead."

"Avernus?" Sancha wrinkled her nose. "What's that?"

"The latest poetical sensation." Ten sonnets had been published lately under the pen name of Avernus (the entrance to the underworld! How very mysterious!), written to the glory of some anonymous beloved named Aurora (the goddess of dawn, bringing light to Avernus's darkness! How very romantic!). Whoever he was under his pen name, he had not overlooked a single cliché in the entire classical repertory of gods and myth as far as I could tell. And now of course, every woman in Rome fancied *she* was the inspiration for Aurora.

Except Giulia Farnese—she just shrugged and said quite without jealousy, "I know they weren't written for me. You have to be chaste to be a poetical inspiration. Well, either chaste or dead, and thankfully I'm neither. No one dedicates poetry to live harlots!" Unfortunately, this conclusion did not stop my mistress from reading the wretched book cover to cover.

I dismissed bad love poetry from my mind and tilted my head back at the Princess of Squillace. "So, *madonna*, whom might you be meeting? Cesare Borgia?" Everyone in Rome whispered that Sancha was bedding her brother-in-law. Among many others.

Sancha tossed her head. "I could have you flogged, you know."

"No, you couldn't. I belong to La Bella, and while her taste in poetry is appalling, she's very protective when it comes to her servants. Even ones as rude as I." I flicked a page of my book over. "If it's Cardinal Borgia you're waiting for, then you will have a long wait. He was here, visiting Madonna Lucrezia, but he set off an hour ago."

"What?" Sancha's blue gauze veil drifted as she turned her head.

"The Holy Father, I understand, required his services. Some disturbance among the papal guard. The Duke of Gandia is their new Gonfalonier, but the Duke is out whoring and not to be found."

"And Cesare just galloped off with never a thought?"

"Not of you, certainly." The fire in his eye had all been for the troops His Holiness had conferred to the Duke of Gandia's command. Cesare Borgia would certainly not pass up a chance at Juan's post just for an afternoon tumble with his little brother's wife.

"If he thinks I'll be waiting here for him like a tame dog once he's done, he can think twice," Sancha sniffed. "Arrogant bastard."

"He is at that."

"He's talked of you, you know." She gave me a sidelong glance. "Leonello, isn't it? He says you're clever."

"We play the odd game of chess now and then. Sometimes I even beat him."

"Does he ever mention me?"

"No."

"You're a rude little beast, you know that?"

"Yes."

She flung herself down beside me with a great lack of grace, sighing. I would have wondered why a princess would talk to a dwarf, but bastard-born Sancha of Aragon was not much of a princess. I'd never spoken a word to her before, but I'd observed her the past few months after she and her sulky little husband Joffre had come from Naples. It wasn't for nothing that my mistress referred to her as the Tart of Aragon. "Spread her knees for the nearest page boy, she will," I'd heard one of her maids whispering to another. "Then tease her little husband about it, just to see his chin quiver!"

"An afternoon wasted," Sancha complained, jamming a pearl pin further into her piled hair. "Cesare said we'd have the whole day after he was done visiting with Lucrezia!"

"How efficient of him," I said. "Visit his sister, then pick up his sister-in-law on the way home for a good romp."

Sancha cast her blue eyes at me. "Does that shock you?"

"Nothing shocks me," I said, but thought of my friend Anna again. Her death had shocked me profoundly—staked out on a tavern table by a knife through each palm, and her throat cut afterward. She had a dimple in her cheek, her one claim to prettiness, and it had had a drop of dried blood in it by the time I found her dead on the table.

"Cesare might be able to shock you." Sancha laughed. "He'll do anything, you know. I had him take me once on the altar over there, in his cardinal's robes."

Time was, I'd thought him capable of sins a good deal more sinister than fornicating in a church. Three men had killed Anna: a guardsman and a steward from the Borgia household escorting a young masked man hunting through the slums of Rome for a whore. The steward and the guardsman I'd hunted down myself, but I'd never found the man in the mask. Time was I thought it might be Cesare, or maybe his vicious brother, Juan. And there had been other girls after Anna, found table-staked and throat-slit and raped. Five in all . . .

But the last had been a year and a half ago, the night after La Bella and I had been captured by the French, according to the gossip I'd gleaned on my return. Juan Borgia had been off in Spain then, and Cesare Borgia had been pacing the floor in the Vatican, witnessed by a hundred eyes as he tried to reassure the frantic Pope that his mistress would not be murdered by the French King. La Bella and I had not died that night; another girl had—but since then? Nothing.

The masked man who had killed first my friend and then a string of others was either gone from Rome or dead. Or had perhaps never existed at all, except in a series of coincidences and a dwarf's overheated imagination. It would not be the first time my flights of fancy had led me into trouble.

Sancha twisted her neck at my book. "Why would anyone bother teaching a dwarf to read? All you have to do in life is juggle."

"Why would anyone ever bother teaching a princess to read?" I retorted. "All *you* have to do in life is flop on your back and produce babies."

"I've got the first part all right." She let out a giggle, buffing at her nails. They could have used a good scrubbing. "What's that book there?"

"De Vita Caesarum."

"It sounds dull."

"It's salacious imperial gossip about the old Roman emperors. I find Latin smut is much easier for a poor scholar like me to parse together than Latin prayers."

Her lips curved. "Is there anything dirty?"

"Well, Emperor Domitian liked to depilate his concubines—pluck their hairs out one by one with tweezers."

"Which hairs?"

"Which do you think?"

"Oooh." Her eyes widened deliciously, and then she laughed. For a beautiful girl, Sancha of Aragon had a surprisingly nasty laugh. "Can you see the Holy Father doing that to Giulia Farnese?"

"Keep your tongue off my mistress, *madonna*."

"Well, aren't you the little champion?"

"I'm paid to be." No use explaining friendship to a spiteful tart who didn't believe dwarves had any more feeling in them than dogs. I turned a page.

"I don't see why everyone thinks Giulia's so special." Sancha sounded resentful. She'd cut quite a dash at the Neapolitan court, and no doubt she'd intended to do the same here—but in Rome, it was Giulia Farnese who set the fashions. The virtuous women of the Holy City might shudder at the Bride of Christ's reputation, but they devoured every detail of her appearance down to the last tassel and ribbon. Let Sancha of Aragon show herself at Mass in blue striped velvet, or Lucrezia Borgia in pink-and-silver checkered silk—if Giulia Farnese tripped out in pale green with a matching furred capelet, every woman in Rome was soon sporting the "Farnese green" and the "papal *mozzetta*."

"Really, I don't think she's so beautiful at all," Sancha continued peevishly, picking at her nails again. "I've got a far finer figure. Don't you think, little man?"

I allowed my eyes to travel over her. "I'd have to make a comparison, Madonna Sancha."

"You must have sneaked a look when La Bella was dressing." Sancha tossed her head. "If you saw me without my shift, you'd give me the prize."

I'd never seen Giulia naked, nor to my knowledge had any man who wasn't the Holy Father, but I had no intention of saying so.

Joffre Borgia's wife looked down at me through her long lashes, and I saw a spark of interest in her eyes—a spark I'd seen before in the eyes of other women. "Tell me, are you little and stunted everywhere?"

Ah, the eternal question. Female curiosity; it's put more women in my arms than you might think. Though never a princess. "Am I stunted everywhere?" I repeated, giving Sancha a slow, cool smile. "Perhaps you'd like to find out for yourself, *madonna*."

She leaned down, smelling of overripe flowers. Her breath was hot and spiced on my face. "All those dirty things in that book, little man. Is that what dwarves like? Do you like to pluck out hair too?"

Dio. I linked my fingers around the back of her neck and yanked her mouth against mine, just to shut her up. She gave a gasp of surprise, but then her tongue darted into my mouth, and her teeth scored my lip.

I drew back, touching my lip where she'd drawn a bead of blood. Private rumor among the guardsmen had it that Sancha of Aragon liked rough handling, both giving it and receiving it, and for once rumor appeared to be correct. "I don't need books for inspiration," I said finally, and flipped *De Vita Caesarum* closed before she could ask any more sordid questions about the plucking out of hair.

She looked pleased at my daring, and her hand strayed to toy with the lacing at my shirt. "Cesare has some books that would make a churchman go blind. Any churchman but him, that is." Her fingers petted my chest as though she were caressing a lapdog. "Cesare likes to tie me down, you know. Like a crucifix, with my arms out, and then he does whatever he likes to me." She lowered her voice. "And what he likes is to hurt me."

My fingers froze, moving through her hair. "Does he, now?"

She arched a little, giving a shiver and a purr at once. "Sometimes I think he won't stop. Not till I'm dead." She didn't appear too disturbed by the thought. To girls like Sancha of Aragon, rough play is all a game, just another way to lead a man about by the balls. She'd shriek bloody murder if the rough play ever got dangerous. But it never would, because who dares seriously hurt a king's daughter? No, she'd play her little games around the fringes of the dark things, fancying herself so daring, and the girls like Anna were the ones who died when they did the same.

"You should be careful, Madonna Sancha," I said finally. "I've known five girls in this city who died bound down. Their arms wide, their legs spread, and their throats cut."

"Just whores," Sancha shrugged. "Nothing to do with me. Another died like that two nights ago."

My voice came out too sharp. "You're sure?"

"Staked to a table with knives. Juan told me. He heard it from a guard. What does it matter?" Sancha hesitated a moment, and I wondered if she'd made the same connection I had, but she just looked impatient that we weren't talking about her any longer. *You may be a king's daughter, lovely lady*, I thought, *but you really aren't very bright, are you?*

"You know, Juan's been very attentive to me," she went prattling blithely on. "If Cesare thinks he can keep me waiting, well, he'll find I can have as many Borgias as I like without pining after him—"

I twined my hand through her hair again, and she broke off her complaining to dandle her hand down toward my breeches. She had a gleam of spite in her half-closed eyes that I'd seen before too, on girls who thought it great fun to wait till a man was half clothed and then snap their legs closed with a stream of spiteful laughter. A dangerous trick to pull on a full-sized man who might use his fists, but what can a dwarf do except slink away in shame?

"Why don't you tell me more," I murmured, dropping a string of unhurried kisses down her slender neck as she stroked me. I like being teased no more than any man, but I'd let her do it if it kept her talking. "Tell me everything you know about this woman who died two nights ago. And after that, tell me *all* about Cardinal Borgia and his . . . tastes."

"Is that the kind of thing you like to hear?" She laughed. "You're a twisted little man, aren't you?"

"Oh, you have no idea." I was smiling as her mouth closed on mine, but not because I had a princess in my arms. Another girl was dead, and that was nothing to smile about . . . but perhaps I'd been right after all. Perhaps the man in the mask wasn't a product of my imagination.

And perhaps I had not been so wrong to suspect Cesare Borgia.

Giulia

There's no sight like a girl being alluring with all her heart. The flutter of the lashes, the delicate blush of the cheeks, the rapid rise and fall of the bosom—it's a performance in its own right, just as much an art as the singing of a motet or the execution of a complicated *basse-danse*. Having made quite a study of allurement myself, I enjoyed watching another woman do it well.

But not when the woman being alluring was seventeen-year-old Lucrezia Borgia, Countess of Pesaro, and when the object of her allurement wasn't the Count of Pesaro, but my older brother Alessandro Farnese.

"You must be sure to sit beside me when the singers begin," Lucrezia was saying, having worked her soft little hand into the crook of Sandro's elbow as they stood by a blaze of rosebushes in the Vatican gardens. "These musical afternoons are always so dull, Cardinal Farnese. Giulia!" she cried, catching sight of me. "I'd forgotten your brother could be so amusing!"

"Yes, he's quite the jester." I crossed the stretch of grass to join them, Leonello trailing behind me as usual. "Sandro, don't tell me the Holy Father released you already?"

"He's released a few of us. I believe Cardinal Zeno and one or two others were detained for some additional shouting."

Whenever my Pope hosted one of these musical afternoons to follow a consistory or a more informal meeting of his cardinals, it was a sure sign there was shouting to be done beforehand. If the order of the day was merely business as usual, Rodrigo would harangue his cardinals and hand out orders to his archbishops, and may the Holy Virgin have mercy on them if they didn't get immediately to work. But if my Pope had a difficult measure to force down unwilling throats, he was sure to detain his churchmen after the day's business in the gardens of the Vatican. A dozen furious-faced cardinals and bishops would come stamping down among the grass and the rosebushes, muttering of my Pope's high-handedness, but before they had the opportunity to stew in their own resentment, they would be met by refreshments and wine. Not to mention a dozen women headed by Lucrezia and myself, all of us ordered to laugh and to charm until the storms passed and all those cross old cardinals and bishops went home mellow with wine and music.

"So why didn't the Holy Father keep you behind for a little shouting, Sandro?" I took my brother's other arm. "He should shout at you—you're the most useless fellow in the whole College!"

"True." Sandro doffed his scarlet cardinal's hat modestly. "But I'm the most entertaining. Just this afternoon I made everyone's sides ache when I trotted out that old joke about the friar and the trout. Well, Cardinal Carafa didn't laugh. But I did say the trout looked like him . . ."

I smiled at my brother: six years older than I, slender and dark-haired with a smile of demure wickedness like a fallen angel and his cardinal's cap forever sitting at a rakish angle. I had another brother in my hometown of Capodimonte, and a sister married in Florence as well, but Sandro and I had always been each other's favorites. We had the same dark eyes and the same sense of fun that danced behind them, and both were traits the rest of *la famiglia Farnese* sorely lacked.

"Not only amusing, but handsome as well!" Lucrezia certainly seemed to be admiring my brother's eyes, and her lashes had a quick flutter for the rest of him, too. "Surely the handsomest man in the College! Except for my brother Cesare, of course. A girl must always support her big brother first—Giulia will understand that. Goodness, but it's hot!"

The Pope's daughter fluttered her fingers at the base of her throat, a gesture copied from Sancha to draw attention to her breasts, which had been powdered and trussed and laced into the lowest-cut gown I'd ever seen her wear. Orange-red brocade embroidered within an inch of its life, too ornate for a simple summer entertainment, but Lucrezia had been piling it on in these past months: wider skirts, lower necklines, more paint, more embroidery, more jewels; anything to make a splash. I couldn't help looking at her thoughtfully as she chattered at my brother again.

"—we'll be hearing more of those dull motets, I suppose. Ugh, but I don't care if I never hear Josquin again. There's something new, though; one of the court musicians set the Avernus sonnets to music." Another sweep of lashes. Someone really should tell her not to overdo the lashes. "Surely you've read Avernus's sonnets to his Aurora? I favor Sonnet II, but Giulia prefers Sonnet VI. Just because it has Aurora as Europa, borne off by Jupiter as a bull—"

"You know my fondness for bulls," I said lightly, and Sandro gave a brief scowl. He'd never entirely reconciled himself to my status as the

Pope's mistress. It's not precisely what most men want for their favorite sisters, is it? *My little sister, the Pope's mistress.*

Lucrezia was still chattering on about poetry, which had the usual effect of making Leonello, at my back, put his thumbs in his ears, when an undulation of purple satin swished up. "My dear Lucrezia," Sancha of Aragon purred, looking at Sandro through half-closed lids. "And Cardinal Farnese, of course. You look nothing like your sister, do you know that? Fortunately. Golden hair is all very well, but I do prefer dark suitors." She reached up to twine a strand of his hair about her finger, and Sandro looked faintly startled . "Lucrezia, I won't allow you to keep this luscious fellow all to yourself!" Sancha went on. "Cardinal Farnese, perhaps you will take a turn about the gardens with me?"

"I fear I must steal him," I said firmly, and led my brother away. "Sandro, come see these roses over here, don't they look just like those little yellow ramblers our mother used to grow in Capodimonte . . . ?"

As soon as I had my brother out of earshot, I plucked one of those little yellow roses off its bush and pointed it at him thorns first. "The Tart of Aragon is fair game, Sandro, but *don't* flirt with Lucrezia. I know you've never been happy with the idea of the Holy Father and me, but don't think to even the score by seducing his daughter!"

"What do you take me for, *sorellina*?" Sandro gave a great show of mock outrage. "Besides, please note who was flirting with whom." He peered over my shoulder at Sancha and Lucrezia, giggling softly with their heads together. My brother had been away these past months, on business for the College of Cardinals, and as usual he had managed to find time to dally in the country with his little mistress. He hadn't seen much of either Lucrezia or the Tart of Aragon this summer, not the way I had. "Are they always like that?"

"Sancha's always been a cat in heat." I plucked another pair of roses, making a little nosegay. "I do wish Lucrezia wouldn't imitate her so much."

"Better than having them at each other's throats, surely." Sandro tugged me companionably against his side, leading me through the clipped hedges away from the crowd gathering rapidly round Lucrezia and Sancha like bees round their queens. "You thought the fur was going to fly when they first clapped eyes on each other!"

There had been a certain period of scrutiny between the Pope's daughter and daughter-in-law when they first met this spring. A certain covert amount of measuring dark hair against blond, a fuller bosom against a slimmer waist, a collection of Roman gowns against a chest full of Neapolitan dresses. Now they had nothing but giggles and gossip for each other, and that disquieted me sometimes as I saw Lucrezia drinking every salacious whisper from her new sister-in-law.

"I heard Cardinal Michiel say it's all to be expected, Sancha acting like a tart, because she's bastard-born!" I gave an indignant sniff of my sweet-scented little roses, watching Sancha wind her arm through a young bishop's. "'Born in lust means lust in the blood'—have you ever heard such rubbish? Lucrezia's bastard-born too, and she's always been such a sweet little thing." At least, she *had* been. "And if anyone ever said my Laura had lust in the blood—"

"Or my Costanza!" Sandro clapped an outraged hand to the place he would have been wearing a sword if he'd been a *condottiere* rather than a cardinal, with a flourish because even when he was being outraged he had more flourishes in him than a pantomime actor. Really, he should have been a pantomime actor rather than a cardinal. "Did you know Costanza's learning to move about already? Not crawling, exactly; more like rotating herself across the floor like a little rolling pin—"

I listened for a while to my brother's recitations of Costanza's latest achievements—his first child from his much-adored mistress, so naturally she was perfection embodied. She really was a little dear, if not quite the miracle that was my Laura, but proud fathers must be allowed to gush. I did wish sometimes that Rodrigo would gush a little more about Laura . . .

My Pope made his appearance then, followed by a flock of bad-tempered cardinals. They must be fuming over the notion of Juan leading the papal armies as Gonfalonier, not that I blamed them. Cardinal Zeno stamped off without even the pretense of a courteous exit, and Ascanio Sforza would have too if I had not accosted him. "Cardinal

Sforza, I will need you desperately once the music begins, for it's all in French and you know how wretched my French is. Perhaps you will translate for me?" I smiled and charmed until he thawed, and then I nodded sympathetically as he muttered veiled complaints about these consistories where one's opinions weren't even consulted, and had anyone listened to his proposal that one of the Sforza clan be considered as Gonfalonier? Perhaps even the absent Count of Pesaro; he was the Pope's son-in-law, after all, yet had anyone even *pretended* to consider his name when Cardinal Sforza suggested it?

"The Holy Father hears all suggestions," I soothed, and made my usual discreet promise that I would carry Cardinal Sforza's concerns directly to the papal ear when it was next close to mine. He bustled off looking mollified. This was my own part of Rodrigo's seemingly idle social gatherings: to listen, to promise, and to decant all for my Pope's dissection later. In truth, I had no idea why anyone tried to bribe or wheedle me into using my influence with Rodrigo, because he kept his own counsel when it came to the business of Christendom. He was not a man to be swayed just because a soft voice whispered in his ear across a pillow, nor did I believe it my place to sway him. God's chosen Vicar on earth had far more exalted sources than me to consult for advice— namely, God Himself. No one had elected *me* Pope, after all, so I kept well out of papal business, merely giving Rodrigo a dutiful recitation of what others so hopefully whispered into my ear. He drank it all in, chuckling at their efforts to recruit me.

By the time the music began, I'd soothed another pair of cardinals and smiled at the Neapolitan ambassador's attempt to find out if Gonsalvo de Cordoba, or any of the other Spanish generals, or possibly a mule, would be aiding Juan in leading the papal armies. A little array of choir boys were paraded out into the gardens, looking unnaturally solemn, and the cardinals and the ladies took their places on padded stools as the first pure treble launched the melody. Normally I'd sit at my Pope's side, but he was weaving some scheme with a pair of sourlooking ambassadors from Queen Isabella of Castile. Lucrezia had abandoned flirting with my brother and was now eyeing one of her father's papal envoys.

Impulsively, I caught at her brocade sleeve. "Come sit with me, Lucrezia."

"I can't," she said flippantly. "Our dresses will clash." She twitched her bright scarlet skirts against my ice-blue gauze. "These pale colors of yours—I'm determined to set the style for something bolder. You'd better look to your laurels if you want to keep leading the fashions in Rome, Giulia! You know, Sancha told me her robe makers had a dozen orders for caps with peacock plumes the instant I was seen wearing one to Mass? And Perotto over there—Father's new envoy, you know the one? Pedro Calderon, but everyone calls him Perotto—says I'm an absolute *vision* in bright red like this!"

"You're making talk, you know." I tried to say it lightly. "All this flirting with my brother, and with Sancha's pages, and now with papal envoys. Don't you think—"

"You sound like my mother, Giulia Farnese. Are you getting old and prim?" And off rushed the Pope's daughter—"My dear Perotto, you must sit beside *me*!"

Taking a deep breath, I claimed a seat of my own beside the last woman in the world who wanted me at her side. Claimed my seat and smiled, and gestured for the earnest little choir of boys to continue their singing, and said low-voiced, "Vannozza, perhaps we should talk about your daughter."

She looked at me down the long, high-bridged nose that she'd also passed on to Cesare Borgia. Vannozza dei Cattanei: my well-preserved auburn-haired predecessor, still handsome in her russet velvets and many rings. Vannozza, who had stayed at Rodrigo's side a full decade and given him four children. "La Bella," she said, and smiled in that special way that both indicated her innate superiority *and* concealed those horse teeth. "What has my daughter to do with you?"

"I love her," I said bluntly. "As much as my own daughter. But Lucrezia needs reining in."

That surprised Vannozza; I could see from the peevish fold that suddenly appeared at the corner of her eyes. Because *blunt* wasn't how we ever began things, Vannozza and me. Most of time we managed to ignore each other altogether. If forced into conversation, there would first be polite noncommittals, then a few exchanges of edged courtesy punctuated by an oversweet bout of cooing, and then perhaps one of us would unsheathe claws. Usually Vannozza, because I could outcoo absolutely anyone, much less my spiteful, wasp-waisted, wasp-tongued predecessor.

This time, however, I had sidestepped all the pleasantries.

"Lucrezia is being talked about," I went on under cover of the music, before Vannozza's bright eyes could narrow any further. "It's Sancha's example—remember the incident at Pentecost? People whispered for weeks."

At the Feast of Pentecost in May, Lucrezia and Sancha had traded jokes and whispers all through the long sermon in the Basilica San Pietro—and had finally abandoned their seats altogether to clamber into the choir stalls with all their ladies, bringing the service to a complete halt as they settled their skirts and called for refreshments. Johann Burchard, the beleaguered little German who had the thankless task of acting as Rodrigo's master of ceremonies, had run about shrieking and tearing his hair afterward as he bemoaned the horrendous impropriety of it all, and even I had been surprised. Lucrezia was merry by nature, but she'd always been respectful.

"My daughter," Vannozza stated as though bringing the Eleventh Commandment down from on high, "is merely high-spirited."

"Rodrigo said that too," I said, and her eyes flared at my use of her former lover's name. Oh, Holy Virgin, would she just stop bristling? I hadn't taken Rodrigo away from her; they'd already been long parted when he swooped me off my feet, but there was no use telling Vannozza that. One of those women who always finds an excuse to feel slighted; aren't they tiresome? "His Holiness won't listen to a word about Lucrezia," I tried again. "You know how he is—'Bah, Lucrezia's just in high spirits! I like seeing a pretty young filly kick up her heels—'"

Vannozza gave an unwilling snort through her long nose. I leaned closer, lifting my nosegay of yellow roses to cover our conversation as the choir began a new tune. A good many eyes had flicked avidly in our direction, seeing the Pope's current and former mistresses bend their heads so close together. "It's not just about Lucrezia giggling and misbehaving during sermons," I went on. "She listens far too much to San-cha, and Sancha is *not* a good influence."

"That girl is a harlot," Vannozza deigned to concede. Not the kind of girl a mother wants for any of her sons—and surely she had to know by now that Sancha was sleeping with all them (having recently added Juan to her collection to complete the trifecta of Borgia sons. I ask you). I pressed my advantage.

"Do you want Lucrezia to be a harlot too, Vannozza? She's fluttering her lashes at that new papal envoy now, *and* my brother, *and* any other handsome man at court who crosses her path. And she used to be so in love with her husband; it floated off her like perfume."

Maybe that was what truly troubled me. You could look about Rome and see any number of young wives who loved to flirt and giggle, and if you saw the fat or sour or graying men they were married to, you usually couldn't blame them. But Lucrezia had always been different. Something of the maiden in the tower about her, surrounded by protective Spanish father and brothers as she was—and then Giovanni Sforza had come along and swept her away from the walls her family had put up around her, and I'd seen her blossom like one of these yellow roses in my hand.

I didn't like seeing that glow of love turn into common, roving-eyed flirtation.

Vannozza dei Cattanei broke into my speculations. "Maybe it's just as well my daughter is no longer so starry-eyed for Lord Sforza."

I looked at Vannozza. My predecessor was looking smug, and that was hardly a good sign. "What have you heard about Lord Sforza?"

A deliberate shrug of those velvet-clad shoulders. "He isn't the match my daughter could have had, certainly. His ties with the other Sforza in Milan aren't anywhere near as strong as he made out when he presented himself for Lucrezia's hand."

"So?"

"You don't know, then?" Vannozza gave a faint smile. "I see Rodrigo doesn't tell you everything, Giulia Farnese."

The choirboys sang on in piercing sweetness—the Avernus sonnets, starting with the first where Aurora was compared to Ulysses's Calypso on her sea-washed isle. Leonello was muttering something under his breath that sounded like *Oh,* Dio, *not those damned sonnets again!* but I wasn't listening to him *or* to that lovely music and its even lovelier words.

"Calypso, smiling nymph of sanded isle—"

Vannozza examined her buffed nails. "Rodrigo still visits me, you know. He so values my advice, he'll quite often come for a cup of wine or two before *cena*."

"Holy Virgin, Vannozza, will you cease trying to make me jealous?" Though she had succeeded, just a little. I knew very well that Rodrigo had an old fondness for his former mistress—he even sometimes referred to her as his *wife*! And then couldn't see why it exasperated me . . .

I put that aside, lowering my voice. "I don't see why it matters, Rodrigo fretting to you about Lord Sforza's shortcomings. Whether he is the ally that was hoped for or not, he is Lucrezia's husband now. And he loves her, I have seen that with my own eyes, and he deserves better from her than flirtation when his back is turned. Even if flirtation is as far as it ever goes." I did not truly believe Lucrezia would stray from her marital bed. She was surely just drunk on admiration and flattery.

"—In whose white arms Ulysses would not sleep—"

"You are hardly one to criticize *my* daughter's behavior," Vannozza snapped.

"Yes, yes, because I'm her father's whore." I brushed that aside impatiently. "Let's not get stuck upon the obvious, Vannozza. I'm the great harlot of the Vatican, and no one expects decorum from me." Which was precisely why I tried to give it. "But do you really want Lucrezia to take *my* path? She is Countess of Pesaro, and the Pope's daughter. There are rules; there are expectations of her. High ones, considering her position, and she does herself no good by flouting them."

"My daughter is the Pope's child," Vannozza dei Cattanei pronounced. The Twelfth Commandment, clearly. "Like her brothers. And they are *above* rules."

"—Calypso's arms, if yours, would surely keep—"

I looked at her a moment, hoping she might be jesting. But no, Vannozza dei Cattanei was utterly, appallingly serious. "You know, my brother Sandro just fathered his first child," I said finally. "A girl, and a sweet little thing too. She has black hair, just like him, and he thinks she's perfection. I thought my Laura was perfection too—I still do. But she's not above *rules*, Vannozza, nor is Sandro's daughter, nor is yours. Where do you get this idea, you and Rodrigo, that your children are above *rules*?"

She smiled at me pityingly. "If your Laura were of Rodrigo's getting, Giulia Farnese, then you'd understand."

"My Laura *is* of Rodrigo's getting, Vannozza dei Cattanei. And I understand that she will soon be her father's favorite daughter, if you allow her sister to turn into a spoiled little tart."

"—*Ulysses from the bed of home beguiled.*"

The song ended, and a smattering of applause broke out. My Pope looked around for me and had a beam when he saw his old mistress sitting with the new. So amicably too, smiling at each other with such great sweetness. Rodrigo couldn't see that I was gripping my roses so hard that my fingers welled blood from half a dozen thorn pricks. How I longed to cram those roses up Vannozza dei Cattanei's nose. "My dears," Rodrigo called, oblivious. "You must both come sit with me! Those new sonnets everyone's talking of, which shall we hear next?"

"I prefer Sonnet VII," Vannozza said, claiming her place at the Pope's other side with great smugness. "The sonnet comparing the poet's beloved to Leda. Such a *maternal* figure, Leda—she produced such beautiful sons, didn't she, alongside Helen of Troy?"

"Of course, of course. And which do you prefer, Giulia?" A papal tweak to my cheek. "You're my Persephone, surely you like Sonnet IX. Aurora as Persephone—"

"They both belong at the bottom of the Tiber," Leonello muttered behind me.

"So does Vannozza dei Cattanei," I muttered back at him, and settled for a grim afternoon of laughter, music, and grave doubts.

CHAPTER THREE

*Nor can the father force his daughter
to become a nun without the cooperation of her free will!*

—SUORA ARCANGELA TARABOTTI, "L'INFERNO
MONACALE"

Carmelina

A ren't you coming with us?" the maids asked me as we left the
palazzo and I split left instead of right on reaching the street. "It's
bound to be splendid, all those handsome soldiers on parade!"

"And we can sing a great hymn of thanks, once *il Duche* is over the
horizon," Pantisilea said with relish. She was one of Madonna Giulia's
maids, far above the kitchen girls in the *palazzo* hierarchy of servants,
but Pantisilea was cheerfully indiscriminate: she slept with all the male
servants and befriended all the female, and that was as much distinction
as she ever made as far as hierarchy was concerned. She paused now to
cross herself and spit at the mention of the Duke of Gandia, and the
other maids did the same. "I can't wait to see him go, God rot him. He
had me over a basket of laundry once, did I tell you? I like myself a
nobleman now and then, don't think I don't, but he smelled like a brew-
ery and lasted about three strokes! Are you sure you don't want to watch
him leave, Carmelina?"

"No," I said, touching my purse and the crackle of paper inside that
was the letter. "Bid the Duke of Gandia good-bye without me."

Pantisilea made a face, and the cluster of maids headed off laughing toward the Piazza San Pietro, where most of the city had flocked to watch the Duke of Gandia receive the jeweled sword and white staff of Captain-General of the papal forces. He would be leading those same forces off against the remnants of the French, not to mention those branches of the Orsini family who had supported the French against the Pope. For Pantisilea and the rest of the maids it was a holiday; Bartolomeo had packed them one of his hampers as though they were off to a picnic. That boy couldn't see anyone out the door without making sure they had enough food for an army; he was worse than a Sicilian grandmother. But I didn't share the maids' festive mood, and I didn't care a bit about the Duke of Gandia's coming campaign. I turned the other direction, shivering even in my heavy cloak.

The Duke of Gandia had not gotten a fair day for his departure—it was blustery, gray, with a spiteful October breeze that tugged at my skirt hem, and the looming threat of rain. I was more concerned with the letter in my pouch alongside the hand of Santa Marta. I wondered what Santa Marta made of the words my younger sister had written in her looping childish hand.

Pray for our family, Carmelina, because a fever took Father to God.

Maddalena went on to say a good deal more—a great many warnings that I was *not* by any means to come back to Venice to bring shame upon the family by appearing at the burial, and after that followed a whole self-congratulatory paragraph on how virtuous she had been for taking our mother into her home. *I suppose she will be fit to look after the children; at least it will save me the need for a nursemaid. Naturally I have not told our mother anything of you, she would hardly approve of my writing, but I have far too forgiving a heart—my husband says I am a perfect saint . . .*

But all I really bothered to read was *a fever took Father to God.*

"Where should I go to, to pray for his soul?" I asked Santa Marta, who was as usual tied up securely in my pouch. "I thought I should go to the Basilica San Pietro, but perhaps Father would think that sacrilegious?"

It might seem silly to talk to a hand, even Santa Marta's, but I always had the feeling she was listening. I wasn't entirely convinced she didn't *move* sometimes—back in the days when she'd been a proper relic in a seemly reliquary with a viewing window, people used to whisper that the hand would make the sign of the cross if Santa Marta had answered your prayers. I never saw that hand make the sign of the cross, but she did have a habit of falling out of her pouch if she didn't have a good enough view of what went on around her.

"Now that I think on it, Father will be utterly furious if I go pray for him. Even if he's dead," I added to Santa Marta's listening ears (well, fingers). "He'll be up there in heaven stamping and roaring that he has no need for worthless prayers from a runaway nun, and he'd be right."

On the other hand . . . *I'm maestra di cucina now, Father.* I'd been told all my life that a woman could never have a position like my father's, yet now I did. I owed my rise to Adriana da Mila's tight grip on her purse rather than my own skills, of course, but I wasn't going to quibble with my luck. I looked up at the gray heavens. "Are you proud of me, Father?"

If he had gone to heaven at all, that is. Surely that was his eventual destination—my father might have clouted me a good deal, and hated me when I ran away from the convent, but I could not in all fairness call him a wicked man. Nor was he exactly a saintly one. Perhaps he was in purgatory for a time, working off a batch of smaller sins like vanity and pride and his tendency to pad the accounts when it came to his wealthier clients. "You had all better be ready for him when he finally does arrive in heaven," I told Santa Marta. "The way he schemed to cook for the Doge, well, that will be nothing to how he'll scheme to cook for God Himself."

A woman with a market basket gave me a startled look, and I realized I was talking aloud like a madwoman. I tugged my cloak closer about me, feeling the bite of the wind, and I decided against the Basilica San Pietro, setting off across the long stretch of the Ponte Sant'Angelo instead. Maybe I could find a shrine to Santa Marta, and just lay some flowers on it in my father's memory . . . but I passed a churchyard first, some small distance from the busy Campo dei Fiori, and the sight stopped me.

Just a small church in this city of churches; no grand dome or expanse of gleaming windows to draw the pilgrims in their hordes. The churchyard was overgrown, the paving stones cracked in places. But this church must have had a little convent attached to it, because I saw two sisters in the weedy churchyard, spading at the wild grass as the wind tugged at their black-and-white habits. One was old and had a tight-drawn face under her veil; the other was young with a crop of pimples by her nose. Both had chapped hands and faces reddened from cold, and even though their lips were moving silently, I knew they weren't muttering prayers. Lay sisters, both of them, because highborn choir nuns never spaded churchyards. The nobly born girls who brought illustrious family names and sizable dowries to the convent weren't required to work. The lay sisters worked for *them*, cleaning their cells and ironing the silk shifts they wore under their habits and making their beds since the choir nuns were allowed to sleep through the endless dawn prayers if they felt like it. I'd spaded my share of herb gardens and churchyards, blowing on my cold hands as my higher-born sisters practiced their Josquin motets or sat in cozy parlors gossiping about the latest fashions with their illustrious visitors.

"If I'd been able to cook," I told Santa Marta, "I might have stayed." Perhaps that was blasphemy, to put a mere earthly occupation above holy vows—but really, I'd been told many times as a child that every man honored God by the work he did with his hands. If I'd been allowed to honor God with the food I cooked, I might still be back in that convent putting prayers into the ovens along with the bread. But as a raw young novice, I'd been put under a savage-tempered old cow whose idea of high culinary discernment was boiling vegetables until gray. Even later when my skill with sweets vaulted me a bit higher up the ladder, there was nothing more innovative than, "Just add more sugar, Suora Serafina!"

The two lay sisters in the churchyard had stopped their weeding, the elder wincing as she stretched her stout back, the younger mopping her sweaty face with a grubby sleeve. "Maybe I still would have stayed," I told Santa Marta. "It's what girls do, after all, when you have too many daughters. The pretty one gets the dowry and the other takes the veil." Or in my case, the daughter who kept her virginity got the dowry, and the daughter who surrendered her virtue to a good-looking apprentice behind an orange crate got sent to the convent. I hadn't been in love with him, and that had made it all even worse—I'd felt enough shame at my sinful lusts that I'd felt I *deserved* the convent. And since I'd been at the age when I was getting a bit full of my own skill in the kitchen, and inclined to argue about it (like Bartolomeo)—well, my father had been glad to pack me out of his kitchens.

No, I might very well have stayed at my convent till I was old and withered. I could have carved out a place for myself in the kitchens, resigned myself to it all. But—

"It was the way Father came *visiting* me," I told Santa Marta. "Every Sunday he'd come to pay a call. He never paid so much attention to me when I lived under his own roof! And it wasn't me he really came to see at all, but of course you know that."

Choir nuns from illustrious families never really leave their noble relatives behind, you see. Every week a stream of velvet-clad visitors comes through those forbidding convent gates, and the nuns sit down with their married sisters and tickle their nieces under the chin and gossip about who will be next to marry and who will take the veil and what the Dogaressa wore at the last procession. The noble ladies who visit daughters in convents have feasts to plan at home; perhaps the celebration of a nephew's marriage or a grandson's christening. And hovering on the fringes of all those clusters of Venetian noblewomen, my father: falling into casual conversation at the grilles, ready with his book of recipes, leaving with yet another client. All with me standing there in the wimple that squeezed my face and the habit that was never long enough to cover my shins, doomed to peel onions and roll out marzipan forever.

That last day, I suppose, had been the seal. "Your fool cousin Marco got himself a patron at last," my father deigned to tell me. "Adriana da Mila of Rome. Ha, she'll realize *that* mistake soon enough." Then he'd abandoned me midsentence in favor of a bejeweled Foscari matron reeling off advice to her postulant daughter, who looked like she'd very much been hoping to leave maternal advice behind by taking the veil, and I hadn't known what I was doing until my hands were actually rifling the pouch my father had left at my feet and slipping his packet of recipes into my sleeve.

"Though I can't really claim the rest was impulse," I told Santa Marta. Taking Santa Marta's reliquary, bribing a fisherman to smuggle me out in his boat—that had all been a half-formed plan I'd been turning over for some months, a plan I hadn't put into action until I thought of a place I could flee and someone to give me work. Once I knew where I was going, well, the rest had fallen into place. Even if the addition to my belongings of a certain severed hand had not been part of the original scheme—she had gotten caught in the folds of my cloak somehow as I bundled up the crystal and silver reliquary, and I hadn't discovered her until it was far too late to give her back.

I gave Santa Marta a pat through the pouch, unable to help a smile. I'd been horrified at first to find myself a desecrator—I could just about settle my conscience when it came to taking the reliquary, considering that the convent had swallowed up the dowry that should have been mine—but nobody could justify stealing a saint (well, part of a saint). Now, however, I wondered if Santa Marta's hand hadn't decided to come along with me of its own free will. The inside of a reliquary box must get dull, after all, no matter how prettily jeweled, and with me she at least had a kitchen to rule over again.

No, I was sorry about many things: sorry to break my vows even if I'd never wanted to take them in the first place; sorry to steal from the nuns who might have been greedy and silly but still hadn't deserved to be robbed; sorry for the shame I'd brought down on my family's reputation. I even felt pangs of conscience over the sin of bedding Marco, who would be in a great deal of trouble if it were ever found out he had lain with a nun. But I no longer felt the slightest twinge of guilt over the fact that the severed hand of my patron saint had now, in however unorthodox a fashion, found a home with me.

And despite all my sins and broken vows and occasional instances of theft, Santa Marta must have liked something about me. Because I was mistress of my own kitchens, in my own right. Because I still hadn't been caught and returned to my convent.

You never will be now, something whispered, and my shiver had nothing to do with the bitter autumn wind. With my father dead . . . well, who *would* catch me? My sister didn't want me brought to justice;

she wanted me as far from Venice as possible. Marco, even if he was angry with me for taking his position, still had a vested interest in keeping my secret—he'd be in as much trouble as me if I were found out. Aside from Marco, Leonello was the only other person in Rome to know my true history, and so far he seemed inclined to keep his lips sealed.

No, I was safe—or as safe as I was ever likely to be.

The two lay sisters looked up at me when I called to them over the low stone wall around the churchyard. "Yes, *signorina?*"

I sketched a curtsy as the younger one came closer, still clutching her spade in one cold-chapped hand. "May I ask that you offer a prayer for my good father, Suora?" I asked respectfully. "I have just learned of his death, God rest his soul."

"Of course." The young nun looked hopeful, and I took a coin out of my purse and pressed it into her work-callused hand.

"One more thing." I lowered my voice. "Will you lay this on the altar in my father's memory?" And I passed her my father's worn packet of ciphered recipes.

"What is it?"

"Just recipes. My father's." I didn't need them anymore; I had them all long memorized. "Give them to your convent cook, after you take them off the altar," I advised. "If she can unpick the cipher—there's a note about how to read it in the back—then I promise you, the whole convent will eat better than queens. Even the lay sisters!"

"That would be something," the young lay sister muttered, eyeing the packet with a bit more interest. Perhaps she *would* take it down to the convent kitchens. Or maybe she'd just toss the whole bundle on the fire. Either way, I'd send my father's recipes out into the world and not really care where they ended up. I made my own recipes now, and they were better than my father's.

"I'll pray for your father," the lay sister promised, pocketing my coin and the packet of paper. "At Vespers, after the Duke of Gandia passes by—I suppose I won't get a good view when he goes by, but there's always hoping." Wistful. "They say he has a pearl in his helmet the size of an egg!"

"That's also the size of his brain," I told her, and took myself back to my kitchens. Enough pensive maundering for one afternoon. Juan

Borgia would be gone soon, and Madonna Giulia would come back shivering from the afternoon's ceremony even though she'd been wrapped in a lynx-lined cloak. She'd want a hot posset, and a good warming plate of stew.

"What do you mean the stew's not ready?" I shouted at Bartolomeo back in the kitchens. No day off for him to see the parade, since he was still on restriction for the ferocious quarrel he'd picked with me. Not the quarrel about the saffron *frittelle*, but yet another quarrel, last week, over whether to cook a calf's sweetbreads with a caul. Of course you cooked sweetbreads with a caul; absurd even to think otherwise, but Bartolomeo had some ridiculous idea about searing them on the spit with slabs of sausage. He had not been nearly as penitent as he should have been, even when I docked his free afternoons yet again in punishment, and now—

"I changed the menu," he said. "The stew will hold for tomorrow. Tonight we're to serve salted ox tongue, a fish pie flavored with oranges, nutmeg, and dates—what are you scowling for, *signorina*?" He took the time to rap out a series of orders to the undercooks, letting me see how they hopped to his words like frogs, and then looked down at me with guileless innocence. "You left me in charge of the kitchens. How was I to know you didn't want me changing the menu?"

"If you think for one moment I will allow an apprentice to change a menu without consultation—"

Yes, definitely enough pensive maundering for one day. My father was dead, and whether I could manage to grieve for him or not, I'd say prayers for his soul and more prayers for the fact that I was now likely safe—safe from discovery, safe from everything. But prayers could wait. For now, I had an apprentice to murder.

Leonello

Bloodshed made beautiful—I could think of no other words for it as I watched Cesare Borgia bring his sword down in one massive hewing sweep and lop a bull's head half off its body. I had never cared for bullfighting, nor for cockfights, dogfights, or the baiting of bears, but the Pope's son made this hideous dance of death into a thing of marvelous grace.

He hewed the bull's head off in two more strokes. The beast continued to stumble toward him for an instant , as though determined to catch the young Cardinal even as its head tumbled onto the stones. Then the massive body crashed in a spray of bright blood, and Cesare put a boot to the great horned head with its glazing eyes and raised his sword for applause. His eyes glittered, his impassive mask cracked into a grin, and as applause roared around the *piazza*, he swept a cocky bow. Burly servants in the Borgia mulberry and yellow rushed out to drag the fallen bull away on hooks, and Cesare Borgia tossed his bloodied sword aside in a careless rattle and vaulted in one lithe motion up to the temporary dais where his sister and the other ladies sat in a flutter of veils and velvets. I had a place there too, though no one would notice my small dark figure amid all the radiance that was the Pope's concubine, daughter, and daughter-in-law.

"Another bull!" Cardinal Borgia called, and Lucrezia struck him on the arm with her fan.

"You'll be gored, Cesare. Two bulls aren't enough for you?"

"Nothing is enough for your brother," Sancha purred, arching her throat.

"At least you make it quick for the poor bulls," Giulia said, and the ladies all made room as Cesare flung himself down in a chair among them, calling for wine. Christmas and all its festivities had passed and the year turned; the sky was steel-gray above and breath puffed white on the air, but Cesare Borgia had declared himself in need of celebration and announced a bullfight. Bullfights were not such a common thing in Rome—"More Spanish oddities!"—but that did not stop the city's idlers from packing into the Piazza San Pietro to watch.

"Why not the Colosseum instead?" I'd suggested. "We could kill prisoners instead of bulls; hark back to Imperial Rome instead of Spain. Far more civilized!" But the ancient Colosseum was a wreck of crumbling stone, and so the Piazza San Pietro was fitted with temporary wooden seats and a chute and transformed into an arena.

"A bullfight in honor of Our son-in-law," the Pope had said expansively, clapping the new-returned Lord Sforza on the shoulder. "To celebrate his return to Us from his soldiers."

"If he thinks we missed him," Cesare said indifferently, not bothering to whisper, and the Count of Pesaro swelled in outrage before his little wife whispered quick assurances in his ear. Lucrezia had smiled at her brother behind her husband's back, though, and even now Lord Sforza sat swamped in all the feminine flurry, bad-tempered and flushed and overlooked. Lucrezia's husband was guest of honor, but no one had eyes for anyone but Cesare, who had stripped out of his doublet after the very first fight and taken on the next bull himself.

"A splendid fight," I said as the young Cardinal tossed down a cup of wine. "To kill a bull with a sword and on foot—tricky." The flamboyant *rejonear* had killed the first bull from the safety of horseback, pricking it to death with the long lance, but that was too dull and safe for Cesare, who had thrown himself against the huge snorting beasts on foot, and with nothing but a sword. "And only three strokes to sever the neck. I congratulate you."

"To sever a man's neck is near as hard." The January day was cold, but Cesare seemed oblivious, lounging back in his half-unlaced shirt with his dark auburn hair tumbled about the faint dent of a tonsure, and his breath puffing white on the air. "I think because men struggle harder than bulls when it comes to dying."

"And women?" I asked. "How do they struggle?"

He grinned. "Just like they struggle beneath you in a bed."

The bloody stones were swept below for the next match. Giulia sat wrapped in a sable cloak, her bright hair shining above the dark fur like a gold coin, while Lucrezia had tucked a dutiful hand through her husband's arm but leaned close to Sancha on her other side, whispering. Sancha was ignoring Joffre and casting her eyes at Cesare, but her gaze flickered briefly to me, and I made sure to blow her a kiss. She hissed at me and flounced her attention in the other direction, slapping Joffre's hand away as he tried to catch her eyes.

Cesare noted her glance at me. "Don't tell me my brother's wife has granted you her favors, dwarf?"

Favors? Not really. Sancha of Aragon had greedily run her hands over my body for a little while, savoring its oddities, and had allowed me a little exploration of her luscious one—and then she'd laughed her nasty laugh and shoved me away, just as I'd thought she might. She then got quite peevish when I didn't curse or groan or grovel for her favors, but merely straightened my doublet, swept her an elaborate bow, and strolled away whistling. What an array of gutter curses to fall from the lips of a king's daughter! "The Princess of Squillace enjoys variety," I said blandly.

"She does," Cesare agreed, unoffended. He did not seem to care one whit that he had shared Sancha with half of Rome including both of his own brothers, but then, he didn't seem to care one whit about any woman at all except perhaps his sister. Sancha was pouting her lips at him, but he dismissed her from his notice as though she'd been a lapdog wiggling for his attention.

"Your Eminence appears cheerful," I observed as he stretched in his chair like a lithe-bodied cat. Usually his moods rose no further than a studied neutrality. "What might the cause be? Have the French captured our good Duke of Gandia?"

"That would be cause for a ball, not a bullfight," Cesare said. "I've had word, however, that he has been wounded at Soriano. A very slight wound, but to the face."

"Tragic when a young man must lose his beauty," I intoned.

Cesare's eyes gleamed. "Tragic."

"And after Bracciano . . ." The Duke of Gandia had enjoyed a few easy victories late in the year, but the fortress of Bracciano had proved a harder nut for his forces. Cesare Borgia's control over his expressions was normally perfect, but I'd seen him turn abruptly to the wall to hide his dancing eyes from the Holy Father when news came that the defenders at Bracciano had returned Juan's offer of peace by way of a mule with a placard about its neck jeering *I am the ambassador of the Duke of Gandia*, and a very rude letter indeed stuffed under its tail. I wished I'd been there to see young Juan's face.

"Nevertheless," I continued, propping my boots on the same table with Cesare's, "I hear the Duke is to take his forces to march against the French in Ostia next."

Cesare's smile disappeared. "He is."

"I hear Your Eminence begged the Holy Father for that command instead."

"A caesar does not beg," Cesare Borgia said, "nor do I."

"I hear otherwise." The fight between His Holiness and His Holiness's most unholy of sons had gone on behind closed doors, but both men had emerged with white furious faces. Perhaps that was why the Holy Father had declined to join us for this afternoon's bullfights.

"It's a slight against me," the Count of Pesaro had said tightly at the Pope's absence.

"Really, husband," Lucrezia had said in a tart voice. "Not everything is aimed at you. Slights *or* honors."

"I'm glad you're not taking the army to Ostia." Sancha had aimed her hot whisper into Cesare's ear. "I'd rather you were in my bed."

"Oh Holy Virgin," Giulia groaned to me privately. "Listen to them all!"

"I try not to."

A roar from the crowd around the improvised ranks of stands, and I looked up to see that another bull had been released into the *piazza*. The creature tossed its great horns, snorting and raking its hooves, and I saw Lucrezia cast a sidelong glance at her husband. "Do you want to face this one, my lord?" she said, wide-eyed. "Bulls are no match for the men in my family. Why do you think we have one as our emblem?"

I wondered if anyone else thought it odd that Cesare Borgia should slaughter bulls with such gusto when his own father was both a Borgia bull and (in Giulia's fond little blasphemy) a papal bull . . .

"I am a Sforza," the Count of Pesaro said stiffly. "A serpent is our emblem."

"Then we'll find you a serpent to fight." Cesare flicked his wine cup aside, rising. "A little grass snake, perhaps. That shouldn't offer too much of a challenge for you."

Lord Sforza reddened, opening his mouth and then shutting it again.

His eyes flicked at the bull, now raking savagely at the stones with huge hooves, and he sank a little deeper into his chair.

"I don't mind taking on another," Cesare shrugged. "A good kill clears the head, and my head needs clearing."

"You should stick to killing whores, Your Eminence," I said in a low, clear voice. "Less dangerous than bulls, surely."

Lord Sforza was hissing at his wife and Sancha was eavesdropping on them without shame; Giulia was trying her futile best to smooth things over, and the crowds were roaring at the sight of their Pope's son on his feet again. Only Cesare had heard my words, and he looked down at me without speaking.

I don't know why I said it. Cesare Borgia and I had been dancing about my private obsession for years—and in latter months, when I'd believed I must be wrong about him, I'd nearly dropped it altogether. Why challenge him now?

Perhaps because Sancha told me another woman had died, another victim after all this time, and I would rather end this game of cat and mouse than wait for even one more death to provide me clues. Perhaps because the young Cardinal seemed in an expansive mood for once, expansive enough to be loose-lipped. Perhaps because I was tired of the game, and after so many hours of wondering I just wanted to *know* who had killed my friend Anna.

Or perhaps because I simply preferred the baiting of murderers to the baiting of bulls.

But for whatever reason the words were out. Cesare Borgia looked down at me, and I gazed levelly back at him.

"Are you hinting at something, little lion man?" His voice was mild.

"Why, yes. I am." If today was to be the day, so be it. I'd lay my cards on the table, and I'd either get the truth or get a knife in my throat. One or the other, I felt certain—because I did not think Cesare Borgia would lie to me.

"Out with it, dwarf," he said to me. "Whatever it is you're thinking. I don't like hints."

"A woman named Anna died in this city some four years ago," I stated.

"Her hands knifed to a table, her throat opened by a masked man from the Borgia household. That I know, because I killed the men who helped him. But he went on alone after that, and killed five more women over the years, one of them with a dagger identified as yours. That one you're wearing now, with the sapphire in the hilt." I took a breath. "I think if I ever saw the murderer of those women take his mask off, I would see Your Eminence's face."

I thought my hands would be trembling if I ever said those words. I thought my heart would be racing, my palms sweating and my words cracking from a dry throat. But I felt nothing, sitting there with my boots propped on a table and my head tilted back to look Cesare Borgia in the eye—nothing, that is, but excitement.

"The odd thing is," I added, "I don't know how you did it. At least one of those deaths happened when you were occupied at the Vatican, soothing your Holy Father over La Bella's abduction. I don't know how you managed that one. But you did. Maybe you succeeded in being in two places at once. Maybe you really *are* the Devil, Eminence."

"You think the Devil would bother killing common whores?" Cesare seemed more amused than angry. "Why would a cardinal bother, for that matter?"

"I think you have dark moods, Your Eminence, that only blood satisfies."

"Do you not have such moods yourself?"

"I do. But I don't kill women to purge them."

Giulia was looking over her shoulder at me now. I saw her frown from the corner of my vision, but I could not look at her. I could not look at anything but those bottomless Borgia eyes.

"Follow me," said Cesare, "and I will give you your answer."

His boots made a crunch as he jumped down from the makeshift dais into the arena. I rose to follow him, and Giulia Farnese gasped, leaning forward to seize my arm. "Leonello, what are you—"

I planted a great loud smack of a kiss right at the corner of her mouth, giving a grin as her hand released my sleeve. "If a man's about to die, he should get to kiss a beautiful woman first," I said with a comic waggle of my eyebrows. "Even a dwarf!" I dashed a salute off to the whole company at large, and a heartbeat later my boots crunched as I swung myself over the railing and strode into the arena after Cesare Borgia.

The crowd must have roared again, but I did not hear it. I only heard the steady thumping of my own heart as I stood at Cesare Borgia's side. He retrieved the bloodied sword from his expressionless man-at-arms Michelotto, as I reached for my own weapons. I had a full set of ten throwing knives: finest Toledo steel with intricate damascened hilts, ranging from the long dagger at my waist to the little inch-long blades that could be tucked inside a wrist cuff. Presented to me as a gift from Cesare Borgia, when he first hired me as bodyguard to his father's mistress. I reached for the pair of blades tucked in my boots, and I had six inches of gleaming Spanish steel in each hand. My wounds from the French had left me with more lingering aches and pains than I used to endure, but my feet were still fleet—and my four-fingered hand could throw knives as fast as ever.

Across the arena, the bull raised its huge baleful head at us.

"Bulls are quicker than they look," said Cesare, conversationally, as though we sat idling over a chessboard. "Don't retreat backward when he comes at you. Dodge sideways instead."

"Noted," I said, and we split away, one to each side, as the bull came for us in a rush of hooves. It turned for Cesare, a storm of death behind two vast horns, and as the Pope's son melted to one side like a lithe shadow, I gave a shout and sent one of my blades winging into the bull's rippling slab of a shoulder.

Surely only a pinprick to a maddened beast, but a pinprick it felt. The bull whirled, quicker than a cat as it thundered toward me, and distantly I could hear the crowd screaming at me to *run, run*, but I did not want to run. I wanted to fight. I bounced on my toes, feeling the blood rush in my ears, and perhaps I was a liar all those years when I said I didn't tumble, because I dived to one side as neatly as though I'd been tumbling all my life. I felt a reminiscent ache from the wound a French pike-man had given my shoulder, but the pain seemed very distant.

Among the roaring of the crowd I heard a woman's cry from the dais as the bull missed me by inches, one massive hoof clipping down beside my shoulder. Perhaps Giulia; she was surely the only one watching who cared even remotely if a bull trampled me to death. She'd tasted like sweet honey and cool water; not a bad taste at all to die on. From everyone else in the stands around her, I heard roars of laughter. A dwarf taking on a bull; what could be funnier than that?

I'd already taken on a bull, though, with the words I'd thrown down on the dais. And of the two bulls, the one without horns was the one to fear.

"Did those girls die hard?" I called out to Cesare Borgia as he whipped in shadow-quick to open a slash across the bull's haunch with his sword. "I know the first girl fought; I found blood under her nails." The bull turned on Cesare, roaring as blood sprayed from its haunch, and now it was my turn to distract it as Cesare dodged sideways. "Was it your blood?" I sent another finger knife whipping through the winter light into the bull's shoulder.

"No." Cesare rolled, came to his feet with auburn hair flying, swept in again with his sword as the bull turned between us, maddened. "No woman's ever scratched me except in passion."

"Was it about passion?" I waited this time until the bull was nearly on me before I flung myself to the side. There was a rhythm to this, a rhythm I felt in my thumping blood. "Did you take them first willing, then kill them for pleasure?"

"My pleasure in women ends when the seed spills." Cesare Borgia opened the bull's other flank that time, with a casual sweep of his arm. "That's all they're good for."

I thought of Giulia Farnese's myriad kindnesses; of the sweetness Anna had showed me when she smiled. "You are wrong."

"Am I?"

My next knife missed, but the bull turned toward me with a roar anyway. "Why leave your dagger with the fourth victim, Eminence? Carelessness?" Not that, I already knew. Cesare Borgia was never careless. "Amusement?" A very black amusement indeed, to challenge all Rome to attach such deeds to his name. "Arrogance?" I dropped into another neat tumble almost under the bull's hooves, and it occurred to me that I was the arrogant one here. All Cesare Borgia had to do to kill me, and my theories with me, was stand back and let the bull trample me to death.

"Careful, little lion man," Cesare sang out, and dived between me and the bull, his blade carving a furrow along its shoulder. I rolled to my feet, flicking another knife into my hand, and we had no breath left for words after that. The bull spun between us, maddened and roaring, blood dappling its brown flanks, and we spun with it as the crowd screamed. I dodged the horns as Cesare attacked the haunches; then Cesare flung himself away from the hooves as I threw another knife into the massive throat, and we pivoted that bull between us like we'd been doing it all our lives. The beast bellowed, tiring and stumbling, and all I felt was a savage release. *Finish it*, I thought, but finish what? Finish who?

Finish it.

My biggest blade winged sweetly through the air, burying itself hilt-deep through the bull's heart. A dying beat of that heart later, Cesare's sword struck the bull's head half off in a single stroke.

The beast fell between us with a crash that sent dust billowing up like the roars of the crowd. Laughter mixed with those roars—laughter for me, of course. In the ancient days when Rome was an empire, dwarves had fought and died in the great arena of the Colosseum, tossed to lions or pitted against teams of cripples and half-wits. Palate-cleansers between the big gladiatorial fights. I wondered if those dwarves had heard these same hoots of laughter as they died.

The shouting faded in my ears to soundlessness, the laughter to an empty ringing. I stood locked eye to eye with a pope's son, both of us panting hard, with a dead bull and a river of blood between us. "My kill," I said.

"Mine," he said. Both our chests heaved like a forge's bellows. "I took the head."

"After I stopped the heart. My kill."

"Our kill," he allowed, and bent to wipe his blade clean along the bull's hide. My knives were buried in that same hide, thrown one at a time, and I dropped to my knees to yank them free.

"Will I get my answer?" I said. With the heady rush of excitement fading I felt the sweat soaking my shirt and cooling rapidly in the winter breezes; a sting in my elbow where I had knocked it rolling sideways; the ache in my thighs that protested all the sprinting and tumbling. Deeper, more distant pains in my chest and hip, more long-healed wounds from the French. "Did you kill those women?"

"I know the ones you speak of," he said. "And I did not kill them."

Strange that I believed him, when a moment ago I had been so ready to think him guilty—but I did believe him. He could kill without blinking, that I was sure of—but lie about it? Not to a lowly dwarf, anyway. He would have flung it in my face just to see the look in my eyes.

"Pity," I said, sliding the last of my little blades home into its boot sheath and rising. "I thought myself so clever for tracking you." Though I should have known, really—how could he have killed that one girl, when he had been at odds with his father in the Vatican over Giulia Farnese being held for ransom? Cesare Borgia was merely a pope's bastard, after all, not the Devil himself. No matter what he said. As for the dagger, it could easily have been stolen and used against him, to attach foul rumors to the Borgia name.

Foolish dwarf.

"Would you have killed me for it?" Cesare sounded curious, looking down at me, ignoring his sister's cheering from the dais and Sancha's imperious calling of his name. "If I'd done it?"

I hesitated. For Anna I'd killed the other two men who had been present at her death—but Anna was four years in her grave, and I could scarcely remember her face. It had been the chase that spurred me since then, not revenge. Boredom, not outrage. Perhaps that was ignoble, but a dwarf cannot afford nobility. "Probably not," I said at last. "I am fond of living, after all, and the Pope would not look lightly on me for killing his son."

"No. The Holy Father and I may not always see eye to eye—he will not give me his army to lead, and he will strike me across the face for daring to say that my brother is an incompetent ass." Cesare slid his sword back into its scabbard. "But as much as my father and I quarrel, he would never allow anyone to harm me. Even if I *had* killed and raped your whores."

I started back toward the dais. "How fortunate you didn't, then."

Cesare smiled faintly, leaning down to whisper in my ear just before vaulting up into the arms of his sister and sister-in-law. Just a handful of words, but they froze me in my tracks.

"Leonello!" My mistress's pale face leaned down from the height of the dais. "Guards, lift him up, it's too tall—Leonello, what were you *thinking*! It's bad enough watching the poor bulls die; you think I want to see you die, too?"

"Apologies, Madonna Giulia," I said woodenly, allowing the guards to lift me up by the arms. They were laughing and ruffling my hair in the way I hated, telling me how funny I looked waddling after a bull, but I barely heard them. My ears buzzed; my legs had turned wobbly as Carmelina's savory jellies, and my chest had gone cold as one of her Spanish ices.

Two short sentences in Cesare Borgia's devil whisper.

I did not kill your whores, he had whispered. *But I know who did.*

CHAPTER FOUR

❖

Into the endless screaming fall of dark
She tumbles, lovely daughter of the earth,
Her golden light extinguished in its birth.
A pomegranate stains her: prey and mark.

—AVERNUS, FROM SONNET IX: AURORA AS PERSEPHONE

Giulia

Illustrious people of great fame and renowned reputation rarely seem to live up to it in the flesh, do they? Well, my Pope being the exception—he was the only man I knew whose fleshly presence dwarfed his rank. But for the most part, people of renown were something of a disappointment when one actually met them. As Maestro Botticelli bowed to kiss my Pope's ring in the great *sala*, I couldn't help but think that he looked nothing like a titan of art whose brush had been kissed by God. He looked like a worn-out man of fifty with pouches under his eyes and gray heavily streaking his hair, and I could hardly understand his rough Florentine dialect as he mumbled his greetings.

"We are honored to receive you," Rodrigo said, expansive. In truth, I think Maestro Botticelli could have done without the honor—he was eyeing Rodrigo as though he'd been put into a cage with a wolf. I'd scolded my Pope when he told me Maestro Botticelli was passing through Rome on a recent journey and had been commanded to present himself at the Vatican to discuss the possibility of painting me. "Rodrigo, really. He's a follower of Fra Savonarola and all his rantings about the

fleshly evils of the world. If he's renounced the painting of sinful subjects, do you really think he wants to paint the Pope's concubine?"

"Bah, he'll be delighted," Rodrigo returned. And then added a more
ominous "If he knows what's good for him."

My Pope was all charm now, sitting through the last of his petitioners as the morning passed, then finally rising with a gesture of dismissal
and ushering the artist to follow him out of the informal *sala*. "I fear
I've a few more appointments this afternoon, Maestro Botticelli—God's
work is never done! Do accompany me, and we can talk further about
this portrait of Madonna Giulia . . ." The rest of us trailed after my Pope:
myself holding the gilt leather leash of my little pet goat, Leonello trotting at both our heels, an entourage of cardinals and bishops and their
hangers-on gathering like a tail. I was the only woman, but I was used
to that within the halls of the Vatican.

"Perhaps you'd like to see the frescoes in Our private apartments,
Maestro Botticelli?" Rodrigo was saying warmly. "Maestro Pinturicchio
has done splendid work, though he does have one figure left to paint in
the Resurrection—"

"Is that figure—Madonna Giulia? In a *Resurrection*?" Maestro Botticelli looked as though he were about to choke on the sacrilege of it all.

"No." I smiled, coming up beside his other elbow. "It's the Holy
Father who is to sit for Pinturicchio this afternoon. He's been putting
it off for months. All my sitting is done, thank the Holy Virgin."

A spark of interest lit Botticelli's sunken eyes. "In my experience,
beautiful women enjoy being immortalized in paint."

His gallantry was rusty, but genuine. "Well, I don't," I confessed,
tugging my little pet goat away before he could start nibbling the painter's sleeve. "It's the dullest thing imaginable. And you are entirely to
blame, Maestro Botticelli!"

"Me?"

"Your *Birth of Venus*, rather." I tucked his hand through my elbow,
guiding him after my Pope, who had broken ahead of his meandering
entourage and was making for his private apartments with brisk strides.
"I was only twelve when you completed the painting, but everyone was
talking of it. Venus on her seashell, and who was she smiling at, and was

it true the model was Marco Vespucci's wife Simonetta. After that there wasn't a girl alive who didn't dream of being immortalized for the ages in paint."

Immortalized by some famous painter who would capture your face for the ages as Venus or the Virgin, and of course be in love with you as well, and the romance of it all was just entrancing, especially if you were twelve. The reality of sitting for a portrait was quite different: hours of shivering in a cold studio, getting a crick in your neck from holding your head at some exquisitely uncomfortable angle, and being chided by the painter, who was generally far too busy trying to match your skin tone in paint to even think about falling in love with you. I told Maestro Botticelli so, and he laughed.

"Madonna Simonetta complained of my cold studio too," he agreed, a faint spark of laughter in his eye, and I liked him. I wondered if he regretted the decision not to paint anything more sinful than an Annunciation—maybe it had been the right decision for his conscience, but certainly not his prosperity. His hose and cloak were far too thread-bare for this winter cold, and he looked haggard as though he hadn't had enough meals.

Well, whether he painted me or not, I'd see he went back to Florence with a full purse. And a new set of clothes!

Poor Pinturicchio looked about to faint as he saw the stooped figure that followed the Holy Father into the Sala dei Misteri. "Maestro—" he stammered, and there was a great deal of bowing and complimenting and demurring over the finished frescoes, and Pinturicchio turned quite white when it became clear he was to *work* in front of his idol. "Surely His Holiness would rather sit for the Resurrection another day . . ."

Rodrigo looked tempted, but I scolded and chivvied him into his pose in the splendid jeweled cope that would show to such nice effect in the finished Resurrection, and he resigned himself. The cardinals and archbishops settled themselves about the walls, whispering behind ringed hands or going through documents as they waited, and the remaining pages, servants, and petty dignitaries squashed in as best they could around the clutter of paint and plaster, buckets and drapes and artist's paraphernalia. Leonello settled on a stool at my feet, pulling out a book and ignoring us all utterly. He seemed to have suffered no ill effects from his hair-raising stint in the bullring—really, I could have clouted him for being so rash! "I shan't kiss you next time you decide you feel like throwing your life away," I'd scolded him. "I'll knock you down and sit on you instead, until the madness passes!"

"Some things are worth risking one's life for." He looked sober and troubled at that, but he still went off whistling the way men always do when they feel they've proved some nebulous moral point with a totally unnecessary act of bravery.

"If Your Holiness will perhaps lift the chin?" Pinturicchio glanced at Maestro Botticelli, glanced at the Pope, and cleared his throat. "Just a touch—"

"We cannot read with Our chin in the air!" I stifled a smile at the irritation already rising in my Pope's face. If there was anything Rodrigo hated, it was sitting idle—he'd looked about for Maestro Botticelli, ready to discuss my portrait, but the papal secretaries had come forward first with baskets of sealed letters and official missives, pleading for the papal attention. "How long will this take?"

"The merest, um—I will do a sketch only; I will transfer the Holy Father's image to the wall in paint at a later time. Perhaps an hour—"

"You have half that," my Pope said, and assumed the pose with his hands pressed together in prayer. He was to be shown kneeling at the tomb of Christ during the Resurrection, though hopefully Pinturicchio could paint that irritated expression into something a touch more exalted. Painted as he looked right now, my Pope just seemed irked that Christ was taking so long to climb out of the tomb.

"Perhaps I can read Your Holiness's correspondence out loud?" I cajoled. "Save your eyes *and* Maestro Pinturicchio's artistic sensibilities—" I sank onto a velvet stool at Rodrigo's side and began reading the latest missive from Florence, as Pinturicchio sketched in quick motions—*Drop the eyes, Your Holiness, and keep the hands pressed together*. A buzz of conversation rose about the *sala*, and Maestro Botticelli wandered into the Sala dei Santi to examine Lucrezia's painted figure as Santa Caterina. I'd expected him to show the impatience of genius, look irked that he was being forced to wait on the Pope's pleasure, but now I rather thought he was hoping the whole idea of painting me would just go away if Rodrigo was sufficiently distracted by official business.

"Goodness, is Fra Savonarola quite serious?" I wrinkled my nose as I finished reading the friar's ranting letter out loud. "Does he really think dice and lip rouge and wine are signs that the world is ending?" I could think of a dozen other omens that couldn't be called favorable—putting Juan Borgia at the head of an army certainly seemed like a recipe for all sorts of cosmic disaster, and last winter there had been reports of a strange dead creature with a woman's face and an elephant's trunk washing up on the banks of the Tiber, and hadn't *that* had everyone wondering if the end was nigh. But lip rouge?

"Apparently Savonarola is going to scourge Florence of all frivolity and make it into a Holy City to point the way for the rest of the world." Rodrigo's voice was very dry. "Cards are to be forbidden within the city's walls, not to mention dicing and drinking and gambling of all sorts. Women are to give up their fine clothes, for fear of bringing heavenly wrath down upon their godly menfolk. And paintings depicting the naked female form are not to be allowed either."

"Such paintings are only forbidden in homes where there are unmarried girls." Maestro Botticelli spoke up unexpectedly in his rough Florentine voice, wandering back into the Sala dei Misteri in time to hear our words. "Fra Savonarola would not have the virgin minds of Florence's womenfolk corrupted."

"But when you count servant girls too, almost every home in Florence has unmarried girls," I pointed out.

"Unmarried, but perhaps not virgin," Rodrigo chuckled. "How does Fra Savonarola plan to tell the difference? Lift their skirts?"

"He is a holy prophet." Maestro Botticelli's lined face was set. "He gives us visions sent direct from God."

"So do you, with your paintings," I said, conciliatory. "I would be sad to see no more Venuses come from that brush, Maestro Botticelli."

"Only clothed Venuses. By Fra Savonarola's decree, to keep us all from eternal damnation."

Really, priests. War and famine all around them; poverty and foreign armies and that dreadful disease with pustules that the French had brought with them, and somehow damnation was at hand because of naked women. Not even *real* naked women—naked women in paint! I ask you.

But I heard a certain subdued rustle of agreement among a few of the watching cardinals, those more straitlaced men inclined to be shocked by my Pope and the earthier of his attitudes. Perhaps Rodrigo heard that rustle too, because his heavy brows came together above his nose. "There is nothing in the beauty of the female form to offend Our eyes," he said in a tone that brooked no discussion. "Did God not create that form with love and with reverence, just as He created the form of man?"

The straitlaced rustle died, and Maestro Botticelli retreated with a flush on his cheeks, perhaps realizing he was arguing with the Holy Father Himself. Rodrigo shrugged irritated shoulders at the whole business, and dictated a rapid response to one of his secretaries. I put the letter from Savonarola aside and read a missive from a Medici in Florence next; then another letter from Lord Sforza requesting money to pay his soldiers—"What is the man, a human drain on Our treasury?" The prioress of a local convent wrote her thanks for a recent benefice, and then there was the report of a Franciscan friar who had shown signs of the stigmata—"Bah, his order needs pilgrims to refill the coffers. That's one way to attract them!"

My Pope kept a team of secretaries on the trot, periodically breaking his pose to sign something, and as one letter followed another my voice grew scratchy. I scanned the next missive, and shook my head. "Another complaint about Sancha, I'm afraid. This time it's the envoy from Mantua—'By her gestures and aspect, it seems the sheep will put herself easily at the disposal of the wolf.'" I wondered if the wolf was supposed to be Cesare or Juan. I'd seen the Tart of Aragon coming out of both bedchambers on a fairly regular basis before Juan left with his army. I wished I could show her to Fra Savonarola, as proof positive that female debauchery would not bring about the world's end. If the Four Horsemen of the Apocalypse could truly be summoned by lecherous women, then Sancha's parade of lovers would have had all Rome hearing hoofbeats months ago.

"Take a sworn declaration," Rodrigo said carelessly to one of his secretaries. "Find someone useful in her household who can testify all things are as they should be. Preferably someone elderly and male. 'In the household of the Princess of Squillace, the government of the ladies is of such good order' and so on. Next."

"She needs reining in," I warned, as I had been warning him for quite some time now, but of course he just chuckled and shook his head.

"Bah!"

"Madonna Giulia," Maestro Pinturicchio called to me plaintively. "Can you *please* stop the goat from eating my supplies!"

I rescued a paintbrush from my pet goat, and Rodrigo had already moved on to the next bit of business. "What of it if Juan's troops are a little wild? Success will do that to a man! Ten castles taken from the Orsini, that's cause to celebrate."

"And Bracciano?" I couldn't help but ask. *That* could not in any way be qualified a success.

"If Juan couldn't take Bracciano, it couldn't be taken." Dictating blithely. "It is Our decision that the Gonfalonier shall mount the attack at Ostia next—"

Ha. Juan had made much this past fall of his rapid capture of ten Orsini castles—but they had been small castles, and I'd heard whispers that Juan's part had involved prancing about at the army's head adjusting his banners and plumes while his generals got on with the work of the matter. Bracciano had been a disaster, whether Rodrigo admitted it or not. And as far as Juan's troops went, well, if I'd been a lordling or a farmer anywhere near Ostia, I'd have been decidedly worried to see the young Gonfalonier and his troops pointed my direction.

"'Rapine and plunder are regrettable things,'" Rodrigo was dictating to another secretary, answering some lord near Bracciano who had written a protest to how his lands had been treated. "'But necessary evils when war raises its banners'—couch that a bit more artfully, will you? Next—"

I sighed. Lucrezia flirting her way through the papal court, Sancha sleeping with both her brothers-in-law, Juan raping his way toward Ostia—"Maybe there's a *reason* popes aren't supposed to have children," I couldn't help saying, but Rodrigo didn't hear me and it was just as well.

"My deepest thanks, Your Holiness." Pinturicchio was bowing now, relieved and eager. "I assure you the figure will be finished in all speed—the final touch upon the Resurrection—"

Rodrigo rose, dropping his hands from their pose of prayer and flicking the secretaries back. "Let's have a look," he said, and shrugged his priceless jeweled cope from his heavy shoulders to the floor. "Hm. Does my chin really droop that way?"

"Of course not, this is a hasty sketch only. I assure Your Holiness that he will be pleased with the final result."

"A very fine work," Maestro Botticelli smiled. Apparently Resurrections met with his approval where goddesses of love did not.

"We would have a portrait from your hands as well, Maestro Botticelli." Rodrigo's gaze found me, and he held out his hand. I twined my fingers with his. "A portrait of La Bella, as We had mentioned previously."

"Just not as the Holy Virgin this time," I warned. "Really, it's too hypocritical for words." Rodrigo preferred the Virgin Mary for his private devotions—he kept various images of her about his chambers, and he always addressed his personal prayers to her ears. I suppose he thought of the Blessed Virgin as yet one more woman he could wheedle: "Oh, Rodrigo," he envisioned her saying as she heard his prayers, shaking her veiled head fondly and going to intercede on his behalf with God the Father. I admit, I too found the Holy Virgin far more approachable than some stern-faced saint. But putting *my* face on that exalted image seemed a bit much!

"No virgins or saints this time," my Pope agreed. "Something more . . . fleshly. You as you first came to me: Persephone, clad only in your hair with a pomegranate in your hand . . ."

Definitely not, I thought. Not as Persephone. Such a very private memory, that was. One of Rodrigo's first gifts to me had been not my great pearl or some other jewel, but a pomegranate. A simple, rosy fruit pressed into my hand as he wooed me with the story of Persephone, whom the god of the underworld wooed in turn with pomegranate seeds. Persephone had eaten the seeds and stayed with her dark lord, and in the end so had I; I'd brought the pomegranate back to Rodrigo on the day I decided I would share his bed, and we'd fed each other the jewel-red seeds, Rodrigo kissing each of my pink-stained fingers like a ritual. Avernus had a sonnet comparing his Aurora to Persephone— *lovely daughter of the earth*, he put it, and how I loved that one!

But I didn't want to *be* Persephone for any eyes but Rodrigo's. I parted my lips to demur, but Rodrigo had dropped my hand and took hold of my shoulder instead, his thumb slipping inside the edge of my dress.

"I want a record of your beauty," he whispered. "*All* of your beauty."

Maestro Botticelli was blushing red as a virgin girl. "Your Holiness, I am honored. But I have sworn to renounce paintings of that kind—if you will please allow me, I shall recommend another painter . . ."

Rodrigo looked at him. "We desire your brush. No other."

"Fra Savonarola, he—"

"His decrees do not hold sway in Our Holy City," Rodrigo snapped. "Which is the only Holy City, Maestro Botticelli. If We wish you to paint La Bella, you will do so."

Maestro Botticelli's eyes dropped to the woven carpet. He fiddled with his shirt cuff, and I noticed its fraying edge. "Yes, Your Holiness," he muttered.

"He doesn't have to," I put in swiftly. "Really, I've no wish to be preserved through history as a naked goddess." I tried for a laugh. "To be preserved as a holy virgin is absurd enough!"

"But I want you as Persephone too," my Pope insisted. "So every man in Rome can see what I have!"

What if I don't want every man in Rome to see what I have? I started to say. But Rodrigo's fingers slipped further along my shoulder inside the edge of my dress, and a familiar spark of desire kindled in his eye like a dark fire. "You could drop your gown and let Maestro Botticelli take a drawing." His breath whispered hot along my neck. "Here. Now."

"Your Holiness, you cannot be serious!" Bad enough sitting chilled and stiff-necked in a Madonna's veil and feeling like the world's greatest joke. I was *not* going to strip out of my gown before half the papal secretaries and pages in the basilica, not to mention a cluster of cardinals who looked equally avid and appalled. I drew breath to argue, but Cardinal Piccolomini spoke up in a shocked expostulation.

"Really, Your Holiness—a naked woman, here in the sacred walls of the Vatican? It is blasphemous!"

There was another rustle at his words, the same rustle that had gone up when Maestro Botticelli quoted Fra Savonarola's pious strictures. Even those bishops and pages whose eyes had been eating me up had a moment's flash of discomfort across their faces, and Cardinal Piccolomini looked at me reprovingly as though this were all my fault. "It would be indecent," he said, crossing himself in great distaste. "*She* is indecent." And my Pope's face went hard all at once.

"Surely we can arrange a private sitting later!" I jumped in, desperately—perhaps I could offer a sop to please both propriety and Rodrigo's pride. "I have been meaning to visit Florence, to see my sister. I could call upon Maestro Botticelli there, in his studio—you could still have the portrait, Holy Father, but painted in proper privacy—"

"We do not require privacy," my Pope said in cutting tones, not to me but to Cardinal Piccolomini and any of the other men who had dared to rumble against him. "Because nothing about you is indecent, Giulia Farnese. Nothing We order done within these walls is indecent. And We refuse to have any man from the College of Cardinals, or any frothing Dominican from Florence, or any pious little sheep of an artist dictate to Us otherwise."

The silence fell, chastened and complete. Rodrigo's eyes raked the room. "Good," he said curtly, and turned in a swirl of robes. "A painting, then, of La Bella as Persephone. Pinturicchio, clear your easel and offer Maestro Botticelli the materials he needs to make the initial sketch. It is Our will that the first sitting be done here and now. You may all watch, my good gentlemen, to be certain nothing *indecent* takes place within these sacred halls." A contemptuous glance over the silent cardinals and bishops. "A pomegranate, have one fetched from the kitchens at once—"

And there were pages at my back, hastening forward at the snap of the papal fingers to take my little goat's leash from my wrist and begin unlacing the gown down my back, and my mind had gone blank from astonishment. How had this all happened so fast? I caught Rodrigo's arm with one hand, feeling my sleeve slide down the other and drop to the floor. "Your Holiness," I said quietly. "They spoke out of turn, and I know you wish to chastise them. But I am yours alone. I am not for common viewing—not for any reason."

Why did I have to tell him such a thing? We had been together more than four years; he had never before—

"Let them see," he breathed. "Let the word carry all the way to Savonarola in Florence if they like. I do what I please, and I will not be censured for it." Rodrigo brought my hand to his lips. "After today, when they see what God gave me in you, I will not be censured. I will be envied. Envied by every man in Rome—every man in Christendom, once the painting is showed to the world."

I could have shouted, I suppose. Thrown a tantrum, stamped my feet, and I drew a breath to do so—but his enemies here from Cardinal Piccolomini down would have mocked him for it. He had made such a gesture, and by now Maestro Botticelli was already laying out paper and sticks of fresh black chalk with a resigned tilt to his shoulders, and the gown was falling down about my feet, leaving me in my shift. I crossed my arms instinctively across myself as the men behind Rodrigo looked at me furtively, either excitement or distaste or some blend of the two in their eyes, and I didn't see a way through them. Not with my dignity, anyway, and Rodrigo's dignity too.

"Take down your hair," Rodrigo whispered in my ear, looking over my shoulder at his churchmen.

Slowly I began to remove pins and undo plaits. Surely that was as far as he would—

But he reached under the curtain of my hair and slipped the shift off my shoulders. It puddled about my feet, and I stood naked in a room full of staring men.

A thick silence had fallen. My Pope retreated to his heavy chair as all eyes drank me, and his cardinals settled around him like chastened children. I could see his eyes drifting from face to face, noting which eyes drank me in and which looked away in shock. A great deal of shock, I thought, feeling the blush of humiliation rise clear up from the soles of my naked feet—even the men who had licked their lips to see my gown drop were now looking uneasy as I continued to stand there, naked in their midst. Had such a thing happened in the Vatican before, or at least openly and before public eyes?

"Maestro Botticelli," my Pope called, enjoying the general discomfiture. "Pose her."

The artist would hardly look at me. "My apologies, Madonna Giulia," he murmured. "One arm across the breast. The other arm curved lower, under the, ah, belly. The hair behind the shoulders—"

I remembered coming to Rodrigo for the first time, wearing his pearl, clutching his pomegranate, summoning the courage to draw myself up naked before him. Nearly five years later, and he was still the only man to ever see me unclothed—my one brief coupling with Orsino had been done beneath the awkward cover of skirts and hose pushed aside. Only one man had ever looked on my naked body, and now twenty or thirty pairs of eyes were drinking me in.

Avernus's Aurora, in her ten sonnets. Aurora as Persephone, desired by Death himself; Aurora as Helen of Troy, desired by everybody; Aurora as Calypso, Leda, Venus, Europa . . . All those couplets and classical tropes, and not one to tell Aurora the most important thing—that *desire* just means *trouble*.

I arranged my arms woodenly, put my shoulders back, raised my head. *You faced a French army*, I reminded myself. What were a few stares compared to that?

"That's how she looked when she first came to me." Rodrigo's eyes had a particular malice looking at Cardinal Piccolomini's tight-drawn face. "'*Domine Deus*,' I remember thinking. 'I'm the luckiest man on earth.'"

You're the luckiest man on earth because my brother can't hear you saying such things about me, I thought. Thank the Holy Virgin Sandro was off in Bologna on some bit of papal business. He'd be out of his chair with his fists swinging for Rodrigo, pope or no. And then for good measure he'd take on the rest of the men in this cold room, every one of them no matter how exalted, because they dared look on his *sorellina* like this. Yes, good thing Sandro wasn't here. I didn't want him in trouble.

My eyes blurred. I didn't try to blink it away. A blur, I thought, would be useful.

"Your pomegranate, Persephone. Actually no one could find a pomegranate. So we shall make do with a lemon, and make good use of our imaginations." I looked down in the direction of the voice, and saw Leonello. His gaze was as cool and his voice as cynical as ever as he put a withered little lemon in my hand, and I was grateful. He looked at me, standing flushed and bare-skinned before him, and then he glanced away as though he hadn't even noticed my nakedness. He looked over his shoulder at the painter instead, and lifted a brow. "Are you sure you want her posed standing, Maestro Botticelli? Surely Persephone would be reclining in her underworld garden—"

"Yes, but if she is reclining we won't see the full glory of the hair." Maestro Botticelli looked suddenly much less like a tortured saint about to be put on the rack for violating his holy oath, and much more like an absorbed craftsman contemplating an interesting problem. "Pull one lock of hair over your shoulder, Madonna Giulia, and let it fall loose . . ."

"Just get the proportions right," Leonello advised as the artist fussed with my pose again. "Your Venus's lines were *very* improbable. No woman alive ever had that long of a neck."

"Of course not." The painter was unruffled; his hands flew as they sketched goddesses in the air. "Venus was intended to represent an unearthly ideal of beauty—her proportions are elongated, perfected. Persephone will be a depiction of earthly maidenhood, riper and lusher . . ."

They descended into a discussion of proportion and shape as related to linear distance, and somehow that thick, shamed, avid silence in the room was broken. Botticelli bustled forward, all business now, directing me this way and that with his eyes narrowed in thoughtfulness rather than lust, and I felt my own eyes clear. I was able to gaze ahead, as the cardinals and pages stared at me in silence. Let them stare. Hungry little boys gazed longingly at the sides of meat that hung in a butcher's yard, but even if their mouths watered, they still weren't allowed to touch.

"A beseeching Persephone, framed by her hair," Botticelli muttered, arranging my unresisting arms again. "The pomegranate cupped in the lower hand, below the belly; the other hand extended across the breast— yes, like that. Six seeds lying across the palm like jewels, offered to the viewer. Tilt the head, part the lips, the eyes lowered just a trifle. Persephone before she eats the seeds, the agony of choice before she dooms herself to the underworld . . ."

I heard scratching as he took up his chalks and began to sketch. I held my pose. Cardinals gazed at me avidly, pages, archbishops, secretaries, all gaping. Johann Burchard, the prim little master of ceremonies, was flushing so dark he looked like a Moor. Cardinal Piccolomini and his supporters still sat tight-lipped. Rodrigo looked saturnine, amused—and so tender, when his eyes rested on me.

"She should have jewels," Leonello observed, looking over the painter's shoulder. "Venus was born from the waves naked, but the king of the underworld showered all the jewels of the earth on his bride, trying to win her love. One wonders how well it succeeded . . ."

"A ruby, perhaps," Botticelli agreed. "Like a drop of blood at the throat, echoing the pomegranate . . ."

I kept my gaze serene, fixed on the Resurrection over their heads. I suppose it didn't take as long as it felt.

"For a first sitting, that will do." Botticelli laid down his chalk judiciously. "I'll mark the colors in later—the red of the pomegranate, drawing the eye in the center; the hair, hmm, perhaps picked out in gold leaf. A dark space behind her, I think; the whirling dark of the underworld . . . Echoes of Eve, with the pomegranate symbolizing the eternal apple . . ."

"If Maestro Botticelli is finished, I think you have all ogled my Giulia long enough!" Rodrigo approached, his eyes gleaming with fond pride as I dropped my posed arms and shook my hair around me again. "What a picture you are, *mi perla*. In paint or in the flesh."

I ignored him, nodding my thanks to Leonello as he handed me the bundle of my shift.

"It will be a splendid painting," Maestro Botticelli said, and oddly my heart squeezed out a little gladness for him. He had a flush in his thin cheeks, a fire of creation in his eye—far better than the worn, graying man who had parroted Fra Savonarola's dictates of damnation. *Leave off Savonarola's hellfire*, I thought, *and go back to painting your goddesses*. He certainly looked happier that way. "Several more sittings will be required, of course. But I am to set out for Florence in two days . . ."

"Then let us continue the sittings in Florence," I said, shrugging my dress up over my shoulders and turning so the pages could fasten the lacings up my back. I was still clutching the lemon that was supposed to be a pomegranate, so hard my nails scored the withered skin. "I am to visit my sister there very soon; we can finish the portrait then. I will be staying some weeks, so there will be plenty of time."

"Weeks?" my Pope protested. "How can I do without you for even one week?"

"Perhaps I'll stay a month." I tossed the words over one shoulder, bending to retrieve the leash of my little goat.

"Giulia—" Rodrigo sounded exasperated but still fond, keeping his voice low. "This was not about you, *mi perla*. You think I like these straitlaced fanatics like Savonarola prating their lunacy at me? My cardinals use the excuse to chastise me, and where does it end? I've sent a message, that's all."

"Next time"—I turned and flung the withered lemon at his feet—"you can leave my public humiliation out of your *messages*!"

My Pope looked at the lemon and then back at me, and maybe that was the beginning of chagrin forming in his eyes. But I whirled away with my gown still half unlaced and left the *sala* behind: the whispering cardinals, my sputtering Pope, the two painters still twittering about new techniques in plaster. A month in Florence? Maybe that wouldn't be long enough. Maybe two months. "I need a respite."

"A respite from what?" Leonello asked. I hadn't realized I'd said it out loud.

"The *Borgias*," I said, and felt myself near tears. "*All* of them."

Carmelina

There." I hurled the little purse at him like a stone. "Eight ducats. Now get out of my chamber."

"La Bella didn't mind, I'll wager." Marco caught the pouch before it hit him, pouring the coins out into his palm. "She's got a purse as open as her legs—"

"Don't be vile!" I would have flown at my cousin and boxed his ears, but he saw the look on my face and hastily retreated behind my narrow bed. "I don't care what you threaten next time. I am never begging money for you or your poxy dicing debts again."

Marco had the grace to look shamefaced. "I wouldn't have told, you know. Not really."

He tried a wheedling smile, but I still had fury roiling about in my chest like a kettle about to boil over. My fool of a cousin evidently did not have enough to do in the Duke of Gandia's half-staffed *palazzo*. In absence of anyone to cook for, he'd been gaming again and had lost three months' worth of pay wagering on Cesare Borgia's bullfights a fortnight ago. Judging from the dark bruises on his face and the puffed cut on his lip, Marco's smile had not succeeded this time in getting him out of the debt.

We hadn't spoken since he'd left the Palazzo Santa Maria with his pack over his shoulder, still full of sullen resentment at me for taking his position. But he'd turned up this morning, shamefaced and shuffling just outside my tiny chamber, and he hadn't been looking for the pleasure of my company.

"Just beg the money from Madonna Giulia. She's fond of you! Eight ducats, little cousin, it's nothing to her. In fact, ask for ten and I'll have a little something extra to put on a *pallone* match—"

"Absolutely not," I'd stated.

He'd tried pleading, and he even tried kissing, and when neither of those worked—

"You know what they'll do to me next?" he'd shouted, pointing at his split lip. "You'll get me those eight ducats from La Bella, Carmelina, or maybe I'll go to Adriana da Mila with a few stories about you! You won't be mistress of these kitchens anymore if that old bitch finds out where you fled from!"

Now, of course, he was not wild-eyed at all. Ashamed again, and cajoling.

"Don't look at me like that," he insisted, as I continued to gaze at him with stony eyes. "I wouldn't really have told that you're—well, you know. Not really. It's my skin too if they find out, after all. I was just desperate. I didn't mean it!"

"Of course not," I said. "Not now you have the coin."

He shuffled a little behind my bed, hooking his thumbs through his belt. My big feckless cousin, so tall and strong with his curly black hair all mussed like a little boy's. Seedy around the edges, though. His shirt was grimy, and his right eye swelled and bruised to the color of the squid ink I sometimes used as a sauce for wide ribbons of pasta.

I could not believe we had ever shared a bed.

"No harm done, is there, little cousin?" Marco continued in the face of my silence. "Madonna Giulia didn't mind giving you the coin, did she?"

"That's not the point." Of course my mistress had opened her purse at once when she heard my fumbling flame-faced story about an orphaned cousin arrived from Parma. She gave money away like water, to her servants or to the beggars in the streets or to anyone who asked for it. "Madonna Giulia isn't the point at all, Marco. You *threatened* me."

"I had to get the money!"

"And now you're leaving." I pointed to the door. "Madonna Giulia departs for Florence tomorrow, and I'll need to prepare her a few treats for the journey. Get out, you lying caul-brained goat turd."

"Well, now, no need to be so hasty. I thought I'd pay a visit to my kitchens, see everyone—"

"They aren't *your* kitchens, Marco!" I bundled my cousin toward the courtyard. "They haven't been your kitchens for a very long time. So *get out*."

I banged the door on his indignant face and contemplated my own imminent future with a scowl. I should have been accompanying Madonna Giulia to Florence, really. "No journey is complete without a little basket of your pastries," she'd declared. "I always eat when I'm traveling! Especially those little kerchiefy-shaped *crostata* things with the honeyed strawberries . . ." But I was supposed to be tending my orphaned cousin from Parma, the fictitious one for whom I'd begged eight ducats, and of course Madonna Giulia had given me leave to stay home from her Florentine visit. She was far too generous with her servants, not just in money but in time she allowed for us to miss our work. Making up for Madonna Adriana's stinginess with our wages and our free hours, I always thought, and the other maidservants took shameless advantage—but this was the first time I'd abused my mistress's easy generosity. So I guiltily made an extra basketful of those little kerchiefy-shaped *crostata* things with honeyed strawberries for her to share with her golden gabble-head of a daughter on their journey, and went back to my kitchens alone.

The Palazzo Santa Maria seemed empty without her. Madonna Lucrezia was still dawdling in Rome, finding excuses to postpone her return to "that backwater sinkhole" that was Pesaro, but she spent more nights dancing and banqueting through the various great *palazzi* of the city than she did at her old girlhood home. Madonna Adriana was no longer really needed to chaperone the Pope's daughter and had taken herself off to spend the winter with her niece in Liguria who had just delivered a baby. Without Madonna Giulia drifting about the house like a joyous bubble, playing games with her daughter and sunning her hair and singing tuneless little love songs, the loggias of the *palazzo* seemed cold and empty.

So when I woke one night to the delicious golden smell of something frying, at first I thought I was dreaming.

If so, it was a good dream. I'd been having the troubling kinds of dreams lately, the kind where I swam out of sleep still feeling a hard male chest against mine, seeing the loom of strong broad shoulders overhead, tasting the salty tang of a man's sweat on smooth warm skin . . . not any man I knew, just a man with a shadow for a face. It's the sort of dream a woman has when her life has no particular passion in it, and probably never will. It's not a very helpful dream, either, because I'd made my choices, I'd chosen my life with clear eyes, and I'd known love would have no real part in it. So all in all, dreaming about frying food instead of shadowy lovers seemed a great improvement.

But then I sat up in bed, sniffing more strongly, and realized I was awake.

"What are you doing?" I demanded, prowling into the kitchens. "Bartolomeo, it's past midnight!"

My apprentice turned, skillet in one hand and a broad spoon in the other, but rather than look guilty he just gave me a delirious grin. "Couldn't sleep, *signorina*! Neither could you, by the look of it."

I doubted my apprentice remained sleepless for the same reason I did. The excessive emptiness of my bed might keep me awake sometimes, but surely not Bartolomeo—he had passed his eighteenth year not long ago, and the maids who had once whacked him on the head for getting underfoot were now looking at him speculatively. And why not? A skinny, penniless pot-boy is one thing, but a promising young cook with a bright future and no mother is entirely another.

"Can't you just steal a cask of wine to put yourself back to sleep, like all normal apprentices?" I said through a yawn. "You have to build up a fire and start frying everything in sight? That's good kindling you're wasting!"

He hardly seemed to hear me. "Look, I found these at market yesterday." He thrust some odd brown tubers at me like a bouquet of roses. "Aren't they wonderful?"

"They look like warts." I poked at them with a dubious finger. "What are they?"

"Some kind of root. Not so different from a turnip, but the texture has more starch to it. The vendor claimed they came clear across the ocean from those new lands the Spanish found, but I wasn't swallowing *that* nonsense." Bartolomeo snorted. "I've been experimenting with them all day. Boiling, chopping, spicing, and the texture wasn't coming out how I wanted. I was just getting into bed when I thought I'd have one more try at frying them." His eyes had a gleam of enthusiasm as he whirled back to the trestle table where a bowl of chopped tubers or whatever they were waited for him. "A little coarse salt, a little olive oil . . ." He tilted a generous splash of oil into the pan. "Is Madonna Adriana still cross with you for buying the expensive oil from Apulia? She thought she'd save money, paying you less than she did Maestro Santini, but you never skimp on ordering good supplies the way he did.

Doubt she's saved too many *scudi* by the end of the month after your olive oil bills—"

"Careful," I said, as a drop of that hot oil splashed out of the pan. "You couldn't put a shirt on, Bartolomeo? You'll burn yourself."

"Already have," Bartolomeo said, unconcerned. When his urge for the frying pan had hit, he'd clearly not bothered to pull on more than a pair of worn breeches before racing for the kitchens. The flagstone floor was chilly beneath my slippers, and despite the crackling kitchen fire I still shivered in my linen shift, but Bartolomeo was evidently feeling no cold as he padded barefoot about the ovens. Feeling no heat either; among the cinnamon-dark freckles splashed over his milk-pale chest and arms I could see red splotch marks where hot olive oil had spattered, but he was whistling happily between his teeth.

"You shouldn't be using my kitchens just to experiment on strange tubers, you know." I hesitated, wondering if I should order him to desist, but for once my rebellious apprentice was being cheerful instead of argumentative, and that seemed like something to encourage. "You're lucky I feel like a bit of a nibble," I finally allowed. "Let's have a look at these roots of yours."

"The first batch burned," Bartolomeo admitted, jerking his chin at the trestle table toward a plate of what appeared to be little scorched black disks. "They fry up fast, whatever they are. Sweet Santa Marta, don't let me burn the next batch or I'll be out of tubers—" He touched the little wooden crucifix hanging about his neck on a cord. "You think she listens?"

"Santa Marta?" I couldn't help a little smile. "I know she does."

"I think so, too. Not that the Heavenly Father doesn't," Bartolomeo allowed. "But He's busy. He's got His hands full finishing off the French; I'm not going to burden Him with my kitchen woes."

"His Holiness the Pope is the one with his hands full when it comes to the French," I pointed out. "He's the one waging war on them."

"It's all the same," Bartolomeo shrugged. "The Heavenly Father and the Holy Father—they're both about equally far above a kitchen apprentice with a pan full of tubers, aren't they? Pure, powerful, perfect—

things I can't ever aspire to. Except maybe in food," he added, and gave the pan a swirl.

"I would hardly call the Holy Father pure," I snorted. "Or are you going to tell me he loves Madonna Giulia like a daughter?"

Bartolomeo grinned. "Even the Holy Father was a man first, and Madonna Giulia would tempt God Himself. Come to think of it, God Himself was a man once, too. He'd understand."

Belatedly, I reined myself in from further gossip. It was one thing to encourage my apprentice's good cheer, but too much free rein was another thing entirely. Bartolomeo might be only eighteen, but the other apprentices listened to him, and so did the undercooks who should have been giving him orders rather than taking them—he'd even gotten clever lately in how he challenged me! He no longer picked open quarrels when we disagreed on what to put into a sauce or how to roll out pasta; instead, he followed me about with ostentatious humility saying, "If you please, *signorina*, just a touch more mint? And if you please, *signorina*, if we could roll out the *tagliatelli* with a comb to give the sauce more grip? And if you please, *signorina*—" Always during the busiest hour of pre-*pranzo* rushing. Until finally I would snap, "Oh, do what you please with the *tagliatelli*, Bartolomeo!" and then see his wide grin and realize I had been played like a viol. So it went against the grain to give him a free hand with anything, even just with a bunch of tubers and a line or two of conversation in the small hours of the night, because if you gave Bartolomeo one pinch of independence he'd have your whole kitchen turned upside-down in a heartbeat.

But whatever those unpromising-looking tubers were sizzling in the pan, they were just starting to turn golden about the edges and they smelled marvelous as I took a long sniff over my apprentice's shoulder.

"Passable," I said. "Give them a flip now—"

"No. They need a bit more browning on this side." A drop of olive oil leaped out and sizzled on his bare arm, but he paid no attention. He flipped a slice neatly out of the pan to the notch-eared tomcat, who pounced with a rusty *mrow*.

"Don't feed that beast!" I scolded. "He's spoiled enough, the way the maids coo over him—"

"Why are you so hard on that cat, *signorina*?" Flipping another disk out of the pan to the floor.

"It's no use being sentimental about animals, Bartolomeo. Either they earn their keep or we eat them. I haven't any use for a cat that doesn't catch mice." I craned my neck at the pan as he gave it a shake. The little disks had gone golden all over, and my mouth was watering. "Take them off the heat!"

"All in good time . . ." He flipped them expertly, gave another swirl and a nod as the other side crisped, and turned them out into a clean bowl. I reached for one of the crisp little golden disks, but he nudged my hand away. "They're too hot, *signorina*, so wait till you're asked."

"My kitchen, apprentice." I gave him an absent rap on the shoulder as I always did, and it surprised me when he caught my wrist and held it.

"Stop doing that," he said. "I am eighteen years of age, so quit whacking me like a scullion. And it's my recipe even if it is your kitchen, so I'll tell you when you're allowed to taste it."

I felt my brows fly up in surprise, and I almost told him he was an insolent lug, as I had last week when he dared add beaten mint to my dish of salted tuna belly. But his voice now was firm rather than belligerent, and his eyes were steady as they looked down at me. My apprentice *was* eighteen years old, and perhaps we'd been arguing too loudly for me to notice that the unsteady wobbles of his young voice had settled into a confident tenor, and his milk-pale shoulders were as broad as Marco's. Just last week I'd watched him step between two of his fellow apprentices as they started a shoving match, haul them out in the yard, crack their heads together until they yowled, and then deliver a stern tongue-lashing that could have come straight from me. They'd *listened*, too, muttering and rubbing their sore heads, and it didn't seem to occur to them that he didn't have any real authority over them. My erstwhile pot-boy had grown up, it seemed, and I wondered if I should think about raising him from apprentice to undercook.

"Pass me the pepper," said Bartolomeo, releasing my wrist. "If you please, *signorina*. And a block of the good Parmesan, and a grater."

"Yes, *maestro*," I said with just a bit of a sniff so he'd see the concession I was making, and I fetched both. Bartolomeo tossed the crisp golden disks with pepper and just a little fine-grated cheese, and popped one into his mouth. He chewed. I waited. "Well?"

"Needs more salt," he decided. Another sprinkle, another taste, as I shifted from foot to foot. My mouth was watering again, and Bartolomeo's cheeks creased in a smile as he proffered a fried golden coin of tuber. "Here."

Taste exploded in my mouth—the crunch of salt flakes and faint burn of fresh pepper, the crisp fried skin on the outside giving way to something mealy, mild . . . and quite wonderful.

"Hmph," I said, swallowing the last heavenly crumb. "I'd add a dash of rosemary."

"At least you didn't say cinnamon," Bartolomeo said, and then he kissed me. Not a boy's clumsy peck but a young man's kiss, too hard, too hungry, too eager, but I was too astounded to pull away as he cupped one big hand around the back of my neck and pulled me up against him.

I tasted flakes of salt on his lips from the fried golden disks we'd shared, tasted pepper and Parmesan and the good olive oil from Apulia. His lips parted mine hungrily, one hand sliding up into my hair and the other gripping my waist, and I didn't pull away as fast as I should have because he tasted so *good*. Cooks were better for kissing than anyone else. Cooks had sweet breath from chewing mint rather than drinking rotgut beer; cooks smelled of rosemary and nutmeg rather than sweat and smoke; cooks were hard-bodied from hauling kegs and carcasses all day rather than soft-gutted from sitting about a barracks or a shop counter. A guardsman or a clerk gripped you in hairy arms, but a cook's skin was smooth to the touch because his arms were singed hairless by hot ovens . . .

My lips parted under his before I could think of moving away. A mistake, because he lifted me to the edge of the trestle table, one hand smoothing my hip through my shift, the other still twined in my hair.

"Stop," I managed to mutter then, though his hand moving from my hip down the outside of my thigh burned me. "Stop, we can't—I can't—"

"Why?" His mouth had moved to my neck, and he was drinking the skin of my shoulder where my shift had slipped down. "Why not?"

"Because—" Because he was my apprentice, because he was eighteen, because I had a position to maintain in this household, and the respect that had to be maintained with it—because—

I should have pulled away. I should have pulled away at once, but he had ambushed me as neatly as the French army, my apprentice boy who had somehow stopped being a boy when I wasn't looking. I wound my hands into his bright hair—to pull his head back, to shake some sense into him—but my bed had been empty such a long time, and now I had a pair of smooth hard-muscled arms about me again, and a kiss that tasted as good as those fried golden things. I was lonely and hungry and cold, and my apprentice smelled of wild thyme and his flesh was warm as a kettle on rolling boil. "Bartolomeo—" I managed to say.

"Mouths shut," he murmured against my lips, "and hands moving."

His big kitchen-scarred hand slipped up to span my breasts, and my whole body juddered at the touch. It was all he needed. He scooped me up so my legs wrapped his waist and it was only a few short steps to his tiny cubbyhole beside the wine cellars. If it had been farther, if he'd put me down to walk—if we'd had to stop and fumble with boots and ties, apron knots and a gown's laces—but my shift billowed to the floor half a heartbeat after he kicked the door shut with one bare foot, and his breeches followed another heartbeat later, and there was no time to think, no time to think and no desire to think either. Just hunger, a ravenous tearing hunger as though the flesh had been starved instead of the belly, and on the narrow straw-stuffed apprentice's pallet on the floor we flung our bodies down like feasts and tore at each other, savored each other, ate and drank each other, until there was nothing left but crumbs.

And it's only when the crumbs are left and you're scraping the dish that you begin to feel the shame of having acted like such a glutton.

I lay gasping and covered with sweat on the lumpy pallet, the hard shoulder and hip of my apprentice—my *apprentice*!—still pressed against my side. I heard Bartolomeo's breath slowing and I closed my eyes and prayed as I had never prayed in my life. *Sweet Santa Marta, just let him fall asleep.* Marco had always promptly fallen asleep when he rolled away from me. If Bartolomeo did too, surely I could creep off to my own chamber and pretend this had all been some fevered nightmare. Surely. *Sweet Santa Marta, please let him sleep.*

"More Parmesan," Bartolomeo said up to the ceiling.

"What?" I replied before I could switch to my other plan, which was to pretend that *I* was asleep. Or perhaps dead.

"More Parmesan." He turned his head, looking at me over the thin pillow. "On those fried tubers. And a dash of rosemary. You're right about that."

"Oh." I felt my face flaming.

"I'm going to write that recipe up," he said cheerfully. "I write up all my recipes. The ones that work, anyway. I had an idea for shaved ice and frozen fruits and cream that was a disaster. I wanted it all creamy and cold and smooth, and it just melted into a great sticky puddle. But the fried tubers, those were good. I'm going to make a book someday—all the best recipes, *and* the best advice for cooks." He reached out, smoothing back a curl of hair that was sticking to my neck. "You could help me write that part."

I moved away from his hand, sitting up.

"Where are you going?" He sat up too, sliding his arms around my waist from behind and kissing the back of my neck. "You think I'm letting you up yet, as long as I've wanted to get you here? Just give me, oh, the length of time it takes to say a rosary, and then . . ." He buried his nose in my loose hair. "Sweet Santa Marta, maybe I won't even need that long. You smell like cinnamon."

"It's very late." I pulled away from his arms, keeping my words stern. "I'll need to be back to my chamber before anyone's awake to see me come out of here."

"Why shouldn't they see?" He fell back on his elbows, admiring me as I rose. "They'll know soon enough anyway."

"Oh, will they?" I snarled, fumbling for my shift. Men, always boasting about the women they'd wheedled out of their skirts. What an achievement for a mere apprentice: getting his own *maestra di cucina* to flop on her back. What a *joke* for the scullery.

Bartolomeo shrugged, unfazed. "They'll know when we make the announcement."

"Announcement?" I found my shift, yanking it gratefully down over my head. My whole body felt flushed and awkward with embarrassment. "Announcement of what?"

He grinned. "Marry me."

I stood there goggling like a goose about to get its neck wrung.

"You think I'd bed you and not marry you?" He raised his eyebrows at my aghast silence. "What sort of man do you think I am? I know we can't wed before I'm done with my apprenticeship, but I'm near finished anyway. I'm already better than half the undercooks Madonna Adriana hired on the cheap—"

Sweet Santa Marta, I thought again in utter horror, but the prayer stopped short this time. My patron saint clearly wasn't going to be any help in situations like this, good as she was for keeping a roast rare on the spit or a sauce from breaking. *This* was far out of her control.

Bartolomeo must have taken my frantic, silent hunt for words as some kind of permission, because he rose from his pallet and came to slip his arms about my waist. "Summertime, do you think? We could save a little, go to the priest then—"

My mouth was dry, and my heart hammered. In the light of the single taper I could see every detail of this tiny cubby of a chamber: barely big enough for a pallet and a stool and a bag of clothes but exquisitely neat for all that; a bowl of crushed mint leaves that he must have placed to keep the windowless air sweet; a packet of scribbled papers that might have been the start of his recipe collection. A tiny chamber not tall enough even at its highest point for my apprentice to stand up straight, but he was standing in the middle of it now, utterly naked and proposing marriage to me.

A tiny, astounded part of me thought back to the words that had drifted through my head when I first woke up, just an hour ago: *This is the sort of dream a woman has when her life has no particular passion in it, and probably never will.*

"These will be our kitchens, yours and mine, we'll run everything between us!" His words poured fast and eager now, like warm olive oil out of a jar. "The two of us, we'll be the greatest cooks in Rome. Sweet Christ, Carmelina, I've never known a woman who could cook like you! Even," he conceded, "if you put too much orange juice in everything."

"I do not," I couldn't help saying, even though it rocked me clear back onto my heels to hear him say my name instead of *signorina*.

"Yes, you do, but that's not important. We'll learn, we'll both of us learn, we'll travel!" His arms had tightened around me now, and he was gabbling faster. "We don't have to stay in Rome, we could go to Milan; Lodovico Il Moro keeps a court there to rival the Pope's. Then to Lombardy where I was born; I can show you how the French influence comes over into the recipes, and I know you scoff about the French and their sour spices, but there's something to be learned there—"

"You've gone mad!" I had a handsome young man before me proposing marriage in all seriousness—was the world just laughing at me? What woman has to dodge marriage proposals *after* becoming a nun? *He doesn't know that*, I thought disjointedly, *and you certainly can't tell him, so find some other way to dodge it.*

I made myself plant a stern hand on Bartolomeo's hard chest, pushing him back, but that might have been a mistake because I could feel his heartbeat speed up under my touch. Maybe mine too, but that was just more panic. "Bartolomeo, this has all been a mistake." I spoke calmly, reasonably. "A very great mistake, and I do apologize for that. I am *maestra di cucina*, and you are an apprentice. I am seven years older than you, and I should never have—"

"And I've wanted you since I was fourteen." His eyes burned me, bright as cinnamon. "When you threw me my apprentice apron for the first time. When you let me make smelt in green sauce for Madonna Giulia. When you put your head on my shoulder after we were captured by the French, and let me put my arm around you—sweet Christ, I nearly kissed you right then." His voice bubbled faster, a torrent of words like wine out of a breached cask. "I get weak in the knees just watching you beat *eggs*—when you're slinging spoons at me just because I'm the only one in these kitchens brave enough to tell you that your recipe's wrong—"

"Don't be ridiculous." I wrenched away, feeling a film of his sweat on my fingertips from his broad freckled chest. Bad enough to handle an apprentice in lust; boys were always in lust. But an apprentice in love? *How can he be in love with me?* a small inner voice thought in wondering astonishment. *I don't do anything but shout at him!*

Never mind how it started, I thought harshly. *Squelch it. For his own good, just squelch it.* "This is just silly moon-eyed calf love," I told him. "All boys go a little soft for their first girl. It means nothing."

"You didn't think I was such a *boy* down there." He jerked his chin at the rumpled pallet, grinning. "And as a matter of fact, you aren't my first girl."

I seized on that. "Then go marry her, if you're not the kind of lad who'd bed a girl and then leave her!"

"I did offer to marry her. She laughed at me. Nicely, though, and then she kissed me and said I was a lovely boy but if she married all the boys she broke in, she'd have enough husbands for an army. I liked her, but not the way I love you, though, so all in all I was very relieved—"

Sounds like Pantisilea, I couldn't help thinking, but shoved the thought away. This whole argument was slipping out of my hands. "Well, I can't marry you. You work in my kitchens"—I groped—"and you are *under* me, and—"

"Not last time, I wasn't." He grabbed me around the waist again, pulling me back toward the pallet. "But *this* time I'll be under you if you like, Carmelina—"

"You do not have leave to call me that!" I shoved away desperately, trying not to look at the hard freckled length of his body against me. "We rolled about in a bed, but that does not mean you have leave to call me by name. You are my *apprentice*. And even if you weren't, I have no intention of marrying anybody, much less you. Rolling about in a bed doesn't change that either!"

"Why not?" He folded his arms across his chest, looking down at me in challenge. "The two best cooks in Rome, married to each other. Why *not*?"

Because I'm a nun, I almost said. *Because the vow didn't disappear just because I ran from it. Because you'd face charges if we were caught.* Charges of profanation, desecration, adultery—crimes meriting at the least exile, at the most death, for marrying a nun who already had her Lord for a husband.

Bad enough that we bedded once—but if that was found out, Bartolomeo could at least claim he didn't know my secrets. Likely he'd be spared as the innocent dupe of a wicked seductress. But if I were ever mad enough to *marry*, then my so-called husband's guilt would be assumed, and his whole future in ruins. Oh, maybe I'd shared Marco's bed on occasion, but Marco knew my past, knew the risks and the sins attached, and he certainly knew he couldn't marry me. Bartolomeo didn't know anything of the kind. *You want to lay that on his conscience?* my own conscience snarled, raking guilt through me like a lion's claws. *A boy who can't bed a girl without offering to marry her after, and you want to tell him he's violated a nun?*

All my life I'd been taught that girls grew up to be wives, or else they became nuns or whores. I'd said that once to Madonna Giulia, when we first met. But she occupied an odd limbo between *wife* and *whore*, and I occupied an even odder one myself between *whore* and *nun*. There were shadowy spaces between the stark trinity of futures I'd been offered as a girl—but however you defined me, there would be no marriage in my future. I felt a moment's pang of regret go through me like a sword, but I hardened my heart. I'd made my choices: work, only work, and the occasional casual tumble with men like Marco who knew about my past. Or maybe lordlings who liked to bed servant girls and were too high and mighty to care about consequences.

Bartolomeo was neither.

"Is it Maestro Santini?" Bartolomeo said, as though reading my mind. "Don't tell me you mooned after him too like all those silly maidservants, just because he's handsome and has *curls*. He'll waste every *scudo* he earns, and besides, he couldn't cook his way out of a flour sack. He lost his place here, and he'll lose his place with the Duke of Gandia too."

"It's not Maestro Santini," I said at last. "It's a vow I made—to myself." I wished I had a shawl to cover my thin shift. His eyes were still devouring me, making my skin prickle, and I folded my arms across my breasts instead. "I don't need any husband. I've a good trade and a good position in this *palazzo*—" I was talking too much, too fast. Does a cook bother to explain his decisions to his subordinates when explaining a menu? A proposal of marriage should be no different. "I do not wish to marry," I concluded with as much finality as I could muster. "Not Maestro Santini, and certainly not you."

"But you get lonely." Bartolomeo reached out and touched a curl of my hair, winding it around his finger. "I can always tell. It shows in your *tourtes* first, those marzipan ones you make for Madonna Giulia. They get sweeter, and you add more ground almonds. And it takes you half the time to whip up egg whites, because you get vicious when you're sad, and you take it out on the eggs—"

He bent his head to kiss me again, surely one of the few men in the *palazzo* tall enough to do it, not that he was really a man; he was a boy and he was seven years younger than I and sweet Santa Marta, how did I get into this mess and why was I kissing him again and why wouldn't he just put some clothes on before I did something else stupid?

"Enough!" I pushed him away, sweeping back my hair where he'd twined it about his hand. "I will forget this, Bartolomeo," I said sternly as he opened his mouth. "But not if I hear one more word about it, from you or anyone else, so don't even think about boasting to the other apprentices." Dear God, I knew how fast gossip could spread through a kitchen. A cocky boy who has just made a conquest always wants to boast to his friends, but a cocky boy I might have been able to silence. A lovelorn moon-calf of a boy who had just been rejected in his first heart-felt marriage proposal? Had I been too busy worrying about Bartolomeo's future to worry about mine?

All he had to do was burst out bitterly to the first friend he saw in the scullery, or the first pretty serving maid who took him to bed and consoled him with what a coldhearted bitch I was. And after that, the whole household would know how a kitchen apprentice had seduced the *maestra di cucina*, and I'd have not a single crumb of authority left. The maids and the pot-boys would all be giggling behind my back, and once it got up to Madonna Adriana . . . maids in this household were dismissed if they gained reputations as whores. Pantisilea was our resident harlot, and as much as everyone liked her, she would have been packed out years ago if Madonna Giulia had not intervened. And a *maestra di cucina* would be held to an even higher standard—if she could not keep order among her underlings, she was worth nothing. How my underlings would love whispering about Carmelina, the inviolable Madonna of the kitchens, revealed as no better than Pantisilea.

Stupider than Pantisilea. She was at least clever enough to keep her belly flat using all those prudent tricks with halved limes or cups of pennyroyal extract. I knew those tricks too, but had that stopped me? Had I really been so foolish and lonely and lust-drunk that I hadn't even thought of pushing a halved lime into myself before my apprentice pushed his way in after it? If my belly swelled, it wouldn't even matter if Bartolomeo held his tongue. I'd be out on the streets the moment my apron showed a bulge, and even Madonna Giulia wouldn't be able to save my position for me.

Dear God, I was going to lose everything. All because I couldn't keep my legs closed. My father was right—I really was just a slattern.

"Not one word to anyone," I said desperately, jabbing a finger into Bartolomeo's chest. "You will take my orders, you will do as I tell you, and you will *never* presume to touch me again."

"Carmelina—"

"Or call me anything but *signorina*," I rode over him. "You are an apprentice, and you are a silly boy, and I should never have let you touch me. It was a mistake, you hear me? A *mistake*."

He stood there with his hands hanging at his sides, still naked except for the cross about his neck, looking at me. He flushed slowly, so dark his freckles disappeared all the way down his chest. He turned away from me, fumbling for his breeches, and I felt a pang. But I kept my stony expression. I'd suffered calf love too when I was his age—painful though it was, it went away quickly. He'd forget about me with the next maidservant to bat her lashes at him. Far better for his future if he did.

If he would just not ruin *my* future by talking . . .

"Good night," I added in the same severe tones, and turned for the door. My cold and empty bed now seemed very welcoming indeed. Though before I collapsed into it, I'd have to rush for a jar of the strongest vinegar we had, and rinse my body out with a prayer that it wasn't too late to keep myself from quickening . . .

But even in all my confused fear, I couldn't stop myself from hesitating as I opened the door and smelled the waft of olive oil and coarse salt from the plate of now-cold tubers in the kitchens. I looked back over my shoulder and saw that Bartolomeo had not moved, still standing beside the rumpled pallet with his arms folded across his chest and his bare feet looking rather pathetic below his flour-dusted breeches.

"Bartolomeo," I said. "You were right about one thing. Those fried things you made, whatever that vegetable is—they're delicious. I'll have you cook them for Madonna Giulia as soon as she returns."

"Go to hell," said my apprentice, and slammed the door in my face.

CHAPTER FIVE

❖

Evil is often spoken of me, but I let it pass.

—RODRIGO BORGIA, POPE ALEXANDER VI

Giulia

I f there's anything you must never say to a Florentine, it's that Florence is the little sister of Rome. Any Florentine citizen will puff up like a toad and then proceed to list all the glories of their fair city, from the enormous dome of the Santa Maria del Fiore ("*Far* finer than the Basilica San Pietro!") to the bridges over the Arno ("Far fewer dead cats in *our* river than in your Tiber!"). So unless you have a great deal of time to spend listening to a huffy lecture on all of Florence's admitted glories, it's better just to keep from making any comparisons at all. But Florence *is* a little sister to Rome, and in more than just her size. Rome is a courtesan in her prime, ripe and perhaps decaying a little under the façade of her cosmetics, but flaunting herself in spite of it: luscious and foulmouthed and funny, praying and swearing and laughing all at once, speaking a dozen languages and spreading her skirts and her arms wide for all the pilgrims and travelers of the world. Florence is a girl just come from a convent: beautiful but self-contained, a little wary, a little prim. Rome is the hub of all Christendom; you can see a thousand new faces a day and never repeat a one, and Romans react a thousand different ways to any dilemma. In Florence everyone seems to know each other, and whether for good or ill, they all react as one.

And in January when I went to visit my sister, Florence was not only an insular city but a frightened one. Frightened, but strangely exalted, and what a mix it was to see on people's faces.

"It's all the fault of that wretched Savonarola," my skinny and acerbic older sister fretted. But even in the safety of her own cozy *sala*, she gave a quick glance to make sure the maids were busy clearing the *credenza* at the other end of the room, and the servers occupied decanting the wine rather than eavesdropping on our conversation. I hadn't been in Florence a day before I knew about Savonarola's Angels: the young men and boys of Florence who had answered all that Dominican thundering from the pulpit to join God's militia. That nice young page with the chestnut curls—who knew if after *cena* he might slip out of the house, don a white robe, and join bands of fellow Angels in singing hymns and roaming the streets looking for sinners to reprimand? Best to be careful; Savonarola had a great many Angels. Much like God Himself, I suppose, though I doubted God's angels were quite so obnoxious and pimply.

"So it's not enough now that we've been instructed to forswear sloth and luxury and idle pastimes," Gerolama complained as she passed me a cup of warmed wine. "We're now to be *inspected*, to make sure our houses contain nothing ungodly! It's all for that wretched bonfire Fra Savonarola's determined to build—you can already see the pyre being built in the Piazza della Signoria. We're to toss everything vain onto it—jewels, lip rouge, perfumes, cards—"

"Then Madonna Giulia will return to Rome with no baggage at all," remarked Leonello from his corner. It did not matter whether the room my bodyguard entered was my private chamber, the great Sala dei Santi in the Vatican, or my sister's overdecorated little chamber with its too-ornate *credenza* and garishly embroidered wall hangings—Leonello's hazel eyes always flicked briefly in each direction, measuring angles of attack in the event of any assassins lurking about, and then he took the corner with the best view of the room regardless of who might already be seated there, propped up his black boots, and took out a book. Currently the book was some salaciously illustrated volume of tales from the Orient that he had borrowed from Cesare Borgia's collection, and Leonello flicked the pages with great interest. "Such utter rubbish," he remarked. "I must be sure to finish it quickly, as I'm sure this city's dirty literature will all be required as fuel for Fra Savonarola's bonfire."

I made a private note to keep my jewels in their boxes during this visit. I didn't really see any reason why God would want me to burn up my teardrop pearl necklace or my diamond hair roses. Besides, according to Fra Savonarola and his ilk, a woman of my stature was thoroughly damned anyway, so why not at least go down to hell in all my finery? And how can you *burn* diamonds, anyway?

"I'm already storing away a few things," my sister confided. "My better gowns, of course, and the good silver, and the pendant my husband gave me on our wedding. Though I may just let those hideous earrings from his mother get into the pile," Gerolama added thoughtfully. "Not to mention that ghastly *credenza* from our great-aunt Lella ..."

"Mamma, Mamma!" My Laura dashed into the *sala* in a whirl of bouncing blond curls. "Giuseppe the cook gave me a sugar lump! And he says there are *angels* in Florence, angels on every street corner—"

"Not the kind of angels you want to meet, *Lauretta mia*." I lifted my daughter up into my lap, dabbing at the sugar on her cheeks. Nearly four years old now, plump and golden and giggling, and every time I looked at her my heart squeezed utter happiness. Even with the rest of me so unsettled.

"You'd better put her in a wool dress when you take her out." Gerolama sniffed at Laura's apricot velvet gown with the sleeves trimmed in fox fur, a miniature copy of mine. Laura had at last outgrown the stage of wanting to run about naked; these days she took a very keen interest indeed in her dresses. "Swirly skirts!" she always demanded of my robe makers. "With *sparkles*." Sparkles were all she thought about now—Laura had wanted earrings for her last birthday, and so I relented and let Leonello pierce her little ears with a heated needle. She'd been so determined to have pearl eardrops of her very own, she hadn't made a peep at the pain. "You spoil that child, Giulia," my sister scolded as I kissed the top of Laura's blond head.

"Of course I do," I said without shame, and tickled my girl until she shrieked laughter. She had exactly the same ticklish spot at her waist as my Pope.

Gerolama eyed her: a shrewd farmer's wife pricing a lamb to see how much it will fetch at market. "Still an Orsini, is she?"

"In name at least." But in blood—well, blood was beginning to tell. Laura's face was emerging from its infant roundness into a character and shape of its own, and from certain angles I thought I could see a chin that might turn out like Lucrezia's, or an arch of eyebrow exactly like Cesare's. And she definitely had Rodrigo's nose. *Laura Borgia?* I wondered, and thought I could see my Pope wondering too lately as he looked at my daughter.

"Has His Holiness spoken of a marriage for her?" Gerolama pressed. "That would seal the connection for our family, you know."

"She's not four years old," I protested.

"And you told me yourself Lucrezia had a betrothal at seven. It's never too early to start planning a daughter's future, Giulia."

Says the mother of none, I thought unkindly.

"Besides, you'll lose your looks someday, and the Pope's favor with them, and then where will we all be? But if you've managed to betroth Laura to an Este or a Gonzaga, well, that's something we can all fall back on."

"I am touched by your concern for your niece," I said tartly.

"I only want her properly married," Gerolama retorted. "A countess or a duchess, think of it! Or are you going to groom her to take your path instead?"

My voice slid from tart to freezing. "My daughter will *never* be an old man's plaything."

The words startled me, coming out so fast and unthinking. Perhaps because it wasn't quite the fate I had pictured for myself, when I was a little girl who also loved sparkles and swirling skirts.

Laura soon slid off my lap and bounced away to go play with the new litter of kittens in the kitchens—"Can I have one, Mamma? Can I, can I?"—and Gerolama was soon complaining of the insolence of her maidservants and the difficulties of keeping dust off her carpets. Eternal topics among respectable women, and perhaps there were more benefits to being a harlot than I'd previously thought, like the fact that most respectable women refused to talk to me. They rushed to copy any item of clothing I wore on my sinful body, but my sinful conversation was entirely shunned.

Still, I was glad I'd come to Florence, even if my sister did grate against me. I could play with Laura all day long now, brush her curls and tell her stories and applaud her as she took up her miniature lute with great seriousness and fumbled through her first simple song with every bit as little musical talent as her mother. All the time with my daughter that I wanted, without being interrupted by some obsequious archbishop murmuring about how much he would appreciate a new benefice from the Pope. In Florence I could relax my morning routine, leave off dressing my hair in those elaborate plaits and curls that took hours and left my neck rigid, without having the Tart of Aragon make some pointed comment about how sad it was when a woman stopped taking trouble with her looks. I could rise early to watch the dawn if I liked without being exhausted from some endless banquet the evening before; I could throw on any gown I liked for Mass because nobody cared if I had worn the same thing to Mass two weeks ago; I could go riding without Lucrezia always trying to make sure her riding dress was just a little finer than mine. I could spend an entire morning in my shift if I wanted, savoring my way through Avernus's sonnets and reading bits out loud just to annoy Leonello. "Listen to Sonnet VIII; surely even you have to admit it's marvelous. He compares his Aurora to Helen of Troy—"

"No more, I beg you." Fingers in ears.

I just read louder, giggling. *"'A golden Helen for a golden war—'"*

"Kill me, please. Kill me at once."

It was all just another of my forays into the ordinary world, I suppose. And even if Florence felt small and fearful under Savonarola's rantings and his Angels, it was a foray I enjoyed.

A respite away from my Pope.

"I shall have to give His Holiness a good excuse if I wish to stay longer," I told Leonello one morning as I was lacing Laura's little dress up her back.

"No, you don't. He doesn't own you, after all, and I've heard you say so yourself."

"True," I agreed. "But the letters are getting irate. He started out apologetic, begging me to come back soon and saying he'd die a slow and horrible death if I was still angry at him. But now *he's* getting angry that I haven't answered any of those letters, so I'm getting missives about how I'm an unfeeling minx for leaving him so long."

"Tell him Fra Savonarola refuses to let you leave until you have given all your jewels over to his bonfire." Leonello distracted Laura from her wriggling by picking up one of Gerolama's prized glass ornaments from Murano and balancing it on the very tip of one finger. "You'll get another week in Florence, *and* the Holy Father will finally excommunicate our good fire-and-brimstone friar."

Laura clapped her hands at Leonello, crying, "Make it dance, Leo, make it *dance*!" Leonello would juggle for no one but my daughter. He set three of Gerolama's fragile vases to whirling above his stubby hands as I recaptured Laura's little wrist and stuffed it into her sleeve. My daughter had nursemaids, of course, but I would far rather dress her myself. Left to her own devices, Laura would beg the maids to steal my rouge for her cheeks and my pulverized malachite to smear around her eyes. Just because I was a harlot did *not* mean I was going to let my daughter start painting herself like one at the age of not-quite-four.

Laura squealed delight as Leonello tossed one vase high and caught it with a hand behind his back, and I tilted my head at him. "You're so good with children, Leonello. Why on earth don't you marry and have a few of your own?"

"What woman would have me?" His eyes followed the dance of the vases in the air. "A stunted little fellow who only comes to her waist?"

"Nonsense, you're not so small as that." I'd seen many dwarves; jesters and tumblers in the Duke of Gandia's household or the Tart of Aragon's, and Leonello overtopped them all by at least a hand's breadth. He really stood only half a head below me. "A great many women would consider you handsome," I informed him. "If you'd only make yourself pleasant to them!"

He turned a circle, still juggling for Laura, and I saw that the back of his neck reddened as it always did when he was exasperated. I did adore exasperating him. "Women like to point at men like me, Madonna Giulia. That does not mean they find me handsome."

"Why not choose a woman like you, then?"

Leonello gave a snort of derision. "Because one dwarf is an oddity, but two together are a freak show. No."

"You aren't very nice to your own kind, you know." I'd seen him watching Juan's Spanish dwarves when they bounded out to entertain after *cena*. They looked at him in curiosity and envy, my bodyguard in his rich blacks standing so proud with his dark head thrown back, and he gazed back at them with no expression at all. "You've found yourself a soft billet," I'd once heard a wizened little woman in motley tell Leonello, eyeing his livery cynically, and he gave her a smile of slow scorn. "Why don't you ever seek their company, Leonello?" I persisted. Surely there was companionship to be found among those like him, but I'd never once seen him look for it.

"They envy me," he said briefly. "And I despise them."

"Why?"

"They wish they had a place in the world. A place where they are not laughed at." One by one, Leonello caught the fragile glass vases. "And I scorn them because they never taught themselves any skills, nothing that would raise them above laughter. Instead they took the easy path, and let the world mock them. Eventually it turns them sour, and then they turn to drink, and most of the time they die badly. And as far as I am concerned, it's their own fault."

I studied him. "That seems very harsh."

"The world is harsh, Madonna Giulia. I was born as I am, and I see no reason to whine about it. At least I can make certain that I never marry, never sire children, and never pass this deformity of mine to some unfortunate infant. Stop whimpering," he said sharply to Laura as she clamored for more of his juggling, and I bit my lip. I did like to tease Leonello, but I would not hurt him for the world.

He turned to put Gerolama's vases back in their niches, and when he turned back I saw his eyes were glass-cool and he was done with the subject. "Maestro Botticelli's painting of you," he said, all business. "You did promise him you would complete your sittings while you were here in Florence."

I made a face, grateful for the change in conversation. "I suppose if I string the sittings out, I'll earn another few weeks here. If I want them."

Laura was still looking hurt, and Leonello tweaked her nose in apology for snapping at her. "You've been putting it off, Madonna Giulia. Sitting for your painting."

"I don't want to do it," I said simply.

My bodyguard regarded me, head tilted. He hadn't spoken of the day I'd posed naked and cold in the papal apartments surrounded by leering men, and I hadn't either. I wondered if Leonello would say something cutting and careless about it—we called ourselves friends by now, but that had never stopped him in the past from carving me up with his viper's tongue if he was in the mood, and he was certainly in the mood now after the way I'd probed him. But his voice wasn't mocking at all when he spoke. "If it's any consolation," he said instead, "you carried it off rather splendidly."

But oh, going to Mass that first Sunday after my portrait-sitting had been agony! I was used to being stared at as I took Communion at the Basilica San Pietro—mostly it was the women who stared, craning their necks to see if my sleeves were cut in the French fashion or the Neapolitan, or if my collar was lace or marten fur. That particular Sunday it had been the men staring, trading the latest rumors in a hot whisper about how I'd stripped naked before the entire College of Cardinals and posed on my hands and knees as the Mary Magdalene, or with my legs spread and an apple in my hand as Eve. What a great many whispers had flown through Rome in just a few short days. I'd closed my eyes, cheeks burning as I opened my mouth for the Holy Wafer, and I heard one of the altar boys whisper to the other, "Do you think she goes on her knees and opens her mouth like that for the Holy Father?"

How was I supposed to carry *that* off splendidly?

Leonello was still looking at me, thoughtful. "Will you refuse to finish Maestro Botticelli's portrait then, Madonna Giulia?"

"Maybe." I turned Laura around, stroking a comb through her hair. She was already begging me for chamomile pastes to help it grow as long as mine. "Maybe not. Sitting for Maestro Botticelli, well, it won't be so bad with just him in the room. I don't mind that so much. But after the portrait's done it will be displayed everywhere, and I don't know if I want that."

"Perhaps His Holiness will keep it for his private apartments."

"He won't." Once, yes—Rodrigo would have been too possessive to let any other man see what I looked like under my gown, even if just in a painting. That Rodrigo would never have pressed me to strip naked before a roomful of cardinals either . . . I struggled to pinpoint the change, dividing Laura's hair to plait. "He'll enjoy watching them be envious. So he'll show the painting to everyone, and all Rome is going to know exactly what my breasts look like, not just a handful of cardinals and papal functionaries."

And then my brother Sandro really *would* put a fist into someone he shouldn't, possibly my Pope. The only way I'd been able to calm him after all the rumors that had flown about . . . well, I'd lied completely and told him it was all just vicious gossip. How was I supposed to maintain that little fiction if there was a portrait of me in all my nakedness, and everyone in Rome had seen it?

"You may console yourself with one thing," Leonello said at last.

"What?"

"All Rome has wondered for years what your breasts look like. If you have the painting done, the citywide suspense will at last be ended."

I laughed, feeling lighter somehow. "Will you stay in the room with me, if I go to Maestro Botticelli for another sitting?"

"I thought you wanted fewer men gazing on the breasts in question, not more."

I tied off Laura's blond plait, and sent her skipping out of the *sala* with a kiss to the top of her head. "You don't count."

"No, of course not." My bodyguard's voice had gone sharp and cutting again, and I winced because I hadn't meant to anger him. "Dwarves are not men, to be sure."

"Now, that's not what I meant." I could see him retreating behind his book as he so often did, and I put my hand out and tipped the book down so I could meet his eyes. "You were there in the papal apartments when they stripped me, Leonello, and you were the only one I didn't *mind* being there. Because every other man stood ogling me, but not you."

"I assure you, I ogled."

"No, you didn't. I know you." That didn't please him, I could see. Men like Leonello want to be inscrutable; mysteries unto themselves. It irritated him no end to think that I might have him figured out. But he didn't have that look of cynical anger anymore, so I hid my smile as I went on. "So, I'd like to have you at my second sitting too. Lounging there with your book, making caustic comments about Maestro Botticelli's use of proportion. Because I still don't really want to do this painting, after all, and it will go easier if I have a friend in attendance."

Leonello looked at me for a moment, and then he picked up my hand and kissed it rather carelessly before tossing it back into my lap like a discarded glove. And that was how I found myself braving the streets of Florence with a pair of guards at my back and my friend at my side, making for Maestro Botticelli's studio.

Leonello

Let my mistress tease the Florentines all she liked, telling them their great city was a little sister in Rome's shadow—I did not like Florence at all. I didn't like the furtive scurry of so many of its citizens as they hastened through the streets; I didn't like the fervent gleam in so many eyes as they spoke of Savonarola and his latest dictates; I didn't like the strange, heated excitement that perfumed the air like smoke: excitement laced with fear.

Maestro Botticelli's face as he stood before my mistress in the door to his humble apartments could have been a sketch standing for all Florence: fervent and furtive, exalted and afraid.

"I am most sorry, Madonna Giulia." He spoke brusquely in his rough Florentine accents, avoiding her eyes. "There will be no further sittings."

"Are you ill?" Her eyes traveled behind the painter to his apartments. Normally any artist would have done my mistress the honor of calling upon her, but Giulia put no one out of his way if she could help it and had insisted on coming herself to Maestro Botticelli's lodgings. A shabby little room or two in one of the seedier quarters of the city, stale-smelling and almost bare of furnishings. Maestro Botticelli's lush Venuses of old might have earned him renown, but his new prim Madonnas were clearly not supporting him in comfort. "I can return on your convenience," Giulia said. "Perhaps bring you a hot posset; this cold weather has been—"

"No." The painter had a glitter in his eye, and not the fire of inspiration I'd seen as his chalk flew in the papal apartments and Giulia-as-Persephone emerged on the page. "I have prayed upon it, Madonna Giulia, and I cannot ignore the dictates of conscience. Even for the Holy Father, I cannot sully my paints upon"—looking at her fur-lined robe, the hair she had packed into a net so it could be easily shaken down for her sitting—"lewd subjects," the painter finished.

"Now, really," Giulia said, exasperated. "Why am I suddenly the lewd one? I didn't want to be painted at all, much less with my clothes off, but now suddenly it's all my fault?"

"I do apologize," Maestro Botticelli mumbled. "I will write to the Holy Father in explanation—excuse me—" And he shut the door in our faces.

"Artists," Giulia huffed, and kicked her robe out in a swirl as she stamped away from the rickety overhanging apartments with their crooked rooflines and the gutters with a dirty crust of old snow. "It's a very fine line with them, isn't it? Either you're a great artistic inspiration, or you're a tempting menace!"

"Why the pique?" I didn't bother speeding my steps to keep up with her stamping; Madonna Giulia always slowed without being asked when she realized she was outpacing me. Two stolid guards tramped behind us, looking quite disconsolate that they weren't to see the Bride of Christ shed her clothes this afternoon after all. "You didn't want to finish the painting in the first place, after all."

"There is that," she conceded, and paused to let me catch up, smiling. Her fits of exasperation never lasted long. "Goodness, a free afternoon instead of sitting naked in a cold studio. Shall we go buy some of those tasty little roast pigeon things from the vendor by the old bridge? I always eat when I'm at loose ends. Or shall we catch a look at this pyre they're building in the Piazza della Signoria? I hear it's going to be twice as tall as a man!"

"It will have to be." All through the past fortnight, Savonarola's Angels had been swaggering up and down the streets of Florence, collecting "donations" for the great bonfire that was to come. Anyone who found themselves unwilling to part with their Murano glass goblets and their statues of a naked David might just find that the Angels had tipped the statue over on the way out the door, or broken the goblets with a misplaced elbow, so really it was better just to give and have done with it. Madonna Giulia's sister and her sticklike husband had contributed a few ugly vases, one truly hideous *credenza* in gilt-edged oak, and a pile of silk gowns and velvet doublets that were not only outlawed under the new sumptuary laws, but also thoroughly out of fashion. "Let the men agonize about luxury and sin," Giulia had said, winking at me as we peeked through the shutters to watch those gawky young Angels staggering away under the weight of Gerolama's unwanted junk. "The women will just see an opportunity to clean house!"

I tossed my mistress's copy of the Avernus sonnets into the pile for the bonfire when everyone's back was turned. But Giulia rescued it before the Angels arrived, giving me a look. "Damn," I sighed, and she replied demurely, "Good try, Leonello."

"I do wish I could hear Fra Savonarola preach," my mistress was saying now as we turned back across a narrow *piazza* in the direction of her sister's house. "He's supposed to be thrilling—my sister says you can really *feel* the fires of hell when he's on a good rant. Gerolama does enjoy that sort of thing. She must have been crushed when he started forbidding women to attend his sermons. Really, I don't see why we can't go. It's mostly us he's preaching about, after all. Why don't you go, Leonello, and have a listen for me the next time he gives a sermon?"

"I have no intention of being trampled by the fervent masses," I informed her, and I must have been shielding my face from a gust of freezing February wind because I didn't see the white-clad figures until the rough voice hailed us.

"Ho there! *Madonna*, you'd better have a good reason to be wandering these streets! A virtuous woman keeps to her household."

Giulia's guards braced, and I let my hands drift down toward the daggers at my belt as three swaggering young men in dirty-hemmed white robes approached us. Murkier tales of Savonarola's Angels were told besides their devotion to their master and their singing of hymns—whispers of women harassed, of drunks and gamblers or simply those marked as "sinners" found beaten in the streets. I crooked my wrist at the angle that would bring my finger knife slipping into my hand with another twitch, but Giulia merely bowed her head in deepest greeting as the Angels arrayed themselves before her. "Good sirs," she said, casting her lashes down piously. "I would not have strayed from the protection of my home at this time, but my sister took to her sickbed and required my care. I am only now hastening home."

Apparently Savonarola's Angels were no more immune to a woman's beauty than any common guardsman. Their eyes flicked over her, and she stood meekly with her head bowed. I wondered what they might have said if she'd admitted she was returning from a failed rendezvous with an artist who had reneged on his promise to paint her as a naked, pagan goddess. I suppose there would have been a fight. Maybe my mistress was wise in her pious lies, but I wished she'd told the truth because I could have used a fight. First I'd take on the one in the middle, the stocky leader with his thumbs hooked into his belt and the rash of blemishes on his chin.

He was eyeing Giulia now, and with an interest that I doubt would have pleased the good Dominican friar he served. "I think we have a lady here who has missed contributing her due to the bonfire," he told his fellow Angels, who both laughed. "That's a fur collar I see, *madonna*—"

"*Signora* Gerolama," Giulia said instantly, clever girl. "Wife to *Signore* Puccio Pucci, may God keep him always."

"Well, *Signora*, that's a fur collar I see, and stilt clogs under that hem. You think God does not see vanity, just because it's hidden under your skirts?"

"I wear them only to keep my shoes from the mud—"

"Our Lord walked in mud. You are too good to follow in His footsteps?"

Giulia let her lashes drop over her eyes again and stepped out of her tall stilt clogs. "A donation," she murmured, proffering them with a gesture and then detaching the fur collar from her robe. "I shall feed my womanly vanity into the flames."

"God be praised," intoned one of the other Angels, a stringy fellow not yet old enough to shave. He cast a look at me, and I thought it wise to surrender my worn deck of cards. I'd had that deck for more than five years, since the days I'd made my money playing *primiera* and fleecing sailors out of their wages . . . the other two guardsmen were quick to follow my lead, contributing between them a set of bone-carved dice and a little good-luck charm on a silver chain. I tensed as the stringy Angel sniffed at our contributions. If he tried to take my knives . . .

The stocky leader still looked dissatisfied with Giulia. My mistress had listened to her sister's warnings about the new austerity demanded of the women of Florence, and kept her silks and jewels for the privacy of the *sala*—venturing out today, she wore a gray wool dress under her fur-lined robe, and not even a ring for adornment. There was nothing the Angels could reproach—except the fact that even wrapped in gray wool, La Bella looked luscious and bewitching and tempting enough to inspire all kinds of sin.

"That hair," the Angel finally said. "That's false hair, that is. A hairpiece that might as well be woven of vanity!"

"Vanity and immodesty!" the stringy Angel thundered.

"It's not false hair," my mistress protested. "It all grows on my head, I assure you."

"You're lying, *madonna*. No woman has that much hair."

"Oh, Holy Virgin save me," Giulia said, and in an exasperated jerk she pulled off the net and shook her hair down around her. "Does that satisfy you?"

The Angels all insisted on giving it a good tug to make sure it was real, and I tensed at Giulia's side but her gaze flicked at me in warning.

"You should cut that hair and add it to the fire," the first Angel warned, pulling the long waves through his fingers just a bit more slowly than I thought strictly necessary. "A woman's hair is her vanity. She adorns herself with it, she takes pride in it, and soon enough she is plucking and dyeing like a whore."

"Or like that pack of Borgia sluts in Rome." The stringy Angel spat into the street. "The Pope's daughter, she suns her hair all day while drinking and dallying with lovers."

Giulia's chin jerked at that. "Madonna Lucrezia is the most pious of girls—"

"A slut," the first Angel insisted, and thrust something into my mistress's hands. "Read this if you want the truth of it. Lucrezia Borgia plays the whore for her own father *and* her brothers, and so does that harlot princess from Naples. They pleasure themselves on the altars of the holy Basilica itself, drunken and naked, and the Pope and his pack of corrupt cardinals like to watch—"

"They do *not*!" Giulia burst out, and I breathed shallowly through my nose as all three Angels fastened their eyes on her.

"Contradicting the holy followers of Fra Savonarola," the third Angel said in his squeaking voice, looking at the others. "This woman holds herself very high!"

"Too high." The stocky Angel stepped closer to Giulia. "I think we will cut that hair for the fire after all, *signora*. Kneel!"

"I will do no such thing," Giulia retorted, retreating back a sharp step before he could grab hold of her hair, and on my signal the other two guardsmen waded into Savonarola's Angels.

The sounds of grunts and blows filled the cold street. All three Angels had stout staves, and one of Giulia's guardsmen hissed a curse through his teeth as the scrawny Angel thumped him soundly across the shoulder. But my mistress's guards had short swords, and both flashed out of their scabbards. "Pommels only," I called, both knives drawn before my mistress as I kept out of the fray, because I wanted no bodies in the street today if I could help it. God only knew what punishment Florence's mad Dominican friar would levy on anyone who killed one of his holy thugs. "Pommels," I called again, "or flats of the blade!" Both guardsmen heard me, using their swords as cudgels rather than spilling blood with the cutting edges. One guard had got caught between two Angels, both of them buffeting him with their staves as they gave shrill whoops, and I stepped sideways to see if there was an angle where I could trip the scrawny one. But the stocky leader of the three saw my attention shift, and he darted around me to seize Giulia by the hair. "On your knees, whore" he whispered, and had his knife ready to saw through the gold mass doubled around his hand.

I darted back, my throat dry as a bone, ready to prickle him with steel, but my mistress—oh, my clever mistress. Rather than yank backward against the Angel's grip, she flung herself forward against him and plastered her mouth over his. He went stiff all over in surprise, hand loosening in her hair for just an instant. Quite long enough for me to bump his knee out from under him with a blow of my knife hilt. Giulia helped with a shove of her own to the burly chest, and he fell flat on his back in the muddy street.

"*Guards!*" I rapped out, and both guardsmen lunged back to array themselves before their mistress and me. One of the guards had a bloody nose and the other had a set of knuckles that would be the size of cabbages tomorrow, but they'd left both Angels groaning over smashed shins and bleeding heads.

"Good sir," I said, addressing the stocky Angel with all the bland politeness I could muster as he scraped himself off the stones with a very red face. "I do apologize for any pain we have caused your fellows. Be assured we will be on our way, and my mistress will keep to her household in future like a modest and decent woman."

"She *kissed* me!" the stocky Angel shouted, pointing at my mistress, who was speedily bundling her hair back into its net. "She kissed me, that foul harlot—"

"And this foul harlot has the French pox," Giulia said sweetly. "Enjoy the pustules!"

They started for her again, and I showed them the knives in my hands. "Come one step closer and I will spear your eyes in their sockets like grapes," I said. "I suggest you be on your way. Plenty of sinners in this city, after all, and we have already made our donations to Fra Savonarola's fire. Good day, and God keep you."

The stocky Angel scowled, looking more than ready to continue the quarrel, and part of me hoped he would. But the other two looked bruised and embarrassed, already edging back down the street, and their leader seemed to realize he stood alone now against Giulia, me, and both of our large, grinning, and truculent guards. "Be on your way, *madonna*," he warned her with a dark look, rubbing ostentatiously at his lips where she had glued hers. Somehow I doubted he was truly as sorry about that kiss as he pretended. Sorry, perhaps, that it had not been one whit sincere. "And meditate on your sins! Vanity, pride, and unbridled lust. We put women in the stocks for less in Florence!"

He strode to catch up with his fellows and they regained something of their swagger as they retreated from us, taking up three quarters of the street and forcing the few cloaked and hurrying passersby to squeeze out of their way. I didn't sheathe the knife in my hand until they were out of sight, and only then did I let out the breath I had been holding. "Madonna Giulia," I said, "we go home at once."

She nodded, and we set a swift pace back toward her sister's house.

"Clever trick, that kiss," I said. "Very quick of you."

"You were about to kill him," she said, and quoted my own words at me from just before I had vaulted into the bullring. "'If a man's about to die, he should get to kiss a beautiful woman first.'"

"Very true," I said, and we both fell silent. I kept one unobtrusive hand on my dagger as we hastened along, the sound of my boots muffled in the cold. Florence's streets were empty except for the occasional beggar or harried housewife or drinker too far gone in his cups to be careful. All Florence knew by now it was better to stay in, stay safe, stay behind locked doors where at least they couldn't be seized by Angels and accused of sinning.

The moment we were safe inside her sister's doors, Madonna Giulia sank down on the first wall bench without even bothering to shed her cloak. She was looking at something—whatever it was the Angels had thrust into her hands before the struggle began.

"What's that?" I asked as I took off my cloak, and she showed me wordlessly. A pamphlet: cheaply printed, smudgily illustrated. The familiar bulky figure of Pope Alexander VI showed on the first page, reproduced badly in his papal tiara. He had been printed with a leer on his face and the flames of hell licking around him.

"Do people really believe such things?" Giulia whispered, turning the pages with the very tips of her fingers. "It's—it's *filth*."

"People love to tell filthy rumors of the great, Madonna Giulia." I motioned the guardsmen inside—*Get yourselves a good drink, you've earned it*—and turned back to my mistress where she sat with her snow-damp skirts around her on the tiles of the entry. "Your cloak, if you please."

She surrendered it without argument, still looking down at the pamphlet. "This isn't just filthy rumors, Leonello, it's *foul*. And it's not just—here they say the Holy Father steals the estates of dead cardinals to fill his coffers—that he sells offices and benefices by the cartload—that he promotes his family and his 'rapacious Catalan minions'—really, *minions*? That any king in Europe who wishes to put away a devout queen to marry his mistress can buy a divorce from 'this bastard *marrano* pope . . .'" More pages turned. "That Juan is a murderer and a violator of virgins . . . that Cesare practices the dark arts and fornicates with his sister—how can people believe such things?"

"Because they are true," I said.

Giulia looked up at me from her bench. "What do you mean?"

"Oh, not all of it," I shrugged, hanging up her damp cloak. Servants were approaching with trays and cups of warmed wine, but I waved them back for the moment. "Your Pope is no *marrano*, and we both know Lucrezia does not pleasure her brothers or her father, and I doubt our good Cardinal Cesare practices dark magic. But for the rest of it, well, Juan Borgia has raped more than one virgin who had to be packed off to a convent, and Cesare is certainly capable of murder, and since our departed Pope Innocent VIII left us with empty coffers, his successor has filled them by means of selling benefices. And I believe a rather hefty sum changed hands when King Louis XII wished to divorce his queen and indicated he was willing to pay for the required dispensation."

"How do you know these things?" my mistress whispered.

"It's common knowledge, Madonna Giulia."

"But the rest of it." She shook her head a little. "What that stalk-necked boy said about drunken orgies and incest—"

"Half-truths." I spread my hands. "Cesare Borgia sleeps with his sister-in-law, after all—why not his sister too? The Pope dotes so much upon his daughter that he called her away from her husband to visit him—so surely she shares his bed as well as his table. As for naked women in the Vatican, stripped for the Pope's pleasure while he watches with his friends—well, it might not have been an orgy, but I think you can recall a recent event along those lines."

Giulia stared at me as though I had horns. "This is how people see him? All of them?"

I thought of Cesare, who knew where to find a murderer of innocent women and didn't care a fig about it except to find my silent burning frustration amusing. I thought of the Pope, who in the early days would not ever have exposed his pearl to the world's greedy eyes. I thought of Lucrezia with her rouged cheeks, and Sancha arching greedily against me. I shrugged again.

"But it's not *fair*!" Giulia burst out. "There have been other popes with bastard children—Pope Innocent had sixteen! And Rodrigo is hardly the first to sell a benefice or two, or hand out red hats and bishoprics among his family. So why does *he* incite them to all this hatred"—waving the pamphlet—"and not the others?"

I paused, leaning against the doorjamb and reflecting. A good question, that. "Perhaps because unlike the others, this pope hides nothing," I offered. "In the past, a pope passed his bastard daughters off as nieces rather than marrying them off openly in the Vatican in huge weddings. Popes promoted a few family members—not *all* of them. Popes at least pretended virtue—smuggled their mistresses in through discreet passageways, rather than installing them openly in luxurious seraglios."

This pope pretended nothing, hid nothing, was ashamed of nothing. I supposed that was the most unforgivable sin of all.

The chill February wind gave a moaning gust outside the door, and I saw Giulia shiver. "What will they say of Laura?" she said in a low voice. "Just because she is a Borgia and can be painted with the same brush?"

"She was christened an Orsini."

"She's a Borgia. Rodrigo might doubt it, but no one else in Rome does, and isn't that what matters? What people *want* to believe?" Giulia sounded bitter. "Will they say she's the bastard get of a fallen woman, a little harlot in the cradle?"

"Probably," I said.

Giulia shook her head and rose, the pamphlet still crumpled in her fist.

"Let's get upstairs to the *sala*," I said, and touched her arm. "You look cold."

"I am cold," she sighed. "Cold to the bone."

A whole entourage of papal guards in the Borgia colors awaited us in sour Gerolama's overheated little *sala*. A stolid captain stepped forward, offering Giulia a sealed missive stamped with the Pope's own seal. "We are to escort you back to Rome at once, Madonna Giulia," the captain intoned. "His Holiness will not have you caught in Fra Savonarola's unrest. News of this coming bonfire disturbs him."

Frankly, it disturbed me. I looked at my mistress, wondering if she would disobey him in her anger over being stripped before half the College of Cardinals. But she looked down at the Pope's seal, and her free hand drifted up to touch her head, which must have been aching after all the yanking the Angels had done on her hair. "I will pack," she said, and I let out a silent breath of relief. This was no city for the Bride of Christ, nor for anything beautiful. Fra Savonarola was a man of dust and pain; he wanted everything beautiful rendered to ash. The Borgias might have their sins, but I could not count their love of beauty as one of them.

I n the end, however, we did see the great burning that would be known as the Bonfire of the Vanities. The fires were lit at noon, accompanied by a citywide clamor of church bells, and smoke was roiling up toward the sky when Madonna Giulia's carriage with its envelope of papal guards rolled out into the streets of Florence. Even emptier streets—everyone in this city, it seemed, had flocked to watch the burning. Or else they stayed home and prayed.

"Stop the carriage," Madonna Giulia called to her captain as we approached the Piazza della Signoria.

"Madonna—"

"I said stop!"

The wheels creaked, and we gazed out. A throng of fervent figures choked the *piazza*; men cheering and roaring, women sobbing and casting their cosmetics pots or their mirrors into the blaze; children competing to see who could throw a toy farthest into the flames. A great eight-sided inferno, larger than a house, boiling black smoke in great billows that immediately made little Laura begin to cough. Giulia pulled her daughter away from the window, but I stayed, my stomach rolling sickly. I saw ranks of white-robed Angels singing hymns in their loud fervent voices; Dominicans weeping and lifting their hands up to the heavens as they railed at God. I saw a frail little nun assisting an Angel as he flung a painted panel of nude sea nymphs into the flames; I saw statues and mirrors, velvet hangings and illuminated books and playing cards waiting their turn to be burned. I saw a bent man in a patched robe with tears streaming down his face, praying as he flung armloads of drawings and canvases onto the pyre, and for a moment I thought it was Maestro Botticelli, but I blinked and he had disappeared.

The smoke billowed again, and I saw a black-robed friar with fleshy lips and a great hooked nose, elevated above the others. He flung his arms upward, outspread like a crucifix, howling at the heavens, and I was too far away to hear any of his words, but I heard the answering screams responding to the cries of the beast himself. Fra Savonarola flung one finger out toward his personal inferno, and I saw the figure that had been propped at the very top of Florence's illicit luxuries. The bulky, straw-stuffed figure of a man in rich jeweled robes.

"Is it His Holiness?" Giulia said, low-voiced.

The smoke coiled down again like a tremendous serpent, hiding everything from my eyes. "I don't know."

"Do they really hate him so much?"

"Of course they do, *madonna*. They are sheep, and they believe whatever they are told. Everyone hates powerful men."

"They wouldn't if they knew him," she said passionately. "If they saw how hard he works—how he denies himself sleep and wine and rich food—"

"Not much else," I murmured.

"How he'll receive any petitioner, no matter how low-born, because he says every man should have the right to address the Holy Father— how he wouldn't even *care* that they say these things of him, because he says Rome is a free city and anyone can say or write what they please!" Giulia took the crumpled ball of the pamphlet and flung it out the window, clutching Laura even tighter. "Does that sound like an Antichrist to you?"

"We're in Florence, not Rome," I said, and waved out the window at Savonarola's hell. "This is not a free city to be saying anything."

"Drive on," Giulia called to her captain, and the carriage jolted into motion again. Giulia stared into her own thoughts, stroking Laura's hair, and I watched the enormous cloud of smoke rising into the sky as we pulled away from it. The paintings that would be going up in the engulfing flames, the statues, the works of art, the books. *Dio*, the books.

Just as much trash as art, I told myself. Would the world really be so deprived, losing a few cosmetics pots and pairs of dice and bad paintings of naked goddesses?

But the books, I couldn't help thinking, and a twist of helpless anger curdled my stomach.

"I thought for a moment that I saw Maestro Botticelli in that crowd," Giulia said perhaps an hour outside Florence. "He was tossing his own paintings on the fire. I suppose one of them was the sketch of me."

"I suppose so," I answered.

"Good," said Giulia Farnese.

I wasn't stupid enough to say so, but I couldn't agree with her there. Because I'd seen that sketch take shape under Botticelli's hand, during that one awkward sitting in the papal apartments, and even half formed in chalk lines with the colors just hinted at, it had the look of something breathtaking. He'd caught her expression, a fearful wonder I'd seen as I described the things they said of her Pope, and her hair would have been a marvel of a thing on canvas, picked out in gold leaf and contrasting with the white of her body and the darkness he'd scribbled about her with the half-formed serpents and monsters of the underworld. A canvas that might have rivaled his *Birth of Venus*, and now the world would never see it.

Savonarola's great bonfire was only a smudge on the horizon behind us now, but the wind had caught the whirling cloud of ash and brought it down on the road like a strangely warm storm. Flakes of ash powdered Giulia's hair like deathly snow as we made our way back to Rome.

PART TWO

April 1497–June 1497

CHAPTER SIX

O bawdy Church . . .
You have become a wanton whore with your lust.
You are lower than the beasts, a monster of depravity.

—FRA SAVONAROLA

Carmelina

Carmelina." Madonna Giulia greeted me distractedly. "What do unicorns eat?"

"Um." I blinked. "Virgins?"

"That's dragons. Isn't it? I thought unicorns only got *captured* by virgins." Giulia rummaged in a box before her mirror, back to me. "And then there's the question of what lions eat, and serpents and peacocks and swans. Goodness," she sighed. "It's going to be a disaster."

"What is, *madonna?*" I ventured into her chamber, drying my hands on the apron I hadn't had an opportunity to take off before being whisked upstairs to see my mistress. For a panicked instant I thought I was going to be dismissed. A fortnight's agony of waiting and praying and dousing myself with vinegar had given me the relief of knowing I wasn't with child—but I could still lose my reputation and everything else with it. All Bartolomeo had to do was go beyond glaring at me stonily and let something slip, maybe show the marks my nails had left in his back and tell the scullions what a whore the *maestra di cucina* was . . .

But no: Madonna Giulia beckoned me in with her usual friendly wave, and her chamber bustled with a dozen robe makers throwing swatches of figured velvet and Spanish brocade over everything. Slippers and sleeves lay discarded on every surface, the goat gnawed on a curtain tassel, maids darted back and forth like schooling lake smelt—La Bella's usual cheerful disorder, except for the masks. Dozens and dozens of masks, feathered and jeweled, beaded and eyeless, that lay about the room on every surface staring at me.

"Sweet Santa Marta," I said as La Bella herself turned from her mirror to look at me. "What's it supposed to be?"

"A unicorn." Madonna Giulia doffed her white-and-gold beaded half mask with its tip-tilted eyes and spiraled gilt-and-ivory horn. "I've decided to be a unicorn for His Holiness's masquerade in a fortnight. It's a Menagerie Ball, so we're all to come as animals. So, what *does* one serve a unicorn at a Menagerie Ball?"

I vacillated dubiously between holy water and oats. You couldn't even get a decent *frittella* out of holy water and oats. Then I counted my days and blinked. "A fortnight? That's Easter."

"Just afterward." Madonna Giulia's voice was very dry. "The very instant Lent is done, in other words. The soonest His Holiness could host another celebration for the Duke of Gandia's triumph at Ostia."

I heard a few snorts about the room at that. Juan Borgia had come prancing back to Rome crowing of the victory he had won over the remainders of the French army, which had immured itself in Ostia, but the winds of gossip had it that his generals deserved the credit. Besides, what did a small victory count when all the ground gained over the rebellious branches of the Orsini family last fall had had to be given back already to keep the peace?

"In any case," Madonna Giulia concluded, tossing the unicorn mask aside and picking up a silver-white swan mask with an ivory beak and a cockade of white feathers, "we're to design a menu for the masquerade. I'm not sure what to serve a lot of wild beasts, or guests dressed as wild beasts. I suggest we don't serve it in a trough. The last thing we need to do is give Juan ideas." She wrinkled her nose. "I wonder if he'll come dressed as a jackass."

"He wouldn't need a costume." I moved a death's-head mask from a stool to sit down. Unlike the little Countess of Pesaro, Madonna Giulia did not keep her servants standing during long interviews. "We'll serve a *collatione*, lots of small dishes served on vine leaves, since beasts don't eat off plates. And tiny one-bite sort of nibbles, since beasts don't use spoons either." A great many cold thin-shaved slivers of fine meats; salted nuts and candied curls of citron; endives stuffed with cheese and drizzled with oil; olives and Spanish mustard and a great blood-rare roast of ox shoulder for all the masked predators . . . "And sugar subtleties," I decided. "Molded and dyed in the shape of beasts. I can make a spun-sugar unicorn with a gilded horn for you, Madonna Giulia."

"And a red sugar bull for His Holiness." La Bella's dimple flashed. "He's to come as the Borgia bull, of course." The dimple disappeared. "Oh, dear."

"*Madonna?*" I ventured.

She gestured at the roomful of masks. Three of her maids were giggling and trying on feathered harlequin half masks before her mirror, but their mistress looked somber. "It's not really a good idea, is it? Everyone at each other's throats as it is, and then put them all in masks and tell them to behave like beasts?"

I shrugged, uncomfortable. My mistress had been very sober-faced since her return from Florence, distracted and more inclined to curl up in her chamber playing with Laura rather than join the hilarious evenings of games and cards and song that Madonna Lucrezia and Sancha of Aragon planned every night. It was Lent, the time for somber reflection rather than raucous play, but that had certainly not slowed *them* down. Whenever Sancha of Aragon visited the Palazzo Santa Maria, she always had some whine for the steward about "Carp *again*?" If she even bothered to come to *cena* at all, with all her bed-hopping. It wasn't long before all the maids had picked up Madonna Giulia's name for her, and I had to remind them that they could *not* go about referring to the Princess of Squillace as "the Tart of Aragon," at least not where anyone could hear them.

Madonna Giulia was still looking at the mask in her lap, and I tried to coax a smile from her. "It's just a masquerade, Madonna Giulia.

Harmless fun, you know—and I come from Venice; I know about masquerades."

"Perhaps you're right." Giulia smiled at me, and a thoughtful gleam lit her eye. Seizing my wrist, she pulled me up from the stool and looked me over. "Well, I may not particularly want to act the hostess in a horned mask for this affair, but if I'm to do it, I shall have some fun. What beast will we dress *you* up as, Carmelina?"

"Me?" I nearly blurted out that the last time I'd worn a mask, it had been fleeing a convent during Carnivale while dressed as a man in order to escape charges of altar desecration. "Madonna Giulia, I'm just the one making sugar subtleties and preparing the banquet. Not a guest."

"Nonsense. Every one of my maids is going; we're sneaking you all in for a lark." She gave her enchanting grin. "In a mask and a costume, who's to know? There will be hundreds of guests; no one will ever find out."

"You'd have a costume and a mask made for me, when I'd never wear it but once?" I cast an incredulous eye about the swatches of fine-woven cloth, the fragile costly masks. "The expense—"

"Bother the expense," said my mistress blithely. Of course, she never had to think about the cost of anything. Ten extra costumes so all her maids could attend the masquerade? Why not!

Very few noble ladies like Giulia Farnese bothered befriending their maidservants as she did, but I'd long since gotten used to the informality in the Palazzo Santa Maria. The plain truth was that La Bella had no women to talk to *but* the maidservants. The other highborn wives of Rome were far too virtuous to come calling on the Pope's whore. They envied her looks, they copied everything she wore, they fawned on her at public functions if their husbands needed some favor from the Holy Father—but they were certainly too good to befriend her. So she befriended the *palazzo*'s maids instead, gossiping and giggling with them, lending them her perfumes and hair potions, drying their tears over failed love affairs or helping arrange marriages for them. I couldn't count the number of times Madonna Giulia had come tripping into my kitchens for a plate of *biscotti* or a little cooking instruction (at least until I banned her from cooking instruction, because the woman could set cold water on fire just by walking past the pot).

No, Giulia Farnese was a far cry from most noble mistresses who might confide in their maids but certainly wanted to hear no confessions in return—but I'd gotten used to her hilarity and her mad schemes, and now it seemed her latest mad scheme was to sneak all her maidservants into the Menagerie Ball. Robe makers descended on me with knotted measuring cords even as I protested, marking the length of my arms and the circumference of my wrists, while Giulia stood back with a critical eye. "The question is," she continued, "what animal will suit you best? Pantisilea over there is going to make a splendid cat—"

"A cat in heat?" I couldn't help saying, but Pantisilea just made a face at me as she folded a pair of our mistress's sleeves. I'd never known a greater slut than Pantisilea, except maybe Sancha of Aragon. But everyone hated the Tart of Aragon with a passion, the spiteful bitch, and skinny cheerful Pantisilea was everybody's favorite.

"We've got a gray beaded mask for her with whiskers and pointed ears," Giulia continued, unruffled. "Pia, now, she's going be a dear little blackbird; I've got a mask for her with a jet-beaded beak and a glorious crest of shiny black feathers . . ."

Over by the mirror, Pia bobbed a curtsy at her mistress and traded a shy little smile of her own.

"So," Giulia concluded. "What shall we dress you as?"

I imagined my father's roar of outrage. "Servants don't mix with their masters."

"Don't be ridiculous, servants and masters mix constantly. How many maids in this house have Cesare and Juan slept with?"

"Me, for one," Pantisilea volunteered. "You wouldn't have time to wring out a shirt in the time it took the Duke of Gandia to finish, but Cardinal Borgia—well, let's say he likes some *very* odd things!"

I coughed, remembering. Let's just say Cesare Borgia happened on me once when he was bored, as well. He'd spread me out on a table, pinned my arms out and taken his time, and I'd been willing enough because he was beautiful, as beautiful as his brother Juan and far less of a lout. But I wouldn't say I thought about it much when it was over, or yearned for it to happen again. Lying with Cesare Borgia had been a bit like watching an eclipse of the sun: strange and frightening and dark, if also rather exciting, and once is enough.

"Ugh, don't tell me." Giulia dismissed Cesare and whatever odd tastes he might have, looking at me. "Carmelina, don't argue; you must come to the masquerade. How many banquets have you served in your life? Wouldn't you like to *eat* the food for once, instead of just cooking it?"

I felt a smile tug at my lips despite myself. I could slip away easily once the dishes were prepared—any cook worth her mettle had her kitchens well trained enough to run smoothly without her. "Why not?" I heard myself saying, and Giulia applauded. I gave a little curtsy of thanks. Why not, indeed? A chance to get away from the tense atmosphere that was my kitchens these days; Bartolomeo's expressionless stares and icy silences were infecting the scullions and the undercooks, who seemed to know something was wrong even if they weren't sure what. I tried to address him briskly, nudge him back into his old enthusiasm for what he was cooking—really, a cook was worth nothing if he couldn't keep his own feelings out of the kitchens! But I couldn't quite seem to meet his gaze when I gave him orders now; I had to fix on the wall over his shoulder and ignore the sick swoop in my stomach whenever I thought how easily he could ruin me.

And maybe some of that sick swoop was shame, for the way I'd kissed him and cried out under him and then stamped all over him. *I'm sorry*, I wanted to say. Of course, it wasn't really my fault that he had a whole *palazzo* of pretty maidservants to choose from and he'd decided to fix on the runaway nun, but still . . . *I'm sorry.*

Maybe I *deserved* to be ruined.

In any case, a chance to get out of my kitchens sounded like a far more appealing prospect than it usually did.

"Just don't dress me up as a heron," I warned Madonna Giulia. "My sister called me Heron all through childhood because I was so tall."

"No, no, not a heron." My mistress gave another up-and-down analysis of my lanky frame. "Something very exotic, I think. No common sparrows or kitchen cats for you. What do you say, girls?" she called to her maids. "What animal is tall, exotic, and *very* long-legged?"

"A stag . . ."

"A mare . . ."

"A gazelle . . ."

"What's a gazelle?"

That costume. Looking back, I think you could fairly say it was all the fault of that thrice-damned costume.

Giulia

I really don't know why women bother so much with their gowns. We fuss so much over the cut of a headdress, the width of a neckline, the exact degree to which a shift can be pulled through the slits of a sleeve. I suppose we do it for ourselves, for the satisfaction we get looking in the glass and knowing we can sally out into the world looking our best. Or we do it for other women, hoping that there won't be a single married matron or virgin girl at Mass paying attention to the sermon because they'll all be taking down every detail of your new sleeves with French puffs. We certainly shouldn't bother dressing for men. Because if a man approves of how you look in that new gown, the only thing he wants to do is get it off you.

"Rodrigo—" I could feel his mouth making its way down my neck, and I bumped him in reproof with the gilded unicorn horn of my mask. "We'll be late!"

"Men are always willing to wait for beauty, and they are taught from the cradle to wait for God." The white brocade gown with its sleeves and ribbons of rosy gauze slid from my shoulders under his hands. "You are Beauty and I am God, so they can damned well wait all night."

"Blasphemer," I accused, but smiled. My papal bull smiled back at me, a bull in truth tonight with a mulberry red doublet molding his heavy shoulders instead of his papal robes, a red bull mask with curving gilt horns crowning his head. He should have been worn to the bone after the panoply of ceremony and splendor that had consumed his days during Holy Week. There is nothing on earth more exhausting than Easter. I was so tired by the end of a week's array of relics and parades and sermons that I dozed off in the Sistine Chapel during Tenebrae, right at the place in the Mass where my soul was supposed to be harrowed.

But my Pope had sailed through it all: Parading some truly disgusting relics through the city (the severed heads of various apostles! Really, no one would ever want to be an apostle if they knew how their poor bodies would be hacked apart after death!). Washing the feet of twelve beggars all overcome at the honor they were receiving. Bestowing charity dowries on eighteen girls who should have been overcome at the honor they were receiving but were instead giggling at Rodrigo's roguish winks. Nothing had assailed my Pope's poise that week, not running out of palm branches on Palm Sunday, not Burchard's horror when Rodrigo was too busy blowing a kiss at me to come in properly with the Alleluia on Holy Saturday, not even the tense moment when one of the Spanish generals refused to take a palm from the Pope's hand because he was still furious that Juan Borgia had received all the credit for the recent battles. No, my Pope had sailed through it all, and from the gleam in his eye I could see he was now ready to celebrate. His hands on my bare shoulders were warmer than firelight.

I stood on tiptoe, reaching behind his head for the mask's ties, but he caught my wrists. "Leave the masks," he whispered, and the bull and the unicorn slid entwined to the floor of my chamber. The familiar heat burned between us, our bodies moving with long ease, our mouths drinking and clashing below the masks. That at least had not changed.

We even managed not to get our horns tangled up. How I hate it when that happens!

Rodrigo gave a bull's growl as he helped me dress afterward, lacing up my gown. "You women! How do you manage all these fiddly little ties?" I straightened his horns for him, then sat before my glass to refasten the diamond roses that had come loose from my piled hair.

"I thought you might care to wear this." He sounded faintly anxious, and I felt something cold drop between my breasts. Looking down, I saw a brooch in the shape of a massive diamond rose, matching the ones in my hair. "Pretty, eh? I knew it would suit you."

I met his eyes in the glass, through the eye holes of my mask. Quite a confection, that mask; all white velvet and gold embroidery and tiny winking beads of rose quartz, and perhaps hiding my face made me blunt. "It's beautiful, truly—but I don't need jewels, Your Holiness."

"But I want to give them to you." His lips touched the back of my neck as he pinned the diamond rose at my bosom. "Weigh my unicorn down with diamonds and perhaps she won't go dashing away again."

There was anxiety under his amusement. My Pope had been just a little tentative with me, ever since the debacle of my painting as Persephone. My long, angry silence from Florence, and then his relief at having me back—I think he was half convinced Fra Savonarola would toss *me* on the bonfire. Really, one brush of danger with a French army or a few religious fanatics, and a fond lover sees disaster lurking around every corner! Rodrigo had excommunicated Savonarola, as much for the way his Angels had treated me as for his semiheretical rantings, and showered me with presents ever since my return.

But my anger with him hadn't truly abated until I pointed a finger at my lover some few days after my return from Florence and said quietly, "You will never put me on display like that again."

"I was proud of you! So proud, I wanted them all to see—"

"I don't care what your reasons are." I'd cut him off as I never dared do before. "I am *your* mistress, Rodrigo. No one else's. And in the future, you would do well to remember that!"

A glint of anger had showed in his eye for a moment, but I held his gaze unblinking and then I saw the anger fade, replaced by a faint chagrin. "Never again," he agreed reluctantly, and there was no more talk of having me sit for another painter without my clothes on. "Maestro Botticelli's painting?" he ventured, and when I gave a cold "It's burned up, and a good thing, too," nothing more was said about that either.

My anger had faded since then (well, mostly), but Rodrigo still seemed anxious with me sometimes.

"A whole chain of diamond roses couldn't keep this unicorn from escaping," I said lightly after I thanked him, rising from my mirror.

"Don't you know the stories, Your Holiness? Only a fair young virgin may bind a unicorn. Usually with a golden bridle."

I called for my maids, and Rodrigo broke into a laugh as Laura ran into my chamber. She wore her best gown, pink velvet sewn with seed pearls, and she waved a length of gold ribbon. "A fair maiden to bind me," I explained as Laura clamored to tie the ribbon about my wrist for a leash. It was the best way I could find to leash *her*, really. "She so begged to see the spectacle, I promised her she could come. For a short time only," I added to Laura. "Then it's to bed with you. Masquerades go on far too late for little girls." Not to mention the fact that people in masks seem to get up to all kinds of behavior they'd never dream of indulging in bare-faced. The kind of behavior no little girl should see.

"Yes, Mamma." She added a deeper curtsy for Rodrigo. "Your Holiness," she piped, "you match Mamma. You have *horns*!"

"Indeed," he said, looking fond through the eye slits of his mask. "And I do believe you have my nose, little one."

"Are you the Devil?" Laura said interestedly, still looking at the horns.

I laid my hand on Rodrigo's arm as he roared with laughter. "Shall we?"

The guests made a great roar as the Bull and the Unicorn descended the steps into the throng. The spring nights had grown warm and so the Menagerie Ball had been cast outside, in the Palazzo Santa Maria's largest garden. An Eden for the night: all green moss and starry flowers underfoot, tiny twinkling candles scattered below to echo the scatter of stars above. Small tables and sideboards brought outside and draped with mosses and garlands; food laid out on broad vine leaves rather than silver trays; wine circulated not by servants but flowing freely from the fountain where anyone might dip a cup—or simply lap it up on hands and knees, as I saw one young fellow in a hawk mask doing. Eden, but an Eden peopled with beasts rather than Adam and his Eve. I saw bird masks with huge cockades of feathers; panthers and cheetahs with fanged masks; fantastical masks in the shapes of griffons and manticores and dragons. I saw Sancha in red satin trimmed with fox fur, avid-eyed behind a vixen mask with pointed ears and laughing muzzle. Juan as a tiger, all orange and black stripes across his tight doublet with ivory fangs framing his own mouth, whispering in Sancha's vixen ear.

"Too many of Juan's soldiers here tonight," I whispered to Rodrigo as he led me down into the throng of beasts.

"How can you tell?" The Holy Father lifted his goblet in greeting to someone in a maned horse's mask across the garden.

"Juan's men are the ones who are drunk already." Juan had brought far too many soldiers back from his supposed victory at Ostia. They'd swarmed all over Rome, drinking and whoring and smashing windows—"celebrating their victory," people said at first, but then it had been "celebrating Carnivale." And then it had been "celebrating Lent," even though you weren't supposed to celebrate Lent with anything more showy than a fish bake, and now Lent was done and people were inclined to mutter and hasten across the *piazza* if they saw any of Juan's men approaching. Or anyone in the Borgia colors either, for that matter, but Rodrigo only laughed. As he was laughing now, behind his bull mask.

"Bah," my bull said. "High spirits!" And I could have mouthed the words right along with him, so often did he trot them out in Juan's defense. "They'll liven up the masquerade, mark my words. Ah, is that Cardinal Zeno behind that cockerel mask? Excellent costume for him; I really must have a word about those letters to the Florentines he thinks I don't know about . . ."

I watched his bull horns forge their confident path through the crowd until the ribbon leash on my wrist tugged. Laura was gazing wide-eyed at the Eden below her, bouncing up and down in her pink velvet. "So *pretty*," she breathed, and then gaped as a glittering peacock went to its knees before her in a pool of mottled blue-and-purple velvet skirts.

"May I steal her, Giulia?" a voice laughed, and behind the jeweled mask with its extravagant cockade of peacock feathers I saw Lucrezia's lined and painted eyes. "I think our Laura can get an even better view by the fountain! And if she's only to stay a short time, she should see everything. Shouldn't you, *Lauretta mia*?"

Laura ducked her head shyly. She always went wide-eyed at the sight of Lucrezia—the young Countess of Pesaro, too glamorous for words as she blew in and out of the *palazzo* in her whirl of silks and laughter and ladies-in-waiting. *Lucrezia used to look at me that way*, I thought, and wondered what had gone wrong there. It wasn't just Lucrezia's new sophistication or her flirtations—she had an edge now in her sweet voice when she spoke to me these days.

"You think it's easy for a girl growing up next to you?" Adriana da Mila had said bluntly when I asked her as much.

"But I adore Lucrezia," I'd protested. "And we've always gotten on so well—"

"Yes, but she's never been able to compete with you. At least until now. And now—" My mother-in-law had shrugged. "You're the nearest thing to a sister she's ever had. And sisters always compete with each other."

Lucrezia's eyes behind her peacock mask seemed to have more of their old bubbling warmth, and certainly Laura's eyes were all stars as she took Lucrezia's hand. "Don't take her too far," I said, untying the ribbon that had kept Laura tethered to my wrist. "And keep hold of this; she can disappear in an instant!"

They fluttered off, the peacock and the little girl, and I wondered if it was lack of babies making my Pope's daughter so hard about the edges. Three years of marriage and she'd never even quickened—and at least in the early days, there had been no lack of trying. My eyes found Lord Sforza, trying to drink wine through the snarling muzzle of his dog's-head mask and watching Lucrezia whirl Laura about the garden pointing out her favorite costumes. *Those two need babies*, I decided. *Babies, and lots of them.*

A fresh array of vine-wrapped dishes streamed out for the table, along with another swirl of guests. A new swarm of beasts: a fish mask, all glittering silver scales, babbling compliments at me—"Behind cover of our masks, my fair unicorn, I may admit how much I have always admired you? Perhaps you'd consider meeting me inside the *palazzo* later, if the Bull over there seems occupied . . ." Poor young Joffre, wearing a maned stallion mask and swaggering about with a stuffed codpiece, but snickers followed him: "The little gelding!" as eyes tracked his vixen wife who was letting a tight-hosed, heron-masked soldier go fishing for cherries in her bodice with his long bill. I waved at my little maid Pia in her blackbird feathers, keeping to the side and sipping timidly at a cup of the exquisite wine. Juan's soldiers were lunging for the new influx of food, gobbling down the artful servings of Carmelina's oil-drizzled olives, her blood-rare curls of beef skewered on rosemary spears, the chilled milk-snow heaped in seashells for bowls. I smiled behind my mask, wondering if my cook had made her entrance yet, and reached back for my little bodyguard who stood in my shadow in his customary black velvet. "By the way," I murmured to Leonello. "You should keep watch for Carmelina tonight."

"Our *Signorina Cuoca*?" His voice was cool as ever behind the gold lion's mask with its cockade of scarlet feathers—the *only* concession he would make to a costume. I'd lost the battle over the tawny leonine doublet that was supposed to go with it. "Our prickly cook is to join us? Dressed as what?"

"You'll know her when you see her. She looks ravishing."

"Still trying to make a pair of us, Madonna Giulia?" Through the mask, Leonello's eyes roamed the crowd.

"No one else I know has a tongue sharp enough to match yours, Leonello." I'd long been convinced they were made for each other—you had only to see the way they prickled in each other's company. Nobody prickled like that unless they were intensely aware of someone else, did they? "Wait till you see her," I went on. "I must say, I outdid myself when it came to Carmelina's costume."

"Point her out, by all means. Until then, I'm watching a tiger pick a fight with a serpent. Personally, I back the serpent."

I followed Leonello's stubby finger over the masked and laughing beasts. In the shadow of the loggia under the vines I saw the striped outline of Juan Borgia's tiger-patterned doublet, inches away from a lean figure in scale-embroidered green and gold. The matching serpent mask had jet fangs coming down over the taut, unsmiling mouth, but I knew who it was. "Excuse me—" But of course Leonello tracked silently behind me as I made my way through the throng.

"—you will not speak to me that way," I heard Juan hissing inside the shadows of the loggia. "I will not tolerate such words, and certainly not from my brother in priest's skirts!"

The voice behind the serpent mask came calmly. "You've made our family name a laughingstock, Juan. Bracciano? They sent a donkey to treat with you, and their counteroffer rammed under its tail."

"I made them pay!"

"How? Bracciano still stands. Those branches of the Orsini family who sided with the French should have been made to pay in blood, and they still have everything. Including those piddling castles you originally took from them last fall."

"I took Ostia! The last French garrison on our soil—"

"Gonsalvo de Cordoba took Ostia. You took his credit."

"The Holy Father does not seem to agree!"

"The Holy Father believes your lies, but not the rest of Rome. They know what you are, and so do I."

"If you think you'll take the title of Gonfalonier from me—"

"Cesare!" I stepped into the shadows of the loggia, smiling warmly at the fanged serpent. "There you are. Your father wishes a word. Juan, you will forgive me if I steal your brother a moment?"

"Steal him to Hades," Juan snarled, and I latched a firm hand into Cesare's elbow and eased him away.

"Is my father truly looking for me?" Juan's voice might have been rising in their quarrel, but Cesare's sounded calm as ever.

"No." We skirted the fountain, still splashing wine in ruby streams. "I thought it wise to separate you, since the purpose of this menagerie is entertainment and not bloodshed."

"Then we should not have worn masks. Bloodshed happens much more easily when one is masked." A nod behind me. "Your little lion understands something about that."

I felt Leonello at my back, taut and watchful. Cesare's eyes on him were half taunting, half amused. I pushed up my unicorn mask, capturing Cesare's gaze again.

"Let us speak without masks, then," I said. "Why do you needle Juan, Cesare? It angers your father, and gains you no favors from him."

"Why do tigers scratch?" He pushed up his own mask. "Why do snakes bite?"

"They bite when they are threatened."

"They bite because it is their nature."

I looked at my lover's eldest son. Twenty-one years old, a year and a half younger than me, and handsome enough now to make the breath catch with his auburn hair and inscrutable eyes and rapier-lean body. But for all I'd seen women flutter and grow silly in his presence, making fools of themselves for his favor like Sancha, I'd never felt tempted by the son over the father. Maybe it was because Rodrigo loved me, loved his children, loved life—but I wasn't sure Cesare loved anything, certainly not a woman. I'd never seen him regard any woman as anything more than something warm into which he could periodically spill his tensions. And any woman at all would serve for that.

"You're cleverer than people think, Giulia Farnese," he said calmly, noting my gaze. "And you're very good at keeping my father occupied. I like him occupied."

"I like him happy," I retorted. "He'd be happier if you mended your fences with Juan."

"Stick to keeping my father happy," Cesare said. "Not acting the peacekeeper. You aren't a Borgia, Giulia. Don't try to understand us."

"I gave birth to a Borgia. Isn't that enough?"

"Only the children of my mother are true Borgias. If my father were a prince of the realm and not of God, she would be his wife and you would still be the concubine."

I wanted to spear him on my mask's horn, but I wouldn't give him the satisfaction. It was Cesare's way, needling people just to see their reaction—he was like Leonello in that, and the best way to foil either of them was to wear a different kind of mask, one of utter indifference. I gave a faint smile, tilting my head and looking over the green-and-gold velvet that fit the lithe boneless grace of Cesare Borgia's body like a coat of scales. "A serpent," I said. "How apt."

He plucked an apple from a silver bowl nearby and offered it to me. "A bite, my fair lady Eve?"

"No, I've already fallen far enough from grace." I gestured at the mossy green paradise around me. "I don't need to be expelled from Eden too."

"Besides, what need do you have of apples?" Cesare lobbed the apple into the wine fountain with a splash. "My father already seduced you with a pomegranate. Or was it a pearl?"

He tugged his fanged mask back down over his face and slid off through the crowd.

Leonello

I don't like masks; no bodyguard does. The falsity, the restriction in vision, the notion that anyone at all could approach our charges behind a harlequin's false smile. And what was the use of a mask for a dwarf? The thrill of a masquerade is that identity is disguised. My identity shouted itself loud and clear whether my face was visible or not.

Besides, the world looks very different through a mask. The eye holes limit the sight; you can see straight ahead, but everything to the side is shadows, and half the shadows at this party were beaked or toothed, menacing until you looked at them straight and then that threatening shape turned into Cardinal Zeno, stiff and embarrassed behind a coxcomb's half mask. But just behind Zeno would be something else not quite seen. Maybe just the Count of Pesaro, perspiring crossly behind a dog's head. Or maybe something that would bite you.

Or in the case of Cesare Borgia behind his serpent fangs, something that would bite you with his mask or without.

I lowered the snarling gold lion's mask Madonna Giulia had ordered for me despite my protests. A lion's mask for a little lion, so what did the serpent mask make Cesare?

Tell me. Months now my eyes had been begging him. *Tell me the killer; tell me, tell me.*

No. His eyes stayed amused, and he no longer sought me out for games of chess. Why should he? He had a far more amusing game to play with me now, and it required no effort from him at all except silence. Only a small game, of course—the young Cardinal Borgia had bigger games to play by far, weaving alliances for his father in the chambers of the Vatican, weaving other alliances in private with Spanish generals and Neapolitan ambassadors against his brother. But this little game of keeping me dancing in my suspense had its mild amusements. As long as it did, I supposed, he would refuse to tell me a thing.

I'd resumed questioning his guards, but not one of them would talk with me. I'd tried his servants, but they were silent, too. I'd even tried buying a drink for Michelotto, the granite-eyed *condottiere* who kept to Cardinal Borgia's side like a shadow, but Michelotto was all but mute. Unless Cesare Borgia decided to begin the game again, my trail was dead.

And so was one more girl—a tavern maid in the Borgo, three weeks ago.

In one hand, I held a goblet of green glass; it turned the wine inside black. I swirled it but did not drink.

Shrill laughter. Ladies lolling on silk cushions in the grass, the men curling up on their skirts, laying masked heads in velvet laps. More wine splashing. Giulia in her white brocade with its touches of rosy gauze, like a unicorn viewed in the pink light of dawn, dancing with her favorite brother Sandro Farnese. The cheerful young cardinal had discarded his red hat for a bright-feathered mask as a parrot, and had been annoying his superiors all night, parroting anything they said with great glee behind his beaked mask. Behind their graceful figures I glimpsed the massive red bull that was our Pope, holding easy court in his seraglio-turned-Eden among a circle of lesser beasts who were his uneasy cardinals. "We have issued warning to the Florentines. They will give Us Savonarola on a platter, or face Our displeasure—" Scheming and dealing even in a menagerie.

I took a swallow of wine, swinging my lion mask. I'd not have picked a lion—too grand for me. Of course everyone picked the beast they most wanted to be. Mostly savage swaggering beasts for the men: tigers, dragons, bulls. Poor little Joffre with his stuffed codpiece, pining to be a stallion—I remembered him as a boy of ten, pop-eyed and blinking, giving me a nervous smile when I offered to teach him how to throw knives. Now I saw him backhand a page boy who didn't fetch his wine quickly enough, trying for the effortless arrogance of his big brothers but achieving only petulance. Someone should have told him arrogance doesn't come from a mask.

The women in this mossy Eden, they aimed for loveliness as the men aimed for savagery, swans and butterflies and other beasts of beauty dominating among the masks. Bolder ladies like Sancha of Aragon were foxes or cats, though one tall beauty with a touch more originality had come as something foreign and exotic that I couldn't quite identify: a long-nosed, long-lashed mask and skin-tight dappled hose like a man's, the better to show off endless slender legs that were anything but masculine. The Duke of Gandia was already eyeing her through the slitted eye holes of his ferocious fanged tiger's mask. But this tiger had the glassy-eyed sway of a common gutter drunk.

Lucrezia lolled in the grass beside the fountain, giggling behind her peacock feathers as she watched little Laura take a sip of wine from her cup and sneeze at the taste. "Isn't she darling? Try again, Laura, you'll get to like the taste! And another, that's it, swallow it down, it makes you feel dizzy and *marvelous*—" I moved toward Laura, who was holding the cup in both little hands and taking another game swallow as Lucrezia and Sancha laughed above her, but Giulia swooped in with a swirl of white-and-rose skirts, knocking the cup of wine aside. "*Lucrezia!*"

"My dress," Lucrezia complained as the wine went flying over her peacock-patterned hem.

"I told you to watch out for her!" Giulia dabbed wine off Laura's chin, glaring. "How *dare* you!"

Lucrezia heaved a put-upon sigh: so soft and slender in her jewel-colored feathers and velvets, but the eyes behind the mask were cool.

My mistress looked as though she were about to say something else, but her lips sealed in a hard line and she moved a hiccuping Laura to her other shoulder. "Time for bed, *Lauretta mia*." She stayed me with a gesture, making for the stairs. Lucrezia shrugged, looking at Sancha, who whispered in her ear as they filled their wine cups again and Giulia vanished upstairs. Her pet goat trotted after her with a *baaaa*, turned into a unicorn himself for the night with a pearly horn tied on to match his mistress.

A certain supple green-and-gold serpent caught my eye again as he offered some woman an apple. *Tell me,* I sent my thoughts howling after him, *tell me, oh, tell me, you bastard!*—but he shifted to one side and I saw that the girl before him was the long-legged beauty in the dappled hose. Something about her brought me up short. The way she looked away from the masked serpent to critically rearrange the candied nuts on a tray . . . I raised the lion's mask to my face again and made my way through the crowd to her side.

"You are familiar," Cesare Borgia was saying, his interest seeming to me more curious than lustful. "Have I made your acquaintance?"

"One could say that," said Carmelina Mangano, muffled through her mask.

"Surely not. I would remember you."

"I wasn't memorable, Your Eminence." Her tone was discouraging, and Cesare Borgia gave a languid shrug and glided off without further ado. I saw her give a little sigh of relief as he disappeared, and stiffen all over again as I spoke.

"Signorina Cuoca."

Carmelina's head jerked as she looked down at me. "Is it so obvious?" she said, exasperated.

"Not at all. Unlike Cardinal Borgia, I recognize the way you can't help assessing all the food." I lowered my mask for a long stunned glance over the *palazzo*'s cook. "What are you supposed to *be*?"

"Something Madonna Giulia called a *giraffe*." Plucking at her own mask, which had golden and white dapples over a long nose, a pair of stubby horns, and an outrageous fringe of lashes with which her own darkened lashes mingled. "I have no idea what a *giraffe* is—some kind of rare exotic desert creature, she said. One of the Milanese lords managed to import one for his private menagerie, and Madonna Giulia saw an engraving. She said it had long legs and a long neck, so it would be perfect for me. Personally, I think she might have just made it up to get me into this costume."

"Then it was a lie worth telling." In her usual woolen work dresses

and enveloping egg-stained aprons, our scowling Venetian cook generally looked lanky, flat-bosomed, overtall, and cross. But in a man's doublet cut to expose an unexpectedly supple throat, with skintight hose
hugging every taut inch of legs almost as long as I was . . . *Dio.*

"I think you had better leave," I couldn't help saying. "You are going
to attract entirely too much attention to remain anonymous."

"I wasn't going to stay," she admitted. "It was Madonna Giulia's
idea—she sneaked all her maids in, too. That's Taddea over there in the
swan mask trying to eavesdrop on the Pope, and Pantisilea is the gray
cat flirting with Angelo Colonna." Carmelina peered about. "I thought
all this would be more entertaining. Is this really what they do, all the
people I cook for? Loll about drinking wine and giggling and ignoring
the viol players?"

"Mostly," I said.

"I think I'd rather be cooking." Carmelina glanced down at me
through her mask's outrageous eyelashes. "Are you going to tell anyone
I'm here?"

"Why should I?" I crossed my arms across my chest, leaning against
a pillar of the loggia.

"Because you've threatened to tell a lot of things about me."

"So I have."

"Why haven't you *told* any of them?"

"Well," I pointed out, "you did threaten to poison me if I tried."

"Is that really why you haven't told?"

I swirled the wine in my cup, pondering an answer. But a slurred
voice slid itself between us before I could find the words.

"Well, well, what can this lovely lady be?" The Duke of Gandia
pushed his tiger mask atop his head, the ivory fangs framing his eyes
crookedly as he grinned up at Carmelina, who at once looked wary
through her eye holes. He still bore a livid mark by one eye where he
had been wounded at Soriano—not much of a wound, but he had picked
at the healing scab and dabbed it with lime, to ensure it would leave a
scar. *He thinks it makes him look like a warrior,* Giulia had snorted to
me privately. *I ask you!*

"Perhaps you're a doe," the Duke continued, pushing a cup of wine unasked into Carmelina's hand. "Is it a doe, with those eyes? Or a gazelle?"

"A giraffe," Carmelina said uneasily.

"What's that?"

"I don't know, your lordship." She looked for somewhere to put the unwanted cup, and Juan Borgia took hold of her shoulder.

"So, giraffe lady. Who are you? I thought I knew all the lovelies here tonight, but I've never seen you. One of the Princess of Squillace's new flock?"

"No, I—Madonna Giulia invited me. Um." Carmelina did a fair imitation of Madonna Giulia's more educated accents, and Juan was too drunk to notice the occasional Venetian clip when her mimicry faltered. "Giovanna, ah, Serrano."

Juan lowered his voice. "I don't like women who are taller than me," he confided.

Carmelina looked relieved.

"But for *you*," he slurred, "I'll make an exception. If you'll promise to fold those legs around my neck when I—"

"If you please, your lordship." Carmelina yanked her shoulder out of his grip. "I'm not staying."

"You are if I say you're staying." He wrapped a hand around her wrist and gave another hard-edged grin. "You see the bull down there? You know who he is, don't you? Then you should know who I am, my long-legged lovely."

"Your lordship—"

"Why don't we slip away, you and I? You want to find out how much cock a tiger has—" He yanked her hand forward, clapping it on his codpiece. Carmelina jerked against his grip, but his fingers tightened. "Back behind the loggia with you. I want to see if that bum looks just as ripe peeled out of that hose—"

"I do believe it's the hero of the hour," I broke in loudly. "Our Gonfalonier, the hero of Ostia. Or Bracciano. Hero of somewhere, anyway."

"Eh?" Juan squinted muzzily down at me. "Don't tell me you're sniffing around my giraffe, dwarf. Need a ladder to get all the way to her cunt—"

Carmelina yanked hard against his grip on her wrist, and at the same time I dropped my goblet on his foot. Wine spattered up to splash his fine curly-toed shoes, he let out a loud curse, and Carmelina was free. I flicked my eyes at her, and she was gone into the loggia. "What a shame," I clucked as Juan Borgia hopped on one foot, looking about for her. "It appears giraffes can outrun tigers. Perhaps just drunken tigers."

Juan leveled a finger at me. "I know who you are behind that mask!"

"Oh, do tell. What gave me away? The eyes? The hair? Or could it be the fact I'm not even up to your chin?" I bowed. "Good night, Gonfalonier. I suggest you set your eyes on a slower mount than a giraffe. Or at least a drunker one."

I strolled off, humming a jaunty tune through my mask, and lost myself speedily in the crowd. Only when I was sure I'd outstripped his drunken gaze did I double back through the loggia.

"He won't forget that," Carmelina whispered in the shadows.

"Nor will he forget those legs of yours." I whistled at the endless dappled length of her. "Whatever prompted you into a nunnery, Suora Carmelina? You could wear silk hose every day and command any price you liked as a courtesan."

"I think I'll leave the courtesan's life to Madonna Giulia." The exotic long-legged giraffe snorted, stripping off her mask and turning into the sharp-edged Venetian cook again. "I'm going back to my kitchens, thank you. At least if Juan Borgia comes sniffing around me there, I've got plenty of knives to fend him off."

"Wise decision."

Carmelina hesitated, looking down at me in the shadows. "Why did you help me? With the Duke of Gandia, I mean. You don't like me."

"And you don't like me," I returned.

"You haven't told my secret," she said. "What I am."

"Because secrets are power," I said airily. "The more people know your secrets, the less power I have over you. And what if I decide I want something from you someday? After seeing you in that doublet, I admit I have a few ideas—"

The hesitant friendliness in her face disappeared. "Don't be vile," she snapped, and stamped off in the direction of the servants' stairs.

I whistled soundlessly, watching those splendid legs all the way down the loggia. Carmelina Mangano really was wasted in skirts.

Carmelina

My father had been a proper bastard, God rest his soul, but he was right. Servants *shouldn't* mix with their masters. I hadn't even been at that wretched masquerade the length of a sermon! I wasn't sure what was worse: that I'd had to fend off the Duke of Gandia, or that I'd needed that ghastly dwarf's help to do so. Give me my kitchens any day, where I was mistress of all I surveyed with my very own patron saint and plenty of quaking underlings.

It was all Madonna Giulia's fault. Why couldn't she have dressed *me* as a blackbird or a cat? Why did I have to be the one in men's hose? "You should never wear anything else!" she'd said admiringly, and somehow everything sounded like a good idea when it came out in that rich laughing voice of hers. I suppose it wasn't really her fault—I didn't have to listen, after all; I could have put my foot down and refused to put on the hose. Not to mention the absurdly high boots that boosted me near as tall as Bartolomeo. "No, Carmelina, you are *not* too tall," Madonna Giulia had argued when I protested the boots. "The key to beauty is to turn what should be a fault into an asset. Don't think of yourself as too tall—think of yourself as built like a goddess! Cultivate a good haughty stalk in those boots, and men will trip over themselves for the privilege of gazing up at you!"

I couldn't do anything about the boots now; they were tight as a second skin and I imagined I'd have to do a good deal of hopping and cursing in the privacy of my chamber to peel them off, no doubt with the hand of Santa Marta snickering at me, if a severed hand could be said to snicker. But I paused in a crook of the stairs to the kitchens and shook my hair down from the high-piled arrangement of curls that Madonna Giulia had insisted made my neck look longer, and scrubbed at the smoky stuff she'd had me line about my eyes as well. The arrogant kitchen cat prowled past, and I swear the notch-eared bastard was laughing at me. Santa Marta save me if any of the scullions saw me in this ridiculous ensemble; I'd never hear the end of it! Fortunately the kitchens were at full boil, trotting out one tray of dainties after another, and everyone would be far too busy to notice if I slipped through the storerooms to my own chamber. I'd be back in my apron to supervise the spun-sugar bulls and unicorns in no time.

"Little cousin?"

I yelped and whirled. My cousin Marco stood half through the doors leading to the outside courtyard, staring at me. I hadn't seen my cousin once since giving him Madonna Giulia's money. He'd been far too busy to visit me once the Duke of Gandia returned to Rome, too busy feeding the endless stream of soldiers, toadies, and whores Juan Borgia brought to his *palazzo* on a nightly basis for debauches that went till dawn. But now here he was: Marco, standing here looking at me after months, and why in the name of all that was holy did he have to turn up *tonight*?

I had a fleeting urge to clap my giraffe mask back on. If I'd been wearing the mask he might not have known me—in my outlandish male finery, in the dim light of the back passage, maybe he'd assume I was some noble guest who'd gotten lost. Perhaps one of Sancha of Aragon's notorious Neapolitan ladies-in-waiting, sneaking off to some dark corner to meet a lover. But no, my mask dangled from my hand and Marco's eyes had gone huge at the sight of me.

I attacked first. "What are you doing here? If you've come for more money, you might as well go home. I'm in the middle of a banquet, and I've no time for your wheedling. Or your threats."

"I've a night to myself with the Duke of Gandia going out for once instead of entertaining," he began automatically. "His guardsmen invited me along in the entourage; we all know each other now after all the *zara* games we've played. Thought I'd slip down, see everyone . . ." Cadge a few delicacies too, no doubt, and the odd coin anyone might feel like lending him. Marco trailed off, and his eyes flickered over me. "What are you wearing?"

I groaned. "Will you just get out of my way, Marco? So I can get to my chamber and take *off* what I'm wearing?"

The same frank admiration I'd seen in Leonello's eyes now filled Marco's. "I'll help you take it off."

"Oh, be serious." I looked over my shoulder toward the hum of commotion from the kitchens. So far it seemed no one had missed me. I'd told everyone I felt ill, needed a breath of air. "Keep the mouths shut and the hands moving until I'm back!" I'd said in conclusion, or started to say, but in the end I slipped out without saying it. It was a phrase I'd stopped using since Bartolomeo had said those same words to me, but murmured against my lips.

"Who knew you'd look so well dressed as a man?" Marco caught me around the waist. "Not my usual tastes, but just this once—"

"Marco, let go of me. I'd rather sleep with a Tiber eel, don't you dare—"

But his lips dove down on mine. "You're beautiful," he murmured. I tried to evade his kisses, and he pulled me against him with a heat he hadn't shown for me in a long time. That heat had been pleasant enough, but when compared to the passion with which my apprentice had seized me . . . "Did I ever tell you you're beautiful?" Marco said wetly into my neck.

"No, because I'm not." I gave his hand a sharp smack as it tried to find its way inside my doublet. "Sweet Santa Marta, what is wrong with you men? I put a pair of hose on and you all go insane! Marco—"

"*Signorina*," a distinctly cold voice called. "That idiot Ottaviano's gone and broken the horn clean off the sugar unicorn. I'll repair it with a little egg white." A hesitation, and diffidence crept into the voice. "Are you still feeling ill, or—"

Then that voice broke off like it had been cut with a knife.

I groaned, feeling the urge to thump my head repeatedly against the wall. Preferably until I achieved unconsciousness. "Bartolomeo," I said, closing my eyes. "Go. Away."

"Egg white, yes." Marco sounded offhand, breezy. "That should patch your sugar subtleties for you. I can lend a hand if you like; I've a night free from my own kitchens!"

Bartolomeo ignored him, frozen in the act of scrubbing his big hands on his apron as he stared at us, at Marco's arm still slung around my hip. It was the first time he'd looked me in the eye since the night we—well, *that* night. I saw the same dark flush spread slowly up from the collar of his shirt until his freckles disappeared. "So," he said in a strange flat voice. "You don't care after all if a man can cook or not, do you? Or if he's a fool. As long as he's got curls and a smile. As long as he's not a *boy*."

I could feel myself blushing. "Bartolomeo—"

He took off his apron, balled it up, and flung it at my feet. "I quit."

"You can't!" I wrenched away from Marco's arm at my waist. "Bartolomeo, we're in the middle of a feast—"

"Bugger that. Someone else can fix the damned unicorn's horn." Bartolomeo looked at Marco contemptuously. "Hire him back, if you want another apprentice. Egg white and a small brush should do it, *Marco*. If you even remember how to cook, after all the wine and the cards."

"See here, boy," Marco began, glaring, and Bartolomeo hit him so fast I almost didn't see it. He was as tall as Marco now, and even stronger with all the hauling of barrels and carcasses that was an apprentice's lot. The muscles bunched under the freckled skin of his arm as his fist exploded into Marco's jaw. Then my cousin was flat on his back on the flagstones, blood dripping from his lip, and I heard screaming and wondered if it was me. But it wasn't me, it came from upstairs. Even Bartolomeo, hauling Marco up by the collar and preparing to wallop him again, paused to jerk his eyes upward in puzzlement at the shouting now drifting down from the gardens.

I groaned, stealing Bartolomeo's favorite expression. "Santa Marta bung me with a spoon!"

He turned away from Marco, who was muttering and gingerly feeling at his lip, and toward me. "Carmelina—"

"None of that!" I jabbed a finger into Bartolomeo's chest. "Help my cousin up and for God's sake stop hitting him. We will discuss your position here later!"

His voice was low and steely. "If you think I'm going to watch you drape yourself all over that bungling ham-handed ass after you kicked me out of my own bed like a stray dog—"

"*Later*, Bartolomeo!" I left Marco groaning against the wall and my apprentice eyeing him with balled fists. The shouts coming from the garden had redoubled, if anything—could something have caught fire? Those torches dotted all about the garden . . . I ran back toward the stairs for a quick look, slipping the giraffe mask over my face again. My hose and boots were indecent, but I had to admit they were far easier to run in than skirts and clogs.

There was already a clot of servants clustered at the narrow servants' entrance, where the servers had been whisking the platters in and out of the garden all night. "What happened?" I heard someone say, shouting to be heard over the commotion in the garden, and someone else yelled, "It's the Duke of Gandia!"

I should have gone back to my kitchens to sort out the mess that had erupted, but I could see over everyone's heads in my tall boots, and the sight of a tiger and a bear rolling on the grass made me hesitate. Bestial grunts came from beneath their masks as they swung and clawed at each other, and for a moment I wondered if I was imagining things. Had I come outside at all? Surely it was Bartolomeo holding down the bear and administering great hammer blows back and forth with his fist; surely it was Marco leaking blood through the mouth of his mask. But then I recognized the tiger—the tight striped doublet, the mask flying off to land in the crushed grass—and I heard Juan Borgia's drunken howl as he shouted something foul in Catalan. The watching crowd howled back, half of them cheering, half of them swearing, and with the strange effect of the mask's limiting eye holes, I thought for a moment that all those beast masks had become beast heads in truth, beast heads resting on sumptuous brocade doublets and velvet bodices. They froze me to the spot in horror.

Sancha of Aragon was watching with lips parted below her fox muzzle, dress dragged off her shoulder and one nipple showing darkly above the fox-fur trim of her bodice as she shouted for Juan to *finish him off, finish him off!* A cardinal in a horse's long-nosed mask was whinnying drunkenly, laughing and calling for more wine. I saw Madonna Giulia on the very fringe, trying to call for order, but Leonello dropped his lion mask into her hands and swept her behind him, lion's eyes flickering in all directions.

"*Enough!*" someone roared in a bull's bellow. The strange bestial roaring died away, not slowly, as heads turned toward the masked bull with the curved horns. The Duke of Gandia and his opponent were the last to pull apart, rising with a final mutual snarl, panting and heaving. "Brawling before our guests!" the Pope shouted at his son, and descended to a rattle of furious Spanish.

"Your Holiness!" Juan cut him off, swaying in the grass. Glassy-eyed drunk; I could see it—drunker than when he had fumbled at my hip. "Do you know what he called me? The offense could not be borne!"

His opponent snarled, clawing off his bear mask. I recognized him—one of Ascanio Sforza's party and a friend of Lucrezia's husband; a young lordling who had once sent down a compliment for my salted ox tongue. "You said a pig's mask would suit me better than a bear," he spat at Juan. "Called me a lounging glutton!"

"And he insulted my birth!" Juan roared to his father. "Insulted my lady mother, called me a bastard!"

"We are," Cesare Borgia noted dryly from one side. Juan Borgia's elaborate tiger doublet was torn and dirty now, his face smeared with blood, but his brother in the glittering serpent mask was chill and immaculate as new ice.

"*I will not hear my name insulted,*" Juan howled, and I half-expected him to fling himself on the ground like a screaming child. "Your Holiness, I demand justice!"

The figure in the bull mask stood still, arms crossed over a burly chest. I wished I could see his face, but the bull's muzzle gave nothing away.

The Count of Pesaro shouldered forward, square-faced and earnest beside his exquisite peacock of a wife, giving his friend in the bear mask a reassuring clap on the arm. "Your Holiness, surely we can blame this quarrel on the wine. My friend will be more than happy to apologize for any offense—"

"Of course, Your Holiness," the young lordling said, starting to look nervous, but the Pope ignored them both utterly and gave one careless gesture to the guards.

"Hang him."

No bestial howl this time; only silence. The young lord with his silly bear mask stood frozen. He only began to struggle when the guards seized hold of him. "Your Holiness! I never—I didn't—"

"Your Holiness," Lord Sforza began.

"I will not hear my children insulted," said the bull, and then the shouting broke out again. Some pushing to see, some pushing to move away, Juan standing with his head thrown back and triumph in his eyes. I saw Madonna Giulia threading swiftly to the bull's side, speaking in tones too soft to hear, but he only swatted her away. The young lord was screaming as they called for rope, a length of rope, and for a moment of sickened hope I prayed there was no rope. But someone found rope, of course they did, and the guards looped it about the young man's throat.

"You're mad!" the Count of Pesaro wailed. "You're all mad, you bloody Borgias—"

"Then leave us," Cesare Borgia said carelessly. "We have no need of you, Sforza. Not now." And putting his serpent's arm about Lucrezia's shoulders, he walked her away as guardsmen tossed the free end of the rope up to the high rail of the loggia overhead, and the bear-headed lordling just shrieked.

I did not watch him hang. I turned away, half blind in my mask, and pushed through the crowd back to the servants' door. I tore off my giraffe's face, feeling the gorge rise in my throat. "What's happened?" Marco greeted me, holding a wad of cloth to his bleeding lip, but I shoved past him and fled to my tiny chamber, ripping the dappled hose and doublet away with shaking fingers. The next day it was whispered everywhere in Rome that the masquerade had continued its merriment after the man hanged—that the Pope and his concubine trod a happy *basse-danse* under the jerking boots. Lies, all lies. The guests trailed out uncertainly, hiding their masks under their cloaks like shameful things. Giulia turned away from her bull before he could approach her, fleeing upstairs, and her brother Cardinal Farnese barred the Pope from following. I saw her later at the window of her chamber, still clutching Leonello's lion mask, looking ghastly sick as she stared out over the city.

No one ate my sugar subtleties. The spun-sugar unicorn, the swan and the peacock, the bull with its molded horns I had painstakingly applied with gold leaf; none of them were even carried up to the garden. I stood down in the kitchens long after the stewards and undercooks and the rest of my uneasy scullions had gone to bed, staring at the sugar unicorn. Its horn still lay broken off beside its prancing gilded hooves; no one had mended it with egg white and a brush, and that was when I realized Bartolomeo was gone.

CHAPTER SEVEN

❖

*A greedy youth, self-important, proud, vicious, and
irrational.*

—A CONTEMPORARY'S DESCRIPTION OF JUAN BORGIA

Giulia

Everyone dislikes their mother-in-law, and at the beginning of my
marriage, I was no exception.

Adriana da Mila had brokered the arrangement between Orsino
and the Pope—the arrangement that had turned her son's wife into the
Borgia concubine—and as a bewildered new bride I had found that very
hard indeed to swallow. Complain all you like about *your* mother-in-law;
mine was a procuress.

But that old bitterness had softened since our mutual stint of captivity with the French. There's nothing like shared terror to bring about
camaraderie. Adriana had been most courageous in the way she'd helped
me calm the maids and tend Leonello's wounds. And she did absolutely
adore my daughter, even if Laura wasn't really (except in name) her
granddaughter. A mother can forgive a great deal of someone who loves
her child, after all, and I was no exception. So I wasn't pleased at all
when I came upon my mother-in-law, sitting with her face crumpled in
deep lines of bewildered hurt.

"Adriana?" I had just returned from confession when I saw a stream of maids passing in and out of her private chambers with armloads of gowns and shoes and linens. "Adriana, are you leaving for a journey?" Properly speaking, I should have addressed her formally as was customary for a dutiful daughter-in-law, but we had been through too much to be anything but equals.

"Yes. I'm leaving." In the middle of the bustle she sat still, a plump figure in violet velvet slumped on a footstool. Her hands were still too, and that was something different—she was never without a piece of embroidery or a list of plans for the next banquet, or more likely the *palazzo*'s account books with their figures lovingly totted and checked down to the last *scudo*. "Yes, I'm leaving, Giulia. I'm going to my niece in Liguria, and I don't think I shall be back soon."

"Is your niece ill?" I came into the chamber, moving a pile of embroidered linen shifts and taking a seat. "You said she'd had a baby not long ago. I can accompany you—"

"No, I'm going to stay with her. I'm not needed here anymore, you see." Adriana looked up at me, tried to smile. "Little Joffre and Lucrezia grown and married with households of their own; they don't need me to supervise them. And you don't need a chaperone either, Giulia. You've long since proved yourself a good faithful girl."

"But why now?" Because I could see pain in her eyes, bewildered pain like a puppy who has just been kicked, and it was a strange image to pair with that of my sleek and self-assured mother-in-law. "What's happened?"

"Oh, just Lucrezia." Another attempt at a smile. "Goodness, but girls of her age can be tiresome! Be on your guard when Laura turns seventeen—"

"*Adriana.*"

"It's nothing, my dear. Really nothing. Lucrezia sitting with Sancha, down in the garden just now, sunning their hair. I came out to sit with them. It's a nice thing about being an old woman, you know; sitting in the sun without a hat because you don't have to worry anymore about ruining your skin—"

"You're not so old as that." I motioned the maids back out of earshot. "Go on."

"Well, that Sancha. She made one of her little jokes—oh, what a nasty piece she is, Joffre deserved better! She joked about lending me that expensive cream she rubs into her face. Not that it would do me any good, she said, because I had wrinkled old skin like a lizard." Adriana's hand crept up to touch her own cheek.

"Sancha's a tart," I comforted. "A thoughtless little tart who probably has the French disease by now. We'll see how much she pokes fun at other people's looks when she starts coming out in pustules."

"But Lucrezia laughed!" Adriana's eyes flew up to mine, and I saw her chin quiver. "She laughed too, and there was a plate of *biscotti* they were sharing, and she said I wasn't to have any because I was getting too plump." Adriana plucked at the generous lacing over the bodice of her violet velvet gown. "That sweet girl I helped raise, *mocking* me. Not for the first time, either. A week back, she was twitting me about my hair; said I was too old to be using curling tongs . . ."

I could feel my teeth grit. "You know she didn't mean it. Not really."

"Oh, I know." A gusty sigh. "But Lucrezia's changed, you know—they've all changed. Rodrigo, well, you didn't know him as a boy like I did, but the boy I knew wouldn't have hanged a guest at a party for a few insults!"

My thoughts froze on that. A corpse at a masquerade, hanging from a railing like a dead chicken on the walls of Carmelina's kitchens, and Rodrigo had treated it like nothing. As though the man were no more important than a dead chicken. "Bah!" he finally snapped when I'd railed at him too long. "Leave it, Giulia! People can say what they like of Us; We are God's Vicar. But they will keep their tongues off Our family! We would have strung the man up for making any insult to you as well!"

Not five years ago, you wouldn't have, I couldn't help thinking.

Adriana was still talking, that quiver running through her voice. "They're all different, you know. Juan brawling like a mad dog; he's always been a wild boy, but the things I hear about his army outside Bracciano . . . not to mention his goings-on in Spain. Joffre getting sulky and bad-tempered, hitting the servants and kicking the dogs out of the way when he used to be so good-natured. And Cesare, well, what to say about him."

"But you don't have to leave." Once I'd have been delighted to get rid of my mother-in-law's watchful eye, but not like this. "They need you."

"No, they don't." Her eyes met mine, tired and watery. "And whom they don't need, they discard. I just never thought it would be me, after all I've—well, never mind."

That silenced me. Adriana's loyalty had always been to my Pope—something to do with the way he had protected her and the young Orsino when her husband died and the wolves began circling for Orsino's inheritance. She'd been loyal to Rodrigo ever since, and that had been another thing that had once made me resentful, because who wants a mother-in-law who tattles to the Pope himself whenever she gets wind of misbehavior in the family?

And now she was to be tossed aside, after all that loyalty, with a few casual insults.

"Lucrezia will apologize," I said. If I had to break every bone in her body, she'd apologize. "Surely then—"

"No, I'm done." Adriana dabbed briskly at her eyes, the efficient housewife again even though her chin still wobbled. "I'm going to my niece. She's always been like a daughter to me, and she's worried that her first baby isn't thriving as he should. She'd welcome a helping hand, and I'd rather go where I'm needed."

Not mocked. We didn't say it, but we both thought it.

"I'll miss you, Adriana," I said, and I meant it. Because my mother-in-law's loyalty might lie with the Pope on most things, but she'd sealed her lips tight on one secret just for me: the little matter of the French general and that night we'd been captured, when I was invited to dine with the French officers. I'd come back with cheeks a dull red and blotches on my neck, but I'd come back with a surgeon for Leonello and a store of blankets and supplies for all the maids too. Adriana had wordlessly helped me adjust my gown and never said a word to my Pope afterward. Just parroted my bland assertions that the French general had been a *perfect gentleman.* I must admit I was grateful to her for that.

She patted my cheek, giving a watery little sigh. "You're a dear girl, Giulia Farnese."

I spent an hour helping my mother-in-law pack, folding linens beside the maids and tucking little sprigs of her favorite dried lavender between the sleeves so they would smell fragrant in their chest. I called a few of the household's sweet-voiced page boys to give us some music, poured her wine, and got her smiling again when I bemoaned how the *palazzo*'s finances would surely fall down in ruins with a flighty girl like me holding the purse strings. I persuaded her to lie down for an afternoon doze, and when I had ordered a cold cloth for her head and another cup of wine, I stormed out to find my lover's clever, lovely, newly cruel daughter.

"*Lucrezia!*" I yelled, not caring who in the *palazzo* heard me. She had gone in from sunning her hair, leaving her sun hat and her fan and her missal on the grass for the maids to retrieve, and evidently she had decided on a cool bath after the heat of the afternoon sun because I found the Countess of Pesaro lounging in the huge marble bath with its mosaic mermaids and trays of fragrant oils, her newly sunned and dried hair pinned very carefully on top of her head. The Tart of Aragon had evidently flitted off to her latest lover or had perhaps just gone to find a dockside tavern to hawk her wares. All in all that was a good thing because I had a quarrel to pick with Lucrezia, but Sancha I only wanted to murder. If I murdered her, then there went the alliance with Naples and my Pope would not have been pleased.

"Giulia?" Lucrezia looked up as I stormed into the *bagno*. "Whatever are you shouting about?"

I seized the water jug one of the maids had left after filling the bath and upended it over Lucrezia's head.

"You look like a drowned rat," I told her as she spluttered and coughed and tried to rescue her drenched hair. "Your eyes are all red and squinchy, and your hair is getting overbleached and nasty, and that horrid lip rouge you wear has smeared all around your mouth so you look like you've been drinking blood. And now that I've been as thoroughly horrid to you as you just were to poor Adriana, perhaps you will feel moved to creep up to her chamber like the nasty little rat you've become, and make your apologies for being so cruel."

"*Giulia!*" Lucrezia gasped.

I folded my arms across my breasts, scowling down at her. The maids had all fled, though they were probably eavesdropping just outside the door, and I had no mind to lower my voice and spare the Pope's daughter her dignity. "How could you?" I demanded. "Adriana da Mila *raised* you."

"She is not my mother," Lucrezia muttered. "And neither are you!"

"No, the mother who birthed you was only too happy to give you up, and don't pretend any fondness there because I see the sighs of relief you always heave as soon as her visits are done." Vannozza dei Cattanei did not visit often, thank the Holy Virgin, and when she did we spoke with icy courtesy. I was too angry to summon ice now with her daughter. "Madonna Adriana raised you in her household, and you owe her the respect of any daughter. Just as I owe her the respect of a daughter-in-law." I thought of Lucrezia's little envies this past year whenever she compared our gowns, our jewels, our hair. Our anything, really. "Adriana and I *both* deserve better from you."

"Oh, the faithful daughter-in-law!" Lucrezia cried out. "As if you've made Adriana's son such a marvelous wife!"

"I admit I'm no one to lecture you on wifely behavior," I said crisply. "But that's a lecture you need as well, because Lord Sforza deserves better, too. Your brother *threatened* him at the masquerade, and you said nothing. You didn't even go with him when he fled back to Pesaro the next day. Fled in utter terror with his tail between his legs!"

"I was the one who warned him he should go," Lucrezia protested. "I said it would be wise to put a little distance between himself and Cesare. You know my brother when he decides he dislikes someone."

"Then you should have gone with Lord Sforza. Sided with your husband, Lucrezia, and not your snake of a brother."

Lucrezia started to rise, but I jabbed two fingers into her breastbone and sank her back into the water. No woman is really at an advantage sitting naked in a tub full of water with wet hair straggling into her eyes, and Lucrezia at a disadvantage was exactly how I wanted her.

"You were always a good, sweet girl, Lucrezia." I shook my head. "What's changed you? I don't think we can blame it all on the Tart of Aragon."

"You will not call her—"

"She *is* a tart, and you're well on your way to becoming one. Traips-

ing around Rome with those Neapolitan harlots she calls ladies-in-waiting, painting your eyes and flirting with Juan's bravos—Lucrezia, do
you know what they say of you, outside Rome?" Fra Savonarola's rantings, that foul pamphlet that had made my fingertips burn. Leonello's
cool voice: *They believe such things because they are true.*

"I don't see how *you* have any right to call me a poor wife!" Lucrezia
lashed out. "My father's whore—"

"And do you want to be a whore?" I demanded. "I don't recommend
it, even if the jewels are marvelous. It's not a path I'd ever want for my
own daughter."

"Well, I don't have a daughter, do I?" Lucrezia's little face was bitter.
"Just a husband nobody wants anymore—Father says I'm to use any
excuse I like to keep from sharing a bed with my Lord Sforza; a baby
will inconvenience everything now—"

"What do you mean, inconvenience? Inconvenience whom?"

Lucrezia hesitated, pushing at the wet bundle of her hair. "The Holy
Father wishes to annul my marriage to Lord Sforza."

My mouth dropped. "You cannot be serious!"

Lucrezia tossed her head. "He doesn't tell you everything, you know."

"Annul your marriage? The legality alone—"

"Cesare says I deserve better than a Sforza lordling. He says a duke
is none too good for me, and our father thinks the same."

"But Lord Sforza—" My thoughts whirled. "You loved him. I saw
your face, in this *palazzo* just three years ago. I let you sneak him
into your chamber to consummate your marriage, and you looked so
happy—"

Lucrezia shrugged. "And he used to write me poetry, but he doesn't
bother anymore. Too busy droning on about his soldiers and his horses.
Besides, Pesaro is *so* dull. I'd rot away if I had to live there forever."

"All excellent reasons to cast off a husband, I'm sure," I snapped.
"The law will require something a trifle more substantial than your
boredom."

"Cesare says something can be managed. An annulment—we'll find
some pretext. Consanguinity, maybe. People are always getting marriages annulled for consanguinity, aren't they?"

"He's not your *brother*, Lucrezia, he's not even a distant cousin! There isn't *any* shared blood between you, much less enough for a legal pretext. There's no pretext at all to annul your marriage, not one that anyone would believe!"

"You don't understand, Giulia." Lucrezia sounded patronizing now. "It's not what people believe. It's what we *tell* them to believe."

I stared at her.

"Cesare says I'll be a duchess by this time next year." Lucrezia rose from her bath, and this time I didn't push her back down. "Or even a princess. Then *I'll* be the first woman in Rome, Giulia Farnese—not you. I'll be the one setting the fashion and heading every parade. Sancha says—"

"Sancha says, Cesare says." I cut her off as she reached for her robe. "What do *you* say?"

"Sancha—" Lucrezia stopped herself, looking annoyed.

I looked at her, my middle no longer roiling with rage but with something much colder. My lover's daughter looked ungraceful and young, lips pushed out in a stubborn pout, hair coiling in wet strings down her neck. Without all the sophistication of paint and powder, you could see she had a red spot on her chin. *Seventeen*, I thought, *she is seventeen*. Not much younger than I had been when I went to her father's bed.

"You didn't use to hate me, Lucrezia," I said finally. "In fact, I thought you loved me. I have certainly loved you, ever since I first met you."

Lucrezia avoided my eyes, slipping into her loose wide-sleeved robe.

"I didn't think you hated Madonna Adriana, either." I paused. "So why were you so cruel to her? You've been thoughtless sometimes, but I've never seen you cruel."

"I didn't mean it." Defensive. "Sancha just made a joke. I thought I would too."

"A very unkind joke."

"Oh—" Lucrezia piled her wet hair up again, jabbing pins through the mass of it. "Really, such a fuss. I'll go apologize to her later."

"You'll have to do it quickly, because she's leaving."

"What?" Lucrezia turned, still pinning her hair.

"You *hurt* her, Lucrezia." I enunciated the words. "Madonna Adriana has decided to go back to her niece in Liguria."

"All because of a little joke," Lucrezia muttered, and that was when I slapped her. First with the flat of my palm; I paused to let her look shocked and then slapped her with the back of my hand, as I'd seen her hit clumsy maidservants.

She took a step back, holding her cheek, and I wondered if she'd slap me back. But she stared at me another moment, and then she burst into tears.

"I *hate* you," she sobbed, and flung herself down on the marble edge of the *bagno*. "I hate you, Giulia Farnese—everyone looks at you instead of me, they all do, and Sancha says you're just jealous I'm the Pope's daughter so you take all my attention away. Father loves you more than me, and when Laura grows up he'll love her more than me too, because she's *yours*, and anything *yours* is perfect."

I didn't know whether to feel more exasperated or astonished. "Lucrezia, really—"

"Even my husband—I saw how he looked at you when we went to Pesaro three years ago, and all the ladies arranged themselves in tableaux for that contest of beauty. I was Primavera in a special dress, and that proud slut Caterina Gonzaga came prancing out half *naked* as Venus, but all you did was cast your lashes down and drop to your knees like a Resurrection saint—you didn't take a stitch off, and every man in the room was *still* panting for you. Including *my* husband." A great moist sniff. "Not that he's to be my husband much longer. Who knows whom I'll marry next, maybe some hideous old man. I've been a good wife, I *have*, I tried to put up with Pesaro, and I put up with all my husband's stupid unshaven captains putting their boots on my table, and what do I get for it?" she cried. "What do I get for it? I get my marriage annulled, and I don't even get any babies! You're not a proper wife at all, and you get everything in the world. You're beautiful and everyone loves you and you even got a pretty little girl who looks just like you, and why can't I?"

Lucrezia just sobbed then. "I'm sorry," I heard indistinctly through the tears. "I'm *sorry*—" And my surprise and exasperation melted away into pity. I sat down on the edge of the *bagno*, and she put her head on my shoulder and cried.

"I don't really have everything in the world, you know," I said quietly, but she was making too much noise to hear me, and when do girls of seventeen ever hear sense anyway? I'd been little older when Madonna Adriana had to deal with my tantrums and shoutings, and now I could feel some sympathy for her. I put my arm about Lucrezia and stroked her wet hair, and finally she lifted her head.

"Is Adriana really leaving?" Wiping at the reddened slits of her eyes. "I didn't mean it, what I said. I was just trying to make Sancha laugh—I don't mean half the things I say when I talk to her."

"Then go up and make Adriana a good heartfelt apology." I smoothed the hair out of her eyes. "And I do wish you would stop trying to impress Sancha of Aragon."

"Perhaps you're right." Lucrezia sighed, wiping at her eyes again. I felt my way carefully.

"Perhaps a change is what you need." I looped up a wet lock of her hair and pinned it back out of her eyes. "Someplace quiet, peaceful. Someplace you can think."

"That would be lovely." Lucrezia scrubbed at her cheeks. "Was Rome always so noisy and hectic, or was I just too young to notice?"

I thought Rome was the same as it had always been; it was the Borgias who were worse. But what did I know? "The Convent of San Sisto," I said instead. "You've often spoken of it, how much you enjoyed taking your lessons from the sisters there when you were a little girl, how many friends you made among the sisters. Perhaps you could go back for a short visit. Pray, rest, see your friends. Get away from all the noise here in the city."

"You think so?" Lucrezia brightened. "Would the Holy Father allow it?"

"I'll make sure he does," I promised. "A retreat for you—I'm sure you could use the time to reflect in peace and quiet, if it's really true the Holy Father wishes to annul your marriage." I half-hoped she'd made that up, but she just gave a little shrug.

"He doesn't need the Sforzas anymore," she said, and sounded remarkably offhand about it all. "It's the Neapolitan alliance he needs to reinforce now, in case the French get restive again."

"I see," I said, and wondered why Rodrigo had said nothing of it to me. *He doesn't tell you everything*, I heard Vannozza dei Cattanei whisper in my mind, from that warm afternoon in the gardens of the Vatican when I had first spoken of my doubts about her daughter's behavior.

Just how long had my Pope been planning to rid himself of Lucrezia's husband?

"I wouldn't mind seeing the sisters at San Sisto." Lucrezia's little face had brightened again. "I can tell the Holy Father it will keep me safe out of reach from my husband, in case he decides to return from Pesaro for me. Even my Giovanni isn't so crude he'd storm a convent!"

She giggled at that, good humor apparently restored now that the tears had been cried out. "I'll go to see poor old Adriana now," she said, rising. "And I shall be absolutely *abject*, I promise. I really didn't mean to hurt her. She knows that."

"Of course," I said.

"Then I shall apologize to you all over again," Lucrezia added. "I get stormy when I cry, you know—I don't hate you, not at all. I just said that. You'll forgive me, won't you? Of course you will. Then we shall go sit in the garden and sun our hair together; I have to dry mine all over again now that you've gotten me soaked, and maybe Laura can sun her hair too! It's never too early to begin caring for your looks, you know." Lucrezia strolled over to pick up her hand glass, pinching her cheeks to make them pinker, admiring her fine white teeth in a dazzling smile. "I don't think Laura's going to be as pretty as me, so she'll have to work with what she's been given . . ."

Carmelina

You'd never think a whole household could be thrown into such an uproar by a visit to a nunnery. Hours after *cena* it was, but the Pope's daughter was keeping every servant under this roof at a trot, packing and unpacking and repacking for her forthcoming sojourn to the Convent of San Sisto. I flattened myself against a wall to let a man-servant bent double under a loaded chest stagger past, followed by a maid with an armload of little slippers and another maid with a basket of shifts for mending, and crept back through the dark kitchens toward the wine cellars.

I cast my usual critical eye over my domain, but the fires glowed softly, banked for the night, and the floors were immaculately swept. Much quieter than usual. A fishwife from the docks had been sentenced to hang tonight for strangling her husband with his own fishing line; my carvers and undercooks were all wild to go see the execution. I gave my permission after their work was done, and most of my people tripped out just before the sun was beginning to set, already taking odds on how long it would take the murderess to strangle and planning where they would take celebratory drinks afterward. I had already sent up a plate-ful of honeyed figs and a plate of toasted salted almonds for Madonna Lucrezia to nibble as she packed—now, I had a rare evening to myself.

"Marco had better not take up much of my time," I grumbled under my breath to Santa Marta, who rode in her usual pouch at my waist. I'd seen my cousin only once since the masquerade, when he'd appeared in the Duke of Gandia's train among the guardsmen during a visit to the *palazzo.* "And what is a cook doing nobbing with guardsmen instead of tending his kitchens?" I'd asked.

"We play the occasional game of *zara* together." Of course they did. "The Duke of Gandia plays with us too, sometimes—he's not too proud to have a laugh and a game of *primiera* with his guards. Or with the cook either, come to that. Not like that brother of his who's too good for anyone else on this earth. At least the Duke of Gandia always brings good wine."

"And gold too, I shouldn't wonder," I couldn't help warning. "It may sound very fine to play cards with a pope's son, Marco, but he can afford to throw a hundred florins down on one bet, and you can't."

"Don't harry me," Marco snarled, and that had been our last words to each other since the masquerade. But evidently he was sorry for being short with me, for I'd received a hasty note today in the afternoon. *I can repay you the money I oh you,* my cousin wrote me in his none-too-literate scrawl. *Meet me in the palatso wine celler after cena? Its quiet and Im trying to avoyd the others—I stil oh Ugo 10 scudi.*

"I doubt he'll have any coin for me," I told Santa Marta. "Likely he just wants to borrow more."

Santa Marta agreed with me, and I hoped again that my cousin wouldn't take up much of my precious free time this evening. A real cook hardly ever *has* any free time, and I'd had an idea scratching at the back of my mind for a while now, like that tattered-ear cat tickling my hem with his claws when he wanted another meal he hadn't earned. I had a notion that I just might follow my father's example and write up my recipes in a proper collection. Santa Marta had seemed to approve of that idea, too.

"Though you have to wonder why I should bother," I added as I descended the stone steps toward the barred cellar doors. Leave a wine cellar unlocked, and every cask in it would be empty by morning. "The only point of noting down your recipes is so you can pass them on to someone worthy. And there isn't anyone in these kitchens worth giving my secrets to."

Bartolomeo, I thought immediately, but frowned. My red-haired apprentice was gone; he'd cleared out that tiny immaculate cubby in which he slept and taken himself off before the noosed and silent body of the murdered Sforza guest had even been taken down at the masquerade. And perhaps it was no bad thing he was gone: he'd had the temerity to both fall in love with me *and* tell me my recipes were wrong. I must have threatened to send him packing at least nine times over the past year of stormy shouted arguments . . . but just now, I had to admit as I paused at the cellar doors to light a taper, I missed him. I had a kitchen full of dullards who were happy if they could get the dishes cooked and out to the *credenza* in time, unambitious undercooks and pinheaded apprentices who looked at me blankly when I required anything more creative of them than boiling water. Bartolomeo might have been an arrogant young jolthead, but I'd somehow gotten used to exchanging a triumphant glance with him when a roast surpassed my expectations, to relying on his finely tuned nose when my own wasn't sure if a game hen was quite fresh or not. If I stood frowning over a sauce, it was always Bartolomeo who took a taste and suggested a pinch of pepper or a dash of wild thyme. Half the time I scolded him for being presumptuous, of course, and said that if I wanted an apprentice's opinion I'd damned well ask for it—but as soon as his back was turned, the pepper or the wild thyme usually went in anyway.

I'd missed that silent complicity, during the weeks when he'd been too furious to even look at me. And now he was gone altogether, and he never *had* told anyone about that frenzied, famished hour we'd spent coiled together on the lumpy pallet. The twinge of shame in my stomach had now quite eclipsed my panic over losing my position. Shame for thinking he ever would tell and wreck my reputation. I'd not only bedded him and then—what were his words? Kicked him out of his own bed like a stray dog?—I'd done him the insult of thinking he was a common braggart who would ruin me out of spite.

It did not sit at all well.

"Never mind," I said to Santa Marta, who I think had liked Bartolomeo because she'd had a habit of falling out of her pouch when he was about. "He was too old to keep on as apprentice anyway. Time he made his own way in the world. If he has a grain of sense, he'll find some cook with a plain daughter, make his way up the ladder, marry the daughter, and take over her father's position."

I brushed away a flash of memory—pale shoulders dusted with freckles like cinnamon and smelling like wild thyme, a long hard body stretched over me, and that was a thought that had returned a touch too frequently to my mind for comfort lately. Perhaps it really *was* well that Bartolomeo had left.

I flicked it out of mind like a dusting of flour off the fingertips and cupped the flame about my taper as I went into the wine cellar. The smell of must and stone, wine and wood; casks in orderly rows with their neat labels in my writing. I kept a far closer eye on the wine stores than Marco ever had—he seemed to think he should leave it all to the *palazzo* steward. "Marco?" I called. "Marco, are you here yet?"

"Maestro Santini's lent you out for the night," a male voice slurred from the shadows. "I'll be the one entertaining you this evening, my pretty."

I turned and saw a handsome young man leaning against the cellar's stone wall. Very handsome, in fact; lean and well-built in an embroidered doublet and curly-toed shoes like a Turk, auburn hair falling in his eyes. The Duke of Gandia had already broached one of the wine casks stacked all around us. He toasted me with the cup in his hand, dark eyes gleaming.

Marco, I thought frozenly. It had been Marco's writing on the note he sent; I knew it so well. But I was looking at Juan Borgia, and my heart began to thud like clods dropping on a coffin.

Marco, what did you do?

"You're not really very pretty at all, my pretty," the Duke of Gandia continued as genially as though he had not noticed my horrified stare. "Not in a gown, anyway. Put you in hose and boots, though—" He gave a leer and whispered, "*Signorina* Giraffe. Or was it a *giraffa*?"

That thrice-damned costume. Why had I ever let Madonna Giulia—and how had he ever recognized—never mind. I pushed both those thoughts aside, giving a wary curtsy with the taper still clutched in my hand. "Gonfalonier," I said, keeping my eyes on the floor. He liked to be addressed by his military rank now, rather than his ducal title. Oh, the great conquering hero. "I'm sure I do not know what you mean. But if you and your men—man"—yes, just one guard standing impassive against the stone wall beside the cellar door, one of Juan's uncouth unshaven soldiers—"require refreshment, I will be pleased to see you fed in the kitchens."

"Why not?" Juan Borgia shrugged, and gave an elaborate bow as I sidled back toward the doors, every hair on my head feeling as though it wanted to stand on end. *Get to the kitchens*, I thought, *get to the kitchens where the lights are. Where people can walk through at any moment.* Anything but this very dim, very empty cellar with its insulating stone walls through which you could hear almost nothing. *Get to the kitchens where the knives are.*

But it didn't do any good, because Juan's guard seized hold of me the moment I approached. "Bend her over," Juan said, and I let out an earsplitting yell and began to flail. I knocked the hat off the guardsman and he staggered a moment. I flung myself against the cellar door and got it open halfway, making a desperate lunge, but the guardsman just grabbed my elbow in a grip that numbed my whole arm and hauled me back, cuffing me across the head. My ears rang from the blow, as my skirts were pushed up for the Duke of Gandia's inspection.

"That's the bum I remember!" he crowed behind me, and I heard a crash as another jug of wine was smashed open. "Bar those doors, Paolo, and let's haul her back here where there's room to work!"

I lunged for the half-open doors again, feeling the pouch-strings at my waist snap, and Santa Marta's purse ripped away. But the guardsman spun me and shoved me in one motion so I tripped over my own feet and nearly fell as he dropped the bar on the doors. The cellar was freezing even on this warm June night, and I felt my skin shrink and prickle all over. Or maybe that was the terror, as the guard let me go and I came up painfully hard against the trestle table where the stewards decanted wine for *cena*. My gaze flew like a panicked bird around the cellar, but there was nothing here but casks and spouts and decanters. The guardsman had brought several branches of candles—oh, everything had been well prepared—and I had enough flickering light to see the Duke of Gandia stagger toward me. I made myself straighten before him.

"Gonfalonier—" *Eyes on the floor, shoulders rounded, meek and timid; that's it.* Santa Marta save me, I had no trouble sounding timid. "If you wish me to entertain you this evening, I am pleased to obey." I forced the words out through dry lips. I'd hoped that if I could just get away, run for the kitchens and disappear into the *palazzo*, Juan Borgia would slouch off in search of easier prey or maybe just get drunk enough to forget all about me by morning. But if I couldn't get away, I'd have to endure it. Plenty of the other maids in this household had had to do the same—I'd had to myself, a few years ago when Cesare Borgia had passed a disinterested eye over me and decided to bend me over a table.

But you wanted that, the thought whispered. Cesare Borgia had been frightening, but he had at least been beautiful. Juan made my whole skin crawl across my flesh like it was trying to escape my body altogether.

It doesn't matter, I told myself. Juan Borgia had recognized me from the ball—Marco's doing too, no doubt—and if the Pope's favorite son wanted me, I'd have to grit my teeth through it. Grit my teeth and douse myself afterward with good strong vinegar.

"Did you fuck my brother?" he asked casually, taking another swallow of wine.

"W-what? Gonfalonier, I don't—"

"Saw him looking at you too, at that ball. You prefer snakes to tigers?" He clapped a hand over his own codpiece. "I can tell you now, a tiger has the bigger cock."

Sweet Santa Marta, maybe there was a way out of this unholy mess. "Cardinal Borgia has been gracious enough to honor me with his attentions," I said meekly. "If that means you do not wish to have me—"

But my sliver of hope died, the hope that the Duke of Gandia would spurn his brother's leavings, because Juan Borgia backhanded me across the face without any change in his expression at all.

"My brother's attentions aren't any kind of *honor*," Juan spat as I watched a spray of blood fly from my nose across the cellar floor. "I'm the Holy Father's favorite. I'm Gonfalonier of the papal armies. I defeated the French at Ostia!"

"Yes, Gonfalonier," I mumbled around my own blood running down from my nose into my mouth.

"—and if I decide I want to poke your smelly kitchen cunt, you should be honored. *Honored*."

My eyes hunted behind him for a weapon. More casks, more cups. A spiderweb. I couldn't attack the Pope's son, I *knew* that, I knew it—if I did, I'd be as dead as that guest at the masquerade who had ended up hanging from the loggia. But I wanted my favorite kitchen knife. I wanted it so badly I could feel the weight of the hilt in my hand, almost see the comforting gleam of the sharp edge. Because I didn't think the Pope's son would be satisfied with a poke and a fumble, not tonight. There was a strange glassy gleam in his eyes that wasn't wine, and he padded toward me with a soft-footed prowl utterly unlike his usual posing swagger.

"I've never fucked a giraffe," he remarked, and raised his arm to hit me again. I ducked his fist this time and ran for the doors again, so stupid because the guardsman stood in my way with folded arms, but I couldn't stop myself from fleeing the Duke of Gandia in a raw surge of panic. I rebounded off the guard's hard shoulder, and then I felt the Duke's hand in my hair, jerking me back. I staggered into a branch of candles, knocking it flying. It tumbled into Juan Borgia, and I hoped it would set him on fire, but it didn't; it just doused him in hot wax, and I heard him yell in surprise. A giggle of pure hysteria burst out of me to see the Duke of Gandia, the Gonfalonier of the papal forces, the Pope's beloved son, covered in hot wax like a message case.

Stupid of me, so stupid of me to laugh.

"Bitch!" he howled, and when he began hitting me again I couldn't duck this time. The guardsman came forward, stone-faced, holding me in place like a piece of furniture as Juan Borgia rained blows on my head and my ears rang like a kettle. "Down on the table," I dimly heard him snarl, and I felt myself being lifted, slammed down on a hard surface. *Don't fight*, I thought disjointedly, *don't fight him*—my head cracked against the trestle boards, and I couldn't help crying out. "Shut the bitch up," Juan snarled. I could hardly focus my swimming eyes, but I could see him coming toward me with that terrifying prowl again, and everything in my blood shrieked warning. I didn't even know I was moving until I got an arm free and lunged.

"You *scratched* me." Juan sounded shocked, sincerely shocked, and I felt the strange hysterical urge to giggle again. If I hadn't been bleeding from the nose and mouth by this time, leaking tears from the eyes, my ears ringing and my skin crawling with more raw wailing terror than I'd ever felt in my life.

"Bitch drew blood," I heard the Duke of Gandia mutter, pettishly. "Hold her hand out. The one she scratched me with."

The guard locked my body down this time, forcing out my left arm. I had a sudden flash of Cesare locking my body down on a table, spreading my arms just like this, but he had held me down to keep me from moving as he tasted my skin an inch at a time—

The vision disappeared in a flash of agony as Juan took the dagger from his belt and slammed it in one casual motion through my hand and into the wood below.

It hurt—sweet Santa Marta, but it hurt! Had Leonello hurt so badly when he lost his little finger to the French? If it had pained him half as much as this, he should have trumpeted my secrets all over Rome in revenge. My bloody lips parted, but I couldn't make a sound. The quivering blade neatly bisected my palm, now slowly filling with blood.

"Good," Juan panted. He cuffed blood off his cheek from where I'd scratched him, and I could see a bulge in his codpiece that wasn't just fashionable padding. He was reeling drunk, but dear God, he was hard as a kitchen spit. *God help me,* I thought, *God help me, God help me*—but why would He bother? I'd been wedded to His Son, and I'd fled them both.

"Hold down her other hand," Juan Borgia ordered. "Hold it down, and give me your knife." The guard had no resistance from me this time as he spread my limp arm across the trestle table. But he hesitated as he took the knife from his belt and began to give it to his master, hesitated with a strange little grunt, and I opened my swimming eyes to see the puzzlement in his gaze as he looked down at the blade suddenly growing from his shoulder.

"Stop this at once," said a cold voice from the cellar doors.

Bartolomeo, I thought idiotically. But the figure in the doorway was far smaller, a dwarf with a knife in each hand who fixed the Duke of Gandia and his guardsman with an implacable gaze and said, "Let her go."

Leonello

A spill of yellow candlelight making jagged shadows over the stacks of wine casks. A girl's long body arched and writhing across a table like an agonized female Christ. The knife through her hand, its hilt throwing a cruciform shadow in stark relief across the flagstones. The blood pooling in her palm, dripping slowly through her fingers to the floor as Juan Borgia bent over her other hand.

I saw it all in one horror-filled instant. What a thing to see, when all I wanted was a cup of wine and a little sleep.

I didn't even know I'd thrown the knife until the guard staggered back, clapping a hand to the blade in his shoulder. Carmelina contracted into a trembling ball about her staked hand. And Juan Borgia just straightened in slow arrogance, darkness writhing in his eyes.

"Get out of here, dwarf," the Pope's son rasped.

The Pope's son. So I'd been half right all along. I'd just had my eye on the wrong son. No wonder Cesare Borgia had seemed so entertained.

"You will take your thug, Gonfalonier," I said. "And you will remove yourself at once."

Juan's voice scaled up. "How dare you!"

I felt the same floating emptiness I'd felt when I swept Giulia behind me and faced the French army with nothing but the blades in my hands. I had a blade in each hand now, though I couldn't remember drawing either, and I pointed one straight at the Duke of Gandia.

"You wouldn't dare," Juan snarled, and started for me. I flicked my wrist, and Juan stopped as the blade winged through his hair, carving a thread-fine furrow along one temple. A hair's width of blood welled up. *He'll see you dead for that,* I thought, but I didn't even remotely care. I whipped another knife out of my boot top and held it between two fingers.

"There are only two of you," I said, quite conversationally. "And if you think I cannot kill you both with ease, you are sadly mistaken. I believe you have no weapon, Gonfalonier, since you were careless enough to leave it stabbed through that girl's hand, and your guard is on the other side of that table. By the time he rounds it, you will be dead and I will have seven more blades to spare for him."

I heard Carmelina's soft gasping from the table, and I saw Anna's murderer hesitate. I could see a flush creep up from his collar. A red wave of it, like all the blood he'd spilled over the years. "When the Holy Father hears—"

"The Holy Father will hear a great deal," I said, wondering in some quarter of my brain how my voice was coming out so calm when my insides were such a vicious coil of tension and rage. "Carmelina Mangano might be only the cook, but Giulia Farnese counts her a friend. You wish to upset La Bella, Gonfalonier? She is the only person in this world whose side the Holy Father will choose over yours. Cause any further damage to her friend, and I assure you she will bring your father's wrath down around your ears."

Another pause, one I counted not in heartbeats but in the slow drops of blood from Carmelina's staked palm.

Drip. Drip. Drip.

"I won't forget this," Juan snarled.

"Ever original," I murmured, but I felt a violent squeeze of relief in my chest. If he had rushed me—

He would never have rushed me. A man who had to nail a girl's hands down before he killed her would never rush even a dwarf.

I stood well back from the cellar doors, not lowering my eyes or my knives until the Duke of Gandia snarled something at his guardsman, and the two of them stalked out of the wine cellar.

I heard one great gasp from the trestle table behind me as the footsteps receded. "Th-thank you," Carmelina gasped. "Thank you—"

"You're quite welcome." I still stood in the doorway, watching the quivering shadow of my murderer disappear up the stairs. Once he turned to look back, and I saw a parallel rake of three lines across his cheek where Carmelina had scratched him. Blood on his face and murder in his gaze as he looked at me.

But not tonight. Tonight he would take his unspeakable urges to bed unslaked. My masked murderer.

Don't be wrong, I thought coldly. *Don't be wrong this time, dwarf.* After all, a girl had been killed while Juan Borgia was in Spain; that alone had made me scratch his name off my list when I was looking for my murderer.

But only *one* girl while he was gone in Spain, one girl in three years. Things had gotten so quiet during those three years, I'd convinced myself I must have constructed the whole thing from my imagination. But they hadn't been so quiet after all. Juan Borgia had probably been killing girls in Spain instead, girls turning up staked to tables in Gandia and Barcelona instead of Rome.

He could not have killed the one girl in Rome during that time. I didn't know who had killed her—but he had killed the others. He had killed Anna. I was sure of it.

Five years, Anna, I told my friend. *It took me nearly five years, but I found him.*

I heard Carmelina's voice again behind me, a thin quiver. "Is—is he gone?"

"Quite gone." I sheathed my Toledo blades, kicking the cellar doors shut.

"How did you—" I heard the rustle of her skirts, saw her try to sit up on the trestle table. "How did you come to be here?"

"Lie back down, dear lady, until I can get that knife out of your hand." With some effort, I dropped the bar back across the cellar doors into its bracket first. I had no desire for Juan to sneak back and surprise me as soon as my back was turned and my knives sheathed. "As for my presence here, a night's insomnia proved useful for once. I thought to fetch a little wine—a cup of Chiarello and Nestor's speech in Book IX of the *Iliad* always puts me to sleep." I spoke lightly, conversationally, giving her time to slow her gasping breath. "The door was barred, and I thought I heard struggling. Then it wasn't barred, and in I came."

"But they did bar the door."

"Perhaps it gave way." I bent down and picked up the thing on the floor that had almost tripped me as I entered. "And what is *this* disgusting thing?" A grisly souvenir from one of the Duke of Gandia's prior victims?

"Santa Marta." Carmelina gave a watery half laugh, half sob. "Did she unbolt the door for you, or did the bar just fall out of the bracket?"

"I said lie back." I surveyed the knife through her palm, taking hold of the hilt. "Count to three."

"One—"

I yanked it out. "Good," I said as the cry choked off between her teeth. "Sit up, that's it—clap your apron round it, while I find some bandaging." I thought of trying to get her on her feet, get her out of the cellar and upstairs for some proper care, but she was still shaking, clinging to the edge of the table, and I doubted her feet would carry her up the cellar stairs yet. She looked sadly frail, this prickly self-assured girl I had sparred with for so long; frail as Murano glass and about as likely to shatter into pieces. I wanted to pull her head onto my shoulder and promise her all would be well, but Carmelina Mangano was no fool, and she was no child—she knew all was very far from well. So I turned my back and rummaged through the cellar, finding a wad of thin cloth some maidservant must have left behind after straining wine, not turning around until I heard her get her shaky gasps under control. Then I offered her the jug of wine that had been half emptied by Juan Borgia as he waited.

"Drink," I advised, wrapping her uninjured fingers through the handle. "And keep drinking while I bandage that hand. Let's have a look, now . . . it's not so bad, really. The blade went straight through, between the bones. It should heal clean if you can keep it out of the food for a few weeks. You shouldn't need a surgeon." I was no expert, but it seemed the right thing to tell her. "If you ever decide to go back to your nunnery, you can pass the scar off as the stigmata, eh?"

"Why are you being kind to me?" Carmelina took a deep drink of wine as I began blotting and wrapping, and I heard her teeth chatter against the rim of the jug. "You don't like me. You lost a finger to the French because of me—"

"My dear lady," I said quietly, "I believe we can overlook that at the moment."

She swallowed more wine.

I tied off the ends of the bandage and tried, for the first time in all my conversations with this lanky girl, to be tactful. "Our good Gonfalonier, did he . . . take you?"

"N-no. That was—next." She gave me a watery smile. "You were very timely. I don't like to think what would have happened after he'd staked me down."

"Something much worse than you imagine." I'd seen for myself the feral glitter of his eyes, the tremble of anticipation in his moist lips. Perhaps he hadn't come here with the intention of killing her—perhaps he only wanted to see those long legs again, and wrapped around him this time. An adventure, lying in wait for an unwilling girl. But somewhere, maybe when she'd scratched him, things had gone bad. As they had for Anna, who had probably been his first.

"What do you mean, worse than I imagine?" Carmelina's voice still wobbled, but the shakes in her hands were subsiding. "What's worse than *this*?"

"Never mind." I took the wine jug from her hand, downing a healthy swallow myself. "You will have to leave here, you know."

She curled her good hand about the bandaged one, looking away from me. The light from the remaining tapers sank into the black hair knotted at her neck, danced merrily over the bruises I could see rising dark and puffy on her cheeks and throat.

"Madonna Giulia would gladly make a fuss on your behalf, of course," I continued. "But even for Giulia, the Pope will never punish his favorite son merely for assaulting a maidservant."

Juan would suffer no justice for Anna's death either, or the string of women who followed her. What were a few low women, against a pope's son? *He will never pay for killing them.* What a waste, finding my long-sought murderer only to discover he couldn't be punished. But I banished that thought for another day. Carmelina came first—surely the first of Juan's victims to escape him alive. That at least was no waste.

"The Duke of Gandia, you may be assured, will not forget you." I addressed the words to the cook's lowered head, as she would not look at me. "He will not forget how well you looked in that giraffe costume, and he will certainly not forget how you marked his pretty face with your nails tonight."

"He won't forget you either," she managed to say. "Running him off like that."

"But I have the Pope's other son as my protector, and Cesare would like nothing better than to irritate his brother with my presence." I didn't really know if I could rely on Cesare for protection, but Carmelina had her own future to agonize over. It seemed unfair to burden her with mine, too. "Unless you want to risk rape or worse, you will have to leave here. And very soon."

"Leave?" She looked around the rows of wine casks, but I didn't think she was seeing them. I saw the scrubbed cheer of the *palazzo* kitchens in Carmelina's big tear-filled eyes, with her bustling scullions and obedient apprentices and Madonna Giulia tripping down the steps calling *"Tourtes! Biscotti!* I always eat when I'm happy!"

"Leave," I repeated. "You must."

Leave everything she'd built here, all because of a Pope's lecherous, murderous son.

"I know," she said, and began to cry.

I dared to hop up onto the trestle table beside her then, my boots swinging freely above the floor. I took the jug of wine from her hand and tugged her head down on my shoulder.

"I don't have anywhere to go." Her hand clutched my sleeve as she wept into the black wool of my doublet. "Not anywhere. Not in this wide world."

I thought of Anna, of a fruit seller named Eleonora, of the other women whom I had not been able to save. The ones who had died in agony. But not this one—not this one.

My voice came out somber and measured, echoing off the cold stone of the cellar. "I swear I will see you safe."

CHAPTER EIGHT

❖

In the affairs of this world, misery alone is without envy.

—BOCCACCIO

Carmelina

"A re you sure it's enough?" Madonna Giulia looked anxious as I weighed the purse she'd given me.

"More than enough." Close to a year's wages, by the feel of it. "Thank you, Madonna Giulia."

"I understand one can buy a few luxuries even in a convent." She smiled. "And the Convent of San Sisto, Lucrezia tells me, can be rather worldly. Silk petticoats and strawberry *crostate* for all the nuns, from what I hear!"

My smile thinned. My convent in Venice had been worldly too, at least for the well-born Brides of Christ. Not so much for the lay sisters.

"I shall miss you, Carmelina," my mistress told me, wistful. "I've been relying on you and your marzipan *tourtes* since my wedding day, you know. I shall never forgive that lout Juan for forcing you out."

It had been Leonello's idea to enlist our mistress in my retreat from the Palazzo Santa Maria. I'd protested. "Since when does the lady of the house involve herself in a cook's doings?"

"La Bella does," he'd retorted. "Don't you know her at all by now?"

"Well, what do we tell her?"

"The truth. A portion of it, anyway."

And Madonna Giulia's warm sympathy had rushed out at once when Leonello dropped into her ear the news that Juan Borgia had been pressing me ever since seeing me in my costume at the masquerade. "It's all my fault," she'd fretted, summoning me at once. "I should never have dragged you along that night. If you wish to drop from sight for a while, I don't blame you. Juan's a brute; you aren't the first maid I've had to—well, never mind. Where shall we send you?" The Duke of Gandia was immured in the Vatican today, dancing attendance upon his father for various formal audiences, but I had no illusions that he wouldn't come back. "Let's see," Madonna Giulia mused, and in the end she hit on the perfect solution.

It wasn't her fault that her solution made my skin crawl.

"The Convent of San Sisto," La Bella said triumphantly. "It's perfect. Lucrezia leaves tomorrow anyway, and she's taking a retinue—her maids, her chests of clothes. She's even stole my Pantisilea away from me, lured her away with promises of higher wages and handsome men at the papal court after she leaves the convent—well, why not let Lucrezia take you, too? You can keep Lucrezia fed during her convent rest, and you'll be safe doing it. Even Juan can't get past a nunnery's walls!"

Back to a convent. Back to black-and-white habits and suspicious eyes under veils, prayers and Masses and stale convent bread that was half sawdust. *Surely not,* I told myself. No stale bread for the Countess of Pesaro, not if she was taking me and not if I were to cook for her. I would still be Carmelina Mangano. Not Suora Serafina, as I'd been in my convent in Venice.

I hadn't thought of my nun's name in a long time. It whispered over my skin like a dead breeze.

But this time it won't be forever. I repeated that like the beads of a rosary. *This* sojourn behind convent walls would be strictly temporary. Lucrezia Borgia wouldn't stay in the convent more than a few weeks, a few months—when she left, I could leave too, and by then I'd have found something else. Something far away from Rome, where Juan would never think to look for me. But until then, at least the convent walls would be safe.

"Perhaps you can come back, after . . ." But even Madonna Giulia's smile faded. After what? After Juan forgot me? The Duke of Gandia never forgot a slight. If he'd hanged a lordling at a party for daring to call him illegitimate, I didn't want to think what he'd do to me for scratching him across the face, or watching him be so thoroughly humiliated by a dwarf.

Somehow I didn't think a knife through the hand would be the end of it. Or even the beginning.

I shivered, touching the bandage on my hand, and of course Madonna Giulia saw. "I'm getting you a salve for that wound," she said, and rummaged in her store of vials and potions. "Juan's a ravening beast; I'd stick him with that dagger myself if I could see him now—"

My face flamed. As much as I needed her help, I hated seeing the sympathy in her big dark eyes as she looked at my bandaged hand. It was what everyone looked at—the only visible sign of what Juan had tried to do, and everyone stared at it when they thought I wasn't looking. The only one who didn't look on me pityingly was Leonello. His eyes had been somber when he saw me that night, but they lacked pity. Leonello might have seen me shaking, crying, and bloody, but he did not seem to find me pathetic, and for that I was grateful.

Madonna Giulia finally let me go—"I'm keeping you from your packing, I know you've got to be traveling by dawn"—and I left her chamber with a purse full of ducats and a vial of salve and another vial of that herbal rinse she concocted that miraculously took the frizziness out of my curly hair. "Just because you're in hiding doesn't mean you can't keep tending your looks. Frizzy hair depresses me terribly even when there's nobody but me to see it. And then I just end up eating more than I should and getting plump, because I always eat when I have frizzy hair."

Back in my little chamber I wondered, as I packed my few clothes and linens and Santa Marta in her box, if I'd ever cook marzipan *tourtes* or strawberry *crostate* for my mistress again. I wouldn't stay in the Convent of San Sisto forever, of course—"You stay in hiding there until Lucrezia leaves," Madonna Giulia had declared, "and by then I'll have found you a post somewhere outside Rome. My brother in Capodimonte would hire you in a moment, if you can stand the country—" But somehow I couldn't see anything past the convent.

Well, the convent and the *cena* I'd have to prepare this evening. My last one, and I should have been aching to use my kitchens this final time. In truth I'd have gladly taken a knife through my other hand just for the privilege of lying down on my bed with the door bolted against the world.

My apprentices and undercooks and scullions were all waiting for me when I appeared in the kitchens. They stared at me, and I saw two pot-boys whisper to each other behind their hands. Of course every servant in the house knew by now that the Duke of Gandia had tried to force me. Juan's guardsmen had probably talked, and anyway, news like that never stayed secret in a household this size. One or two of the maids said they'd been forced by him too. "You shouldn't have struggled, Carmelina. I just lay still and gave him a giggle or two, and it was over in a heartbeat! No bruises either. Next time just don't fight it."

"And end up pregnant or poxed?" I'd retorted. *Or dead.*

I couldn't help another shiver.

"*Signorina?*" one of the stewards ventured, and I realized I'd been staring at them all in silence.

"For *cena*—" I cleared my throat and realized I'd planned nothing at all for the evening meal. I didn't even remember if we had hens or geese or lamb ready on the hooks, or if anyone had gone to the fish market this morning to see what was fresh from the docks.

I cleared my throat again. "Ugo," I said, and jerked my chin at the most senior of my undercooks. A young man of twenty-two, short and shiny-faced, who had already been told he would be taking over the kitchens in the interim before another cook was hired to replace me. He looked entirely too pleased about it. "Ugo, a menu, if you please. You will be doing this alone by tomorrow night, so you might as well begin now."

He began reeling off dishes, too many of them and too fancy. It was just a simple summer *cena*, and with Madonna Lucrezia still keeping the house in a frenzy deciding if she wanted one more chest of gowns or three, no one would notice what they were eating tonight. Bread and fruits and a few cold meats would have been sufficient, and I opened my mouth to tell him so, but then closed it again. This wasn't my domain, not anymore.

"I want to see mouths shut and hands moving," Ugo concluded, alight with his own importance, and I just winced.

The sizzling sound of butter hitting a skillet; the rapid *whack-whack-whack* of knives against trestle blocks; the *glug* of olive oil being poured. The sound of a kitchen coming to life, and a spit-boy looked at me strangely because I was standing in the middle of the growing bustle, standing still as a statue, and I made myself move. I reached automatically for my apron, but just tying the knot at my back sent a jolt of pain through my palm. *Don't ever give me the stigmata*, I thought to Santa Marta. *If it hurts like this, I don't see why saints pray for it.*

I settled everyone at their tasks and looked about me for something to do. I couldn't hoist a heavy saucepan with this hand, but there were herbs waiting to be chopped for the stew. An apprentice's task, but the herbal tang in my nose was green and comforting. Rosemary, sweetly medicinal; garlic with its crisp sting; mint to flavor the refreshing ices that would come to the table after the food was done. But I couldn't press the heel of my hand on the knife, and I had to chop one-handed. I made such a mess of it. I hadn't chopped a sprig of rosemary so clumsily since I was five years old. "You finish this," I told one of the apprentices brusquely, shoving the knife at him, and as I turned away I realized I was crying. All day that had been happening, and I couldn't seem to stop it. I'd be cataloguing spices on the racks one moment, and then realize my eyes were leaking again.

"Not enough sugar," I called out to one of the apprentices, dashing at my eyes as he stirred a simmering kettle of pomegranate wine sauce. "Six parts sugar per every unit of wine, and don't forget to skim the top. Here—" I reached out with the skimmer; surely I could do that with a bandaged palm? But my hands were shaking, and I just thrust the skimmer at the apprentice and turned away before he could notice. Shaking hands, leaking eyes—when had I turned into this whimpering quivering ninny? So a brute had knocked me about and tried to pry my legs apart—that wasn't so uncommon in this world. Plenty of women had brutes like that for husbands. *You're lucky*, I reminded myself, *you're very lucky. You didn't even get raped; Leonello stopped that from happening!*

But I was finding it very hard to feel lucky.

"Wine," Ugo was calling out importantly. "Only the finest Magnaguerra will serve for this royal sauce."

"The Lagrima will do," I snapped, finding a stew I could stir one-handed. "That Magnaguerra is far too expensive for ordinary occasions."

Ugo gave a great sigh to show me how he suffered. I was already regretting leaving him in charge, but who else did I have? "The Lagrima, then," he allowed. "A small cask from the wine cellar."

My throat closed up at the mention of the wine cellar. I fumbled with the ladle in my hand, nearly dropping it into the stew, and the bandage about my palm must have come loose because one end trailed in the simmering mix of chard and borage and thick fragrant chicken broth. "Santa Marta," I swore, and then I did drop the ladle because I could see that my hand was bleeding through its bandage again, and all I could hear was the steady *drip-drip-drip* of blood through my fingers onto the cellar floor as I waited to see if Juan Borgia would kill me.

"Excuse me," I muttered, gesturing an apprentice at the stew, which looked about to boil over. "I'll just tend this—can't go about bleeding into the food!" And I stretched a rictus grin over my face as I marched out of the kitchens, past the cold rooms and storerooms, tripping over the cat to get to the courtyard outside.

A lovely summer sunset painted the sky over Rome, laying an orange glow on the kitchen courtyard with its wheel ruts and straw-scattered stones, but all I could see was a blur. At dawn this courtyard was all abustle: carts arriving every other instant with my daily deliveries of salt pork or baskets of fruit or dew-wet herbs; harassed-looking apprentices carrying crates of hissing geese that poked their long necks through their cage slats; the occasional death squeal as a pig's throat was briskly slashed and the carcass hauled into the kitchen for the spit. I could wring a chicken's neck or slaughter a lamb without one drop of Madonna Giulia's sentimentality, but now I found myself averting my eyes from the stream of dried blood between the stones where a ewe's throat had been cut this morning for mutton chops.

I sank down on the upturned barrel beside the cistern and unwrapped the bandage, running my bleeding hand under the flow of water. Such good water they had here at the Palazzo Santa Maria, deep wells with water clean as any spring that ever welled up in Eden itself. Another reason I had so loved working here, because I didn't have to worry about whether my water was good enough for mixing with the wine. Convents never had such good wells. I'd miss the water. Wine too—dear God, but I wanted some wine. Maybe then my hands would stop shaking. Leonello had poured half a jug of wine into me last night, and it was the only way I'd gotten to sleep.

"Carmelina?"

I started violently, erupting from my hunched seat on the barrel and whipping out the knife I'd been carrying under my apron all day. So stupid because how was I supposed to use a knife with this hand? But I still couldn't put it down.

"I'm sorry." Bartolomeo held out his big freckled hands, placating. "I never meant to startle you."

"Well, you did!" I couldn't quite put my knife down, even seeing the familiar red hair and wide shoulders of someone who was decidedly not Juan Borgia. "What are you doing here, Bartolomeo? You quit, and that was a good while ago!"

"I've found work. A new position." He indicated his neat new doublet and the bundle of a fresh apron under one arm. His sleeve was marked with a badge that seemed familiar. "Or rather, Madonna Giulia found me a new position. She heard I was departing, and she said she always loved my fried lake smelt, so she'd be happy to recommend me for a new post. I've been hired today, undercook in the household of that Neapolitan lord, Vittorio Capece of Bozzuto." Bartolomeo's eyes as they looked on me had none of the sullen anger he'd shown since the night we shared a bed. "I thought I'd come back to give my thanks to Madonna Giulia."

"I see." I should have been happy for him, should have congratulated him. All I could think was that it was my fault he'd left the Palazzo Santa Maria in the first place. I averted my eyes from his gaze, feeling a flush mount up from my neck.

"Also," he said candidly, "I came back so I could lord it over you. 'Call me a boy now, *signorina*'—that sort of thing. But Maria the laundry maid's already told me that you're to leave with Madonna Lucrezia tomorrow."

"Yes." I looked down at my still-bleeding hand, the bandage that trailed over one shoe like a dead snake, and found that at least I was able to lower my knife.

His voice was very neutral. "I know why you're going."

"Maria the laundry maid tell you that too?" I managed a bare modicum of tartness, if not quite enough to cover my pride, as I began washing out my bandage under the cistern.

Bartolomeo's face had no expression at all as his eyes fastened on my bruised mouth, then flicked to my hand. "How badly did he hurt you?"

"Not near as badly as he wanted to. Leonello came along." I wrung out the bandage and began wrapping it around my palm. The bleeding looked to have stopped. *Sweet Santa Marta, Bartolomeo, just go away.*

"I never liked Leonello. He was always eyeing you. And he's got charm, you know, for all he's a dwarf, so I was afraid you'd start eyeing him back." Bartolomeo hunkered down on his heels beside me, a lock of hair falling into his eyes. "Then again, I didn't like anyone who gave you the eye besides me."

"Well, most of the time I just thought Leonello was horrible, so nothing to fear there." I struggled with the wet bandage. "But there's no denying those knives of his can be very useful."

"I'll have to thank him, then." Another pause. "Maria said it was your cousin Marco who was to thank for it. Something about a letter he wrote—"

"Leave it, Bartolomeo!" I squeezed my eyes shut. I didn't even want to think about Marco. Just the sound of his name made me sick. I didn't know why he'd helped lure me for the Duke of Gandia, but I had a fair idea money was involved. I didn't care if I ever saw my cousin again in this world.

Bartolomeo reached for my injured hand as I fumbled to knot the bandage. "Here, let me—"

I flinched back.

"Or not," he said, and stood up again. I clumsily tied off my hand, and he stood looking at me in the fading orange sunset with his arms folded across his chest. *Please not another proposal of marriage*, I thought, but his gaze was thoughtful rather than moony. "You should be resting, you know."

"I've *cena* to finish." My hands were shaking again, and I felt a childish urge to hide them under my apron. "I can't leave them all unfed, I—"

"You're a wreck, Carmelina." Bartolomeo's voice was mild. "You're trembling, you're white as rice broth, and I doubt you can chop so much as an onion with that hand. Lie down in your chamber, drink a great deal of wine, and try to sleep."

"But I can't—"

"Yes, you can." Somehow Bartolomeo steered me back into the scullery without touching me. He rummaged behind a door and took down a spare apron. "I'll take charge of *cena* tonight."

"You don't work here anymore," I protested. "And even if you did, you're still junior to Ugo and all the undercooks. They'll never listen to you—"

"They will. Because I'm a better cook than any of them, and they all know it." His voice was calm and confident. A man's voice, not a boy's, and his touch on my shoulder was a man's too, brooking no argument as he steered me back to the chamber he knew was mine. "Take that knife inside with you, and bolt the door if it makes you feel better. I'll knock twice after *cena*, bring you some wine and some hot sops. I doubt you feel like eating anything, but try for me."

"Bartolomeo—" I felt a wave of such weariness, leaning against my chamber door. I wanted to sleep. I wanted to cry. My erstwhile apprentice just looked at me, his eyes warm as cinnamon and his body even warmer as we stood in the close shadows beside my door. He wanted to kiss me so badly, I could see it in his eyes, and my stomach gave a viscid roll because I thought I would shriek and shriek and shriek if I ever felt any man's hand on me again.

"Stop looking at me like that," I blurted. "Stop it, you hear me? Because I'm a *nun*, Bartolomeo, I'm a *nun*. I was called Suora Serafina and I hated her, but just because I ran away from my convent doesn't mean I ever stopped being her. Suora Serafina can't marry you, because you'd lose your life for violating a Bride of Christ, and *that's* why I kicked you out of your own bed like a stray dog after we—I had to; I had to, and I'm sorry. I'm so sorry. So will you stop looking at me like that and just—just go find someone else to moon over? Someone good, like you. Someone who deserves you. Please just go away."

My eyes had blurred all over again, so I couldn't see what expression was on his face. Surely revulsion. A boy with not a stain on his soul, not a sin on his conscience that couldn't be confessed to his priest, and I'd made him a despoiler, an adulterer against God Himself. Surely he had to be thinking that.

But Bartolomeo just picked up my hand, the wounded one, and his kitchen-rough fingers brushed very lightly over the bandage. "Go lie down," he said. "I'll finish *cena*. Then I'll make you a hamper to take to the convent."

And as I shot the bolt on my door and toppled trembling into bed, I could hear a man's authoritative voice in the kitchens, calling out, "Dear God, Ugo, venison in royal sauce *and* stuffed fingers of veal *and* gilded *capirotata*? Who do you think you're feeding, the King of France?"

Strangely comforting, that voice. I fell asleep to the sound of it, and I did not dream of Juan Borgia.

Leonello

I will kill you.
    Words most of us have spoken at one point or another in our lives. Usually in the heat of a quarrel. Few of us mean it. What happens when you *do* mean it?

A question I'd gone to the roof of the *palazzo* to ponder, throwing my knives over and over the length of the loggia as the sun sank in the sky beside me. Below I heard the rumble of cart wheels in the streets, the clop of hooves, the shouts of vendors packing their wares for the night, shopkeepers shuttering windows and latching doors. The smells of night soil, mud, horse manure, the stink of the river in summer's heat rising even as high as my loggia. *I will kill you.* I'd seen those words in Juan Borgia's eyes when he last looked at me, and now I said them to him, silently, as I threw my blades into the makeshift target where I still performed my daily hour of practice.

Killing a man is easy enough, if one has the will. But killing a pope's son? That is a different question altogether. And a question I must answer, because as surely as Juan Borgia would come for Carmelina because she dared to escape him, he would come for me because I had dared to humiliate him.

How fortunate, then, that I could think of nothing more pleasant than coming for him first.

If I could puzzle out how. Because as much as I wanted to conclude this deadly business with Anna's long-sought killer, I had no desire to pay for it stretched on a rack or dangling from a rope.

"Will." I sent a blade winging the length of the empty loggia. The sun was a fiery ball at my right, sinking into a mass of charcoal cloud. Yes, I had the will. Perhaps it was a great sin, but murder had never troubled my conscience as long as I could justify it, and the Gonfalonier's worthless soul would not be missed by any but his blind and doting father. No, I'd not blink an eyelash at the thought of removing Juan Borgia from the world. Finding the opportunity would prove more difficult. For that I would need—

"A site." I sent the dagger at my belt whipping at the target. The killing ground would have to be chosen in advance. Somewhere secluded enough for the asking of questions, for the telling of answers, because killing the man who'd killed Anna was not enough for me. I wanted him to look me in the face and admit he'd done it; I wanted him to explain how his brother's dagger had turned up on one of the bodies; I wanted to know how the one girl had died when Juan had still been far away in Spain. And I would therefore require a site far away from the *palazzo*, to lead suspicion from the household here and anyone in it. That was why I hadn't killed Juan on the spot in the wine cellar, though the thought had flashed briefly through my mind. If he died in the *palazzo*, everyone in the household would become suspect. And I fully intended to walk from this without a shadow of suspicion attached to me.

"A lure." I winged the knife from my boot top after my waist dagger.

Juan Borgia would not be easily drawn to remote killing grounds. He had enemies aplenty: the Orsini whose castles he had attacked last fall; the husbands and fathers of the women he had despoiled—even his own brothers. Cesare, who wanted his position, and little Joffre, who looked at him with helpless hate for bedding Sancha and soiling her reputation all over Rome. The young Gonfalonier went nowhere in Rome without his armor, his retinue, and his guards. A lure would be needed; something to get him alone and helpless.

"An accomplice." I hesitated, and the wrist knife wobbled as I flicked it away and missed the target altogether. I could see no way to spring an ambush like this without a second pair of arms. Strong arms, too, because Juan would need to be dragged from his horse and bound securely. I was stronger than I looked, but I could not haul a full-grown man off a horse, much less if he was struggling.

How hard is it to kill a pope's son? What do you need to do it?

Will—yes. A site—I had a few places in mind. A lure—that too could be managed, maybe. But an accomplice—that was where my brain stopped. Because I had friends, but no friends I could ask to help in a matter such as this.

Almost I thought of Cesare. He hated his brother, after all, and lusted for the opportunities that Juan had squandered. And he knew about his little brother's hobby; Cesare Borgia knew every secret the family had. He hadn't bothered to expose Juan, of course—any secret against a rival brother would be kept until the day it proved useful.

Might he . . .

No. If Cesare Borgia ever turned Cain against a member of his own family, he would do it for his own reasons. Not merely to avenge a few lowborn serving girls and tavern maids.

The sun was gone by the time I descended from the loggia with my knives sheathed again and my dilemma no nearer a solution. I had missed *cena*, so I took myself to the warren of small chambers behind the kitchens, looking to find my wounded *Signorina Cuoca* and perhaps cadge a little food. But I had no answer at her chamber door, and I wandered out to the kitchen courtyard with a shrug. Where I saw a young man standing in the shadows, one elbow propped against the wall and his face buried in his arm as he aimed the other fist over and over, with great softness and precision, into the stones. "I will kill you," I heard him mutter indistinctly. "I swear to Christ, you filthy whoremonger, I will kill you—"

"Kill who?" I called across the courtyard.

His head jerked up, and I recognized Carmelina's red-haired apprentice. "What?"

"You seem to be planning violence." I sauntered closer, watching my shadow dance in the dim light of a rising half moon. "Violence is my business."

"And my business isn't yours." He straightened from the wall, and I could see that his knuckles were bruised from where he'd driven them into the stones. Bruised, but not bloody—even in fury, he was taking great care to save his fists. For a more specific target, I would wager.

"Let me guess." I smiled, taking out my dagger and stropping it against my boot top. "Could your distress have something to do with our *Signorina Cuoca* leaving for the Convent of San Sisto tomorrow morning? Or perhaps *fleeing* for the Convent of San Sisto would be more accurate. And you've been in love with our bad-tempered Venetian cook since you were, oh, fifteen?"

"Carmelina said you saved her from the Duke of Gandia," the boy cut me off. "So I'll thank you for that. But don't twit me, Messer Leonello. I'm no boy anymore."

"Debatable," I said, but Carmelina's apprentice had grown since I'd last bothered to notice him. A strapping young fellow, really, standing with one shoulder jammed truculently against the wall of the courtyard and his face leveled down at mine in a cool stare. Whipping egg whites and cream tops might not be as noble a calling as the sword, but it evidently built men every bit as strong.

"So you have heard what happened to Carmelina," I said, and pushed the knife back into my boot top. "Regrettable, but hardly uncommon. I hope you're not thinking you can take on the Duke of Gandia in revenge?"

"He's too high for me," Bartolomeo returned. "I'd sink a meat cleaver in his skull if I could, but I don't want to die or be excommunicated just for crossing the Pope's son. I'd rather live, marry Carmelina, take her to Milan so we can learn how they do that leavened citron bread of theirs, and come back to Rome someday to cook for the next Pope."

I whistled. If this redheaded boy had gotten through all the thorns around the heart (or the bed) of our prickly *palazzo* cook, I was prepared to be impressed. And possibly ask for his secret. "She's going to marry you, is she?"

"I'm working on that part."

"Making any progress?"

He ran a wide, scarred hand through his hair. "Slowly."

"Fair warning—she has a secret or two that might inconvenience your grand plans."

"You mean that she's a nun?"

My eyebrows shot up. She had trusted him with that, had she? Interesting.

Bartolomeo shrugged, seeing my expression. "It's a wrinkle, I admit."

"Surely more than that." I inspected him. "Don't tell me you mean to run away with a bride of Christ! Don't you know what they do to despoilers of nuns? And you such a stainless young man—"

"It's a wrinkle," he repeated, chin jutting.

Dio, the dreams of young men. "So, if not *il Duche*, whom are you thinking of killing on her behalf?"

"No one." A level look. "I wouldn't quibble at killing him, but I don't want to swing from a gibbet. And I don't want blood on my conscience, either. I'm no murderer, like you or that dead-eyed thug Michelotto—"

"You flatter me," I murmured.

"—but that pretty-faced, mush-brained cousin of Carmelina's lured her to the Duke to get a debt erased, and he's going to pay."

"With his life? What about 'Thou shalt not kill?'"

"Our Lord never said anything about 'Thou shalt not beat him to a pulp.'"

I felt my smile widen. "He didn't, did He?"

"Maestro Santini *wagered* her!" Bartolomeo burst out. "They're cousins; they learned to cook in the same kitchen; maybe they even shared a bed—" A bitter twist of his mouth at that. "He must have been *fond* of her, with all that behind them. And he still gave her to the Duke of Gandia! Even though he'd have seen the other maidservants in this house who have caught the Duke's eye, the same ones I saw with their bruises and—" The red-haired boy stopped, a pulse beating fast and furious in his jaw. "Sweet Jesu, I've never seen her like she was tonight. She's quivering like a jelly. If I'd been there in that wine cellar—"

"You'd have defended her gallantly, I'm sure," I said. "And you would have been killed."

"Maybe," he said with a steeliness that pleased me. "And maybe I can't touch the Duke of Gandia. People like him never pay for the things they do. But Marco Santini's no higher in this world than I am, and I'm going to break every bone in his body."

"Excellent idea," I said. "I can help."

"I don't need help."

"But I do." I pushed away from the wall, advancing on him. "What if I told you the Duke of Gandia wasn't as out of reach as you think?"

"What do you mean?"

What do I need to kill a pope's son? I thought.

The will—yes. The site—I had one in mind. The lure—trickier, but I had an idea there too. And as for the final piece, the accomplice. Someone tall, someone strong, someone resolute. Someone with good reason to hate Juan Borgia.

"Sit down, Bartolomeo." It was quite dark now, but that was good. Murder is better planned in the dark, where the angels cannot eavesdrop. "I have a proposition for you."

CHAPTER NINE

He who places great trust will end up greatly deceived.

—BARTOLOMEO SCAPPI, MASTER COOK

Giulia

You," I informed my Pope's favorite son, "are not welcome here."

Juan Borgia laughed, throwing his auburn head back so it gleamed in the morning sunshine. I continued to look down at him cold-eyed from the marble steps where I'd come to block his path from the courtyard into the *palazzo*, my pet goat at my heels.

"Can't a fond brother come visit his little sister?" Juan was very much the handsome young gallant this morning in his embroidered hose, his velvet cloak with the red satin lining, his spurred boots and the mirror-bright breastplate he now wore at all times to emphasize his position as Gonfalonier. He struck a pose for the courtyard full of grooms and rushing pages and bustling squires. "Don't be sour, Giulia Farnese, let me in to see 'Crezia—"

"Lucrezia left for the Convent of San Sisto already, as you would know if you had bothered to ask Cesare or Messer Burchard or the Holy Father, or anyone else." My lover's daughter was just a day departed, and after the whirlwind of packing and unpacking and repacking, the *palazzo* seemed very empty without her. Or perhaps the *palazzo* just *was* empty: Adriana gone to her niece, Lucrezia to her convent, Cesare preparing for a journey south since he had just been made papal legate to Naples (and hadn't *that* ruffled a few feathers, given his youth). Rodrigo was not much in evidence either; still embroiled up to his ears in the wake of a consistory so private and secret that it had taken a full twenty-four hours for the news to spread across the city that various papal fiefs—Pontecorvo, Terracina, not to mention the Duchy of Benevento—were all to be given to Juan.

I didn't dare tell Rodrigo just what a dreadful idea I thought *that* was. As if Juan needed any more reasons to puff himself up!

"If you wish to visit Lucrezia, you are too late," I continued crisply to the Duke of Gandia and Benevento and all the rest. "She missed you yesterday, when she made her departure. I can't think why."

"Then let me in to visit my other sister," Juan said, not turning a hair. "My dear little Laura. Can't a big brother play with his favorite girl?"

"I don't like how you play with my daughter, Juan." Far too roughly: tossing Laura overhead first until she squealed, and then until she screamed. Or if it wasn't tousling and pinching and pushing, he was jesting in that mean way I so disliked: hiding Laura's favorite doll, the one she loved so much it was bald and faceless, as she hunted all over the *palazzo* weeping.

"Why so cross, Giulia? Don't tell me you're breeding again. That always makes a woman bad-tempered!" Juan's squires and soldiers behind him gave obedient snickers. Juan grinned, offering me a bow as I glared, and presented me with the little nosegay of fresh violets and rosebuds that he had presumably brought for Lucrezia. "Even when you're scowling, you're beautiful—"

I took the nosegay and handed it to my pet goat. "I'll not have you over my threshold right now, Juan Borgia." The goat munched placidly at the mouthful of violets, and I spoke loud and clear so my voice carried to the guardsmen standing behind me, to Leonello who watched from the door's shadow since I'd ordered him to stay out of Juan's sight, to the squires and soldiers at Juan's back, and the grooms still holding Juan's horse in the courtyard. "Not when you attempt to ravage my cooks and my maids. I won't have you over my threshold again until I have a promise you will conduct yourself decently in future." I had no hopes I could bar Juan from my door forever, but I'd settle for vows of good behavior, particularly if I could get my Pope to add a stern lecture. Not that either would stick for long, but I could at least keep a very close eye on Juan in future whenever he crossed my threshold. *And tell all the maids to travel in groups.*

"What stories have you been hearing, Giulia?" Juan wheedled me with another smile, sauntering closer. I refused to back away as he put one boot on the marble step where I stood, drawing his handsome profile close to mine. "Is some maidservant telling tales about me again? I'm not near as bad as my reputation, you know." He lowered his voice to what he probably thought was a sultry whisper. "In fact, I'm better."

He tried to slip an arm about me, but I gave his wrist a smack like I smacked my little goat whenever he tried to eat my sleeves. Juan's smile vanished. "It's not your threshold, Giulia Farnese," he warned. "I do what I wish here. And if you're talking about that long-legged bitch in your kitchens, she's a slut and a cock-tease, and she shouldn't mix with her betters at your banquets!"

"I assure you, she was not mixing with her betters if she was mixing with you," I said coldly, and turned in a whirl of blue velvet skirts.

"I assure you, the bitch liked it." Juan seized me about the waist and yanked me back, pulling me up against him, and to my shock I tasted his wine-sour breath as his mouth leeched onto mine. I wrenched my head away, spluttering, hearing his soldiers hoot, and I would have slapped him but he had locked my arms fast against my sides with his own. He smiled, watching me struggle, and I felt just how strong he was. He could hold me all day if he wanted, and I felt a disquieting pang of fear thrum through my stomach. I had never feared Juan before—he was such a lout!—but his eyes had a fever-bright gleam now that pinned me like a doe pinned by spears on a hunt. *Did Carmelina see that look in his eyes?* I found myself wondering, and swallowed around the sudden lump in my throat.

I made myself stop struggling against his grip, made myself look into his face as though quite unperturbed. "Don't be an ass, Juan. The whole *palazzo* is watching."

"I don't care, not if you don't." His voice was still a hot whisper, and one of his hands dragged upward toward my breasts. "You want it too, don't you, Giulia? Just like that tall kitchen bitch. All women want it, I can give it to you—"

"Good morning, Your Holiness," Leonello said brightly, strolling out of the doorway's shadows to my side and aiming a bow behind Juan as though Rodrigo had just arrived in the courtyard. Juan's arms dropped away from me like two limp strips of pasta. He whirled, smoothing a hand over his mouth, but the courtyard was empty of anyone except guardsmen and goggling servants. Juan turned back with a glare for my bodyguard, and the pang of fear in my stomach deepened to a needle-sharp shaft piercing all the way through me. I didn't know the details of how Leonello had come to clash with Juan over Carmelina, but I knew it had happened, and I'd ordered Leonello to stay out of sight of the Pope's favorite son. But I'd never had any luck yet trying to give Leonello orders, and here he stood at my side: arms folded across his chest, looking up at Juan with that cool insolent stare of his that would madden a saint.

"You and I have business to finish, dwarf." Juan snapped his fingers to the half-dozen guardsmen at his back. "Seize that little monster at once. I'll have him strung up!"

My breath froze in my throat, but Leonello merely smiled. "The first man to touch me," he said, unfolding his arms to show the knives already in his hands, "gets a blade through the eye."

"You think my men can't hang you up by your heels in this doorway, dwarf?" Juan spat.

"Of course they can," Leonello agreed. "Five will be more than enough."

"I have six men!"

"No," Leonello corrected gently. "Five. Because I'm going to kill the first one who lays a hand on me. Likely I'll only get one, and then the other five can string me up as you please. But the first one dies, and that I promise. So—" he gave a benign smile, stropping one of his daggers along the top of one boot. "Who wants to be first?"

Juan's guardsmen, who had started forward obediently with hands on dagger hilts, suddenly looked a trifle uncertain. One or two even looked shamefaced—after all, plenty of the Borgia guardsmen rather liked Leonello, who often joined the house guards at their card games when he wasn't guarding me. Whether out of fright or out of consideration, they hesitated, and I took a step forward up to my bodyguard's side, repressing the urge to put myself between him and the danger just for once rather than the other way around. His pride would never stand for that. "May I add, good sirs, that this man is under my protection?" I fingered my huge teardrop pearl, reminding them just who had given it to me. "Which is to say, the protection of the Holy Father Himself."

"The Holy Father does what I say!" Juan snarled, but his men had fallen back a step, looking between my gleaming jewels and Leonello's gleaming blades. Leonello's mouth had tilted in a smile of faint contempt, gazing at Juan who stared back in flat loathing, and I laid a warning hand on my bodyguard's shoulder. Juan was hard enough to handle without being further stoked by Leonello's jibes.

"Go home, Juan," I said, and wiped an ostentatious hand along my mouth as though to wipe the taste of his kiss away. "Get out now, and perhaps I won't say anything to the Holy Father. How you threatened my bodyguard, *or* how you put your hands on me."

"Tell him," Juan shrugged, with a final narrow look for Leonello. "I'll say you led me on. He always believes me, don't you know that by now?" The Duke of Gandia lowered his voice. "And you do lead me on, Giulia Farnese. I know what you want. You're too much for an old man, you're wet for something younger—"

I whirled and stamped into the *palazzo* then, hearing Juan's snigger behind me as the doors shut. "I'll find you another day, dwarf," he called in a parting shout. "When you're not hiding behind a whore's skirts!"

Leonello merely yawned. "You shouldn't taunt him," I scolded as the guards bolted the doors and I heard the retreat of bootsteps from the courtyard. "He never forgets an insult, you know that."

Leonello fingered his damascened knife hilts. "Then I'll give him some new insults to remember."

"You had better not!" I scrubbed at my lips, still tasting the sour wine on Juan's breath. Ugh, ugh, ugh, but I wanted a bath! Just a kiss, and I felt slimy all over.

"Gossip in Rome has it three to one that the Duke of Gandia goes to Naples soon," Leonello volunteered. "Perhaps he'll stay there."

"For both our sakes, I hope so." Ever since receiving his new papal territories, Juan had been swaggering all over crowing about his new acquisitions, boasting how one day he'd add Naples to those same acquisitions, and maybe he'd just march down with his armies and make himself king there by force rather than wait any longer. I didn't want him king of anywhere, except maybe hell, but if he went to Naples maybe he'd stay there.

That odd gleam in Juan's eyes kept coming back to me throughout the day. The bright gaze, and that enjoyment as he gripped me so tight and watched me struggle. What *had* he been thinking? Juan had always liked to ogle, but to kiss me in front of his soldiers, the maids, the guards, anyone in the *palazzo* who might talk—was he utterly mad? Did he really think his father would laugh it away as he did all of Juan's other antics?

I scrubbed at my lips again. I didn't really think Rodrigo would believe I'd encouraged his son in any kind of familiarity. Still, I decided I'd tell my Pope about this the very next time I saw him. I'd have to make light of it—"Oh, Rodrigo, that son of yours was tipsy again, you'll never believe what he did!" But I'd make sure—very sure—he heard *my* version first, heard it and believed it, just in case Juan decided to make trouble . . .

I had very little patience for my Laura when she put up a fuss that afternoon about her lessons. Maybe because she looked startlingly like Juan when she pushed her lip out and sulked.

"I don't want to learn letters! I want to sit in the *garden* and sun my hair—"

"You are too young to be sun-bleaching your hair," I said shortly, marching my daughter along the loggia. "And today is not the day for sitting in the garden. Today you are to practice your letters. And I will have you start on French soon, too, because everyone says you will learn it faster if you learn it young."

"Don't like French," Laura muttered. "Leonello says they're poxy horses."

"Horses?"

"I believe I said 'whoresons,'" Leonello volunteered, swinging along behind us.

"Thank you for teaching my daughter foul language," I said tartly. "Laura, you *are* going to learn French. And Latin and Greek too someday, just like 'Crezia. Wouldn't you like that?"

"No." Another glower beneath the cloud of blond curls. "'Crezia wouldn't make me learn letters. 'Crezia lets me do whatever I like!"

"I've noticed. But today you will practice your letters." My daughter might only be four, but it was already time to consider her future education, and I found myself wanting more for her than the usual subjects that had been laid out for me at her age. All I had ever learned was dancing and prayers and embroidery stitches; how to keep a household's books and twang very badly on a lute. I wanted more for my daughter.

Not that she appreciated it. Laura whined, and then she wailed, and then when I administered a brisk smack to her bottom through her skirts, she roared. But I marched her along to the pleasant sunny chamber where the balding tutor I'd engaged waited with some apprehension at the sound of his pupil's yelling. "You will sit up straight for Signore Angelotti," I said, cutting off her indignant howls with a little shake. "You will be courteous, and you will be obedient. Yes, *Lauretta mia*?"

Her lip still pushed out, but she gave a sulky bump of a curtsy for me. "Yes, Mamma."

"Good girl."

"You don't speak Latin, Madonna Giulia," Leonello pointed out as I shut the door on my daughter's rebellious mumbling and set off down the loggia toward my own chamber again. "Or French, and you can't translate Plato, either. So why do you want Laura to be a little scholar?"

"Because she's getting spoiled, and the discipline will do her good. I don't want her growing into some pouting featherbrain who thinks she can never do wrong." *Like Juan.* I really did not like it at all, that petulant push of the lower lip Laura shared with my Pope's favorite son. "Laura's going to have every advantage to turn her into a fine woman," I said, and it was a vow I intended to keep if it killed me. Or her. "She'll learn dancing and music and embroidery, but she'll have languages and philosophy too, and I'll teach her to give to beggars and feed stray dogs and—and everything else I can think of. Everything that will make her thoughtful and kind—"

"The other Borgia children grew up with much the same advantages," Leonello said. "And none of them are particularly thoughtful or kind, are they? I believe it takes more than a few tutors to instill good character, Madonna Giulia."

I shied away from *that* thought. "It can't hurt, can it?" Lessons, discipline, a little quiet. Maybe it wasn't such a terrible thing, having Laura to myself for a while without Lucrezia forever breezing in to flatter her and dress her up and urge her to bleach her hair. I already missed Lucrezia, but there were times I wanted to tell her that if she wished for a daughter to spoil and play with like a trained monkey, she should have one of her own.

If Lucrezia had any daughters, though, they wouldn't be coming from Lord Sforza. My Pope was quite open about it now—a way was to be found to annul Lucrezia's marriage to the Count of Pesaro, and he wasn't fussy about what way, either. "If consanguinity won't do the trick," Rodrigo had mused, "perhaps we can pretend Lucrezia's previous betrothals weren't properly reversed?"

"Really, Rodrigo," I'd said. "You'd make your own daughter a bigamist?"

"So she can someday be a duchess rather than a countess? Of course."

Poor Giovanni Sforza had stamped all the way up to Milan to beg assistance from his more illustrious cousins, but I did not think much of his chances. My Pope was utterly unfazed by the sight of the French King on his doorstep with an entire army; he didn't bat an eye when the Orsini threatened to overrun the papal states; and he laughed openly when the College of Cardinals threatened revolt over Juan's newly acquired territories and titles. What chance did Lucrezia's poor nervous husband have of standing down the Holy Father?

Juan's overbright eyes and wet mouth; Lucrezia's convent retreat; poor Lord Sforza's fuming. Really, was the whole world going mad? I felt too weary to think about any of it anymore, and I couldn't help another little sigh as I entered my chamber and sank down on the cushioned wall bench. Two of my maids sat in the corner gossiping and sewing, and Leonello took the opposite corner and picked up his latest book. It was the romance of Tristan and Iseult, which I'd begged him to read out loud while I sewed or practiced my music—he had such a fine deep voice for reading. Not to mention the added pleasure it gave me to watch his ears turn red with irritation during the more overwritten love scenes. Just by looking at those earlobes, I could calculate how long it would take him to groan and heave the book across the room. But he seemed too distracted to read now; his voice kept trailing off, and a description of Iseult's glistening sapphire-hued orbs didn't even move him to a snicker, much less his usual humorous tirade on dimwitted maidens and their even dimmer romantic escapades.

"Never mind Iseult," I said at last, picking up my ivory-fretted lute and giving it a twang. "There's no point if you're not going to joke and grumble about her. Talk to me instead, if you're not going to tease me about my terrible taste in books. I'm thinking of another visit to the country—will you promise not to get homesick for the city this time, if I promise to make it a short visit?"

"Where in the country?" Leonello eyed me. "Perhaps Carbognano? I noticed one of those short, dull letters just arrived from your husband again. No doubt praising the summertime beauties of Carbognano in his execrable spelling."

"Don't be rude," I chided. "And why shouldn't I go to Carbognano? A stint in the country would do Laura good." And I wouldn't mind being away from Juan for a while, either.

"If you go within spitting distance of Orsino Orsini," Leonello pointed out, "the Holy Father will explode."

"The Holy Father may do as he pleases. As long as Laura is not a Borgia, then she should have a chance to see the father whose name she *does* carry. We will live with him again someday, after all."

"Oh, you will, will you?"

"You know he has always wanted me back." Not that he ever really had me to begin with. It wasn't precisely the passionate declaration I might once have hoped for from my husband—an earnest promise that he would consent to take me back once Rodrigo was done with me. But it was a practical consideration for the future, Laura's as well as my own, because I knew that the day would come when Rodrigo was no longer part of my world—when he died, or when his passion for me did. I hated to think of his love ever failing, and certainly it had not waned at all in more than four years—but, well, mistresses *were* discarded. My sister was forever reminding me of that, usually as she nagged for some papal favor that I must obtain for her *now*, while the getting was easy.

Much as I shrank from the thought of being discarded, even worse was the thought that my vital, virile, cheerful Rodrigo would ever be laid beneath the earth.

Oh, Holy Virgin, what a prospect! Could I not have any cheerful thoughts today? I crossed myself, heaving another sigh. Even Leonello seemed gloomy, fingering the book's spine and looking thoughtful. "What is it?" I said, and picked up my lute again. "Don't tell me I've dragged down your mood, too."

"I've been wishing to ask you for a favor, Madonna Giulia."

"Of course. Is it about Carmelina?" I missed my sharp-tongued cook with her sweet hands. I thought Leonello missed her too—he had saved her from that oaf Juan quite romantically, after all. Who says a small man can't act the hero?

"It's not a favor for our *Signorina Cuoca*." My bodyguard sounded uncharacteristically somber. "It's something for me."

"Then I'll gladly help." I looked down at the lute, dubious. "I think I'll save this for Laura when she's older. Surely she'll be more musical than I am. Of course, a turnip would be more musical than I am . . ."

"I need a letter. A letter in your writing, Madonna Giulia, just a few lines. I'll tell you what to write."

"A letter to whom?"

"No name." Leonello did not look at me as he recited, in a toneless voice, the words he wanted me to write. I'd laid aside the lute to go fetch the fine scented paper on which I wrote all my letters, but his flat emotionless words arrested me before I had a chance to rise.

"Leonello—what *is* this? You know I can't write that!"

"You don't have to sign it."

"What does that matter? His Holiness knows my writing. If he saw this, he really *would* explode!"

"I know." My bodyguard looked at me. "But I am asking anyway."

"What for?" I didn't know whether to be more puzzled or horrified. "What can you possibly need this for?"

"You want the truth?" Leonello's hazel eyes were unblinking, pinning mine. "I am looking for a man, Madonna Giulia. I have been looking for him since long before I came to this household. I have found him, and now I am baiting a trap for him. I need only a few words to do it, but they must be words in your hand."

"Then this person is someone I know?" Puzzlement was definitely giving way to horror now.

"He knows of you."

"Everyone in Rome knows of me!"

"You will be in no danger—"

"I'm in danger just by writing those words down!" *You have no right to ask this of me*, I nearly said—but I remembered the way my bodyguard had stepped between me and a French army, the way he had bled and screamed and nearly died for it. *He has the right to ask anything of me*, I thought, but this made me shiver. "If the wrong person saw this letter—"

"No one will. You have my word I will destroy your letter when it has served its purpose."

"And what purpose is that?" I stared at him helplessly. "Holy Virgin, Leonello—"

"Madonna Giulia." His voice cut me off, and his eyes were straight as a sword. "I have not asked for anything in all our acquaintance, and I would not ask this now if it were not . . ." He trailed off. I had never seen my bodyguard look so fierce, not even when he stepped between me and the French pike-men.

I hesitated. "If you could only tell me—"

"I can't." He massaged the stub of his missing finger, the finger that had had to be amputated after those same French pike-men stamped it into a broken mass of blood and bone shards. "Madonna Giulia . . . please?"

I'd never heard him say *please* before in my life.

He looked square into my eyes. "Do you trust me?"

The words came unthinking. "With my life."

"I assure you that if you put your honor in my hands, it will be equally safe."

I held his gaze a moment longer, and then I fetched my scented paper and sharpened a pen. I wrote the few brief sentences for him in my looping sprawl that had never managed to conform itself to the elegant formal hand that girls of rank were supposed to master, no matter how much I practiced. I folded the note and sealed it with the fragrant wax and personal seal that anyone close would know for mine.

"I do trust you, Leonello." I passed my bodyguard the note. "With my life *and* my honor. So I hope you know what you are doing."

He was utterly silent as he took the note from my hand.

Leonello

Night came swiftly over me in the Piazza degli Ebrei. A night darker than murder, and murder was common here where the streets sloped sharply away from the decent houses toward the foul, narrow quarters that were grudgingly given over to house the Jews. Ill deeds happened every night here, because the darkness pressed the eyes like black velvet and once dawn swept it away and revealed the bodies left behind, well, they could always be blamed on the Jews.

I stood in an inky pool of shadows, looking out over the *piazza* with a knife in each hand already drawn, to ward away any drunks or footpads who might decide I looked like an easy mark. But the drunks and footpads passed me by, staggering or slinking to their next drink or victim. It would be hours yet before I needed to draw blood. The trap had been laid and baited, and tonight the strings would begin to tug.

Pay attention, now.

Imagine a spacious villa on the Esquiline Hill. One of the fabled seven hills of Rome; Nero built his Golden House here, and another emperor built a bathhouse where the likes of Marcus Aurelius later sat in the steam and quipped in Latin. Today there were churches and shrines instead, and the bathhouses and Roman villas were all in ruins, but the hill was still a pleasant place with enough open spaces to build vineyards and rambling houses for those who didn't quite wish to leave Rome in order to get a taste of the country. Nothing but the best for Vannozza dei Cattanei, the Pope's thrifty former mistress, who knew that if she wished to scold her two eldest sons, she must promise to wine and dine them first. One or two other guests came to her pretty little villa near the church of San Pietro in Vincoli, but why bother listing them? They would not be important tonight.

Vannozza's sons: the swaggering young Duke of Gandia and the even more elegant young Cardinal Borgia, not trading much beyond sharp-edged pleasantries and dark looks, I imagined, but managing enough courtesy to please their mother. Vannozza herself: sleek and self-satisfied, if not as lovely as her successor, and she presided over her guests like one of those Roman matrons must have done in their own villas when Marcus Aurelius ruled this city rather than Rodrigo Borgia. An evening *cena* eaten outside in the summery green warmth of her little vineyard; elegant low tables and servants with flagons of wine; sweet music and low conversation among the guests; salads of endives and edible flowers, cold ox tongue laid in tissue-thin slices over vine leaves, grapes and melons and ices of the kind Carmelina would describe in loving detail.

Pay attention, now.

A masked man interrupted the evening briefly—a tall figure, broad and silent in black doublet and a cap in the Borgia colors of mulberry and yellow, a black mask below it covering his face. More men in masks; how they had haunted this whole bloody business, but in truth they were not so uncommon in the Holy City. Every lord who sent a gift to another man's wife or a bribe to an underling put his messenger in a mask; every boy trying to duck his tutors for a little after-hours hilarity did the same. At Carnivale, even the respectable in Rome went masked. My masked messenger made straight for the Duke of Gandia, who turned from the dark-haired beauty he was romancing and looked on irritably as a letter was presented. "I await your answer." The words came muffled behind the mask, and the Duke snorted as he broke the seal.

But his irritability faded fast, color rising in his face, as he saw what fell out of the folded paper, and he dismissed without another glance the piqued brunette he had been planning to bed that evening. "At nightfall," he told the masked man, who whispered some discreet directions and then took himself away. And when the Duke of Gandia seemed in high spirits for the rest of the evening, his mother pinched his cheek fondly and Cesare Borgia just sat back to watch.

"I don't know what you put in that letter, but it worked." Bartolomeo's freckled face appeared ghostlike in the air before me as he took off the mask. It was still not even twilight at that point in the night's narrative, and my accomplice lowered his voice from the passersby hurrying on their way home before dark. "The Duke of Gandia says he'll come at nightfall."

"Did he say anything else?"

"He said, 'I always knew she wanted me.' Who did he mean?"

"Never mind. You know where to wait; be ready when he splits from the others. Do you have the letter?"

Bartolomeo gave it back to me. *A good boy*, I thought. He looked drawn and nervous, but determined. I hoped he would not lose his resolve for tonight's work.

Silky purple dusk gave way to black velvet night. I slipped the letter in Giulia's writing back into my doublet. Now that it had served its purpose I'd destroy it, just as I promised her. I had not really thought she would write it for me—even with no signature and no name, any such note in the Bride of Christ's hand would have enraged the Holy Father. But she'd written it anyway when I asked—evidently my giddy little mistress really did trust me. I smiled at that thought as Vannozza dei Cattanei's elegant vineyard *cena* wound to a close, her guests departing with elaborate compliments to their hostess. The Borgia sons were last to leave, of course, lingering for motherly advice and motherly kisses. They departed together, side by side on a dark horse and a pale horse, a pair of stoutly armed squires behind them for guards.

"How will you get rid of the Duke's squire?" Bartolomeo had asked me when we planned this. "And the guards?"

"I'm to have this evening free, as I do all Wednesdays. Normally I stroll down to the printer's in the Borgo where I used to rent a room, to see what new books might have arrived, and I arrange an extra duty of guardsmen for La Bella's safety when I am gone. But this week—" I shrugged. "It slipped my mind. And by the time I looked to rectify my error, the other guardsmen were all assigned, so I was forced to suborn the Duke of Gandia's men instead, just this afternoon when he visited before departing to his mother's *cena*."

"And it worked?"

Of course it worked. I was a man of importance in the Palazzo Santa Maria, after all; I played *primiera* regularly with all the guards, who had come to regard me with a little amusement and more than a little trepidation. And since my authority when it came to La Bella's protection was paramount, and La Bella was still the Holy Father's most cherished possession outside his children, the Duke of Gandia's guards obeyed me without even a grumble.

"And Maestro Santini?" Bartolomeo had pressed. "How did you get him to stand in for the squire?"

"Easily. He's a big strapping fellow, more than adequate to act as a guardsman for a few short hours on a fine summer night. And he was already part of the Duke's entourage that evening. He often is, these days—the guards like him; they all play cards together. To make doubly sure of Marco's presence I'd discreetly tipped one of Juan's regular men to bring him along, pretending I wanted to settle a debt. Then one more bribe to Marco himself, and the deed was done. When did Marco Santini ever turn down money?"

"Sorry to inconvenience you." I'd grimaced as Marco took hold of the other guards' horses when they tramped off to guard La Bella under my orders, leaving the Duke of Gandia raging and spitting for his escort, Cesare making impatient noises about their mother expecting them, and Juan refusing to rely on Michelotto for his own safety, as that snake would likely put a knife in his back rather than guard it. Everybody had been scrambling to obey him, placate him, anything, and I'd taken a coin from my purse and shown it to Marco. "Can't you act the squire for *il Duche* tonight?"

"Me?" Marco looked down at me from his vastly superior height.

"I'm his *maestro di cucina*, not a squire. The guards only brought me along to finish out a *zara* game while they wait for him at Madonna Vannozza's house."

"So you've already left your kitchens behind for the night. It's not as if you have work to go back to." I looked at Marco, exasperated. "Look here, I'll pay you thirty *scudi* if you volunteer as his escort. I want him gone before he troubles my mistress again. He tried to kiss her last time he came here, and I didn't like the look in his eyes at all when she told him to get out."

Marco, of course, had heard nothing beyond "thirty *scudi*." He eyed the coins in my hand. "I'm not trained in the sword, you know . . ."

"Oh, all you cooks are lethal with your knives. Besides, don't you owe the Duke of Gandia a favor? Something to do with a long-legged girl he wanted? Surely you can guard his back for an evening."

Marco had flushed at that. "How did you hear about . . ."

"I hear everything. Apparently *you* haven't heard I was the one who rescued your cousin from the ducal affections. Things got a trifle . . . rough."

"I heard," Marco muttered. "I'm glad you—that is—"

I hadn't intended to raise the subject of Carmelina—it would be better if Marco Santini didn't connect me to her, not in any possible way—but I was too curious to keep from asking. And he, I thought, was too dense to give much thought to my curiosity, or to anything outside his cards and dice. "Why did you do it, Maestro Santini?"

"The Duke plays *zara* at the guardhouse, sometimes." Defensive. "I owed him money."

"You could have asked Madonna Giulia for the coin." I kept my own voice studiedly neutral. "I understand she has paid your debts before— or rather, Carmelina begged her for the money to pay your debts."

"The Duke didn't want money this time," Marco mumbled. "After the masquerade, seeing her in that costume . . ."

"He wanted those legs of hers, didn't he?" I gave a whistle. "And you didn't think she'd part them willingly, so you didn't bother telling her about this little arrangement you'd made with the Duke?"

"Now see here, I wouldn't do that to my own cousin. He just wanted a chance alone with her, that's all. Said he fancied her. If I could just make sure to get her some place quiet, he'd try offering her a little wine and a few pretty words, see if he had better luck."

"And you *believed* him?"

"Why not?" Marco gave a shrug. "People like us—if the great take a fancy, well, that's that. If she'd just gone along with him—"

"Women are so unreasonable," I agreed silkily.

"Besides," he burst out in a sudden eruption of spite. "She stole my *place*!"

"Mmm. Well, if you don't want that thirty *scudi* . . ."

He snatched the coins from my hand and took himself to the Duke, doffing his cap, and Juan Borgia was so impatient to be gone that he barely noticed who took the squire's place at his back. "Keep up, cook," he ordered, and was gone in a storm of hooves to his mother's villa, Cesare at his side looking back in the saddle to give me the faint flick of his smile.

But that was all this afternoon, hours ago. This was now, and night had fallen: a night without footsteps, a night when devils dance. I stood in my pool of shadows, fingering the blades I'd spent the day sharpening to a whisper's edge.

Marco Santini would be yawning now, riding beside silent Michelotto as they trailed their masters through the twisty nighttime streets of Rome away from Vannozza dei Cattanei's *cena*. I wondered if Marco was regretting this excursion; he should be in bed by now, dreaming of the day he'd win five thousand florins in one turn of the dice, and live like a lord all the rest of his days. Ahead of him, Juan and Cesare traded their usual barbed remarks, but finally they fell silent as they passed by the *palazzo* of one of the Sforza cardinals, scattering the nighttime traffic of beggars and drunks with lordly unconcern. Perhaps Cesare was tired, but Juan's eyes glittered in the dark as he looked around him. And the young Duke of Gandia laughed when he saw Bartolomeo step out of his own pool of shadows, face hidden again by the black mask.

"You go on," Juan Borgia said to his brother, and his voice rang excitement. "Go back to your priest's hole, brother; I've got other amusements waiting for me tonight. Prettier amusements than any you've ever had." He swung his horse about, a great pale beast with a white mane, and set off toward the Piazza degli Ebrei. Cesare looked after him for a moment, then shrugged and turned toward home with Michelotto trailing behind him. Good. I had not wanted to face Michelotto on this night's work. That was why I had angled so carefully to get Marco Santini to fill in for Juan's squire. I didn't want my careful attack complicated by any of Juan's hardened soldiers or professional guards; someone alert who could defend his master if things went wrong. A lazy substitute who could be easily distracted and separated from the Duke of Gandia; that was what I wanted.

In the darkness, I thought I could hear the distant ring of hoofbeats. What I *imagined* would turn soon enough into what I *saw*.

Pay attention, now.

Juan turned to Marco, still trudging dutifully along behind him. "Look here," the young Duke said, impatient, and now I could very definitely hear his words, indistinct through the dark as well as ice-clear in my mind. "You stay here, will you? I'll return in an hour."

"Your lordship," Marco began, eyes darting around him at the looming dark of the empty *piazza*. Of course, the night in this part of the city was never quite empty. There were always beggars and vagrants curled in gutters, pickpockets with little knives out for purses—and larger men with larger knives, looking for solitary travelers in the night.

"Wait an hour," Juan Borgia rode over Marco's voice. "If I've not returned by then, you have leave to return home."

"Yes, your lordship," Marco muttered, and I hissed silent satisfaction through my teeth. Any of Juan's usual squires or guardsmen would have insisted on following at a distance—would have insisted on doing their job. Not indolent Marco Santini, who was going to regret very much that he had taken my thirty pieces of silver.

Juan was looking about for Bartolomeo now, who stepped out of the shadows in his black mask.

"Ride ahead, your lordship," he said with a bow, taking care to keep his words low so Marco would not recognize a familiar voice. "Not too fast. You know the place. I'll double back, be sure you aren't followed."

The hooves of Juan's big horse clattered against the stones as he trotted ahead. I slid through the darkness to join Bartolomeo, who was already looking back to where Marco obediently loitered.

"There he is," I said. "Here's your chance. The Duke of Gandia will be out of earshot by now. Make sure you aren't recognized—"

But Bartolomeo was already moving, low and fast through the dark. I heard him draw a rasping breath, and then he flattened Marco Santini with one massive backhand blow.

This was the part of the plan I liked least, but Bartolomeo would not budge. He wanted to give Marco Santini a beating, and he wanted it done before we followed Juan Borgia. I didn't like the delay, but I needed Bartolomeo for what was to come next, and I did not think he would help me if I took his chance for vengeance away. That was something I understood well enough.

Grunts come through the dark, muffled swearing, gasps, short heavy blows that meant fists were finding ribs, and then the dull crunch that was the sound of a nose breaking. I hoped it was Marco Santini's. He might have been caught off guard, but he was still a big strong fellow, and I saw his fist glance off Bartolomeo's cheekbone. Bartolomeo's head snapped back, and his mask went flying.

Oh, *Dio*. I had a moment's hope that the dark would hide a familiar face, but—

"What are you doing, apprentice?" Marco slurred through bloody lips. Bartolomeo's face was just a pale smear in the dark, but there was no mistaking that bright hair, even in faint starlight.

"This is for Carmelina, you bastard," Bartolomeo growled back, and hit him again with another backhand swing of his doubled fist. I groaned inside, darting closer. Marco hadn't been supposed to see who attacked him in the dark, that had been utterly crucial—

"For *Carmelina*?" I heard Marco pant through the dark, shoving his former apprentice back. "Don't tell me the bitch is spreading her legs for pimply apprentice boys now—"

Bartolomeo just let out a snarl, coming for him again, and that was when I saw the flash of a knife in Marco's hand. "Blade!" I called through the dark, darting closer with my own blades. I'd put the big cook down myself if things turned ugly, regardless of whether it angered Bartolomeo. But the red-haired boy had already seized Marco's wrist, forcing the knife aside, and it flashed between them as they struggled. Blades in the dark now, instead of fists, and that changed the game.

I tensed, moving forward, but they were nothing but a lurching tangle of limbs in the shadows, no clear target to be had. I heard a hiss of pain, a lurch of boots and a scrabble of fingers skating across a knife hilt—and then the solid, punching thud of a knife finding its target. Bartolomeo gave a choked gasp, staggering. Marco reeled backward, giving a gurgling cough of his own, and in the faint light of the stars I saw him stumble and fall. There was another solid thud of skull against stone.

I lunged forward and caught the redheaded boy by the arm. "Are you hurt? Where did he hit you?" My heart thudded. *Dio*, to lose this chance for a boy's rashness—

"I'm not hit," Bartolomeo gasped, still reeling. His face was linen white in the dark. "Sweet Jesu, I stabbed him—"

I dove for Marco Santini then, finding his limp form. I had a blade in my fist, ready if he made a move for me, but the big cook lay limp under my searching hand. "Not dead," I called, making my examination by touch. I felt the stickiness of blood on his shirt, but the wide chest rose and fell raggedly. "You caught him in the gut with the knife, but he's alive." I felt my way over the fallen form, finding a swelling knot under the curly hair. "Knocked his head on the ground when he fell, it seems."

Bartolomeo's voice quivered with relief. "I didn't kill him?"

"No." Soundly unconscious, at least for now, but the knife wound— you could never be sure about wounds to the gut. I thumbed through calculations. Marco had recognized us, or at least Bartolomeo. If he died . . .

"What if he dies?" Bartolomeo echoed my thoughts, but almost certainly not for the same reasons. He gave a gulp of the foul night air, his hand stealing unconsciously to the wooden cross about his neck. He was a good boy, after all; he went to Mass weekly and did penance for his small sins with good cheer. He hadn't wanted murder on his conscience, because of course he found the thought appalling—as I no longer did. "I didn't mean—I never meant to stab Maestro Santini. I was only trying to get the knife away from him, but it twisted in his hand and I got it from him and he came at me—"

"He drew the blade on you, when you were unarmed and looking only to avenge a woman's honor with your fists. I'd say your conscience is clear." I rose, rubbing the cook's blood off on my breeches. "On your feet, now. Come along before we lose *il Duche* altogether."

"We can't—" Bartolomeo stared at me through the dark, hardly more than a black shape. "I'm not leaving an unconscious man to bleed to death!"

"He sold your girl to be raped by a madman," I said. "I'd leave him." Better if he died in the street, rather than lived to identify Bartolomeo as having any part in tonight's work.

"I won't leave him. I wanted to give him a beating, not kill him." Bartolomeo's voice was still shaky, but there was steel there and it made me start cursing inside as he took a breath and began to lecture me. "Marco Santini got a beating, all right. He got more than I bargained for, and I'll live with that, but I won't live with abandoning a wounded man in the middle of the slums to be robbed and murdered."

"We've no time for your conscience, boy!" I snarled. But Bartolomeo was already hoisting Marco Santini up over one shoulder like a dead pig bound for the spit. It would have been too much weight for most men, but the boy was fueled by fear and used to hauling carcasses through his lady love's kitchens, and as he staggered into the dark under the cook's heavy form, I cursed viciously and allowed myself a moment's violent envy that I had not been born so tall and strong. If I had been, I'd need no one's help to deal with Juan Borgia, much less a moonstruck apprentice too principled for his own good. Juan Borgia, my masked murderer, drawing farther away on his horse with every moment we wasted, approaching the trap I'd laid for him—I didn't mean to lose this chance just to make sure some gambling fool of a cook got a bandage and a cold compress.

Briefly I considered leaving Carmelina's apprentice to his idiotic chivalry. But like it or not, I hadn't been born a young giant with the muscles of a Hercules. For this night's work to succeed, I needed Bartolomeo.

It seemed an age to wait, but it was only moments before Bartolomeo came bounding back out of the dark, masked and anonymous again. "I left him at the nearest house," he panted. "Gave a knock, then stood back—I saw them pull him inside; they were calling for water and bandages. At least they'll see his wound tended, even if they summon the constables—" Bartolomeo bent over suddenly as though he felt sick. "Oh, Jesu, what if he dies? What if I killed him?"

"So what if you did?" I said coolly. "I'm more worried if he talks." The plan had been to let Bartolomeo beat Marco into the required pulp, and then let Marco run off ignorant of who had ever attacked him. I knew Marco Santini; he was far too yellow-bellied not to run if he was getting the worst of a pummeling. He'd have run off, and Bartolomeo and I would have been free to follow Juan Borgia with no one any the wiser about who had made both attacks.

But since he now knew Bartolomeo was neck-deep in tonight's work, I was improvising.

"We can't follow the Duke of Gandia now," Bartolomeo was groaning. "Marco will say I attacked him. When he finds out Juan Borgia was beaten, too, he'll assume I—"

"If Marco Santini lives, or at least lives long enough to talk, all he knows is that the Duke of Gandia left him to go see a mistress." I cut Bartolomeo off before he could panic any further. "And then you came along, and the two of you got into a fight over a girl. I'll act as witness, and threaten to have him arrested for drawing the knife on you. I'll threaten to get him hanged for attempting murder, unless he leaves Rome. He'll be too terrified to open his mouth about Juan Borgia."

"But—"

"No buts!" I should have been frightened—already the plan had deviated, and that wasn't good, but improvisation in danger had always been a gift of mine, and mainly what I felt was focus. I was coming for Juan Borgia, whether the plan blew apart or not. "You want to go back and fan Marco Santini's brow till he wakes up, boy?" I seized Bartolomeo's arm and lowered my voice to a steel-hard growl. "Or do you want a chance to beat the Duke of Gandia bloody, like we planned? We won't get another opportunity like this, so make up your mind!"

Bartolomeo gulped. "Blessed Mother of Mercy, forgive me," he muttered, crossing himself, but broke into a jog beside me as I plunged into the dark after Juan Borgia.

Good boy, I thought, but didn't say it.

The circuitous route Bartolomeo had given to the Duke of Gandia took him looping back on his own footsteps—an absurd route, really, but young men love to feel they are being covert. "Must make sure we aren't followed," Bartolomeo said through his mask when he whispered the directions, and the Duke had breathed, "Of course." Really the route was designed to buy time, time for us to deal with Marco Santini. We'd wasted more time than I liked; I had to run hard to close the gap, and the twisted muscles of my thighs stabbed like knives. But Juan Borgia rode on a long rein, taking his time on his ambling stallion, and though my heart throbbed in my throat, it wasn't long before we caught up with him. I would have been looking about me constantly in such dangerous streets, but Juan whistled a cheery little tune and never looked back to spot me sliding along through the shadows behind him like a fish. He was a dreaming idiot, and I dearly hoped no footpads would realize what an easy mark he was and take him down before I had my chance.

I heard Bartolomeo gasping at my side, and not because he was winded. "Santa Marta save me," he said in an unsteady voice. "I've never stabbed anyone before. I think I'm going to be sick."

"That usually happens, the first time." At least the boy was still here. He could have panicked at the unplanned bloodshed, stumbled off and left me to deal with the Duke of Gandia on my own, but he did not. I was beginning to have a certain regard for Carmelina's apprentice, who I suppose was now *my* apprentice, albeit in a darker trade than the whipping of egg whites and the kneading of bread dough. "Clamp your teeth down on the nausea, and let's close the gap on that horse," I whispered in brisk tones, and he obeyed me numbly. The numbness was common too, that first time one drew blood.

I hoped he would not have a second time. Far better this apprentice stuck with Carmelina's trade than mine.

Juan was fast approaching the place I wanted, the place where he thought he would get what *he* wanted. He was singing now under his breath, riding along on his pale horse as happy as a bridegroom to a much-desired bride, and in a way I suppose that was what he was. He had wanted her so long, after all. I'd seen the lust in his eyes as he took her in his arms in the courtyard and plastered his leech of a mouth over hers. She was the woman he couldn't have, and that made her even more irresistible than she already was. And of course, any man as vain as Juan Borgia assumes all women want him too, even if they protest the opposite. *I know what you want,* I'd heard him breathe in her ear even as she struggled. *You're too much for an old man, you're wet for something younger.*

When Juan Borgia broke the seal of the letter Bartolomeo passed to him in Vannozza dei Cattanei's vineyard, he'd have felt nothing but a thrill of triumph.

> *My love, I cannot resist you any longer—you have finally made me realize that. If you follow the man who gives you this letter, he will bring you to me tonight. We must be very cautious—but I must have you.*

Unsigned, but surely Juan would know Giulia Farnese's easy looping writing by now, her rose-imprinted seal, the familiar honeysuckle and gillyflower scent that breathed even from the writing paper she used. Even if those details escaped him, I'd added one final touch: one of Giulia's doeskin gloves, soft and perfumed and embroidered with her family crest, which I'd slipped into my sleeve when her back was turned and then added to the folded note.

Juan Borgia had recognized the glove the moment he saw it— Bartolomeo said the Duke had held it to his nose when he opened the letter at Vannozza's *cena*, held it and inhaled Giulia's scent. Not just the smell of honeysuckle and gillyflowers, but passion; the passion she brought to everything she did. It wafted from the glove, from the note she'd written; a passion to make the blood boil in any man's veins if he read the words on that scented page and thought they were meant for him. Never mind that she'd written those words under my direction with nothing but disquiet; the passion was still there. No wonder Juan Borgia sang under his breath as he went to cuckold his father.

He halted his horse, eyes searching through the dark for the door that Bartolomeo had described from behind his mask. A door with faded green paint, marking the entrance to a tall building with a sagging roof. Perhaps once a merchant's dwelling with a shop below and a place for wife and children and a servant or two above, but this quarter of the city had deteriorated, and now the house was divided into small apartments rented by the week, by the day, by the hour to whoever wished to flop there among the fleas. If Juan had a brain in his head, he'd wonder why Giulia Farnese had arranged an assignation in such a sinkhole, but fortunately for me, Juan Borgia did not have a brain in his head. And even if he did, I doubted his head was his primary working organ at the moment.

I saw a beggar limp past on a crutch, half visible in the light of the torch over the door. I'd put that torch there myself when I rented the room—or rather, when I paid a half-drunk fellow at a wine shop a few coins to rent it for me, as I had no intention of being remembered by the man who rented out the rooms.

"Giulia?" Juan called hopefully toward the door, halting his horse. "Are you already wet and waiting for me in there, my girl? You like it dirty, flopping down in a slum like this? If you want it filthy, wait till you see the things I can do to you—"

I hissed to Bartolomeo through the darkness. *"Now."*

Bartolomeo bounds forward with a great leap to Juan's side, seizing the Duke's booted leg in its stirrup. The knife he borrowed from me makes a slash in the dark and cuts the stirrup leather clear through, slashes the leg too from the surprised cry that rises from Juan. The stirrup falls, clanking on the slimy stones underfoot, and the Duke's balance is gone with it. He falls heavily, almost at Bartolomeo's feet, and Bartolomeo scrabbles to get a grip on his arms, but Juan is quick and lithe-muscled even if he is an idiot, and he is already rolling and reaching for the sword at his belt. Even Juan is not fool enough to go unarmed into these squalid streets; he sent Marco to bring his half armor before he even set out from his mother's villa on this journey that he assumed would end between the thighs of his father's mistress. He parries Bartolomeo away, staggering to his feet, and Bartolomeo's answering slash of the knife clangs off the breastplate beneath Juan's cloak. "Attack the Duke of Gandia, will you?" Juan hisses, and his sword whips toward Bartolomeo again.

Juan's torso might be well protected, but half armor does not cover the legs, and I am already moving around the startled horse in the crab-like scuttle that carries me with much speed if very little dignity. I hit Juan from behind with both blades drawn, slashing twice across the hamstrings and slashing deep.

Juan's voice scales upward in a howl as he collapses, blood spurting down his boots on each side. He does not know it, this arrogant young killer, but he will never walk again.

"Take his arms," I snap to Bartolomeo. "Drag him inside while I tether the horse and douse the torch. And *Dio*, will you stop his screaming?"

Darkness turns to light as we drag our victim inside the little rented room. Plans turn to action. And *can we do it?* turns to *it is done*.

Whenever I thought back to that little room afterward, I saw only the flare of light from the cheap tallow tapers I'd brought. Light flaring yellowly over an open hole of a mouth, and the bright spill of blood dripping steadily to the floor from the Duke of Gandia, who sat roped into the chair I'd brought at the same time as the tapers and the rope. Juan Borgia, terrified and furious and already in utter agony.

"*You twisted little bastard, I'll see you dead!*" he howled when he saw me come around the chair from checking Bartolomeo's knots and look him very deliberately in the eye. "*How dare you lay a hand on the Pope's son—*"

"What are you doing?" Bartolomeo whispered fiercely at me from behind his mask. "Bad enough Marco saw me—you insisted we couldn't show the Duke of Gandia who we were! You said we'd lure him here and blindfold him and give him a beating, but he couldn't know who it was. He recognizes you now, are you mad? He'll have you killed when we let him go—"

I spoke softly, under cover of Juan Borgia's raving. "Here's the part where I tell you I lied."

Bartolomeo reared back. "About *what*?"

"About letting him go."

Bartolomeo just stared at me through his mask, and I could see the white around his eyes through the eye holes. I looked at him a moment longer, waiting to see if he'd bolt and leave me now, but he continued to stand in horrified silence, and I shrugged and pulled up a chair before Juan Borgia. I listened to the Pope's son rant for a while, idly flicking my little finger knife back and forth, and when he showed no signs of stopping I slapped him casually across the face like a lackey. That seemed to shock him more than the blood flowing from his legs. He stared at me, and then he began to froth and threaten again. This time I whipped the blade about in a slash that opened a shallow six-inch cut across his thigh; Juan gave a scream, and I motioned Bartolomeo.

"Shut him up, will you?"

Bartolomeo didn't move. "What else did you lie about?"

"He's getting more than a beating, I can tell you that. He's going to answer some questions first."

"*Why?*"

"You're about to find out. Sorry to deceive you, but you wouldn't have helped me otherwise." I'd said very little of why I wanted revenge against the Duke of Gandia, only that I had my reasons, and Carmelina's would-be lover had been too focused on his own reasons for revenge to give a thought for mine. Nor had he questioned my glib assertions that all I intended for Juan Borgia was to drag him off his horse to a prearranged room where we could give him a swift and anonymous beating, and then let him go. "You're a good boy, but you still have things to learn," I told my apprentice kindly. "The next time someone talks you into violence, check *all* the details first. Now, kindly gag that monster in the chair and let me get to work."

I didn't know if Bartolomeo would do it—he looked ready to bolt, away from me and my dark lies and my even darker intentions. But I looked at my apprentice, and he looked at me through his mask, and then he came forward silently and stuffed a rag into Juan Borgia's mouth.

"Now, Gonfalonier," I said, rising from my chair. "No screaming, please. Few people bother answering screams in this quarter of the city, but I'm not taking any chances. We're going to have a long and uninterrupted chat, you and I. It's not how you anticipated spending the evening, I know." I shook my head at the stained walls, the warped boards of the floor, the sounds of barking dogs and muttering drunks coming through the bolted shutters. "And you thought Giulia la Bella would meet you in a place like this," I couldn't help saying. "Because you think she is just a whore, I suppose, and all whores of course like it dirty? *Dio*, it's a good thing the killer I was hunting turned out to be you instead of your brother. Cesare would never have been stupid enough to fall into such a trap."

"My brother—wait, what killer?" The young Duke's eyes narrowed at me after Bartolomeo took the rag away on my nod. "If you release me now—"

"Seven." I folded my arms again. Roped into his chair, Juan was shorter than I, and I took a perverse pleasure in the advantage of height.

"What?" He felt Bartolomeo pace behind his chair and twisted his head in a futile effort to see. "Seven what?"

"Seven girls, Juan Borgia. Seven at least here in Rome, and God only knows how many in Spain when you went to claim your bride. Seven girls staked to tables by knives through their palms. Raped. Their throats cut."

I saw the flare in his dark Borgia eyes. A flare of fright, but behind it something else. A furtive kind of greed, and I felt the familiar savage thrill bloom in my chest. *Yes*, I thought, *yes, oh yes*. I had not thought Juan Borgia had wits enough to get away with so many killings, or tastes twisted enough to move from simple rape to this kind of dark and compulsive murder—but I had been wrong. That furtive gleam in his eye had the base cunning of a rat, and a lust black enough to see a thousand girls staked and screaming on their backs beneath him.

So many wrong turns, but not now. Not now.

"Leonello?" Bartolomeo whispered. "What *is* this? There were more of them? More girls besides Carmelina who he—" But I paid no attention.

"I will make you a bargain, Juan Borgia." I rocked back on my heels, looking almost fondly at my precious, long-sought murderer. "I've no interest in the later girls; I didn't know a one of them. But the first was someone rather special to me, and I believe you will remember her too, because she was your first. No, don't argue. Not the first girl you ever bedded, I'll wager, but your first kill. That's why you botched it when you slashed her throat. Do you still think of her? Because she did take your virginity in another way, didn't she? She made you realize just how much you like the occasional spill of blood to go with that piss-poor stuff you spill between women's legs." I met his eyes. "Tell me her name, Juan Borgia. Tell me her name, and I'll let you go."

Juan licked his lips.

"Seven girls?" Bartolomeo whispered. *"Seven?"*

"Staked down," I said without shifting my eyes from Juan. "When I walked in to see him putting a knife through Carmelina's palm, I knew."

"I don't know what you're saying." But Juan Borgia's eyes flicked, and then he screamed again because a knife flashed out and tore a great slash through his cheek. Not my knife—this one was clutched in Bartolomeo's fist, and it mirrored the triple slash of faint scabbed lines still visible on Juan's cheek where Carmelina had raked him a little over a week ago.

"Tell me!" Bartolomeo roared, and tore off his mask.

"Yes, do tell." I pulled up my chair and sat down as Juan shrieked again, from the pain of his cheek and his thigh and the agony of his hamstrung legs, which had already bled a pool around his feet. "Tell me why you feel the need to stake women through the hands before you kill them. Tell me how many you killed in Spain. Or just tell me the first one's name, and I'll let you go."

It was a messy, bloody business. I asked questions and Juan answered them, and whenever he balked I calmly opened a slash in his arm or put a blade through his hand in imitation of the stakings he'd dealt out so many times. Bartolomeo threw up twice in the corner, but he stayed, stayed with horror in his eyes. I could see an even greater horror growing in Juan Borgia's gaze, every time I cut him. The horror of knowing that his father could not save him, his position and birth could not save him, his money could not save him. That nothing could save his brash and privileged life from the implacable vengeance that was me.

He was screaming at the end, bleeding from four more wounds I'd dealt out in shallow and controlled fashion over his arms and legs and hands whenever the answers slowed. But for the most part, the answers came quickly. Yes, he liked killing girls. He killed the first because she fought too hard, because he was too drunk to finish the job between her legs and too humiliated to let her walk away knowing she'd unmanned him. He killed the others because—well, that part was less clear. He began to sob then, and his words came more and more indistinctly. He killed girls when drink made him incapable, when he was angry over some insult or failure, if the girl was ugly, or if he knew no one would miss her. One girl he had killed with his brother's dagger, simply to spread ugly rumors about Cesare—a going-away present to his older brother, right before leaving for Spain. He thought he had killed three or four in Spain; he couldn't remember. And no, he had no idea who had killed the girl who died when La Bella and I had been in the hands of the French, and Juan himself had been in Spain.

"Pity," I said, and filed that mystery away for another day.

Bartolomeo stared at the Duke of Gandia in utter revulsion. Juan Borgia was still weeping, tears dripping down to mix with the blood on his face. He'd long since soiled himself; piss and shit mingled with blood on the floor. "Why?" Bartolomeo whispered, clutching at the crucifix about his neck as though fending off a devil. *"Why?"*

But I didn't care much *why*. Never had. Even when I hadn't known the man I was hunting was Juan Borgia, I knew Anna's murderer had killed her and all the others because he wanted to.

Because he liked it.

"Please, little man, please, I won't do it anymore, I won't do it, I swear, and I swear I won't say a word about you, if you'll just let me go—"

"Do you remember the first girl's name?"

His head drooped. "No," he whispered, and I still felt not one drop of pity.

Bartolomeo was white as a bowl of milk, and I rose from my chair on legs that had gone stiff, and drew him to one corner. "Wait outside, boy," I said quietly.

"No." Bartolomeo's voice was just a thread, but a steady thread. "He wouldn't just have raped my Carmelina—he'd have killed her. Like the others. I owe him for more than I thought." A flick of a glance at me. "And you."

I liked him for it, and I felt sorry because I could see the revulsion in his eyes when he looked at me, me and my bloody hands, and I could tell he wouldn't forgive me at the end of this night's grisly work. He might well hate me.

"So be it."

I turned back to the sobbing, bleeding wreck that was the Duke of Gandia, the Gonfalonier of the papal forces, Pope Alexander VI's most beloved son. "Juan Borgia," I said quietly, "look at me."

He lifted his head, sobbing. He had been handsome, but he was not handsome now, blood on his cheek mingling with sweat and tears, his auburn hair hanging in limp strings over his eyes. "I'm sorry," he choked. "I'm *sorry.*"

"You're sorry you were caught," I said. "And her name was Anna."

With that, I cut his throat.

CHAPTER TEN

*The Pope is a carnal man
and very loving of his flesh and blood.*

—CARDINAL ASCANIO SFORZA

Giulia

I had never seen my Pope more frightened. In fact, I had never seen him frightened at all. I had seen him raging, passionate, frustrated, amused—but never one whit terrified by anything that God or Fortune had ever thrown into his path.

"Juan would have sent word by now." Rodrigo could not keep still. He flung himself into his carved chair; he rose again to pace across the Sala dei Santi, he paused with a jerk to finger an exquisitely engraved astrolabe in brass and gold sitting on a small table, and then he was pacing again. But over and over his eyes went to Pinturicchio's fresco on the wall overhead—the disputation of Santa Caterina, where a grandly turbaned figure on a horse oversaw the saint's pleading with the fixed and arrogant face of Juan Borgia. "He would have returned by now, or he would have sent word! To have him disappear like this, and not *one* of his men knowing where—"

"It wouldn't be the first time Juan lost himself sporting all night, and then slept all the next day." I reached up from my chair to touch Rudrigo's arm. "Cesare did say Juan was going to some woman after leaving Vannozza's *cena*. Isn't he very taken with that new Milanese girl, Damiata?" I tried to coax a smile. "You should be glad he's developed enough sense not to be seen leaving a courtesan's house in the middle of the afternoon! He was just waiting for night to fall, for discretion's sake." *As though Juan were ever discreet*, I thought, but did not say it. My Pope needed soothing, not more causes to worry. I couldn't really manage to worry about Juan, but this absence was rather strange.

"But his horse—"

"Horses stray, everyone knows that." Juan's horse had been found by the papal soldiers Rodrigo had dispatched to search for the Duke of Gandia—just the horse, which would not have been so unsettling if the great stallion had not been found with one stirrup cut away and a splash of blood on its flank. Not horse blood, either, because the horse was uninjured. But I gave my Pope as reassuring a smile as I could muster. "Someone no doubt tried to steal the horse when Juan left it tied for the night, and it got loose. How many horses has Juan managed to lose this year, after all?" Usually by riding them until they dropped, and of course there was the one pretty little mare whose throat he'd cut with his own dagger because she had the temerity to throw him off in front of his soldiers . . . but Juan *did* have a fair number of horses stolen, since he could rarely be bothered to tie them properly, much less stable them.

"But we were supposed to meet today, to discuss the campaigns I've planned in Romagna!" Rodrigo burst out. "Even if he were dallying with some woman, even if he lost his horse and went looking for another, he would not have left me waiting with no explanation!"

Cesare looked up from the elaborate globe in the corner, where he had been fingering the etched coasts of the new land that Genoese sailor had discovered. Much of what we knew of Juan's latest activities came from Cesare: his brother's high spirits at Vannozza's *cena*, the masked man who had come to deliver a message, the way he split from Cesare on the ride home and rode off toward the Piazza degli Ebrei, leaving his squire behind. "You have never worried overmuch when I kept you waiting, Holy Father," Cesare murmured.

"Bah, you never forget yourself when dallying with women." Rodrigo gave a distracted clap of the hand to his eldest son's shoulder, and

Cesare's immobile face looked more masklike than ever. He had a hard tension running through him like a strand of fire, a tension that made me wonder if he just might have planned a beating or some other unpleasant surprise for his brother. But Cesare had been fully accounted for the rest of the night after Juan rode off, playing cards until dawn with Michelotto and some of his other soldiers. And if Cesare ever came to blows with his brother, I knew he'd do it himself and not hire bravos.

I wondered if my Pope would ever bring himself to think the same thing. If he did, he'd never speak the words aloud. *He'll never admit the thought that* la familia *could ever turn on each other.*

"Perhaps an accident in the slums . . . I swear, I'll have that rat's nest by the Piazza degli Ebrei swept clean after this!" Rodrigo swept a hand back through his graying hair, and I found myself wondering if it was grayer than it had been. I was so used to seeing my Pope as invincible, confident as Alexander the Great, from whom he had taken his papal name. Perhaps only when he was worrying so visibly could I see any signs that he was old.

He looked older still when nervous little Burchard burst in. "Your Holiness, something has been found—"

"Juan is hurt?" Rodrigo's face drained.

"No, he is still—unaccounted for. But his squire has been found. Or to be precise, the man who was acting as his squire." Burchard addressed his words to the woven carpet. "That man was found stabbed last night."

"Last night?" Cesare's voice lashed like a whip crack. "And only now are we hearing of this?"

"He was found stabbed, unconscious but still alive . . . he had been dragged to the nearest house, but the household was too frightened to make any report to the constables until day had risen. By then, the man was dead." Burchard cleared his throat; the sound fell like a stone into the room. "It appears he died without saying a word—about the Duke of Gandia, or who attacked him. Them, I mean. Attacked them." A sigh. *"Gott im Himmel."*

Rodrigo went so gray that I ran to his side, but Cesare got there first.

"We will keep searching, Father," he said, gripping his father's arm in steel fingers. "I'll have my own men out, down to the last page boy. We will find my brother, but you should rest."

My Pope hardly seemed to hear him. Cesare looked over at me, command in his eyes as though he addressed one of the papal guards. "Take my father to bed and keep him there," he ordered me. "Allow no one to disturb him, for any reason—not until I send word, and I won't unless we find my brother."

I found myself nodding tersely.

"Sweet Christ—" Cesare made the same gesture his father had, rubbing a hand over his hair, only his hair was still auburn and vigorous. "My idiot brother. As many enemies as he's made, and he goes haring off alone into the night with a man in a *mask*? What possible temptation could have made him act such a fool?"

A cool little voice suddenly echoed through my head. *I am looking for a man*, it said. *I have found him, and now I am baiting a trap for him.*

My palms began to sweat. But I pushed the voice away, leading my stunned and frantic Pope back to his private chamber, where I disrobed him, soothed him, whispered hopeful nothings, listened to him fret, and finally coaxed him off to sleep with his head on my breast. Where I lay all through the night, as Cesare's men and the papal guards tore the city apart looking for Juan, and I stared into the dark thinking unimaginable things.

It was afternoon the following day before we heard more.

"Your Holiness," the man whispered, crashing to his knees the moment he laid eyes on my Pope. A common man in a dirty linen shirt and sturdy breeches, deeply tanned from a life spent under the sun, rough-voiced and rough-handed and plainly terrified. His wide eyes darted from the rich mosaics to the Moorish designs about the frescoes, the exquisite ornaments of silver and gilt and fragile glass to the papal guards standing huge and immobile at the doors. Cesare stood just as silent in his cardinal's robes, impassive of face, glittering of eye, one long finger tapping his own elbow. Joffre and Sancha had arrived and stood pressed together in unaccustomed accord, Joffre frightened and trying not to show it, the Tart of Aragon looking almost tearful for her brother-in-law and sometime lover. I stood by my Pope, his hand closed in both of mine—and to a common man like the one staring up at us, the Pope with his magnificent robes and sunken-eyed fear would have been most terrifying of all.

Rodrigo's voice was only a whisper. "Rise."

The man rose, visibly trembling. "I'm Giorgio Schiavi, I am—I didn't do no wrong—"

"Occupation?" Burchard interrupted, pen poised. Johann Burchard always looked relieved when the world slowed enough so he could take proper notes. I was glad to see someone here was soothed.

Giorgio Schiavi twisted his cloth cap between his hands. "Timber merchant."

Wood seller, in other words. "You are safe here, *poveruomo*," I said softly, and he threw me a startled grateful glance as he spoke again.

"I get my wood unloaded from boats in the Tiber," he began, eyes flicking about the *sala* again. "By the hospital of San Girolamo degli Schiavoni. I keep watch over my wood at night—terrible rough it can be down there, thieves everywhere looking to rob an honest man. At midnight two nights back, I see two men come to the riverbank—checking to see that everything was clear, that nobody was watching. They didn't see me, did they? I know how to get out of the way . . ."

My Pope looked on steadily, but his profile looked somehow shrunken to me. Gaunt.

"Two more men, they do another sweep—and then a man on a horse comes along. Big white horse, it was, and it's got a body draped across the saddle. Feet on one side, the head dragging along the other."

Rodrigo's hand jerked in mine.

"They pull the horse up, right near where I'm hiding, and I'm hiding by now, Your Holiness. Hiding and praying. There's a spot where the sewers come into the water, it's full of rubbish . . . they drag the body off the horse, and they give a great heave and into the river it goes." Giorgio Schiavi licked his dry lips. "The man in the saddle, he asks if the body's been sunk. They all say 'Yes, my lord'—he sounds like a lord, you know. I didn't get a look at his face, but he speaks good. Even though he's a small man in that saddle compared to them, they look at him like he's the one giving the orders."

I was the one to start trembling then. *Oh, sweet Holy Virgin*—but I firmly shut away all thoughts of the utterly impossible.

"The body's gone down," the wretched wood seller yammered on, "but his cloak's still floating. So they throw stones at it till it's gone too, and then they leave." Sancha of Aragon gave a great sob, clutching Joffre's arm, and our witness came to a halt. "That's all," he mumbled. "Your Holiness."

"Why did you not report this?" Cesare said in his velvety voice.

For the first time, Giorgio Schiavi looked too startled to be afraid. "I've seen a hundred bodies dumped there," he said. "Until today, when guards came about asking for any information on murders done that night—that's the first time anyone's made inquiries about any of them."

"Dumped," Rodrigo echoed. His eyes stared at the carpet, seeing nothing. "They *dumped* him there, with the rest of the sewage. Like my son was trash—"

"We don't know that." I folded my poor Pope in my arms, not caring when I heard Burchard's click of the tongue for Rodrigo's papal dignity. "We don't know it was Juan, you heard Messer Schiavi, a hundred bodies have been put into that river—"

"We'll have the Tiber dragged at once." Cesare was snapping orders to the guards. "Summon every fisherman and boatman who can be found. Ten ducats to the man who brings up the body—you'll see, Father, surely it won't be Juan—"

Sancha was crying noisily now. Joffre tried to comfort her and she struck at him. My Pope was shaking in my arms, shoulders heaving under his cope, and silly Burchard was still taking notes as though that would put everything right. Poor Giorgio Schiavi looked about him with open mouth. When a wood seller imagines the glories of the Vatican, the illustrious dignity of God's Vicar on earth, I doubt he imagines anything like this. "Thank you, Messer Schiavi," I said, disentangling myself from Rodrigo for a moment and ushering the poor wood seller out through the chaos. "Your loyalty and honesty will not be forgotten."

I pressed all the coins I had into his hands and flew back into the *sala*. "We will all pray," I said, and no one could hear me over Sancha's wailing so I gave her a good slap. Why not, she'd already hit Joffre and he wasn't making any noise to speak of. That shut her up, and I clapped my hands.

"We shall all pray," I repeated, taking out the rosary beads in black amber and gold that my Pope had given me at Easter, and slowly other voices joined mine in saying the Rosary. *"Credo in unum Deum, Patrem omnipoténtem, factorem cæli et terræ—"* I gulped out the words, suppressing the tears that wanted to follow them, because I loathed Juan Borgia but I wanted him to live. I could not bear the terrible, frozen grief on his father's face, so I bowed my head over my rosary and prayed to the Mother of Mercy that my Pope's most beloved son was alive.

But the Mother of Mercy was not merciful that day. Because as the bells for Vespers were ringing over the city a few hours later, tolling so sweetly they caught at the heart, the Tiber gave up her dead and Juan Borgia was dragged from the water.

They took him to the fortress of the Castel Sant'Angelo, to be washed and dressed in his military finery. "We should wait," Cesare said, stone-faced as ever. "We should wait until he is tended, Your Holiness." But my Pope just gave one great cry, a cry that split me like a sword, and rushed from his private apartments.

"Sweet Christ," Cesare said viciously. "I didn't want him to see Juan this way—stabbed nine times—"

"Nine?" I whispered, but my feet were moving, everyone's feet moved, and papal guards closed about the whole party of us as we followed the Holy Father to the Castel Sant'Angelo. I had been inside that gloomy papal fortress before, looking down from its great crenellated walls over the lake of surcoats and pike points and lily-strewn flags that had been the French army—but my Pope had been laughing then, making nothing of the trials ahead of him and scheming with great good cheer how he would make this army melt away, bend to his bidding, wish they had never crossed him. Now there was no laughter—only the Holy Father's piercing cry again, followed by hoarse, wailing sobs as I crossed into the chapel where the servants had laid out the corpse of the

Duke of Gandia. I could not see Juan's face, or his terrible mutilated body—only one limp white arm, trailing loose from its bier as my weeping Pope gathered his son up into his arms and rocked him like a child.

"Rodrigo—" I did not try to touch him, but he still struck at me as I approached, burying his head in Juan's torn and waterlogged chest. Juan's limp hand brushed my skirt, and I stepped back with a cry of my own. The palm had been torn open, pierced through by a dagger, leaving a great jagged wound. The river had washed it clean and bloodless, or else it could have been the hand of Christ upon His cross.

I became dimly aware that Cesare was ordering everyone out in a voice like ice. I cast a look at Rodrigo, but he was still weeping, still cradling his dead son tenderly to his chest, and I felt my eyes sting. I turned to go, but Cesare stopped me on the threshold of the chapel, waving the others on. "Giulia," he said, "I have a task for you."

I nodded dumbly, still deaf to anything but those terrible sobs in the chapel.

"I ask you to tend my sister," Cesare said, and I saw the softening in his face that I always saw when he mentioned Lucrezia. No wonder the nasty-minded gossips of Rome thought the love he bore her was some perverse thing—he had no love for anyone but Lucrezia, and love in a man as cold as Cesare was such a miracle that surely people would think it a profaned miracle. "I won't have her hearing of our brother's death from strangers," Cesare continued. "Will you travel to the Convent of San Sisto, to give her the news?"

"But His Holiness . . ."

"His Holiness will not want you for now," said Cesare. "He will not want anyone."

"I can't leave him in this grief!" The howls from the chapel tore at me like claws. "I'll wait here outside the doors all night if I must, but surely I should be here when he needs me—"

"I'll tell him you've gone to Lucrezia; he'll understand that. And besides, better to leave him for a time than to let him realize you are not particularly sorry Juan is gone."

"I don't—"

"Speak truth. It's my father you grieve for, not my brother."

I looked at Cesare, holding himself as calmly as ever. "I don't think you're terribly sorry about Juan either," I heard myself remarking with a ludicrous numb candor. I felt as though I were floating above the ground, wrapped in wool away from anything that was real. "How long will it be before you start angling to put away your cardinal's hat and help yourself to all Juan's military posts?"

"A month or two," Cesare returned, unruffled, and I shivered at his calm. "But until then, I can pretend sadness for my father. You aren't very good at pretending, Giulia, and I don't want him to remember your lack of any real grief later, and resent you. Better you come rushing back in a few days to console him, once he realizes he needs consolation, and he will welcome you as a balm and not a reminder. I will be counting on you, then, to help put him back together."

"How clever," I said. I didn't like Cesare, but I could see the sense of what he said. Besides, I had no energy to refuse him. "I'll go to Lucrezia at once."

"Set off tomorrow at dawn," Cesare said. "The streets will be too wild to travel tonight. Now, she'll want to come back with you, but see she stays where she is. If murderers struck down Juan, I want Lucrezia kept safe behind convent walls."

I turned to take myself home, wincing again as I heard the weeping from behind the chapel door. *My poor Pope*, I thought, and Cesare was right. Juan's death grieved me only for the sorrow it gave Rodrigo. And I thought there would be a good many in Rome to echo that sentiment, no matter what pious platitudes were uttered in the days to come.

Though I did almost come to tears that evening when I saw the torchlit procession that took Juan from the Castel Sant'Angelo to the Church of Santa Maria del Popolo, where (Joffre had told me, through tears that made him look ten years old again) their weeping mother Vannozza had already made arrangements for Juan's burial. Juan in his gaudy Gonfalonier's finery, borne along on a bier surrounded by two hundred torchbearers, his household guards and his military officers, and his crowd of swaggering young Spanish bravos who trailed along now with their fine tail feathers draggled in the dust. I saw one of Juan's little Spanish dwarves trotting along in the jam of the household that followed the bier. Juan had brought a great many dwarf jesters with him from Spain, liking to dress them in motley and set them beating each other with blunted clubs for the amusement of his soldiers after dinner. But this dwarf was toddling after the bier now, scrubbing at his eyes, and I wondered if he was crying for his master or for the position he'd lost. Somehow I doubted it was Juan. . . . The whole procession was ringed by Spanish guards, staring out murderously into the Roman crowd with their blades drawn, but there was no violence—only wailing, and a great unease.

I could see Juan's profile, wax-pale in the light of the torches held over his bier, and his still face had a beauty that stabbed me. A beauty it had never had in life, when any good looks he possessed were gilded by arrogance and vanity and fatuous pride. I could not help but wonder if he could ever have looked as pure and peaceful in life as he did on his bier.

Maybe if he had not been born a Borgia, I thought, and shivered.

Nine knife wounds, to the limbs and body and throat. Nine, and the money not even taken from his pouch. A purse full of gold ducats, far more than a laboring man could earn in a year. Whoever had killed him . . .

"My carriage is arranged for dawn?" I checked with the stewards when I arrived back at the Palazzo Santa Maria. "Good. Can you send Leonello to me, please?" He hadn't accompanied me to the Vatican to wait with Rodrigo; he often didn't, as there were papal guards there to see to my protection. But he always came bounding up as soon as I returned to the *palazzo*, tapping his latest book against the outside of his leg, one finger marking the page where he'd left off—and tonight, I didn't see him. "I want to speak with him at once," I said, and suppressed a shudder. If I could speak the terrible suspicions that lurked somewhere in the base of my throat.

"There'll be no speaking to Messer Leonello tonight, Madonna Giulia." The steward lowered his voice. "Dead drunk, he is. Staggered in an hour ago, and he's still sleeping it off. Not like him, is it?"

"No," I said, and went to my chamber where I lay down fully clothed and spent another sleepless night contemplating unspeakable things.

Carmelina

In a cook's world, and indeed with much of the world, the day divides itself sensibly: that is to say, around meals. The morning, for market and preparation and planning the day's menus. When the noon sun climbs, it's the bustle of *pranzo* that marks the change. Then *cena*, marking the sun's descent, then the scouring and cleaning of the kitchen, at which point the day is at an end.

For a nun, life is governed by bells. Bells at midnight, then at dawn, then regularly through the day, interrupting you the moment you get into a decent rhythm of work, all the way to Vespers and Compline after sunset when all you can do is look at the broken intervals of the day and the utter lack of any properly completed tasks, and stagger off to bed to do it all again in the morning. And the next morning, and the next and the next and the next, because a nun has nothing to look forward to for the rest of her life but bells.

At least I could ignore the bells now. I was no lay sister anymore who had to lay down my ladle and go hastening off to prayers. I had been brought to serve the Countess of Pesaro, who had a suite of rooms in the gatehouse and certainly required to be served. She did not have to attend prayers and neither did I; I could just keep chopping away in the kitchens as the lay sisters straightened veils and wimples and fluttered away like magpies. But the bells got into my head anyway, the placid silvery rhythm reverberating about the inside of my skull, and I don't know how many times I bent over the chopping block once I was blessedly alone and clapped my hands over my ears, trying to persuade myself that the walls were *not* moving in on me, they were *not*. "I'm going mad," I told Santa Marta, whose hand I once more carried about in a pouch beneath my skirt, because in a convent there was no bloody privacy. "Only ten days here, and I'm already going mad."

Her gold ring seemed to gleam at me in sympathy.

At least you're safe here, I told myself firmly—and that at least was true. No matter how many times I woke with a shudder as I imagined Juan Borgia's hands flinging me down on my own trestle table, I knew he would not find me here. The Convent of San Sisto was a worldly place—half the young choir nuns who giggled with Lucrezia and tried on her lip rouge were no more devoted to serving God than any bored girl who spends Mass making eyes at all the men. But even at a convent like this where the rules were lax and the prioress inclined to be indulgent when her richer-dowered novices wore silk petticoats and lilac scent, men were not allowed to stay. The Pope himself had sent a few guards to hammer on the convent gates a few days after Lucrezia arrived, being a trifle irate that his daughter had flounced off to a convent without asking his august permission first, and they had been firmly turned away like any unwanted suitor. So I had no fear that Juan would appear in these kitchens with his leer and his breath that smelled like wine and blood. Even if he came to see his sister, he would be allowed only a brief visit with her in her borrowed *sala*. He would certainly not be allowed to roam about the convent looking for a conquest—should it even occur to him to come looking for me at all. I was safe.

Still, safety was starting to seem a high price to pay for such maddening tedium. I had managed the vast kitchens of an even more vast *palazzo*, with dozens of people under my direct command and dozens more hopping to the sound of my voice—and now I had a drafty gloomy kitchen with a cistern that leaked, a hearth that smoked, and no hands to help prepare *cena* but my own (one of those hands still throbbing too much to be useful). In the Palazzo Santa Maria I had enjoyed a chamber all to myself, even if a small one—and now I shared an even smaller cell in the gatehouse with Pantisilea, who didn't have any men to sneak off and seduce so I could have the room to myself. Working for Madonna Giulia I had served banquets to hundreds, and the most illustrious guests in Rome, too—and now I had only a few dishes to prepare each day, whatever struck the young Countess of Pesaro's fancy.

"You could always whip off a few *tourtes* if you're feeling bored," one of the other lay sisters said hopefully. "The choir nuns, they're all mad for anything sweet. You should see the frenzy whenever anyone gets any good sugar for a *crostata*—"

"No," I said, and they didn't press me. The lay sisters stayed well out of my way; I had full run of the dank little kitchen and no one talked to me while I was in it, which suited me very well indeed. But after a week I could have used *someone* to talk to. Madonna Giulia swinging her little slippered feet at my table and giving her golden peal of a laugh, maybe. Or Bartolomeo. I could have asked him whether he had tried making those fried tubers again for that Neapolitan lord, Vittorio Capece. Or I could have asked him what he had thought when I told him I was a nun . . . if he thought anything at all. If he had any sense, he'd banish all thoughts of me from mind and move his affections to a girl he could actually marry.

Still, I was thankful he'd freed me from having to prepare *cena* that last night at the Palazzo Santa Maria. I'd slept so very long and well—nowadays all my nights were interrupted by *bells*.

I'd worked myself into such a fit of the sulks by the time Sunday approached, I paid no attention to the clatter of hooves and carriage wheels that sent all the nuns flocking to see who approached the gate-house. Who cared if the nuns had travelers begging a night's stay, or if the Countess of Pesaro had summoned some vivacious friend like the Tart of Aragon or that self-important Caterina Gonzaga to lighten her growing boredom? I wouldn't be able to cook anything for them; nothing decent, anyway. "Call this olive oil?" I muttered, and dumped a vicious dram of it into the bowl.

"Is there balm in Gilead, *Signorina Cuoca*?" a familiar voice said from the door. "Or at least balm for a small man's aching head?"

I dropped my ladle into the bowl in surprise. "Leonello?" Spinning about. "What are you doing here?"

"Madonna Giulia has come to call upon the Countess of Pesaro, with some rather somber news. Where my lady goeth—" He shrugged, leaning up against the door frame to the small courtyard.

A pimply young lay sister whom I'd set to whipping egg whites stared covertly at him over her bowl, and Leonello stared back at her until she looked away. "Shoo," he said, and flapped a hand at her. "Or I'll eat you." She fled with a squeak, and so did the sturdy, boot-faced woman whom I'd never once seen parted from the ever-simmering community stew since I arrived.

"There," said Leonello, swinging inside. "Alone at last."

I laughed, surveying him. He pulled a rickety chair over to the trestle table and hopped up, feet swinging as insouciantly as always, but his face looked sunken and grained, and his black cap was tilted well forward over his eyes. "Are you suffering from the effects of too much wine?"

"This morning I was vomiting from the effects of too much wine." He removed his cap with care, stubby fingers gingerly massaging through his dark hair. "Mere suffering seems a great improvement."

"Chilled lemon water," I said briskly. "Nothing like it for a sore head. Not that they have lemons here, or even water that I'd care to serve my guests. So—" I uncorked a jar with a cross carved into it. "Communion wine."

"Stealing from this convent too, now?" Leonello winced at the thump of the jar on the table as I put it before him.

"I robbed a reliquary from my last convent," I said after making absolutely certain the two lay sisters weren't eavesdropping outside in the courtyard. "You think I would balk at communion wine?"

Leonello managed a grin. "Can you possibly be bantering with me, Suora Carmelina? You haven't spoken a word to me in years except to scratch and spit."

"Any man who comes to my rescue with knives drawn must be viewed in a better light," I informed him. "Even if he does know every secret I have."

He studied me. "I would not have told, you know. I did like to torture you with it now and then, but as for truly giving you away?" A shrug. "Even I am not so cruel as that."

I looked at him, my little adversary sitting with elbows propped on the trestle table and his chair tilted back on two legs, hazel eyes serious under cocked black brows. He looked small and wry and unexpectedly kind, not at all as sinister as I'd first found him. And though he was far beneath my eye level as usual, his broad-chested, big-headed little figure in its plain black had more quiet authority than Juan Borgia ever had in his most swaggering finery.

"I am sorry, you know," I told him, and didn't mind the apology. "That I was so prickly with you, and for so long. I misjudged you."

"Most people do. You at least did not misjudge me as a drooling idiot or some fool in motley. For that"—raising his cup—"I thank you."

I gave him an answering grin, wondering if we might have cleared the distrust away for good, and retrieved my ladle and bowl. "So?" I asked as he drank an abstemious mouthful from his jug. "What brings Madonna Giulia here? And why aren't you with her instead of putting your feet up in my kitchen?"

"She has gone to see the Countess of Pesaro in private." Leonello tilted the jug, looking down into it. "To tell her, in fact, that her brother is dead."

I stopped stirring, feeling my mouth grow dry all at once. "Which brother?"

Leonello looked at me straight. "Juan."

I dropped my ladle for the second time as I made a grab for the edge of the table to steady myself.

"Sit down, dear lady." Leonello pushed a stool out for me with one booted foot, and by the time I was seated with a cup of that thin communion wine in my own hands, he'd outlined the bare and brutal details of the Duke of Gandia's death.

"Stabbed *nine* times?" I shivered. "Someone wanted him very dead."

"They did," Leonello said.

I eyed him. "Any ideas who . . ."

"Take your pick of enemies. Rome is swarming with rumors." Leonello waved a hand. "The Orsini, for his attacks on their lands? The Sforza, for the slight done to the soon-to-be-annulled Count of Pesaro? The Count of Pesaro himself, to punish His Holiness for this attempted annulment?"

"Leonello—"

"Or perhaps we must look closer inside the family. There was no love lost between Juan and Cesare, as all Rome knows. Or Juan and Joffre, who could perhaps have been more angry than we all thought about Juan bedding his wife." Leonello looked thoughtful. "Though if Joffre is that angry to be cuckolded, he'll have to wipe out Cesare next, which would be considerably more difficult. And after Cesare, the whole papal guard, most of the palace pages, and everyone else to whom Sancha of Aragon has given her kisses and her greedy little hands. Even myself."

"You? And the Tart of Aragon?" Even with my head still reeling from the news, I couldn't help but make a face. "I thought you had better taste."

"Fortunately for me, her taste runs to the exotic. Even as far as the deformed and short-statured." Leonello waved the Tart of Aragon away with one hand. "Back to Juan. There are, of course, all those outraged husbands and fathers out for his blood, the ones who had to console weeping wives and despoiled daughters. Count Antonio Maria della Mirandola, most recently, whose daughter surrendered her virginity most unwillingly. Who knows how many more like her have vengeful relatives?" Leonello gave a long innocent blink. "So, how are we ever to know who killed our good Duke of Gandia?"

I eyed him back in silence. Maybe he *was* as sinister as I'd first thought, at that. "How indeed."

We looked at each other.

The Duke of Gandia is dead, I thought, and felt a bubble of violent relief swelling in my chest. Probably a sinful bubble, but there was no stopping its rise. I felt like laughing, or weeping, or maybe both. I squeezed my eyes shut.

"Another death will sober you rather more, I think." Leonello nursed another small sip of communion wine. "Your cousin, Marco Santini. He was serving as Juan's squire that night. He was not killed in the initial attack, but he was wounded and knocked unconscious. It seems he was dragged to a nearby house and tended there, but he died without waking."

Sweet Santa Marta. Marco too? My eyes flew open; I gaped a moment, and Leonello looked at me inscrutably. I put the heels of my hands to my face to hide from his gaze. Marco.

Marco dead.

Ever since the attack in the wine cellar, rage had festered in my belly toward my cousin—a flinty, straightforward fury; almost comforting. But now I felt rage muddling together with shock, with disjointed memories of the boy who had first captured my heart when I was twelve with his easy smile and broad shoulders. I thought of the amiable gambler I'd tousled and chivvied out of wine shops and *zara* games, the shame-faced fool who thought nothing of leaving a wedding banquet in mid-preparations just to put a bet on a bullfight, the man whose bed I'd sometimes shared when he felt like celebrating a win at the cards . . .

My cousin, who had given me to Juan Borgia because he owed money, or because I had taken his place in the kitchens, or both. Maybe Marco hadn't really guessed what the Duke of Gandia would do to me, but I was sure he'd been careful not to think about that part. Marco didn't like to think about ugly things. He'd just screwed his eyes firmly shut, lured me into the trap, and told himself nothing ugly would possibly happen.

I made myself take my hands down from my eyes, because unlike my cousin, I could look at things when they were ugly. "Marco *and* the Duke of Gandia, Leonello?"

Madonna Giulia's bodyguard sipped calmly, not deigning to answer me. I didn't know what to think, whether to rejoice at the end of Juan Borgia's life or say a prayer for the end of Marco's. *Is this the price?* some part of me wondered. *Juan Borgia dies, but so does a foolish, laughing man who used to share my bed?* I sat feeling very cold in the hot kitchen, breathing shallowly through my nose and trying to keep my head from flying into pieces, as the dwarf opposite me swirled his wine thoughtfully in its cup.

"You know, I've never seen you drink more than a cup of wine at a time, Leonello." I managed to speak around the confused choke of emotions in my throat. "Much less get reeling drunk."

"Sometimes even I feel the need for oblivion." He tilted a shoulder. "It was a bad business, Carmelina."

"The Duke of Gandia—did he—"

"When there is a viper loose," Leonello said in a neutral voice, "you can run all you like evading the fangs. But sooner or later, someone will have to risk the fangs and kill the viper."

"True," I said faintly. "All the same—please don't tell me any more." If I heard any more, I was going to be sick.

"Ask Bartolomeo for details, then," Leonello said. "When you are ready."

"You involved *Bartolomeo*?" I shot to my feet.

"I thought you didn't want details." Leonello blinked innocently.

"You odious little man, I will hate you all over again if Bartolomeo came to any harm!" Sweet Santa Marta, if he was caught and executed for this, it would be all my fault. Was God so jealous of His brides that I was a curse to any man who laid hands on me? I'd bedded three men since taking my vows: Marco, who was dead; Cesare Borgia, who said he was the Devil and was surely damned to hellfire—and then, Bartolomeo. Who had become embroiled in God knew what dark business, and all because of me.

"Calm yourself," said Leonello, seeing my face. "He's unhurt. Though probably even more hungover than I am. He knew I was accompanying Madonna Giulia to the convent today and made me promise to seek you out. I was to tell you—let's see—" Leonello cast his eyes up to the ceiling. I folded my arms, glowering, heart pounding. "Ah, yes. He's taken a position as undercook in the household of Vittorio Capece of Bozzuto. That Neapolitan lordling who collects paintings and pretty page boys."

"I knew that already. That's all Bartolomeo said?"

"There was a great deal more in the way of flowery protestations," Leonello said. "I shall not embarrass you by repeating it all verbatim. He adores you, he will write to you until you can leave here, he would wait for you forever—"

I could feel my cheeks heating. "He told you all that?"

"He was very drunk at that point, I admit. He came to me troubled in his soul, you see, because he did not regret our actions, and thus feared he could not repent as one is supposed to after the doing of evil. As I was the only murderer and evildoer he knew, he wanted to find out how one made the proper atonement. An odd mix of purity and practicality, that boy . . . he needed reassurance, and even more badly he needed wine, so I broached a cask and gave him a little practical advice about how exactly one confesses the more serious sins to one's priest without giving away the details that get one caught. Sins like, say, accidentally killing a clumsy lout despite doing everything possible to save him."

My heart squeezed. *Oh, Bartolomeo*—"How could you drag him into this? He's just a *boy*—"

"He's no boy." Leonello's tone brooked no argument. "He's a man grown, Carmelina. And he's done nothing he need feel remorse for."

Easy for Leonello to say, with his conscience as flexible as a snake and as impervious as burnished steel. Bartolomeo and his finely tuned sense of wrongdoing were another matter entirely. "He'll never forgive himself," I said into my hands. "Sweet Santa Marta, I wish he'd never met me."

"Do you?" Another arched eyebrow.

"I'm sure he does, too! What if he's caught and hanged because of me?" Dread pooled sickly in my stomach, replacing all my stunned shock. I could not even imagine the vengeance the Pope would unleash on anyone with a hand in the death of his favorite son. "Bartolomeo should take himself away to Naples or Milan, and as soon as possible. He can just as easily build a career outside Rome." Just as easily, and far more safely.

I looked up at Leonello and I couldn't help a shiver, meeting his calm, unrepentant gaze. I didn't see him fleeing to Naples or Milan—he'd see this terrible business out to the end, whatever the cost. "Thank you," I said. "I am grateful, you know. Even if it had to come at such a price."

"I hate gratitude," Leonello said, and tilted his head upward as the bells began to ring overhead, calling the nuns to Terce. "Unless it's the kind of gratitude that offers itself up naked across my bed, but you clearly like your bedmates quite a bit taller and younger than myself."

I felt too worn even to muster a glare. Instead, I leaned across the trestle table, and I touched my lips to his broad forehead. Leonello grinned and rose, and I hoped he wouldn't be damned to hellfire for this unholy business. He didn't seem to care one way or another, but I found that I cared. I crossed myself, shivering again, and he made a dusting-off motion of his hands as if to push my prayers and my sympathies away.

"Now," he said, clearly done discussing vengeance, guilt, and all the rest of it. "Shall we go to Madonna Giulia, then, and tell her you will be accompanying us back to the *palazzo*?"

Back to the Palazzo Santa Maria, back to my kitchens, back anywhere I wanted. Juan Borgia was no longer anywhere in this world to threaten me. "Home," I said, and the first faint stirrings of hope rose in me. *Home.*

"Yes," Leonello agreed. "I'm sure the Countess of Pesaro will be far too busy weeping for her brother to put up a fuss over your leaving."

Madonna Lucrezia was not weeping, however. She was screaming.

The little suite of rooms in the gatehouse for illustrious travelers would have been luxurious enough sanctuary for the Countess of Pesaro all by themselves, but she had brought her own little comforts as well. Silver combs and basins for the washing of her hair, little ivory pots of rouge and hair potions, three elaborately carved and painted chests containing all the gowns and shoes and linens deemed necessary to her retreat, her own fragile Venetian goblets and majolica plates, a pearl-inlaid lute so she could practice her music . . . Just today when I brought the Countess of Pesaro her midday *pranzo* of pastry *pasticcetti* stuffed with milk-fed veal, her little *sala* had been a bower of silks and laughter and bunches of flowers as she read aloud from Ficino's *De Amore* while Pantisilea dressed her hair. "Stupid Ficino, I'm tired of him," Lucrezia had been complaining. "I hear there's to be another book of sonnets from Avernus to his Aurora, but who knows when I shall get them . . ."

Now as I edged into the *sala* wishing I could hide behind Leonello, the bower's peace had shattered right along with the bowl of fresh violets and lilies that now lay smashed on the floor. Cushions had been torn off the wall benches, books lay facedown on the floor, and Lucrezia

Borgia's hair stood out wildly in all directions as she sobbed in the middle of her bed.

"*Lucrezia mia*," Madonna Giulia was saying vainly, trying to put her arms about the young Countess. "Don't flail and gasp like that, you'll make yourself ill—"

"What do you know?" Lucrezia struck her away, gasping. "Have you lost a brother you loved?"

"As a matter of fact, I have." I thought I heard just a touch of asperity in La Bella's normally sweet voice. "My brother Angelo, remember?"

"To a fever! You lost him to a *fever*, not to a *murderer*!" Lucrezia buried her face in a velvet cushion with another howl.

"Weeping will not bring him back. Juan is at rest now." Giulia stroked her back, and I looked down at the bandage that still swathed my hand and made cooking so awkward and difficult. The wound beneath it was either itchy or painful in unbearable turns, and I hoped Juan Borgia was burning in the flames of hell. If I was bound for the inferno myself for all my sins, and I probably was, I hoped the Devil would let me give the Pope's son a turn or two on his own personal spit above the infernal flames. I'd sauce him down with hot oil myself, just to hear him shriek.

"Who would dare lay a hand on him?" Lucrezia was shrieking now. "Who would *dare*? My father will find them, he'll hunt them down and then Cesare will kill them all—"

I couldn't help a glance at Leonello, who was looking nonchalantly at the ceiling.

"I'm sure the killers will be brought to justice," Giulia soothed.

But Lucrezia Borgia would not be soothed.

"It's my husband, I know it is! My lord Sforza, he's furious with Father about our marriage being annulled; he wanted to hurt us any way he could. He had Juan killed, he murdered my *brother*—"

"Now really, Lucrezia—" Giulia gave Leonello a hopeless look as Lucrezia struck her away again.

"If my husband had a hand in it, he'll be sorry," the Countess of Pesaro was shrieking now. "Cesare won't wait for any annulment, he'll make me a *widow*, and for my next wedding—" She collapsed in a wail again, perhaps remembering that Juan had escorted her at her first wedding. Though a distinctly uncharitable part of me wondered if there wasn't a sliver of Lucrezia Borgia that enjoyed the chance to lay aside the gracious dignity required of a pope's daughter, and have herself a good wallow.

"Should we return later?" I whispered to Leonello, but he gave his cynical shrug.

"Why not enjoy the show? *Dio*, one wonders how she'd carry on if a brother she actually liked was killed. Did she forget how Juan used to tease her till she cried about the spots on her chin, and how her feet were growing faster than her breasts, and how her first betrothals ended because no true nobleman could bring himself to wed a churchman's bastard?"

Leonello spoke softly, but perhaps Lucrezia Borgia heard him over her own weeping and Giulia's soothing murmurs, because she lifted her head from its tangled thicket of hair and fixed her swollen, red-rimmed eyes on the dwarf.

"Where were you when my brother was killed?" she demanded. "You're bodyguard to our household, why didn't you ride at my brother's back with your knives when he needed a squire?"

"I am bodyguard to Madonna Giulia," Leonello corrected, imperturbable. "The Duke of Gandia may have needed a guard, but my services were already required elsewhere."

"Don't you smirk at me!" Lucrezia cried, even though his face was entirely bland. "You never liked Juan. That little joke once where he told you to join the other dwarves in the mummer's show—"

"I merely informed the Duke of Gandia that I do not tumble."

"—and even if you *had* been at his back, I don't suppose you'd have bothered to save him! Anything for La Bella, you'd walk on fire for La Bella, but when it's my *brother*—"

"Lucrezia," Giulia said firmly. "That is enough. There is no reason—"

"Oh, but every man is in love with *Giulia*." There was a passing flash of spite in Lucrezia's reddened eyes. "Even the family *dwarf*. It's as plain as the nose on his face; I saw it when he kissed her before he jumped down into the bullring—"

I felt Leonello go rigid at my side, and glanced at him.

"—My brother died, all because Leonello couldn't bear to leave his precious *Giulia* even for an hour, and—and—" The little Countess's chin quivered. "Oh, *Juan!*" She went off into another gale of weeping.

"Lucrezia, don't be absurd!" Giulia exclaimed with a little smile. "Leonello certainly doesn't—"

My eyes flicked down to her little bodyguard. I had never seen his face anything but guarded, quizzical, sometimes amused—but for one horrified instant all his defenses were gone.

Giulia looked puzzled, gazing at him as Lucrezia bawled into a cushion. "Leonello?"

Leonello's gaze touched her for just a split second, touched her and then leaped away again like a drop of water leaping off a hot stove. His usual cool mask blinked back into place half a heartbeat later, but the agony in that one split-second glance sent a ribbon of ice crawling down my spine. I felt a great swell of pity.

Perhaps there were worse things, when it came to matters of the heart, than falling into the arms of your seven-years-younger apprentice after eating too many fried tubers.

"Madonna Giulia," I heard myself saying as Lucrezia continued her oblivious wailing and Leonello stood expressionless and blank-eyed as a statue. "Perhaps Messer Leonello and I may be excused? We don't wish to intrude . . ."

Leonello was gone the moment Giulia nodded, giving a wooden bow and disappearing through the door. I heard his boots retreating down the stone steps, almost running, and Giulia looked after him as if she wanted to follow.

"Don't," I heard myself saying. "Madonna Giulia . . . I wouldn't, if I were you."

"Very well." She sank back down onto the bed beside Lucrezia, who was now weeping more softly, and my mistress's face was now stricken as well as puzzled as I bowed out. It took another hour to calm the Countess of Pesaro. I waited in the passage outside with a hovering Pantisilea, gnawing my thumbnail, Leonello nowhere in sight, until at last Madonna Lucrezia's voice called for her maids again.

"You can't stay, Giulia?" the little Countess was asking as we tiptoed back through the doors. Lucrezia sat up and wiped her face, limp and spent and more or less calm, her momentary flash of spite forgotten. "I'm going to weep all night if I don't have someone to comfort me."

"So will your father, if I'm not there." Gently but firmly, Madonna Giulia disengaged her clinging hands. "I really must go back to the *palazzo*, Lucrezia—I shouldn't have left them all, but I didn't want you to hear the news from a stranger, and neither did Cesare."

"Very well." Lucrezia heaved a gusty sigh. "Pantisilea, fetch some rosewater compresses for my eyes. Carmelina, you go get me a plate of something—I don't care what. Oranges, maybe. They were Juan's favorite." Her chin began to tremble again.

I opened my mouth, but Giulia was ahead of me without needing to be asked. "I'm going to take Carmelina back with me," my mistress said. "She'll be badly needed back at the *palazzo* in all the fuss that's coming."

"Oh, but I need her here." Lucrezia mopped her eyes again. "I'm not going to eat that stale convent bread and gruel, am I? No, Carmelina stays here with me."

"Lucrezia—"

"No." The Pope's daughter put her chin up. "You are not taking her too—I suppose you want Pantisilea back as well? You can't be bothered to stay with me, so no one else is allowed to either?"

Giulia looked exasperated.

"Go running back to my father if you must." Lucrezia flung herself back into the pillows, eyes oozing all over again. "Carmelina stays here."

"I work for Madonna Giulia," I dared to say. "If it please you—"

"It doesn't please me." Lucrezia Borgia looked genuinely surprised. "And it's pleasing *me* that matters."

"I am taking her with me," Giulia began, looking irritated again, but Lucrezia cut her off.

"My father pays all the *palazzo* servants, Giulia. Not you. Not to mention the fact that he endows this convent. If I tell the prioress that Carmelina and Pantisilea must stay here, then they will not be allowed to leave!"

The Pope's daughter would not be budged. She was crying again when Giulia finally cast her eyes up to the heavens and departed.

"Oh dear, I am sorry," Giulia whispered to me just outside the door. "I'd take you with me now anyway, but if I upset her any further, Cesare will have my head. When she calms down, I'm sure she'll change her mind—I'll write her a letter about it in a few days, I promise."

"Thank you, *madonna*." I bobbed a curtsy, and Giulia gave me her own warm glance in return. But her eyes flicked down the stairs where Leonello had fled. "You had best be on your way," I managed to say. "Let me get you a few *biscotti* for the carriage ride."

Her smile definitely looked a little wan. "Yes, I always eat when I'm traveling."

I watched out the nearest window as my former mistress set out across the convent grass for her carriage. Maybe this was my punishment. The man who had hurt me was dead, but I was still locked inside these walls—and who knew how long it would be, before I paid my penance for it, and Fate or Lucrezia Borgia released me?

I heard my new mistress's impatient voice floating from her chamber. "Carmelina, where are my oranges?"

"Coming, Madonna Lucrezia," I called back leadenly, and as I trudged back to the dank and dismal kitchens that were my new domain, I heard the convent bells begin to toll again.

CHAPTER ELEVEN

※

Beauty awakens the soul to act.

—DANTE

Leonello

Even without turning, I knew the moment my mistress stepped into my chamber. The scent of honeysuckle and gillyflower filled my nose, and I took a deep breath of it and kept stuffing shirts into my pack.

Silence built, but I would not be the one to break it. I imagined a dozen things she might say, but her first words were, "You've changed your clothes."

"I think these will suit me better in future." I pushed the sleeves back on my patched linen shirt with the ill-fitting doublet above it. I wasn't certain I'd kept my old clothes, the ones I'd worn when I was first hired to act as bodyguard to a cardinal's concubine, but upon returning from the Convent of San Sisto, I found them stuffed at the bottom of my chest. I put them on in place of the crisp blacks that Giulia had designed for me as my own personal livery, even down to the boots she'd had specially fitted for my twisted legs. *Dio*, but my feet already missed those supple black boots with the reinforced soles and supportive seams, now lying in an abandoned heap with the black doublet and the black hose that actually fit my misshapen legs, and everything else

I was leaving behind. On top of the pile was my deck of cards—the new deck, beautifully painted and gilt-edged, that Giulia had given me to replace the cards that Savonarola's Angels had confiscated in Florence.

I wasn't leaving this *palazzo* with one single solitary thing that had come from her. Not so much as a shirt-lace.

"I haven't seen your chamber since you were recovering from your wounds after our French adventure." Her skirts rustled behind me as she turned, examining the four walls I'd called home for the past few years. "I'd forgotten how small it is."

"A dwarf doesn't need much in the way of space." Except for the fact that it had a high-corniced ceiling and no rats, my chamber in the Palazzo Santa Maria was not so different from the bolt-hole I used to rent in the Borgo in my days as card player. A narrow bed, a chest of clothes, a small shelf of books, a candle to read them by. The difference was all in the details.

I'd retreated to my room the instant the carriage returned from the Convent of San Sisto. The carriage wheels had hardly stopped rolling before I was swinging down into the courtyard and making for the doors. I'd elected to ride on the jolting seat with the driver rather than inside with La Bella as I usually did; I'd been perched up high and staring ahead between the horses' ears by the time she left Lucrezia Borgia in her chambers and come back to the carriage. "Leonello?" she'd said, looking up at me, but I stared straight ahead and she sighed and climbed in.

I'd known, however, that I would not be able to avoid my mistress entirely.

"You're leaving us." Her voice was quiet.

"Your powers of perception are absolutely breathtaking," I said, and rolled up the last of my spare shirts.

"Why?" The rustle of her skirts again as she came closer. I still didn't turn. "Because Lucrezia said—"

"That I allowed her brother to die?" I cut her off. My head was still throbbing, no longer just from the wine I'd drunk with Bartolomeo. "That it was all my fault, due to some astoundingly fuzzy logic? Well, logic is not our little Countess of Pesaro's strongest suit, but she is correct in one particular. It is my fault her brother is dead." I slammed the lid down on the now-empty chest. "Because I murdered him."

I hoped for an outburst or a denial or a cry of horror—anything to make her recoil, rush away in tears, *leave*. But Giulia Farnese only said quietly, "I know."

She sank to her knees beside the pile of my discarded livery. I watched her out of the corner of my eye, waiting for her to intone some platitude about Juan's soul being at rest, but she was silent as she folded my black doublet.

"You know, I'm disappointed you figured it out," I said, stuffing the last rolled-up shirt into my old pack. "I covered my tracks so carefully." Even at the end, when I'd had Bartolomeo put on his mask and hire a few street drunks to help us load Juan's swaddled corpse onto the horse and then into the river, I'd kept myself anonymous. The men had been drunk, and to disguise my height I'd swung myself into the horse's saddle in front of Juan's corpse, and wrapped myself well in a cloak to hide my short legs. Neither the men we'd paid nor the wood seller who saw us toss the body into the river could have recognized the man on the horse for a dwarf. "How did you know it was me, Madonna Giulia? The note I had you write?"

"Of course." There was anger in her voice, muted but powerful like a deep-flowing stream. "You involved me in the murder of my lover's son, Leonello."

"No one will ever know." I strode across the chamber to my bed and began stripping the linens. I would at least leave my room tidied when the servants came to clean it out. "I burned the note once it served its purpose. I gave you my word on that."

"That isn't what worries me! You always keep your word—you think I don't know that?" She stared at me a moment longer, but I refused to look at her, just kept stripping the bed. "*Why?* Why would you risk yourself, risk *me*, to kill him?"

I shrugged. "It isn't important. Suffice to say the bastard deserved it, a thousand times over."

I watched her sidelong as she lowered her eyes to the floor, crossing herself. "I believe you," she whispered, and pressed at her temples with her fingertips as though her head hurt. "And I give you my word, too," she said even more guietly. "No one will ever know who truly killed Juan. Not from me."

"I'm touched. I didn't think you kept anything from His Holiness. Not when he's grunting inside you, anyway."

That brutal tone usually worked well for me, when it came to keeping Giulia Farnese at bay. Say something cutting and she retreated with quiet hurt like a swan folding her wings. This time she merely smoothed my discarded sleeves and added them to the neat pile of black clothing. "Do you really feel you must go?"

"Oh, I think it's time." I finished stripping the bed, heaping the linens together. "Better if I'm out of the Borgia orbit, or I might be tempted to kill off a few more of them." I'd nearly planted a blade in Lucrezia Borgia's long white throat today for her careless offhand spite.

But it wasn't really the little Countess's fault. If I'd just kept better control over my face, shrugged, laughed it off . . .

My mistress's voice again. "Why are you really leaving?"

Don't, I begged La Bella silently. *Oh, don't!* "Perhaps I'm bored with bodyguarding," I said lightly. "It's a dull business, after all, sitting about while you go to confession or get measured for dresses. Besides, I must have read every book in the Borgia collection by now. Time for new pastures."

"Leonello—what Lucrezia said—"

"Leave it, Madonna Giulia." I strode to my small shelf of books, the last things to be packed. The old books I had brought with me: the tattered Cicero, the well-thumbed Ovid and Boccaccio, the ill-printed copy of Marcus Aurelius's *Meditations*. And the new books: the *Chanson de Roland* I had bought from the printer with my first payment as bodyguard, the marvelously translated and illustrated *Iliad* my mistress had given me at Christmastide last year . . . I left the *Iliad* and began sweeping the rest into my pack atop the clothes.

"But Leonello—"

"*I said leave it!*" I roared, and whirled to face her for the first time. Giulia Farnese had dutifully put on black in mourning for Juan, and her skirts pooled around her like the petals of a black rose as she knelt on the floor gathering and folding my dark livery. She always had a way of finding some tactful excuse to kneel or sit when we spoke together; any way she could fit herself to my height so I would not have to crane my neck at her. Her flesh glowed white against the black velvet; her hair gleamed gold in its netted mass, and her eyes were full of tears as she looked at me. Because she was the greatest whore in Rome (hadn't I said that myself once, when I was being cruel?), and the best whores know men to the tips of their fingers. Even better than that, Giulia knew *me*. My face could hide to all the world that I had murdered a pope's son, but it could no longer hide to Giulia Farnese how much I loved her.

"Oh, Leonello," she said softly.

I had dropped my armload of books. I bent to retrieve them, turning away so she would not see the prickle of tears in my own eyes. My heart boiled.

Love. None of the philosophers had it right; what a vile and bitter brew it could be. The ache that had so often swamped me when I sat outside Giulia's chamber after she'd retired with her papal lover, hearing her laughter through the door, and her muffled cries of passion. The jealous bile that filled me when I saw the casual kiss Rodrigo Borgia liked to drop on the nape of her neck in greeting, so I had to hold my hand back from stabbing the Holy Father through the heart out of sheer all-consuming envy. The fury that had swamped me when Juan Borgia and those French soldiers and that thug of an Angel dared lay their hands on her; the raw, clawing determination to sacrifice every last finger and limb I had to keep her from harm. The lust, oh God, when she dropped her gown and stood naked for Maestro Botticelli, and I knew myself no better than those cardinals who ogled her, even though I wanted to beat them all bloody for the humiliation I saw rising red in her cheeks.

Everything in me lifted upward when she laughed, when her voice rippled on in its cheerful breathless chatter, when she dug into a plate of *biscotti* with unabashed zeal, when she shot me one of her teasing complicitous glances as a dull guest droned on at *cena*—and then the shaft of pleasure was always followed by a tang of bitterness, because what in this world can be more trite, more humiliating, more utterly laughable, than the sight of a stunted little man like me pining for a glorious golden beauty like her?

You are a joke. Don't think I didn't know it; don't think I hadn't told myself many times to leave this household, take myself back to the Borgo and my card games. Don't think I didn't rake myself, long and savagely, when I held Giulia's note that had trapped Juan Borgia over the candle flame and found myself unable to burn it. Unable, that is, until I closed my eyes and put my head down on the page that still wafted her scent, and allowed myself to pretend—for ten precisely measured heartbeats—that those words were written for me.

The words that began with *My love, I cannot resist you any longer.*

Laugh at me if you wish. I won't grudge you. I have laughed often enough, long and bitterly, at myself.

My eyes burned as I gathered my books up and stuffed them into the pack, but no tears fell and for that at least I was grateful. Giulia was silent, and for that I was more than grateful; for that I could have kissed her. As if I had not been kissing her a hundred times a day for years, in my imagination. The one kiss I had ever dared plant on her had been a poor excuse of a thing; a comic smack of my lips at the barest corner of her mouth that hadn't in the end been quite comical enough to escape Lucrezia Borgia's sharp eyes, God rot her.

One of my books had fallen face down, the pages crumpled, and she picked it up wordlessly. Too late I saw which book it was. "Don't—!" I lunged, but the collected sermons of the world's dullest Dominican friar had already disgorged their secrets, scattering a handful of loose papers. Giulia looked down at the pages covered in my writing—normally she would not have been able to read my hasty scribble so quickly, but these pages had been bound for the printer and so I had taken great care to write a clear hand. The signature of *Avernus* at the bottom was large and distinct.

Poetry. The final refuge of lovelorn fools. I'd penned all those sonnets in one savage fortnight, after we had been ransomed from the French and I had been recovering from my wounds. Every day Giulia had tended me, seen my bandages changed and scolded me into drinking foul medicines and read me books to pass the time. She'd been kneeling beside my bed one afternoon, deftly adjusting the pillows under my head, talking in her sweet way of anything that would distract me from my pain, and she'd been so close . . . I'd nearly reached out to tilt up her chin with one hand, nearly captured her eyes with my own and said—God knows what I would have said. Horror at that near miss had made me cruel to her instead, snarling at her till she withdrew in hurt bewilderment, and then afterward I wrote poetry for her. She'd once said ruefully that no one wrote poetry to harlots, but I did—a dwarf's pathetic homage to his unchaste muse. Poetry in the name of Aurora; the dawn bringing light to my darkness, oh God, how unbearably *trite*. I'd mocked myself viciously with every line, but all the scorn I'd heaped on my own head hadn't stopped the words coming.

I'd had one copy printed under the name of Avernus—the entrance to the underworld! How very dark and mysterious!—and I'd hoped I could inveigle her into reading it. Cheap thin verse on cheap thin paper, hardly readable considering I'd had it done up by the half-drunk printer in the Borgo who made most of his living printing scurrilous pamphlets, the printer whose spare room I used to rent before I came the Borgia household. *She'll laugh at it*, I'd thought when I looked at my poor offering. *Good*. Hearing her laugh at it would surely cure me.

But she hadn't laughed. She had loved it, my pathetic little collection of sonnets, loved it more than Petrarch's sonnets to his Laura, she said. She'd loved them and sighed over them and read them aloud to anyone who would listen, and soon everyone in Rome was quoting my stunted private passions back and forth to each other.

Even that bitter shame had not stopped me from writing a second batch.

I scrabbled the pages of new sonnets away in frantic haste, but Giulia's eyes had already widened. "Leonello, don't go. *Please* don't go, I—"

"I wouldn't stay if you spread your legs for me right now," I grated, and slung my pack over my shoulder. Maybe it would look suspicious to some, my flight so soon after Juan's death, but so be it. I wouldn't stay here to see Giulia's pity—I would rather die on the rack than bear that. So I took a jagged breath, and turned my back on her.

She rose to follow me, but she had heavy velvet skirts to weigh her down, and I'd dropped into that speedy undignified scuttle that I never used in her sight because I had to be tall for her, as tall as I could manage. I scuttled out of my chamber and slammed the door, and drawing the dagger at my belt, I wedged it fast between the door and the jamb. A few jolts would dislodge it, but that was all the time I needed to disappear from this *palazzo*.

"*Leonello!*" my mistress cried through the door, hammering on it, and I strode away without a second glance.

Giulia

For the very first time in my life I wanted to drink myself insensible. I wanted to sink my wretched body into a warm scented bath, I wanted to cuddle Laura tight and feel her arms about my neck, I wanted to curl up in my bed and weep for a very long time. What I did *not* want, at the very end of this agony-filled day, was Cesare Borgia striding into my *sala* with a curt "Come to my father at once."

"No," I said into my hands. I'd been sitting curled on my day bed with my head in my arms ever since my bodyguard vanished from the *palazzo* like a devil disappearing into a puff of smoke, and I saw no reason to change my plans just because my lover's eldest son was being peremptory. "No, I am not going anywhere. I am not at your beck and call, Cesare, and all I want to do for the rest of this evening is curl up in a chair and weep."

But Cesare was not inclined to take a woman's tears seriously, or her wishes either for that matter, and striding across the *sala*, he took me by the arm and levered me up. "You will talk to my father, and you'll do it now. He's gone mad. Sweet Christ," Cesare swore. "Three days and nights he refuses to eat or speak, and now he's speaking again but he won't speak sense!"

"What's wrong?" Another terrible fear struck me. "Has he—harmed himself?"

"Worse." Cesare sounded grim. "He wants to *reform* himself."

I refused to believe him as he towed me out of the Palazzo Santa Maria, over the marble steps at the threshold where I'd stood for an hour waiting as one by one my guardsmen came back saying none of them had found or even glimpsed Leonello after he'd gone striding off into the teeming streets of Rome. I went on not believing what Cesare had told me, until he ushered me with great speed and none of his customary grace through the passages of the Vatican to the private papal apartments—and then I saw my Pope.

I did not even recognize the bent figure in humble homespun robes, kneeling in prayer not at the elaborately carved and gilded prie-dieu, but on the hard floor itself. Then he turned his head and I saw the hooked nose and gray grief-stricken face of Rodrigo Borgia. All at a stroke, in the days since Juan's death, he had grown old.

I could not resist flying to him, putting my hands to his face. "Oh, Rodrigo," I whispered, and he allowed me to embrace him, fold his head against my bosom. I felt tears drop from my eyes to his tonsured head, but I didn't know if the tears were all for him or for—

"Giulia," the Pope said, pulling away from me and rising. "You should not have come."

"I only wish to comfort you—"

"My son is dead," Rodrigo said simply. "If I had seven papal thrones instead of one, I would give them all to have Juan alive again. No one can comfort me."

I felt rather than saw the Pope's living son fold himself against the tapestries, inscrutable and silent as ever. "God is looking over Juan now," I said, and wondered how many lies, how much blood, had swirled around that name—that vicious, prancing boy surely damned to hell.

Rodrigo was looking at Juan's magnificently turbaned figure in Pinturicchio's fresco. "I will have all this removed," he said, waving a ringed hand that suddenly seemed shrunken to my eyes. "The gilt, the paint, the marble. Simplicity will become me better in future."

"Your Holiness?" I said, cautious.

"God has seen fit to punish Us for Our sins." Rodrigo turned from me, folding his hands into his homespun sleeves. "It is the only explanation. Juan did not deserve such a death."

I bit my tongue at that.

"My son's killers will be found," Rodrigo said in his sonorous Spanish bass as though addressing the whole College of Cardinals, and I bit my tongue even harder. "They will be found and tried, but there must be more. There must be change. There *will* be change. We have prayed upon it; God has spoken to Us. His Holy Church has become a sinkhole, and We have allowed her to be fouled. No more."

I looked at him even more cautiously.

"We summon a consistory tomorrow." Rodrigo turned to look at me again with his ghastly sunken eyes, and somehow the sweep of his plain robes was more regal than all his papal regalia. "There will be reforms made, and men of virtue rather than rank appointed to make them. The sacred offices will be carried out with rigor. Benefices will be conferred upon those who earn them, not those with coin. We shall renounce nepotism, simony." His voice had its old energy now, the passion of planning, though I still heard the ocean of grief behind it. "And Our priests must change themselves as well, if they are to serve the Church as she deserves to be served. Cardinals must limit themselves in income, six thousand ducats—"

"They won't like that," Cesare spoke behind me. "Speaking as Cardinal Borgia, I do not like that."

"Reforms *will* be made," my Pope said, steely. "You will serve God in future, Cesare—not yourself. Give up your fine clothes and your bullfights and your concubines."

Cesare's gaze drifted to me.

"Or you will give up your red hat and give it to one more worthy."

"As to that—" Cesare shrugged. "Throw the red hat in a bullring for all I care. What about the rest of our family? Or am I the only one to be reformed, Your Holiness?"

"Joffre and Sancha can return to Squillace." My Pope's tone was listless again; this man who adored his children above all else now sounded indifferent to them, his eyes dull again as he fingered the plain wooden rosary at his waist. "Lucrezia—she has already retreated to the Convent of San Sisto; perhaps she will be inspired to take the veil. A fitting calling." He closed his eyes in a hard blink. "I must be father to my flock first, not to my bastards."

Cesare turned to me. "Perhaps La Bella will talk some sense into you."

The words came out of me before I was aware I was thinking them. "Perhaps I don't wish to."

"What?"

I studied my Pope, thinking of the vigorous black-haired suitor who had first ambushed me in a garden the day after my wedding. The lover who had claimed me in a half-empty *palazzo*, his dark eyes heavy with passion as he looked on me. The father of my daughter, who had come to my bedside after Laura's birth with a beautifully painted birth tray piled high with candied cherries, and insisted on feeding me every one. The bull in his red horned mask, more cheerful pagan satyr than Holy Father.

This man looked nothing like any of his previous incarnations. This man was weary, heartsick, determined—and stainless. He could have been an exhausted Moses gathering himself to face the Red Sea, or a bowed John the Baptist turning away from the temptations of Salome. This man was not Rodrigo Borgia; he was Pope Alexander VI. A man about whom even Fra Savonarola would have nothing evil to say.

Juan's death. A maelstrom of pain and fury whirling out from the ending of that worthless, wasted life. If something good could come of it—if *Pope Alexander* could come from it—then perhaps all my lover's grief would not be wasted.

"Your Holiness," I said slowly, and dropped to my knees. "May I have your blessing?"

His ringed hand touched my head, stroked just once over the smooth piles of my hair. "Bless you always, my child."

Our eyes met, and I saw love there. But so much weariness, so much grief. "May God keep you," I whispered.

He would have to.

That job was no longer mine.

I remained kneeling as my Pope passed from the room to his private chapel with bowed head and bowed shoulders—but not bowed spirit. Not that, and I was glad for it.

"What are you doing?" Cesare hissed. "I brought you here to talk some sense into him. Not feed this fantasy of his—"

"Is it a fantasy?" I rose. "Perhaps it is a calling."

Cesare regarded me impatiently, fingers drumming on his lean thigh. "He's had these fits of reform before. When my older brother Pedro Luis died, many years ago in Spain—my father was going to renounce us all, give up his *palazzo*, join the Franciscans. As a plan, it lasted a month. Then he was back to his old ways."

"Perhaps he will be back to his old ways this time, too." I looked at the door where Rodrigo had gone, where I thought I could hear a murmured stream of Latin. "But if not, he could do great good."

"Sweet Christ save me," Cesare said in disgust.

"I hope He saves your father," I said, and for the first time all day my sore heart felt lighter. "I would very much like to see what Pope Alexander VI could accomplish in this world, instead of Rodrigo Borgia."

I couldn't help a moment's anxiety for what would happen to Laura—to me. But only a moment. I saw a *castello* in the green countryside, rearing over the bank of a heat-shimmering blue lake. Waiting for us both.

"Go home," Cesare ordered. "Go home, and be ready to receive my father again when he has need of you. Because he *will* have need of you. Once he's found Juan's killers and put this all behind him, he'll want to celebrate, and he'll want to celebrate in your bed."

"Yes, Cardinal Borgia." I swept him an elaborate curtsy, then turned my back on his slit-eyed frustration and glided from the room, back through the papal apartments where my own face looked down from a Madonna's veil, back through the passage to the Palazzo Santa Maria.

"Leonello?" I called in the entrance hall, hoping against hope, but only silence met my ears. I looked about the empty room with its checkered marble floors, its coffered ceiling and elaborate tapestries, and it seemed empty of anything but echoes.

It *was* empty of anything but echoes, I realized. I'd come here full of jubilation just a few short weeks after Rodrigo became pope, and I'd come with a cloud of friends. Adriana da Mila, watching over me even while she irked me; Carmelina feeding me endless sweets and shaking her head in despair when I could not even learn how to whip cream; Pantisilea giggling over her lovers and begging for tidbits about mine.

Lucrezia who had been such a sweet-natured child; Joffre blinking at me shyly when I offered him a hug—and Leonello, my little lion, eternally at my back. The papal seraglio, Leonello had called it. Now every one of those friends had gone.

I thought of the blue lake again, and the *castello* beside it.

"Yes, Madonna Giulia?" A maid answered my summons with a curtsy.

"Go to my daughter's chamber, please, and see her nursemaids pack all her things." I was already on my way to my own chamber. "We are leaving on a journey tomorrow morning."

How strange. I'd always feared this moment's arrival, but now that it was here, I felt nothing but serenity. And sorrow, but that was not for my Pope.

I wrote a brief letter, giving it to the captain of the *palazzo* guards when I departed the following morning. "Give that to Messer Leonello should he return," I said, tethering Laura by the back of her little traveling dress while she in turn held the gilt-leather leash of my pet goat.

"And what should I say to His Holiness?" the captain said curiously, watching the procession of my chests and maids. "Or to Cardinal Borgia, if he asks?"

"You may say," I told him over my shoulder, walking to my carriage, "that the Bride of Christ is no more."

PART THREE

September 1497–June 1498

CHAPTER TWELVE

❖

He has the Pope in his fist.

—ENVOY, WRITING OF CESARE BORGIA

Leonello

"Chorus," I said, laying four cards down across the wine-sticky table. "All spades. The pot is mine."

"Wait," the Genoese sailor across from me protested. "You haven't seen my cards yet!"

"Doesn't matter. You have nothing to beat a *chorus* hand." I leaned forward and began to scoop coins from the center of the table.

The sailor stared at me, suspicious. "How do you know what cards I've got?"

Dio. The same conversations, the same suspicions, the same insults; every time I won. How had I stood it in the old days, years on end of rickety trestle tables and half-drunken gamblers and cards sticky with sour ale? "Mathematical certainty," I said, bored, and then followed the usual argument about what that was, and the Genoese sailor ended up storming off and taking his two friends with him. I was left with the cards and a few *scudi*.

"More wine," I told the sour-faced crone who served the drinks here. She never failed to twitch the sign of the evil eye at me when she thumped down my cup. I missed the days when Anna had worked here and never had to be reminded to cut my wine with water.

I'd come here first upon leaving the Palazzo Santa Maria. "I know you," the tavernkeeper squinted at me. "The dwarf, you used to come here years back. Leonato?"

"Close enough," I'd returned. "I helped you bury a girl named Anna."

"Don't remember."

I sighed. "The one who got staked and killed in your kitchens?"

"Oh, her." Crossing himself. "I remember *that*."

Anna had long been gone from here, but I'd had some thought of talking to someone who remembered her. Anyone—customers who had bedded her, the other maids who had worked by her side. But they either were gone on themselves to other things or had memories as vague as the tavernkeeper's. There was no one at all to care if I had said, *I avenged her death*. More of a dwarf's foolish, oversized dreams.

"A drink?" the tavernkeeper had asked me instead.

"Why not?" And I had stayed, plying my old trade at his wine-sticky tables day after day, too bored to move on.

I lost three hands to a groom with manure on his boots, and recouped it an hour later against a fishmonger too busy reminiscing about the hanging he'd seen to pay attention to his cards. "Horrible, it was," he confided, slapping down a card without looking at it. "The fellow goes black in the face, see, and his tongue comes out all purple. I made a wager he'd keep kicking as long as it took to say a rosary."

"Leave us," a peremptory voice addressed the fishmonger, who gaped briefly at the forbidding figure that had appeared like a black bat at his side.

"See here," the fishmonger began. But a gloved finger pointed at him in emphasis, and my fishy-smelling partner swept up his cards and stole away without another word.

"You could not have waited?" I asked as the man in the mask slid into the vacated seat across from me. "I was about to win my evening meal from that fool."

"Then I shall buy you your evening meal." A few coins landed on the table.

"Very well. Would you care for a game?" I flicked my wrist, snapping the cards together. "We cannot play *primiera* with only two—perhaps Michelotto will join us? No? I must say, Michelotto, I have not missed that blank stare of yours. Perhaps a bout of one-and-thirty then, Your Eminence? A Spanish game, so surely it will be known to a Borgia."

"Of course," said Cesare.

He took one look at my battered and sticky cards and produced his own gilt-edged deck, dealing calmly as the other drinkers in the tavern eyed him from the corner of their eyes. Rich boys sometimes came here, stealing away from their tutors for a whore and a few drinks, but silent velvet-clad figures in masks, not so often. "A drink, *gentilhuomo*?" the tavernkeeper ventured, sidling around Michelotto's statuelike gaze, but Cesare Borgia said, "Keep your swill," without looking up from his cards, and after that no one approached our little table.

"I had not heard Your Eminence had returned from Naples yet," I said, picking up my own cards. "Did King Federigo's coronation proceed in style?"

"Tolerably. A bitch of a Neapolitan girl gave me the French pox, but one hears the pustules go away in time." Cesare tapped the mask covering his face as he discarded a card. "You were hard to find, little lion man. I sent inquiries to Carbognano and Capodimonte first, thinking you had followed my father's little giggler when she departed."

"I am sorry to have misled you, Eminence." I took another card myself.

"La Bella had no notion where you had gone. That surprised me."

"Did it?"

"She seemed very anxious to discover your whereabouts."

I knocked twice on the table: the sign to reveal cards. Cesare Borgia had a hand of seventeen; I had twenty-eight and scooped the coins.

The young Cardinal dealt again. "It was Michelotto who finally caught a glimpse of you, here in this tavern."

I eyed the young Cardinal's favorite murderer, who leaned against the wall cleaning his nails with his knife and ignoring us utterly. "What were you doing in the slums, Michelotto?"

"Michelotto likes the slums," Cesare replied as though the man were mute. "On this occasion, he was having a drink after doing a little work for me."

"Work?" I discarded a card.

"I've orders from the Holy Father to get Cardinal Piccolomini thoroughly unsettled before the next consistory. I'm having his guardsmen picked off at a rate of exactly one a week. It's working nicely."

I paused, looking at him. Cesare smiled, lounging across the rickety wooden chair in his velvet doublet with all the grace of a leopard. "Why admit such things to me, Your Eminence?"

"One man a week—it's a heavy load, even for one like Michelotto who likes his work." A smile for his guard, who looked faintly indignant from his post against the wall. "And I have similar tasks, from time to time, requiring a man of nerve and sharp blades."

I laughed, swinging my feet above the floor, and the tavernkeeper looked up nervously. "You think that describes me? Nerve and sharp blades?"

"I've long had the intention of poaching both for my own service." Cesare Borgia knocked twice, calling for cards. "Your work has been admirable."

"My work was bodyguarding. Trailing about after an empty-headed flirt while she read bad poetry and had her hair plaited." My hand was a measly eleven; Cesare's twenty-nine. He took his coins back and dealt again.

"I refer to your more . . . private work."

My fingers stilled on the new cards. *What do you know?* I thought. *Do you know I killed your brother?*

Three months had passed since the death of the Duke of Gandia, and no murderer had been found. The Pope had publicly exonerated a variety of candidates such as bitter Giovanni Sforza, who according to common rumor would soon be deprived of his little Borgia wife. Even young Joffre Borgia had been exonerated, since he was widely bandied through Rome as a possible fratricide thanks to Juan's liaison with the

Tart of Aragon. But no killer had been arrested, and three months later the scent would seem to be cold. The gossips of Rome had found other things to talk about.

But Cesare Borgia's eyes glittered at me through the eye holes of the black mask, and I felt the old stirring of interest at a puzzle to solve. Did he know? Cesare had had no love for his brother—but for daring to lay a finger on any Borgia, I would find myself on the rack or the *strappado*.

Or perhaps not. Perhaps I would only be offered a job.

"You think I wish to make a career killing your enemies for you, Eminence?" I said at last. "I make a fair enough living here from cards."

"A dull living."

"A safer one. Drunks are not nearly so dangerous as the kind of men you play your games with."

"And don't you miss those games?" He stretched his arms out across the wooden back of his chair. "The hunt? The chase? The kill in the dark? The look in their eyes when they realize they cannot escape you?"

What do you know? my thoughts whispered at him.

Maybe nothing, his whispered back. *Maybe everything.*

I could find out, if I worked for him. Perhaps. A new puzzle, and truth was I'd been bored these past months for lack of puzzles. Though playing that game with Cesare Borgia would be a great deal more dangerous than playing it with Juan.

"Besides," my masked man added, smiling. "Apart from the taking of lives, what else are you good for?"

That hit me in the stomach like a cold fist. "Something, I hope," I managed to say, and the cards felt clammy in my hands.

"Oh?" He raised his eyebrows. "What? Besides shabby little card games, that is."

The thought echoed. *What* are *you good for?* I asked myself. *Alienating friends? Stumbling through Latin books? Writing piss-poor sonnets?*

What indeed.

"Shall we leave it to the next hand?" I said finally, and we turned our cards over in silence.

"Thirty." Cesare Borgia smiled.

I tossed mine down. "Thirty-one."

"So?" He collected all the cards. "What's it to be, little lion man? Will you come and work for me?"

Giulia

I t is every little girl's wish to be a poetical inspiration, preferably one which will live through the ages and inspire love in the hearts of men for all time, and jealousy in the hearts of all women. Or at least it was *my* wish when I was a little girl. I had thought my daughter would be pleased to learn she was named for the greatest muse of all, but Laura was disgusted with her namesake.

"She should love Petrarch," Laura said very firmly.

"She couldn't, *Lauretta mia*. She was already married." I retrieved my daughter's straw hat from where she'd flung it over a rosebush.

"She was mean," Laura decided.

"Well, *he* should have been more sensible. But try telling that to a poet." I kissed the top of Laura's head. "Poets can be quite foolish sometimes. Wait till I tell you about Beatrice and Dante. Beatrice was another great poetical inspiration, you know."

"Was she nicer?" Laura wanted to know, leaning over to stroke my pet goat, who had gotten quite fat on a country diet and now lay snoring in the grass at our feet.

"Well, Beatrice died. But she was nice even after she died." I saw the plump form of our household priest approaching, his tonsured head sunburned from the heat that continued to swelter in Carbognano even in September. "You can read all about Beatrice and Dante someday, but it's got very difficult words for a little girl. Try Leonello's book instead, and see if you can't pronounce all the names this time."

It had been my former bodyguard's gift to Laura just a month or two before he stormed out: a little book he'd bound together out of good parchment and silk ribbon, copied out in his own hand with simple stories from Homer and Virgil and a variety of Greek myths. "She'll hate it," he said, tossing the book rather casually in Laura's lap. "There are no illustrations, and that child of yours won't look at anything unless it has pictures of ladies in fine gowns." But she'd doted on it at once: all those gory old tales of battles and gods, written up in large clear print that she could sound out slowly. At four and a half my daughter was beginning to piece her words together very nicely, and Leonello's book had sped her along far faster than the pious verses Fra Teseo advised.

Really, priests. Did they sincerely think stupid little platitudes made anyone thirsty to learn? I remembered the texts I'd been given as a child: *Put on the slippers of humility, the shift of decorum, the corset of chastity, the garters of steadfastness, and the pins of patience.* How many times had I dutifully copied out *that* little gem? Since I never did put on the corset of chastity or any of the rest of it, I saw no reason why my daughter shouldn't practice her reading on Leonello's less pious but far more interesting *Perseus slew the sea monster with one stroke of his sword, and then he unchained Andromeda from the rock and kissed her.*

I ask you. Which would *you* rather read?

Laura hugged her little parchment book. "When is Leo coming back?"

"I don't know," I said lightly. "Now, if you read the story of Troy and the great big wooden horse all by yourself—"

"I *like* the big wooden horse!"

"Yes, so read about him while I talk with Fra Teseo, and I'll let you take the pony out to the lake this afternoon." I clapped the straw hat back over her little head. "And keep your sun hat on!"

My daughter bent her head over the book, feet swinging again from the stone bench under the shade of the hazel tree. A very old hazel tree, Orsino had told me proudly when he first showed me the *castello* garden. Grown from a nut off the very first hazel tree in Carbognano, if you believed the stories. Carbognano was famous for its hazelnuts; I could eat them by the basketful as I sat under that tree and looked out at the blue surface of Lago di Vico.

The *castello* was square and crenellated and cool, a place of archways and parapets and deep cushioned stone sills for curling up with a cup of warmed wine. A lakeside *castello* like the one where I'd grown up, though this *castello* was both grander and less crumbly. The *sala*'s ceiling had been new-painted to please me with scenes of nymphs and urns and mossy springs, and Orsino in a grand gesture had ordered all the gardens planted with pink roses. "For my little rose," he said, chucking me under the chin. "Giulia Farnese: the Rose of Carbognano!" I really did prefer yellow roses to pink, those tiny rambling spicy-scented blooms my mother had cultivated when I was a child, but Orsino's chin trembled in disappointment when I suggested adding a yellow bush or two among the pink, and I let the matter drop. He had made a very romantic gesture, after all, and anyway the sickly pink blooms all fried in the summer heat like eggs because it wasn't anywhere near the season for planting. Maybe next year I could sneak in a yellow rose or two without Orsino looking quite so hurt.

Yes, on the whole I liked Carbognano very much.

Fra Teseo bowed as he approached, puffing a little from the climb he'd made from the church to the *castello*. "Madonna Giulia," he greeted me. "You wished to be consulted about a new window for the church altar; I have the estimates from the glaziers. And there is that dispute between Messer Bernardo and Messer Guglielmo, the property line dividing their orchard; both have submitted a petition for your judgment. And the harvest festival to be arranged in October . . ."

The day-to-day business of governing a small town. "These figures from the glazier are very dubious," I said, scanning the first set of papers. "He's padding his estimate. Drop a hint, Fra Teseo, and see if his numbers come down. Messers Bernardo and Guglielmo, bring them to me next week and I'll see if I can talk some sense into them . . ."

"Will Signore Orsini wish to hear them?" Fra Teseo hedged.

"My lord husband is involved in greater matters and will leave such small things to me."

In truth, my lord husband did not like to arbitrate any kind of decision. Whether it was a boundary dispute, a charge of theft, or the choice of an Annunciation or a Resurrection in stained glass for the church's new window, Orsino would just blink a few times and say, "I will think on it." Which meant putting the decision off until hopefully it solved itself. I hadn't resided in Carbognano a month before people started bringing such matters direct to me. I did not put myself forward—that wouldn't have been proper, or wifely—but the villagers murmured their concerns to Fra Teseo, he brought them to me in the garden where I sat with my sewing, and Orsino beamed contentment without seeming to wonder why he had so many fewer petitions.

"Mamma?" Laura skipped across the grass with her book. "What's this word, Mamma?"

"You should curtsy to your mother, child," Fra Teseo reproved. "And address her always as 'Madam, my mother.'" But neither my daughter or I paid any attention to him.

"That word is a name," I said, reading the word my daughter's plump finger pointed out. "*Aeneas*. Remember, Laura, he founded Rome."

"Founded? Was it losted?"

Ask Leonello, I almost said. Because Leonello had been my shadow so long, and I still wasn't used to his absence. He was here, surely—I would only have to turn around to see him, boots propped up on the stone bench under the hazel tree as he put down his own book and explained to Laura who Aeneas was. He'd be declaiming the *Aeneid* any instant.

But he didn't, because he wasn't here. And I felt the usual keen ache in my chest as I realized it all over again.

"The festival after the hazelnut harvest," I said to Fra Teseo, giving Laura a gentle push back to her book. "I've already made preparations about the wine, and I believe we should give an outdoor *pranzo* if the weather permits." What I would have given for Carmelina to cook for me, but I'd not heard news of her in months. I'd written to Lucrezia, asking if Carmelina could come to serve me, but had no reply. Well, there had been a reply, but it had been page after page about the new gowns Lucrezia was planning to order from the robe makers, and what suitors were already pressing for her hand even though her marriage vows to the Count of Pesaro had yet to be annulled, and how dull the convent was. Not a word about Carmelina. "Now, I know you've said a bull-baiting is traditional," I continued to Fra Teseo, "but my lord Orsino doesn't like to risk good hunting dogs in a pointless show, and nor do I." Orsino had said nothing of the kind, but I did try to present my decisions as *our* decisions. A lord should be respected by his villagers as decisive in his rulings, even if perhaps he wasn't. "Let us hold a *pallone* match among the village boys instead. I'll present prizes for the winning team . . ."

It wasn't until the last bit of business had been dealt with and the last bit of news discussed (the innkeeper's daughter was with child; perhaps I could do something for her) that Fra Teseo hesitated and turned pink.

"If you will pardon me," he murmured almost inaudibly. "It arrived this morning . . ."

Reaching into his sleeve, he passed me a stamped and sealed packet of creamy paper with a very familiar seal.

"Thank you," I said calmly, and laid the letter unopened on the stone bench beneath the hazelnut tree. "Shall we read the story of Hades and Persephone together, Laura?" I asked, dismissing Fra Teseo, and did not look at the letter again until my husband came striding into the garden a little while later, his eyes lighting at the sight of me as they always did. I allowed mine to light up too, as I saw my lean and handsome Orsino in his riding boots and his fair wind-mussed hair.

"Good hunting today, my little rose," he said, as he said every day, whether he had bagged a stag or a squirrel or nothing at all. And then his face fell as I placed the letter in his hand.

"For you," I said, as was proper because a married woman got no letters that her husband did not read, and so I went back to Laura and looked over her shoulder as her lips moved along the lines of Leonello's clear writing. "*Pomegranate*, Laura, sound it out. That's the present Hades gives Persephone . . ."

My husband had no glances for Laura—he rarely did. He could never help searching her face as though looking for signs of his rival, so mostly he avoided looking at her at all. He stood in the garden staring at the letter in his hand as though it were a snake. "I thought the last one was—well, the last one."

"So did I," I said, and ran my finger over Laura's page for her. "Yes, *Lauretta mia,* you may have a pomegranate with your *cena* this evening, and you may eat all the seeds you want. No one will keep you in the underworld."

Laura looked disappointed. "I *want* to see the underworld."

"Oh, no you don't!"

"Here—" Orsino pushed the letter back at me. "You read it." He always did that, but I still left the letters unopened until he gave me leave to read them. I would give him no cause to think I was writing to Rodrigo behind his back.

"Well?" His hands clasped and unclasped at his sides, crumpling his fine hunting gloves as I broke the seal and read the familiar bold sloping scrawl. "Is it the usual sort of thing? He wishes you to return to Rome?"

"No," I said slowly. "No, he seems to have given up. At least on that matter."

"Good." Orsino looked at me, gnawing his lip. "That *is* good, isn't it? You wrote to him a fortnight ago, you were very firm . . ."

I'd let him read my letter before I dispatched it to the Holy Father. Rodrigo's missives had begun coming for me not six weeks after I left Rome for Carbognano—just as Cesare had predicted. *We would have you back at Our side*, that letter came first, and when that went unanswered, *You pain Us greatly by your absence*, and when that went unanswered too there were a few furious rounds of *Ungrateful, unfaithful Giulia!* The usual sort of thing, in other words, and I won't say I wasn't tempted for a moment to return—return to Rodrigo, to the Palazzo Santa Maria, to the life I'd enjoyed in the Holy City.

But it wouldn't *be* that same life, would it? Not the life I'd had with Leonello at my side, with Adriana and Carmelina and Pantisilea, with Lucrezia still innocent and chattering and young. My friends were gone. And here in Carbognano I had a *castello* filled with a growing band of new friends, and a lake where my Laura was free to run and play as a child should rather than sit still like a doll on display . . . and just like that, the flash of temptation when I opened Rodrigo's letters was gone. I'd sat down a fortnight ago and written him a brief note avowing my future fidelity to my lord husband Orsino Orsini, whose child (I lied smoothly to the Holy Father) I was now carrying. And my prayers went always with His Holiness and the great reforms he had planned after the death of the Duke of Gandia, may God rest his soul.

I knew Rodrigo. That should have been the end of it.

"What is it?" Orsino peered at the lines in Rodrigo's hand. "You said he's not recalling you to Rome."

"No." I passed him the letter, nudging the goat away before it could eat the tassels off Orsino's boots. My husband avoided my pet goat just as he avoided my daughter—yet another thing I'd brought from my former life in Rome. "The Pope is recalling Laura," I said, and my mouth was dry.

Orsino read, and Laura looked up at the sound of her name. My beautiful fair-haired girl, looking the part of a country child now in a linen dress fit for grubbing in the garden and pebble-gathering by the lake. My Laura, who had learned to ride a pony this summer by scrambling on and off its broad back rather than being led formally about by grooms; who had a scattering of freckles across her little nose and no one to admonish her that freckles weren't proper; who ran races and played hoodman-blind with the other children in the *castello* rather than being passed about at parties by giggling ladies who urged her to perform for their amusement. "The Holy Father wishes to arrange a betrothal for Laura," I said through a throat suddenly turned sticky with fear.

"But she's only seven." Orsino was still reading.

Laura was not even five, but I didn't press the point. "Lucrezia had a betrothal at seven," I said instead. And Lucrezia was now sighing her days away in a convent, waiting for a divorce at the age of seventeen. Lucrezia, who had been almost as sweet-natured and pretty as my Laura when she was a child.

And my daughter was *so* pretty, so tall and quick and laughing with such dark mischievous eyes. She'd abandoned her book now, and plopped herself in the grass to weave a flower chain around my pet goat's neck . . . A daughter for any man to be proud of, especially a man who adored his family. A man who had lost one child and might be feeling newly possessive of the rest.

I'd assumed that if I took myself away from the Borgia fold for good, my Orsini-christened daughter would come with me.

"Giulia?" Orsino looked at me, and I took the letter from his hand and crumpled it up in my own, feeling the sun beating down on my head. "Maybe a betrothal would be a good thing for Laura," he said. "She could be a countess someday, even a duchess—"

My sister would have said that. I'd had a great many scolding letters from Gerolama, chiding me for giving up the Holy Father's favor. *This is no time for virtuous flutters!* she wrote indignantly. *Think of the family. Better yet, think of your daughter!*

Well, I was. And if I knew anything at all after watching Lucrezia grow up, her head turned first by one grand match and then another, I knew that no illustrious marriage was worth seeing my daughter change from the happy, unspoiled girl she was into a vain, self-important little ninny.

"No betrothal," I said. "Not for Laura. Not like it was done for Lucrezia. A Spanish count one day and then a French duke the next, or maybe a Sforza or an Este or a Colonna, and all of them tossed aside the moment they prove inconvenient. No."

"How can we refuse? It says here"—Orsino snatched the crumpled letter back, smoothing it out—"if we do not present ourselves within the month, the Holy Father will send an escort! That means *guards*, Giulia. This *castello* can't withstand papal guards!"

I pulled my words in sharply before they could escape me. I laid a hand along Orsino's cheek instead and saw the blossoming in his blue eyes. Even after three months, he still did not seem to believe his good fortune that I had come back to him. I kissed him lightly, and his mouth claimed mine with all the eagerness of a bridegroom. "Orsino," I said, still cupping his cheek, and his smile faded because I so rarely called him by name. I called him *my lord husband*, as was proper and expected. "Orsino, we must go to Rome."

He looked as though I had stabbed him between the ribs. "To see *him*?"

"No." Stroking his cheek. "To fight him."

Carmelina

When the soon-to-be-former Countess of Pesaro took to her bed late in August and declared there was no point anymore in getting up to face the day inside these dreary walls, she was not jesting. "Just leave me here to molder," Lucrezia Borgia said darkly to the giggly younger nuns with whom she'd happily shared perfumes and gossip a few weeks ago. "Let me rot. No one cares a jot, anyway. Carmelina, more wine and some of those little burnt-sugar stars—"

Even confined to her bed, the little Countess kept Pantisilea and me in a trot most of the day. Pantisilea had to massage her feet because they ached, and then her temples because they ached more, and then I would be sent for cold lavender-scented pads for her eyes and perhaps just something to nibble—"I don't know what I want, Carmelina, surprise me. Quince and ricotta *tourtes* again? Well, I suppose." And then she would usually weep for a while, while Pantisilea, who had a sweeter voice than my crow's caw, would sing some soothing little song while I waved a fan until my arms ached, or Lucrezia dried her tears, or both.

And then were the days when the Pope sent his daughter a letter or perhaps a gift of wine or fruit or a length of cloth. Lucrezia did not rise from bed to receive the papal envoy, but she always made sure to bathe first, sending everyone out so she could pat herself all over with rosewater, and then arrange herself back in bed in her best lace shift, and pearls in her ears, and just a bit of red ochre to bring some color to her cheeks. Because the papal envoy, well—

He swept in to make his bow before the day bed: Pedro Calderon, known as Perotto: slender, swarthy, dashing, and handsome. "*Madonna*," he said, with a flashing smile and a sweep of his feathered cap. "Your radiance dims the room."

There was a great deal of fluttering and complimenting, to which Pantisilea and I listened with interest as we hovered outside with trays of sweetmeats and cups for wine, and then finally Lucrezia's silvery voice called for us. "But why won't he *sign*?" my mistress was pouting as we entered with curtsies. She had a new embroidered shawl about her shoulders from His Holiness, and a new letter, too, though she'd tossed that to one side. "Cesare assured me he would sign it!"

"He would have done so." Perotto had an assured courtier's voice, soft and reassuring. "The Count of Pesaro would have signed last week, *madonna*, but the canon lawyers—"

"Oh, bother the canon lawyers. A batch of dried-up old spiders, what do they know? Ah," Lucrezia greeted us, and gestured the wine toward Perotto with a gracious wave. "You may go, Pantisilea. Carmelina, you stay and comb out my hair; the pins are hurting my head and you've got a far lighter touch."

I didn't have a lighter touch, and the pins weren't aching her head either. Madonna Lucrezia just wanted the papal envoy to admire her hair, and she knew I'd comb it out for her without making eyes at Perotto as Pantisilea always did. I began pulling pins and arranging the long blond locks, which had gotten darker since they no longer had their daily sunning, and Perotto paid a few graceful and unoriginal compliments about Venus in her bower. Lucrezia preened herself, but soon she was pouting again.

"Well, you might as well tell me. What *did* the canon lawyers say?"

"They could find nothing in your past betrothals, Madonna Lucrezia, that would invalidate your current marriage." Perotto had the envoy's gift of presenting bad news as though it were good, but even he sounded a little worn at all the back-and-forth legal wrangling that had been going on these past months. "Your past betrothals were formally concluded before your vows to Lord Sforza, so . . ."

"So the Holy Father will have to find some other excuse for annulment." Madonna Lucrezia's rosy little face had gone hard. She'd had a certain guilty sympathy for her husband at first—"Oh, my poor Giovanni, his pride must be hurting him to lose me like this. He does love me so!" But after the rumors he'd lately begun spreading, well . . .

Perotto, who had had to dry a good many of Lucrezia's tears after she'd heard of those foul rumors, changed the subject with alacrity. "Perhaps you have heard, *madonna*? Your eminent brother has returned from Naples."

"Oh, Cesare *is* back! You must tell him to visit me immediately." She shook her loose hair forward over one shoulder in a gesture exactly copied from Giulia Farnese, and flicked a finger at me. "Carmelina, go make some more of those little pastry things with the blood-orange slices in honey. Now, my dear Perotto . . ."

"Isn't he beautiful?" Pantisilea sighed down in the convent kitchens when I entered with the empty plate. "He's even prettier with his doublet off, let me tell you. I had him in Madonna Lucrezia's *sala* last week, up against the wall with his hose around his feet. There's nothing as funny-looking as a man with hose around his feet, is there? But he *was* very pretty, and lovely for kissing. I do like a man with no rotted teeth."

"I wouldn't go boasting about Perotto's kisses if I were you," I warned, arranging more of my little honeyed pastries on their majolica platter. My new mistress ate them by the basket; she was already starting to get fatter under the chin, and they weren't doing her teeth any good either. "He's Madonna Lucrezia's to flirt with."

"But girls like us don't count as flirting! You could have him too if you wanted, Carmelina." Pantisilea never minded sharing her lovers, I would say that for her.

"You're welcome to him." I shoved a curl back behind one ear, feeling the rustle of paper in Santa Marta's pouch. She shared her living space with quite a thick packet of letters by now, all from a certain former apprentice of mine. Santa Marta didn't seem to mind, but I think she approved of Bartolomeo. Her dried-up fingers had always seemed to rustle approval inside their pouch whenever I took a sniff of one of his sauces. "I don't like dark-haired men."

"Well, Madonna Lucrezia does." Pantisilea winked. "Do you think she'll take him for a lover? Perotto, I mean."

"She might, but he won't." I reached for my apron. Perotto flirted with my new mistress, and paid her extravagant compliments, but no more. A very shrewd young man, and you had to be, to make a career under Pope Alexander VI. "Perotto wants to rise, and he won't rise far if he sleeps with the Pope's daughter."

"*If* she's just his daughter." Pantisilea widened her eyes.

"None of that," I said in the same tone I'd always used when gossip among my kitchen apprentices shaded a bit too salacious.

She waggled an eyebrow. "Everyone's saying it."

I glared at her, fists on hips. "How long have you worked in the Borgia household, Pantisilea? Have you ever seen anything, one thing, to justify gossip that foul?"

"Well, no—"

"Then hold your tongue. It's vile and disgusting, and I won't have talk like that in my kitchens."

"They aren't your kitchens, Carmelina Mangano," she laughed.

"They are for now." I rubbed a pinch of sugar between my fingers, wrinkling my nose at the quality. "So, no filthy gossip about Madonna Lucrezia."

Someone should have told that to the Count of Pesaro. Sweet Santa Marta, how the rumors were flying, and it was all his fault! He'd gone stamping and raging off to Milan, begging help from his more illustrious relatives to fight the annulment, and he hadn't been satisfied calling the Pope a *marrano* bastard or a Spanish upstart. No, he'd had to burst out with a lot of resentful whining that the Holy Father only wanted Lucrezia free so he could have her himself.

I don't believe for a moment that he meant it, not the way it sounded. You had only to see the Pope with his daughter to know they were entirely fond of each other, and not in any disgusting way. But the Pope clearly considered Madonna Lucrezia his daughter first and Lord Sforza's wife second; everyone in Rome knew that—and it was the kind of thing to make any husband jealous.

If it had just been the Count of Pesaro doing a little resentful muttering up in Milan, that would have been one thing. But Fra Savonarola had gotten hold of all those rumors clear down in Florence, where he was supposed to be making a Holy City for himself and not just listening for smut. But priests are always listening for smut.

"The nest of Borgia vipers in the Vatican, violating even the laws of blood in their unholy lusts!" Fra Savonarola thundered to his flock, and soon his words were being repeated all the way from Rome to Venice, and in every city, town, and village hamlet in between. "Brother services sister, and father services daughter, no better than beasts wallowing in the mire—" On and on it went, and everyone from Fra Savonarola to Pantisilea seemed happy to embellish the rumors.

I imagine the Holy Father had waved it off as briskly as he waved off any foul rumor. He'd have heard it all before, no doubt. But with Fra Savonarola thundering on about the foul fruits of incest, the whispers had finally penetrated inside convent walls to Madonna Lucrezia's sheltered ears, and she'd stormed and cried and nearly made herself sick with her wailing. And I couldn't help but notice that not nearly so many of her fine friends came to visit now, those other nobly born young wives of Rome who had brought gossip and laughter and the latest fashions to the Pope's daughter in her exile. "No one wants to be seen with me anymore!" she shrieked. "I might as *well* stay here and rot, I can't *face* them, everyone's talking about me—"

Maybe that was when my new mistress's little face changed from hesitant sympathy to cool hardness when Lord Sforza's name arose. Because she'd stay in the Convent of San Sisto now until her marriage was annulled, and after that, the Holy Father and Cesare Borgia between them would find her another husband as fast as possible. "They want me out of *sight*," I'd heard Madonna Lucrezia wailing to the avid ears of Suora Paolina and Suora Speranza. The nuns were the only audience she had left, and all of them clucked delightedly behind their veils to have such drama in their quiet midst. "Not one word of truth in anything my stupid husband said, and Cesare still says I'll have to be married again as fast as possible! And until then I have to rot here until the rumors die!"

"I thought you wanted to stay here, *madonna*." Pantisilea tried to console her. "Didn't you just say you couldn't stand to face everyone with all the whispering?"

More crying then. Logic, I remembered Leonello pointing out once, was not really Lucrezia Borgia's strong suit.

The bells for Sext began to ring. That placid monotonous sound still sent a spike through my temple like a silver nail. I began to assemble the ingredients I'd need for *cena*, something cold because Madonna Lucrezia could not abide anything hot in this weather; something sweet because she could not abide anything spiced; not a salad because I could get no greens that were not wilted by heat and chewed by insects; not fruit because fruit arrived in this kitchen only after the wasps had been at it. You'd think that a wealthy convent like this one would feed its sisters like queens, but you'd be wrong. The choir nuns ate well, but from their private stores: the wine and the fine white bread and the fresh fruit they bought with their allowances or received as gifts from their families. They kept the good stuff locked away in their cells, Santa Marta rot them, and didn't even bother touching the dismal gruel dished up in the refectory. And it *had* to be dismal, in case any sharp-eyed priest made an inspection with his nose sniffing for sin. "We eat humbly here," I'd heard the prioress say piously. "Even the most well-born." And she never bothered to mention that every sister who could afford it just stirred the gruel in her bowl for a while, and then went back to her own cell to dine on fresh bread and apricots and good wine from Ischia.

It had been every bit as bad cooking in the Convent of Santa Marta in Venice, but I'd forgotten how thoroughly, wretchedly soul-flattening it could be when it went on day after day. The murky olive oil and the warped pans and the ovens that didn't heat properly. If I'd seen Lord Sforza in the flesh, I'd have bound him to a spit and cooked him, because he'd done for me as well as his little wife with all those rumors, whether he'd started them in ignorance or in malice. If Lucrezia was bound to stay at the Convent of San Sisto until her annulment could be finalized, then I was bound to stay too. For the past three months, until the end of the year or maybe all the way into the new year, depending on how long it took the Count of Pesaro to give up his wife.

"If I'm to stay here I'll at least be well fed," Madonna Lucrezia had sighed when I ventured to say that my services were required outside convent walls. "You'll stay as long as I do, Carmelina. And who else is needing you, anyway? Not Giulia Farnese, because she's gone back to that dull husband of hers, *and* broken my poor father's heart, so if you think I'm going to listen to any letters she sends—"

Three months. Three months already, and I knew the convent now. I knew the bells were about to toll before they made a sound, I knew the clang of the gates and the rusty squeak of the grilles when they swung shut, and I knew the anonymous black-and-white-garbed sisters who had now become familiar faces: the sleek-faced prioress who visited the Pope's daughter daily with an unctuous smile; Suora Paolina, who came from the illustrious Colonna family and was mad for candied cherries; Suora Cherubina, who had a merry laugh and a liking for figs in honey, and all the rest of them. And I did not want to know any of it.

I found myself praying again inside convent walls, and not my usual quick entreaties to Santa Marta so that my bread would rise or my *tourtes* brown evenly. Santa Marta was cross with me right now anyway, because I never dared take her out of my pouch anymore in the cell I shared with

Pantisilea. But when Pantisilea dropped off to sleep I'd look up into the stuffy dark and make my prayers—not to Santa Marta or even the Holy Virgin, but to the Count of Pesaro. *Sign your wife away*, I prayed. If he could *see* his wife here, whining and wailing the hours as they passed, he'd have given her up in a heartbeat. *Sign and do it quickly, because I want to go home.*

I wasn't really sure where home was, now that the papal seraglio had ceased to exist. But Madonna Giulia would help find a place for me, that was certain. Even in her newly virtuous turn, surely she would aid me if I asked. And of course there was Bartolomeo, cooking away in Vittorio Capece's *palazzo* and writing me letters. He wrote a clear, back-slanting hand, and I smiled at the very sight of it because I'd been the one to tell him at the age of fifteen how important it was for a cook to know his letters, so he could keep his records without being cheated. I told all my apprentices that, but Bartolomeo had been the only one to listen . . . He didn't try to woo me anymore, in all these letters he wrote me, and thank goodness for that. He was long past any calf love infatuation by now. He just wrote prosaically of the new kitchens in the Capece *palazzo*, of the recipes he was making and refining on his own for that book he was still determined to compile. Oh, how it squeezed my heart to open a letter and read: *For a tenderloin in the Roman style, signorina, quarter the leanest part of the meat into chunks and space onto a spit with bacon and sage leaves . . .*

I dredged a dreary little meal together for Madonna Lucrezia, and when dashing young Perotto swaggered away to his horse and went trotting out of the convent gates, Pantisilea and I carried everything up on trays. Lucrezia was admiring her new embroidered shawl, sitting up in bed trying various effects of draping, her cheeks pink with pleasure as they always were after a good dose of masculine admiration. "More of those blood-orange pastry things?" she said, looking up. "You can't imagine how I've been craving them—"

"Yes, and pork jelly for *cena*." I was really rather proud of that jelly. A very substandard pig, but I'd gotten a good flavorful jelly out of boiling the ears and snout and hooves in an even more substandard wine. "Plenty of honey and nutmeg, Madonna Lucrezia; you've been liking everything sweet lately, haven't you? I could only find dandelion greens for a salad, but look how pretty I've made them look with these bugloss flowers . . ."

She looked down at the jelly, which I'd arranged so nicely on the plate: quivering and cold, ringed by bay leaves and slivered almonds. "The smell," she said faintly, pink draining out of her cheeks, and then my jelly went *smash* all over the floor as the little Countess of Pesaro lunged out of bed, stumbled across her chamber, and vomited just in time into the silver basin she normally saved for washing her hands.

"Madonna Lucrezia—" I began to move across the room but then I froze, shards of broken majolica plate and splats of pork jelly all about my feet. I could feel Pantisilea gaping at my side, still gripping the wine decanter, both of us staring at our mistress and realizing just why she had not left her bed in a month and why she bathed herself alone.

She heaved again into the basin and then straightened, pushing her loose hair out of her face and wiping her mouth. She saw us staring at the rise of her belly beneath her shift and heaved an impatient, dramatic sigh. "Yes, yes," she said. "I'm to have a child."

CHAPTER THIRTEEN

✦

*A prince never lacks legitimate reasons
to break his promise.*

—MACHIAVELLI

Giulia

My young friends!" Vittorio Capece of Bozzuto approached with open arms as Orsino and I were ushered into his ornate little *sala*. A sanguine and sophisticated Neapolitan of perhaps fifty, leanly elegant in a sable-furred robe; cheerful, graying, rosy-cheeked. "Your journey was not too tiring?"

"I am too dusty to be allowed in your beautiful home," I informed him, shaking out my limp skirts. "Evict me at once."

"Nonsense, m'dear, you're an ornament to any household. I'm delighted you've chosen to adorn mine." He came to kiss me on both cheeks. "My *palazzo* is yours, as long as you choose to stay in Rome."

"Not long," Orsino hastened to say. His eyes traveled over the coffered ceiling picked out in gilt, the discus thrower carved in exquisite rosy marble beside the doors, the French tapestries of knights and unicorns and maidens skipping through fields of pinks. Fair-haired blue-eyed pages with blue-and-gold livery to match their looks were already taking our dusty cloaks, offering silver basins and rosewater for us to dip our hands, bringing pale sweetened wine in frail-stemmed goblets.

"We will be returning to Carbognano soon," Orsino ventured, looking rather swamped in all the luxurious bustle. "Very soon."

"Such a pity," Vittorio Capece said in his Neapolitan drawl. I didn't think I would ever like any Neapolitans; the Tart of Aragon had spoiled the whole nation for me. But no one could help but be fond of convivial Vittorio, who insisted that even the handles of his doors be works of art. "Haven't you brought that dwarf bodyguard of yours?" he continued, glancing behind me. "Such a clever little fellow; he admired my red marble and ebony chess pieces so much I didn't even mind when he beat me three games in a row. I was looking forward to another match . . ."

"I'm afraid Leonello is no longer in my service," I said briefly, and heard Orsino shift beside me in unstated relief. Even if Leonello hadn't left of his own accord, Orsino wouldn't have wanted to keep him on. My husband would never have been comfortable around my bodyguard's sharp eyes and even sharper tongue, and it wouldn't have been any use asking Leonello to keep his sarcasm to himself, either. Leonello regarded men like my husband as lions regard lambs—fit only for the sharpening of claws. If Orsino had ever addressed me as "my little rose" in Leonello's hearing, my bodyguard would have let out a hoot, struck a lovelorn pose, and composed an extemporaneous sonnet on the spot: "Giulia Farnese, the Milk Thistle of Carbognano." And then he would have followed me about for days saying, "Yes, my little milk thistle?" until I threatened to smack him, and then he'd have grinned his mocking tilted grin and demanded, "Why do women always prefer the trite to the witty? 'My little rose?' *Dio!*"

Oh, but I missed him.

"What a pity, what a pity," said Vittorio, oblivious. "I thought that little lion was your shadow, m'dear! Well, now, you must be tired; I have had rooms prepared if you wish to bathe and change—"

I had thought Leonello my shadow, too. So selfish of me—you can't suborn *people* to be shadows, can you, as if they have no lives of their own? I reminded myself of that, every time I turned to say something to Leonello and then felt the pang of remembering all over again that he was gone. I offered a brief smile to Vittorio and allowed Orsino to lead me toward the stairs.

"It wasn't a suggestion, that little hint about bathing and changing,"

I whispered to my husband as a matched pair of ebony-skinned slave girls whisked us up flights of shallow marble steps. "Vittorio was being very polite, but I could see his agony mounting every time our dusty clothes touched his beautiful carpets."

"How did you make his acquaintance?" Orsino sounded suspicious. He sounded suspicious whenever I mentioned any man's name.

"Vittorio Capece is one of Rome's great collectors of art," I said. "He said I was the most decorative woman he'd ever seen, and he begged to have my hands sculpted as an artistic study. They're here somewhere, my marble hands—he stacks his rings on the fingers when he runs out of room on his own."

Orsino's voice sounded flat as we were ushered into a sumptuous little *sala* with an ornate velvet-hung bed and embroidered satin cushions along the wall benches. "He admires you, then."

"Only as an ornament," I said lightly, dismissing the little slave girls. "Everyone knows Vittorio will never marry."

"Why?"

I thought of pointing out the languid, long-legged good looks of every page boy, manservant, and male attendant in this *palazzo*. And the naked marble figures of Apollo and Pan and David, rather outnumbering the statues of Venus and Diana and Salome. In Carbognano, men of Vittorio's tastes were spoken of only in whispers, but in cosmopolitan Rome such things were far more casually viewed. I had been shocked at first, but Rodrigo didn't care who went to bed with whom, and I certainly wasn't going to spurn poor Vittorio just because ranting men like Fra Savonarola said he was hell-bound. I didn't think Orsino's view of the world was quite so flexible, however. "Vittorio chases art rather than women," I said instead, hanging up my cloak on a silver wall peg. My Pope's letter had offered to house us in the Palazzo Santa Maria when we brought Laura to Rome, but I had taken one look at Orsino's face and written a tactful refusal. I knew any number of noble families in Rome who might have played host for us, even a few of Orsino's cousins from the family's more illustrious branches. But for Orsino's peace of mind I'd chosen Vittorio Capece, whose appreciation of me would be nothing more than aesthetic.

Orsino flushed. "The way men look at you . . ." he began, and trailed off, standing in the middle of the room with his hands hanging at his sides like a little boy. Really, men. Such delicate flowers with their bruised feelings and hurt pride. And they say women are the oversensitive ones!

"The way men look at me?" I kept my voice teasing. "I've seen the way all those wives look at you! Envying me my handsome young husband when they have some dour graybeard!" He brightened at that, as I'd intended, and I kissed his cheek. "Let me settle Laura."

"Surely the maids can do that?" But I pretended I hadn't heard him.

My daughter had been whisked up to a chamber of her own before she could break any of our host's costly knickknacks. She was already careening about the room with her nursemaid chasing behind, another maid with a silver ewer of water and a red-haired manservant with a tray trying their best to keep out of the way. "You must rest before the papal audience, little mistress!" But Laura ignored that blithely, running up to present me with a sticky, sugary fig squashed in each fist. "He brought me my *favorites*!"

"Madonna Giulia." The red-haired manservant bowed to me, and I found myself recognizing him.

"Bartolomeo!" I greeted him. Holy Virgin, could this really be Carmelina's favorite apprentice? He *had* grown.

"I've never had the opportunity to thank you for helping me find my post here, Madonna Giulia," he said with another impeccable bow. "I volunteered to bring up the dishes myself as soon as I'd heard you'd arrived. Sugared figs for the little mistress"—handing another down to Laura—"and marzipan *tourtes* for your own chamber." A grin. "And there will be fried smelt from Lake Bolsena for your plate any day you wish it, regardless of what the *maestro di cucina* has to say." His grin was infectious.

"What, you aren't *maestro di cucina* yet, Bartolomeo?"

"I plan to have his post by next year." Matter-of-factly. "Signore Capece is already a great admirer of my sugar subtleties. 'Food made art,' he says. Many thanks again, Madonna Giulia."

"Don't thank me, thank Carmelina," I smiled. "She trained you, after all. I remember her whacking you over the head with a spoon in Capodimonte, when you were mangling her pasta shapes."

"I've not heard from Carmelina lately." His smile disappeared. "She can't write often; she says the nuns won't have letters delivered without a good fat payment. She did say she'd be able to leave when Madonna Lucrezia did . . ."

"I shall see what I can find out about Madonna Lucrezia, then," I promised. "Surely she won't be staying at the convent much longer."

He gave me another bow and a round of thanks. I'd meant to hunt down Carmelina anyway, and lure her away from the Borgia employ to my *castello* in Carbognano. I'd have to promise her new stoves and new trestle tables and all the spices she wanted, no doubt, but she was worth it. Perhaps this handsome no-longer-apprentice would wish to accompany her . . . Though it would hardly repay poor Vittorio his hospitality if I stole his cook on departure. On the other hand, given Vittorio's tastes for strapping young men, perhaps it *was* a good idea at that.

Orsino was still wandering about our new chamber in his dusty doublet, looking a trifle lost among all the luxury, and I devoted myself to fussing over him for a while in the way I knew he liked: unlacing his shirt with my own hands, bathing his temples in lavender water. He put his hands about my waist, and I knew what he wanted so I smiled and cast my eyes down and let him lead me to our borrowed bed. I lay under the rich green satin bedcover, and then I lay under my husband, and he hardly seemed any more substantial than the satin. He was still so hesitant to touch me, so furtive when his fingers stroked my skin or his weight pressed against me—and it pressed against me a great deal, because my husband very badly wanted me pregnant.

His eyes had lit up when I showed him the letter I had first written Rodrigo, saying I could not return to him because I was carrying the child of Orsino Orsini. "You are?" my husband breathed.

"No," I said, wincing because he looked so crestfallen. "But if I *say* it, he will not want me," I placated. "And it will be true soon enough, surely!"

We'd managed to delay bringing Laura to Rome until November—

and I know Orsino had been hoping to get me with child in that time. It was not just to make my lie a truth, or even because he wanted a son as all men do. Orsino wanted to parade me about Rome with a swollen belly, so that no man would look lustfully at me anymore.

He moved over me, gasping into my shoulder, and I folded my arms about his neck and murmured sweet bits of nonsense. I knew what pleased him by now: soft arms, loving looks, delicate shivers of pleasure. Nothing too bold, because boldness is for harlots, not good and decent wives. I had not always been a good wife to him, but I was now. He deserved that.

I didn't know what I deserved. Maybe just to do my duty—it was what I'd been born and reared for, after all.

"Husband," I scolded softly afterward. "We shall be late."

The Sala del Pappagallo in the Vatican was clustered with ambassadors, envoys, petitioners, flatterers; lords bearing gifts and lords begging favors. How many papal audiences had I witnessed here? The hall of parrots, named for the once-brightly-colored birds painted about the walls in fading splendor. You'd wonder why *parrots* on a wall instead of something a trifle more grand: saints or martyrs, or, if one must follow an animal motif, at least pick a grander animal like the splendid Borgia bull. I think whoever painted those parrots must have had himself quite a chuckle, because a cacophony of cardinals all bickering and backstabbing away in that *sala* could make more noise than any gaggle of birds. And what a great lot of chirping and fluttering went up as Orsino and Laura and I were announced.

I had expected to feel nervous—I had not been so stared at since my arrival in Carbognano, when the villagers looked as though they'd expected their lord's notorious wife to have demon horns and a forked tongue. But it was Orsino's arm that trembled, and I gave his elbow a reassuring squeeze as we approached the glittering figure in the sweeping robes. Rodrigo.

I fixed my eyes instead on a parrot on the wall, a faded green parrot with a cross expression, and I had a wild urge to laugh when I remembered the sulky parrot that had once belonged to little Lucrezia, and how I'd privately named it *Vannozza*.

Orsino's name was given, but the Holy Father had no glance for him. "Madonna Giulia," Rodrigo said formally, and gave me his hand. I bent my head to brush my lips against his ring, and his dark eyes crinkled at me in their old way, and my heart squeezed. Because my former lover had changed so much in only five months. There were deep new lines about his mouth and eyes, graved there by Juan's death, I imagined, and the flesh about his neck hung in loose folds. His hair was entirely gray, and the skin had loosened over the knuckles of the hand he had presented me. But he smiled, and his smile had all its old energy. His fingers gave mine a squeeze and he lowered his voice. "You are looking well, *mi perla.*"

I could see him looking for the pearl he had given me, but I had looped a silver crucifix about my neck instead, an ornament belonging to Orsino's grandmother. I had also made a point to dress my hair low and my neckline high, in just the kind of subdued gray satin gown that a virtuous wife should wear. Voluminous gray satin, too, to hide the belly that was supposed to be showing the first signs of Orsino's child—I'd seen Rodrigo's eyes flit to my stomach at once. "Your Holiness," I said, taking my hand away with great firmness, and cast my eyes down.

I felt my husband let out a silent breath. Rodrigo looked at me a moment longer; I could feel his gaze as tangible as a touch, and more whispers went up along the Sala del Pappagallo. But I went on gazing serenely at the floor, and I heard Rodrigo sigh. "The little one," he said, his gaze moving to Laura. "She has grown."

I had coached my daughter for this moment, and she advanced with great gravity in her small gray satin gown, which was an exact copy of mine. "Your Holiness," she piped, and curtsied as though she had never seen him before in her life, had never squealed with delight when he gave her a string of seed pearls for a present, had never looked at him in his horned mask and inquired if he was the Devil. But she smiled at him, and Rodrigo smiled back, and perhaps it was because I'd not seen them together in almost half a year, but I saw it. Holy Virgin help me, but they had the same smile.

Don't see it, I prayed, and felt a cold shiver run down my back. *Don't see it, Rodrigo.* Once I'd wanted nothing more than for him to believe Laura was his daughter in truth, but now . . .

He threw his head back and laughed as Laura continued to look up at him fearlessly. "What a pretty little thing you're growing up to be, *Lauretta mia.* You'll be pretty as your mother in a few years' time. Come, come—"

And I saw the men craning to look with speculation in their eyes: envoys from Naples and ambassadors from Milan and couriers from Ferrara, sniffing like interested hounds around my daughter as Rodrigo turned her for inspection. I should have known. The Sala del Pappagallo was where the Pope received his ambassadors, the men who brokered brides for their Neapolitan masters or their French masters or their Florentine masters.

"So the little Orsini is a Borgia after all," I heard the Milanese ambassador say professionally to an envoy from Venice as they looked my daughter over. "Too young to breed for a good ten years, but a betrothal might be worth something in the interim."

"No firm amount set for the dowry yet, I suppose . . ."

"Lucrezia Borgia will bring the next husband forty thousand ducats. The little Orsini will be worth more, *and* a virgin . . ."

I saw little Burchard taking his notes as usual. *One Borgia daughter for sale; opening bids accepted from Milan, Ferrara, Naples . . .*

My eyes flew up at Orsino, but he was gazing at the floor, not a glance for Laura. The Pope had not addressed a single word to him, and the tips of his ears had gone scarlet with humiliation. I took my hand from his elbow and bent to recapture Laura as she twirled in her satin dress, laughing now to be the center of all eyes. "If you will pardon me, Your Holiness," I said evenly. "My daughter is too young for such excitement. She needs her bed."

"Yes, yes." Rodrigo looked at me fondly. Remembering, no doubt, the bed we'd shared to create Laura. "We will talk more of her later, Madonna Giulia. Of her future."

No doubt.

The next petitioner came forward, launching into his prepared speech, and Orsino and I were allowed to press back through the crowds. Laura looked up at me, questioning. "Did I do well?" she said, and I swept her up to my hip and hugged her close, crushing the gray satin dress.

"Yes, *Lauretta mia*. You did very well."

"She looks like Lucrezia did at her age." I heard the cool voice behind me, knowing it at once. "I used to carry her about like that too. Juan called me Nursemaid, but I did not mind."

"Your Eminence," I said with another small curtsy. Cesare Borgia, looking as out of place in his red clerical robes as he ever did.

"Giulia Farnese," he returned, without even a glance for Orsino hovering nervously at my side. "I have missed you."

"I doubt that, Cesare. You have never even liked me."

"I like Caterina Gonzaga less. She's arrogant, and she's grasping, and since my father is bedding her now instead of you, I see a great deal of her."

"Caterina Gonzaga?" The wife of the Count of Montevegio, a very pale and very proud beauty indeed who had always made eyes at Rodrigo. I could feel Orsino's gaze on me. "I hadn't heard," I murmured, and cast my eyes down.

"You are surprised?"

"Your father intended so many . . . reforms." To purify himself, and the church with it. A lifetime's work, and I'd seen him filled with its terrible, bowed resolve after Juan's death. A transmutation of sorts: Rodrigo Borgia into Pope Alexander VI.

"What did I tell you?" Cesare gave a lazy shrug. "His fits of reform never last long. He wanted you back within the month, didn't he? The council he'd appointed to head all these great changes was gone shortly after."

My heart squeezed again. I'd known my former lover would not find such a transformation easy—I'd received his letters, after all, begging me to come back to his side. But I hadn't thought—

"Jesu." Cesare looked almost amused, looking at me. "I'd not thought to see you *disappointed*."

"Very." No transmutation of Rodrigo Borgia after all. Base metal would remain unchanged, not turned to gold. Yes, it disappointed me.

Less noble, perhaps, was the small outraged part of me that thought, *Caterina Gonzaga?!*

"Your Eminence," Orsino attempted, pink-faced with chagrin to be ignored yet again, but an authoritative voice overrode him from behind us.

"The Milanese envoy wishes to meet with you, Your Eminence. I'll wager he can tell you if Lord Sforza is finally ready to sign his wife away."

I whirled around, hearing that voice. But Laura had looked first, bored with all this adult talk over her head, and I saw her eyes go wide with delight as she saw the small figure in black and cried, *"Leo!"*

My eyes flew over my former bodyguard. He stood small and proud, holding a place of his own beside blank-faced, stone-eyed Michelotto, who had always given me the shivers. Leonello looked every bit as hard, head thrown back and boots planted, fingers drumming along his dagger hilt as he looked me over with casual eyes. I saw a court lady glance at Michelotto, glance at Leonello, and cross herself with a surreptitious little shiver.

Laura had wriggled down from my arms, running to him with her skirts bunched in her little hands. "Leo, Leo, I can *read* now, I can read anything, I told you I'd learn!" But he disengaged her without even a glance.

"Back to your mother, little one." His deep voice was as cool as I remembered—and on his black sleeve, I saw he wore the badge of Cesare Borgia. Just like Michelotto. "I am no fit company for children."

I was moving toward him, disengaging my hand from Orsino's arm, but Leonello slid into the crowd and vanished.

Leonello

I am no Latin scholar, but I can tell you one thing about the language of ancient Rome: it does not pair well with weeping. Latin is clipped, masculine, cool. Blubbering and wailing your way through terse Latin cadences, no matter how beautifully worded, is no way to impress anyone with your declamation.

"Try again," I heard Cesare Borgia say patiently as Lucrezia broke down in her oration with a fresh welter of tears. "Take it up from the next line."

"Why do I have to bother?" Lucrezia wailed from inside the chamber. When she was unhappy she was piercing, and her voice penetrated clearly through the half-open doors of her chamber to where I leaned against the wall of the stairwell outside. "My husband gave his testimony, he finally signed it before witnesses the way you wanted him to, so why do I—"

"You will confirm his testimony before the court when they hear the petition of annulment." I could hear the smile in Cesare Borgia's voice. "My pretty little sister with her lovely accent in Latin—the canonical judges will be moved."

"I'm too ill to be dragged all the way to the Vatican!" I could see a flash of the Pope's daughter through the half-open door: all but buried in her bed under a mound of furs and lap cushions, her eyes swollen from crying. She had not even risen to greet her favorite brother when he arrived like a dark arrow shot into the convent and sent all the nuns into a flutter. "Can't you just read my testimony, Cesare?"

"It will look better coming from the Countess of Pesaro herself." I heard the bed settle as Cesare put an arm about his sister. They were speaking Catalan, which the family always saved for private moments, but after serving them five years, I had picked up enough of it to understand. "Though you'll soon be much grander than a mere countess, of course. Did I tell you the Duke of Gravina is sniffing for your hand?"

"He is?" Lucrezia sounded less damp and more interested.

"Ottaviano Riario as well, though he has that Sforza bitch for a mother, and I think we've had enough of Sforzas." Another rattle of paper. "So, try the oration again."

The sonorous Latin began, punctuated by periodic honks as the little Countess blew her nose, and I wandered away down the stairs. My head throbbed with every step. Perhaps from the wine I'd drunk to forget the recent things that needed forgetting. Perhaps from the memory of the last time I'd descended these steps, at a dead sprint away from Giulia Farnese's stunned and pitying eyes.

I had not seen what look she had in her eyes when we came face to face in the Sala del Pappagallo. I'd slipped away too swiftly to see, bowed and threaded back into the thickest part of the crowd. Though I'd seen that little Laura had grown taller, in her months in the country sun. By the time the Pope made up his mind on a French husband for her or a Milanese one, she'd probably top me in height.

I found Carmelina not in the kitchens but in the garden, kneeling alone in the barren patch of earth and grubbing at the dirt. I'd have sauntered right past the anonymous figure in the dark nun's habit, but I heard a mutter of Venetian invective behind me and turned for another look. "*Signorina Cuoca*," I greeted her. "Don't tell me you have renewed your vows?"

"I didn't have a dress heavy enough for the cold, so—" She gestured at the heavy wool habit, glowering. "How was I supposed to know to pack clothes for winter? I didn't intend to stay here five *weeks*, let alone five months!"

The coarse black weave turned her olive skin sallow, and even sitting back on her heels in the hard dirt I could see the hem was too short at her shins. "As a costume I prefer the giraffe ensemble," I agreed, and sat down on a sawed section of log that was the only seat the garden had to offer. November's first snow had fallen last night; it showed in dirty gray sprinkles over the packed earth. The sky overhead was like beaten pewter—more snow soon, to be sure.

"What are you doing here, Leonello?" Carmelina uprooted a basil plant with a brisk yank, tossing it roots and all into her basket. "I'd heard Madonna Giulia came back from Carbognano, but you're not in her pay anymore. Not if I know you."

She didn't say *why* I would no longer be taking Giulia's coin, and for that I could have kissed her even though her lips were red and chapped from cold. But she probably would have smacked me. "I work for His Eminence Cardinal Borgia now," I said, indicating my new livery. Much like the old: unadorned black with plenty of hidden sheaths for knives.

Though it missed the subtle tailoring that had made Giulia's livery a work of art, and me in it almost a handsome man.

"You, working for Cesare Borgia?" Carmelina's straight black brows flew up. "Don't tell me you've finally learned how to juggle."

"No." I smiled thinly. "It's my other skills he finds the occasional use for."

"Ugh. Don't tell me." Carmelina yanked up another basil plant.

"It's not as often as people think." Only one task, in fact, since I had been hired. Of course, that one had been quite enough.

"Still, don't tell me." A few sad tendrils of tarragon joined the basil. "So is Madonna Lucrezia still weeping upstairs? She's been weeping for weeks, even when she heard Lord Sforza agreed to have their marriage annulled."

"She's dried her tears enough to butcher the verbs on a very nice little Latin speech written by her brother."

"Don't tell me how nice it is. She'll recite it to Pantisilea and me all week until she knows it. We'll all have it by heart in the end."

"Perhaps you can go to the Vatican in a few weeks and give her testimony for her, then. Swear before God, Pope, and all others assembled that the marriage between you and Lord Sforza was never consummated, not once, and that you are still *virgo intacta*."

Carmelina snorted. "I haven't been *virgo intacta* for a good many years."

"Nor has Lucrezia Borgia, but who's quibbling?"

"Apparently not Lord Sforza." Carmelina shook her head, yanking out a few sorry-looking threads of chives. What a joke it all was. Consanguinity had not worked as a pretext to annul the marriage, and neither had the excuse of Lucrezia's two previous betrothals. Cesare Borgia's solution? Nonconsummation, due to the Count of Pesaro's prevailing impotence. I'd laughed out loud when I first heard it, and so had most of Rome. The Count of Pesaro impotent, when his first wife had died in childbed?

"It will serve him right," Cesare had said coolly. "If he wished for a less humiliating end to his marriage, he should have signed sooner under the betrothal excuse."

But Lord Sforza had stuck his heels in, and for that he would not only lose his wife—he'd be mocked all about Rome as a eunuch. An exquisite revenge, and I was learning what a talent my new master had for that.

"Impotence." Carmelina let out a short laugh. "I ask you, what kind of man would admit to that? Even if it were true, and we both know Madonna Lucrezia and that husband of hers consummated that marriage on every bed in the Palazzo Santa Maria!"

"But the Borgias say they didn't. And they have the power to rewrite truth, didn't you know?" My nails needed trimming, but I had no intention of getting my knife out. I wondered if it still had blood on it. I couldn't remember cleaning the blade since that recent little task I had performed for my new master.

Carmelina pinched a few dead needles off a chilled-looking rosemary bush. "I wonder how they made him do it. Lord Sforza, I mean. How did they make him sign his own virility away?"

"They sent me," I found myself saying.

She looked at me. "You?"

"And Michelotto. This is his sort of work, usually." My first real errand, since donning Cesare Borgia's livery. "Cardinal Borgia sent us to Pesaro, five nights ago. Very quietly. We had a letter in his hand for Lord Sforza, urging that the documents be signed, but the letter wasn't the point."

"What was?" Carmelina asked.

"We were to persuade him what would happen if he did not yield."

"And?"

"And we did."

It had been very quick work, really. All that riding, all the aches in my legs from the saddle, and the whole business itself done in a matter of heartbeats. We were on the way back to Rome almost before the sweat had time to cool on our horses.

"How did you persuade him?" Carmelina's voice was quiet.

"Lord Sforza was in his *sala*—none of his captains there for once, just a page-boy with his wine and his letters. The page . . ." I shrugged. "It isn't important."

"It isn't?"

Michelotto eviscerated him, I almost said. *Dropped the boy's guts onto his shoes in one stroke of the knife. Then broke his neck and slammed the letter on the table in one motion, all before either the page or Lord Sforza could scream.* And then Michelotto had looked at me with his empty stone-colored eyes, and I'd known what he wanted. Known it the way a snake knows the moment to strike its prey; the moment when the eyes go wide and white the way Lord Sforza's eyes looked. And I'd taken the dagger out of my belt and slammed it through Sforza's hand, through the letter and into the table.

Dio. I hadn't even meant to do it.

I—

I suppose Juan Borgia thought that too, when he shoved a knife through Anna's palm.

Carmelina pushed a stray curl back behind her ear with one hand. The scarred hand, which looked like it had healed, but had left a mark the color of a man's liver. I'd seen the page's liver, Lord Sforza's page, when his guts spread themselves on the floor.

Michelotto had given me a nod as I yanked my knife back up. Approval, almost, though it was hard to tell from a man so blank and colorless.

I'd looked over my shoulder at Giovanni Sforza as we left the study. A man of thirty or so, handsome enough with his fashionable beard and less-fashionable doublet, wax-pale and staring at the letter under his spread hand, spotted with his own blood. I looked at him, and he met my eyes. "You don't want her," I said. "You don't want any part of that family."

He'd still been staring as we shut the door. I don't know how he covered the scene, after. Perhaps he claimed he caught the page thieving; no one would bat an eye if a lord killed a servant caught dipping in the gold. It was the sort of decisive gesture men-at-arms appreciated. Everyone liked a ferocious lord.

But Lord Sforza was not ferocious at all. Just a man from the country, a man who liked soldiers and horses and simple things, a man who must have had some sincere affection for his little Borgia wife if he had fought so stubbornly to keep her. Not a ferocious man, not like Michelotto, not like Cesare Borgia. Not like me.

"Good," Michelotto said to me on the way back to Rome. He had a voice with no rise and fall whatsoever, a voice like a sheet of metal. "You did well, little man."

"Will he sign?"

Michelotto did not dignify that with a response. But we heard the next day that witnesses were gathered in Pesaro to watch as Giovanni Sforza, Count of Pesaro, signed the documents stating that he had never laid a finger on Lucrezia Borgia due to his own overpowering impotence.

"Good," Cesare said, brisk as Michelotto, and asked no more.

"Don't you wish to know how we did it?" I couldn't help but ask.

"Why?" The young Cardinal looked surprised. "If one leaves a task to subordinates, one trusts they are capable of handling it. I don't employ anyone unless they are capable. You did your task, the documents were signed, and there's an end to it." He tossed a purse each to Michelotto and me. "Good work."

It *was* good work. He had been right about me. This was the work I was made for.

If only my head didn't ache.

I wished Carmelina would not *look* at me like that, with her suspicious black eyes and the accusing red eye of the scar on the back of her hand staring at me, too. I might have been tempted to put my head on her shoulder and ask her to rub my throbbing temples. But she looked at me that way because she knew what kind of work I could do, the things I was so good at. Unlike Giulia, who had looked so happy to see me when we saw each other in the Sala del Pappagallo. I lied when I said I'd retreated too quickly to read her face. I could read her face in a glance. She'd been glad to see me, lips trembling to speak, and I had no desire to hear anything she had to say.

Oh, but my head ached.

"Have you seen Bartolomeo lately?" Carmelina yanked a bulb of garlic out of the half-frozen ground. Her voice was light, conversational, and I remembered speaking to her in just as soothing a tone when she had been clutching her bleeding hand in the wine cellar and trembling like a horse about to bolt. Did I look like a horse about to bolt? "Bartolomeo writes to me. Mostly just recipes, of course. Perfectly ordinary letters—"

"Of course," I said. "Because you're blushing, and recipes make you blush like poetry."

More light words, coming out in white puffs on the cold air. Any words I could find to replace the images in my head—until Pantisilea came out into the gardens in a flat run, skirts flying about her knees and her face pale as bone.

"Carmelina," she gasped. "Carmelina, he's calling for us, he's calling for us both, he's gone mad—"

"Who's gone mad?" Carmelina rose, basket of herbs over one arm.

"Cardinal *Borgia*!" Pantisilea wailed, just like the little countess. "He found out, Madonna Lucrezia tried so hard, but she felt sick again and had to run to the basin. He saw how she looks under all those blankets and cushions, he *saw*—"

"Saw what?" I began to say, but Carmelina dropped her basket on the ground and sprinted after Pantisilea to the gatehouse where the Pope's daughter was ensconced.

Perhaps Cesare Borgia had been shouting before, but he was deadly hushed now as he summoned the two maidservants inside the chamber. I crept on the outsides of my boot soles along the stairs, barely breathing, because when he spoke in just that hue of quiet I did not want to be caught eavesdropping.

"Who was it?" he said in his near whisper. "Who was it, sister? If that swaggering bravo Perotto dared seduce you—"

"Of course not!" The little Countess of Pesaro was hiccuping and gasping and sobbing all at once; I could hear that very clearly down the stairwell. "I'm not a *whore*, Cesare, I didn't have a lover, it was my *husband*!"

"We warned you," he snapped. "Father warned you to keep out of Sforza's bed, and so did I. Warned. You."

"And I *did*! I *did*, but he came to see me and I—"

"Here? He was allowed in *here*, after all my instructions to the prioress?"

"No, no, it was just before I came here to the convent. He came alone from Pesaro in the night, very privately. He was on horseback and he brought me a poem like he did in the old days. He wanted one last chance to talk. Sancha has a pavilion on the Tiber she uses for meeting—well, you, for one. She lent it to me so I could meet Giovanni in secret. It was *romantic*!" Lucrezia wailed. "There was a *moon*! I felt *sorry* for him!"

"You should have given him your pity with your knees shut. You think his testimony of impotence will carry any weight when you're six months gone with his brat?"

That just fetched a fresh storm of weeping, which neatly covered my startled huff of breath on the stairs. Lucrezia Borgia, heavy with her husband's child when they were trying to prove nonconsummation of the marriage? Oh, *Dio*.

Cesare's deadly quiet voice continued. "Who else knows?"

More tears from Lucrezia, and I thought I heard Pantisilea begin to blubber as well, but Carmelina spoke steadily enough. "Three, Eminence. Pantisilea and I have tended all Madonna Lucrezia's needs—she has stayed in bed, none of the sisters here know—"

"Three. You two, and who else? Perotto?"

"I had to tell *someone*!" Lucrezia hiccuped. "I was in *agony*, and he was so kind—"

"Three," Cesare cut her off. "Good. Perhaps it may be handled yet. You, Pantisilea or whatever your name is, cease your whimpering and fetch wine. You, cook; I remember you. Food, whatever will keep my sister strong, but not much of it. Keep her slim. She is not to leave these chambers, and no one is to see her but you two and Perotto. He will handle her errands outside these walls as they need doing, and you will serve her within. And if any of you breathe one word of the Countess's condition, to the nuns or to any other, I will have your throats slit. Now, get out." Carmelina and Pantisilea flew from the room as though flung from a cannon, faces white as they hurtled down the stairs without even seeing me.

Careful, I wanted to say to Carmelina. *Oh, be careful, Signorina Cuoca, this is not a secret you want.* But from the flash of her set, terrified face as she passed me, I did not think she needed the warning.

Inside the chamber, Cesare Borgia had lapsed back into Catalan. "'Crezia," he said. "'Crezia *mia*, stop weeping. Your speech for the hearing; we will practice it again. Dry your eyes."

"I can't appear before the cardinals like this!" Lucrezia shrieked.

"Of course you can." I heard a yelp and a rustle of bedclothes—it sounded like the Cardinal was dragging the little Countess out of bed. "Look at yourself in the glass—it will all be concealed easily enough. A dress with a high waist and a heavy skirt, a furred cloak. It's deep winter; no one will question it."

"They'll see—"

"They'll see what they are *told* to see: my pretty sister swaddled against the cold. Now, your speech . . ."

Cesare Borgia came from the room an hour later with a brow blacker than midnight, slapping his embroidered riding gloves against his hand, and by that point I was installed well below, making the passing sisters in their black and white flow around me as I sat on my stool over a copy of Pliny's *Naturalis Historia*. "Did you hear?" my new master said without preamble. "Did you hear, little lion man?"

"Hear what?" I asked, chin in hand over my book. "Pliny claims amber will take on a charge when it is rubbed, did you know that? I shall have to test it out."

I do not know if Cesare Borgia believed me, any more than I knew if he suspected my stubby hands were covered in his brother's blood. But he said nothing more of it, and a few weeks later I stood in the Vatican with his retinue, craning my neck to see in the crowd of curious ambassadors and prelates as Lucrezia Borgia was brought from the Convent of San Sisto by sealed coach to give her testimony before the canonical judges. It was just days before Christmas, the breath puffing white in the air even inside the sealed chamber, and Lucrezia stood well-wrapped in her heavy winter velvets and enveloping sable cloak. She flushed prettily as she was called to speak, her sweet grave face a little fuller than usual, giving her the look of an angelic child. She spoke in solemn, perfect Latin (like a Cicero, they gushed afterward), and she testified that her lord husband had not bedded her once in three years of marriage, and she was thus *virgo intacta*.

How Rome rocked with laughter.

CHAPTER FOURTEEN

❖

Lucrezia . . . daughter, wife, and daughter-in-law of
Alexander VI.

—SCURRILOUS ELEGY ABOUT LUCREZIA BORGIA

Carmelina

I was used to blood. I could cut a pig's throat in one double slice, and scrape the blood off my hands afterward without a thought. I'd killed woolly little lambs and big-eared baby goats for my table without a drop of sentimentality. Man's work, and perhaps that was the trouble. A woman's work of breeding babies and bearing them, well, that had passed me by.

Lucrezia Borgia was screaming, bleeding, writhing in her birthing bed, and she terrified me.

"Oh, Jesu, it hurts!" Her matted hair stuck to her sweating face, she clung to Pantisilea's white-knuckled hand, and she was sobbing and praying around her gulps for breath. "Where is Cesare, he said he'd be with me—" She lapsed into Catalan for a few whimpering seconds, and then into Latin. *"Ave Maria, gratia plena, Dominus tecum—"*

"We should fetch the prioress," Pantisilea said nervously.

"What do you think a nun would know about any of this?" I exploded. "We do what Cardinal Borgia said. We sent Perotto for the midwife; now we wait." I had no idea what else to do. My own mother had borne only my sister and me; I'd not helped with the birth of a dozen more little brothers and sisters as so many daughters did. And when my mother went to assist at a friend or neighbor's childbed, well, I'd been so unnerved at all the screaming that I'd always volunteered to heat water in the kitchens or run back and forth for cloths—anything that would keep me out of the way. Now I was beginning to wish I'd stayed and watched at a few more of those childbeds.

"It all began so fast—" Pantisilea bit her lip. One moment our mistress had been lying in bed as usual, eating a plate of my burnt-sugar stars and reading the Avernus sonnets again, though mostly she leafed through them while complaining that Perotto never looked at her now that she was fat and ugly. And Pantisilea had been reassuring her that of course she was not fat, which was even true because for such a slim little thing, Lucrezia Borgia didn't show her pregnancy near as much as she might have. A stroke of luck for her Vatican appearance, that had been. Even now at nine months it was only her face that looked any fatter, and frankly that was from too many burnt-sugar stars. But Pantisilea and I still had to spend a great deal of time assuring her that she was not at all fat or ugly, of course she wasn't—

But this afternoon she had interrupted our reassurances with a cry, and there had been a rush of water across the sheets, and now the whole bed was soaked through. Not just from water but from sweat, and from blood.

"*Benedicta tu in mulieribus*—" She broke off in another cry, and I felt a stab of pity for my little mistress. I hadn't much liked her, not since she had immured me up here just because she didn't feel like eating convent food—I'd have given everything I had to turn my back on her and leave these walls forever. But seeing her writhing in that fouled bed, so swollen and young . . .

"Bite on the sheets, *madonna*," I encouraged. "We must keep you quiet; remember what His Eminence said." Though how Cesare Borgia thought we were going to keep the nuns from knowing their illustrious guest was giving birth in the gatehouse, sweet Santa Marta knew.

Another long and grueling hour passed before the midwife arrived. A plump little woman with a basket over her arm, hustled along by a white-faced Perotto. "No need to hurry me, young man," she clucked. "First babies never come quickly, plenty of time yet, and you did say this was a first—ah, yes, we're well in time." A pat to Lucrezia's sweating forehead. "Best get you up out of that bed, my dear, up and walking. Lean on the maid, that's it—and if the other maid can fetch us hot water, and perhaps a store of cool wet cloths for her face—"

"I'll go," I said, abandoning Pantisilea, who gave me a dirty look as she helped the midwife haul Lucrezia Borgia gasping out of bed. Perotto had already fled the scene, lucky man.

Lucrezia's voice trailed after me toward the stairs, half shriek and half whine: "I don't *want* to get out of bed and walk! I don't *want* to, I'm telling my *brother*—"

"Sweet Santa Marta," I muttered. "Let me never have a child." If I couldn't have been born a man, at least make me barren. I flew down the steps, away from the sound of the midwife's cajoling, and I nearly fell over the convent's prioress.

"Pardon, Mother Prioress—" I curtsied hastily.

"There appeared to be some disturbance in the gatehouse," she said in her smooth voice that whispered of being reared in a *palazzo* somewhere herself, just as her gliding steps whispered of silk shifts under her black convent skirts. "Is our honored guest quite well?"

"She has fallen on the stairs." I trotted out the lie Cesare Borgia had prepared for us all. "It seems her arm is broken. We sent Messer Perotto for a wise-woman to tend her."

"Our infirmarian here could have seen to her—"

"Cardinal Borgia will have none but the best physicians tend his sister." A little head bob of apology. "It seems this woman is versed in the setting of bones. I imagine it will be painful, however—please do not be disturbed if you should hear our mistress cry out."

"Of course," the prioress said smoothly, and I could see not a ripple on her face. Well, if she suspected anything, who was to say otherwise? And where would a nun even take her suspicions? Besides, I would have laid good odds that these walls had seen babies born before. Nuns break their vows too, after all, and erring wives retire behind convent walls in sudden fits of piety when they need to wait out inconveniently swollen bellies in private. I didn't think this elegant prioress would blink at one single thing that was going on in Madonna Lucrezia's chamber right now.

"If you will excuse me, I am to fetch cloths for my mistress—" I took myself down to the kitchens in my ugly black habit that was too short, and flew back up with the wetted cloths. I was back and forth for hours with possets, reels of thread, more cloths, until the sun began its fall and a cold blue twilight fell over the convent.

That was when the gatehouse heard the angry cry of a newborn child.

"Put the little mite to the breast quickly, if you wish to stop those wails." The midwife was already packing the soiled linens, the vials of herbal potions, the tools she had brought with her in her capacious basket. "I've administered a sleeping draught," she told me. "Your mistress will sleep for a time. It's best if she feeds the child herself the first few days, but do try to arrange a wet nurse out in the country as soon as the babe can travel. City air isn't good for infants."

I realized that after all these long hours the midwife had not asked any of our names or volunteered her own. She did not seem curious about the exhausted Lucrezia lying half swooned in the bed, or the tiny collection of swaddled, reddened limbs in the basket of linens that had been padded and prepared as a makeshift cradle. The midwife merely bestowed a twinkling smile on us all, collected a purse from Perotto, and disappeared as swiftly as she had come. A midwife who can be discreet will make herself a good living. There are always women who find a child inconvenient, usually silly girls who have managed to lose their virtue to a poet when they were supposed to be saving it for a husband. A speedy birth in a convent and a quiet payment to a midwife who can keep her mouth shut, no names of course, and everything restored to normal afterward with no one's reputation the worse—I should not have been surprised Cesare Borgia would know how to arrange such a thing.

"What was it?" I asked Pantisilea as we trailed exhaustedly down the steps toward the convent courtyard. Lucrezia was sleeping sound under the midwife's draught, and the baby appeared to be sleeping too in her arm. At least for the moment, and both of us lunged to get out of the chamber's stuffy confines.

"What was what?" Pantisilea yawned.

"The child. Boy or girl?"

"You know, I don't know. I didn't even look."

Whichever it was, Lord Sforza had an heir. Not that he'd ever know it, drinking bitterly in Pesaro with his manhood publicly in shreds. I took a moment to wonder what would happen to the child, if it would be sent away soon into the countryside with a wet-nurse as the midwife had suggested, or perhaps passed off as some minor sprig on another branch of the voluminous Borgia tree. I knew better than to ask.

The moon was just starting to rise, white as frost against a twilight sky. We lingered in the emptying courtyard, watching the nuns in their black and white hurry inside at the sound of the Vespers bell. I took another gulp of the fresh air, savoring the cold after the stifling chamber with its smells of blood and birth. I had a new letter from Bartolomeo, and it had the usual news about how he had packed a hamper yesterday for Madonna Giulia when she took her daughter to see a snake charmer in the Piazza Navona, and how he had really begun work upon his recipe compendium now, beginning with a section on meatless dishes since it would be Lent soon. The same sort of letter he usually wrote, but he had begun it simply *Carmelina* and not the formal *Signorina*, and I wanted to think about that, think about it and study my name as it looked in his neat back-slanting hand—but the last of the nuns disappeared inside to their prayers and soon it would be dark, and Madonna Lucrezia would be needing us.

"We should go in," I said to Pantisilea. "As soon as that child wakes crying she'll wake too, and she'll be wanting warm wine and cold compresses and Santa Marta knows what else."

"My mother birthed six children, and she never howled as much as Madonna Lucrezia did squeezing out the one," Pantisilea groaned, and we were both laughing when hoofbeats sounded.

"My sister," Cesare Borgia rapped out from the back of his horse, almost before it had pulled up in a clatter of hooves. Pantisilea squeaked a little at the sight of the tall dark horse and its tall dark rider, but I stepped forward.

"She is well," I said, and no more than that. He nodded approval; this was a public place after all, even if the nuns had all gone to Vespers.

"I will remove my sister at once. She will rest tonight at the Vatican, with all the comfort she needs."

"She's too weak to be moved," I began, but the young Cardinal cut me off with a twitch of one black-gloved finger.

"I have a horse-drawn litter prepared for her." I could see it trundling into the courtyard with the rest of his men, a great cushioned thing as wide and soft as a bed. "The distance is short, and the Holy Father is eager to see her."

And perhaps his grandchild, I thought. Not to mention that once out of the convent, that grandchild could be hidden safely away. Anyone's child at all, certainly not the child of the Pope's daughter with her reborn virginity.

I nodded. "We will see her things packed."

"We shall send for them later. I want my sister away tonight." Cesare Borgia had brought a small entourage; just the horse-drawn litter and a few guardsmen behind on horseback. His most trusted men, no doubt. "You two prepare to leave as well," he added. "You may ride with my men."

I felt my heart leap at that. I had Santa Marta in her usual pouch at my waist, and Bartolomeo's letters—anything else in the convent, I did not care if I ever saw again. A pair of dresses too worn for decency, a few shifts, and a kitchen whose inadequate ovens I would never need to curse again.

"Where is Perotto?" Cardinal Borgia asked, glancing about.

Pantisilea was already accepting a hand up onto the horse of one of the guardsmen. "Scampered as soon as the noise began. Men always do, at a birth." She swung her leg over the saddle in front of the guard, looking over her shoulder to twinkle a smile at him. "Well now, how are *you*?"

"Pity about Perotto. Well, I shall catch him later." Cesare made a gesture, and the guardsman sitting behind Pantisilea calmly drew a dagger and stabbed her. I saw the blade only as a needle-flash of weak moonlight, but it found its way between two of Pantisilea's bony ribs and she gave a noiseless gasp. Her body jerked, but the guard had his arm hard about her waist and he stabbed her again. Once. Twice. Three times.

There was very little blood. Just the desperate stiffness of her body draining away. She slumped over the saddle, silly Pantisilea who had kept me up so many nights this past year with her prattle about all her lovers. Silly Pantisilea slumped dead over the pommel, and the guardsman pulled her back against him, methodically arranging her head until she looked like a woman who had fallen asleep in the saddle.

"Put her in the river, Michelotto," Cesare Borgia said disinterestedly. "Find the midwife too, and arrange an accident. Something innocuous. That trick with the falling roof tiles, perhaps."

He was swinging out of his saddle now, moving toward me. I backed away, feeling panic freeze in my throat—another Borgia coming toward me, this one much harder to kill than Juan, and Leonello wasn't here this time to save me with his knives and his wit. Or even Bartolomeo with his skillet. Oh, Bartolomeo—

I tripped over a loose stone in the courtyard and fell with a gasp that was half shriek, but Cesare Borgia was already moving past me, toward the stairs that would take him to his sister. "Silence that one too," he said over his shoulder at me, and was gone.

Gone. Pantisilea gone, the midwife gone, Perotto gone. No one left to know that the Pope's daughter had given birth tonight.

The other guardsman swung off his horse, and I felt a squeeze of relief so violent that my heart almost burst from my chest. "Leonello, you're here, I—"

But his eyes were cold this time, cold under the moon, cold, cold. And the knife in his hand was not for my attackers, but for me.

Giulia

Mamma, Mamma!" My daughter looked up at me in glee as I entered the kitchens, her little nose smudged with flour. "I can make *frittelle*!"

"More than I could ever do." I smiled at the sight of her: sitting on the trestle table swaddled in an oversized apron, assiduously rolling out misshapen little balls of dough. "How did you get down here, *Lauretta mia*?"

"*Il Signore* was turning white every time the little one here went careening past his precious statues." Bartolomeo deftly whisked something in a bowl with one hand and pushed a lump of butter around a hot skillet with the other, but he still managed a bow. "The nursemaids had the bright idea of bringing her down here."

"I hope she is not keeping you from your work." I rescued a bowl of flour before it could tumble out of Laura's hands.

"Work was never lost to a more worthy cause, Madonna Giulia." Bartolomeo reeled off a few orders to the pair of pot-boys scrubbing pans under the cistern, more orders to the boy eternally cranking at the spit of hot-roasted pigeons rotating over the fires. "I want to see mouths shut and hands moving," he warned, and turned back to me. "Only a few of us are needed in the kitchens here if *il Signore* isn't entertaining. Most of the others have gone off to see a miracle play in the Piazza San Pietro. The martyrdom of Santo Bartolomeo, and they say he's flayed on the stage so realistically, they had to bring the player back out to show the audience he was still alive. I didn't care to watch my patron saint get killed horribly, so I've enough time to give all the *frittelle* lessons anyone could want." Bartolomeo smiled down at Laura, and she dimpled at him through her lashes. Nearly five years old, and my daughter was already a flirt! Though Bartolomeo had certainly turned into a lad with whom girls of any age would long to flirt. I still remembered Carmelina's favorite apprentice as the scrawny boy who had loped along the wagons on the journey back from France, but this lean young man with the broad shoulders and the shock of fiery hair could have made a nun's heart flutter.

Laura held her breath as her very first batch of *frittelle* went into the skillet, and Bartolomeo handed her the spoon so she could push them around in the butter. "Watch them carefully, little mistress, you don't want them to burn—"

"Carmelina tried to teach me to make elderflower *frittelle* once." I smiled, remembering. "I nearly burned her kitchens down."

Bartolomeo's freckled face lost its smile. "Pardon me, Madonna Giulia—but have you had any news of—"

"No, not yet."

"My last letter came back unopened. The messenger said there was no one of her name within the convent walls." He scowled. "She can't have left the convent already, not without coming to see me! Months I've been waiting and writing; does she think I'm made of iron?"

I tilted my head at him, giving a grin. "So you're her sweetheart!"

"She clearly doesn't think so," he grumbled.

"Well, I shall ask Madonna Lucrezia about her tonight." Orsino and I were invited to see His Holiness again this evening; another of his small gatherings in the papal apartments. Surely Lucrezia would be there. Now that her marriage to Lord Sforza had been annulled and a few months passed for the talk to die down, she had left the Convent of San Sisto for the Vatican. I knew Lucrezia was cross with me; I'd had a few letters arrive in Carbognano, accusing me of breaking her father's heart—but she never held a grudge for long. Leonello would have said it was because she had the attention capacity of a flea.

"My sister is ill," Cesare informed me as I inquired after Lucrezia that night, making my entrance with Orsino. "She broke her arm at the convent, and she is resting quietly while the bone heals. I know she will wish to see you in a week or two, when the pain passes."

"We had planned to return to Carbognano in another week," I began. Holy Virgin save me, how long was this visit going to drag on? We had originally intended to stay in the city only a fortnight or so, but Rodrigo had said we must wait until he decided upon a match for Laura. And then he ruled that *that* would have to wait until Lucrezia's next marriage was settled first, and then he decreed that both betrothals must be postponed until after the Christmas festivities. And now Christmas was come and gone; the year had turned and we were nearing *Lent*, and nothing at all was settled. I missed my square *castello* in Carbognano with a fierceness that surprised me.

And these past few weeks, it wasn't just the Pope who delayed our return home. Orsino was making excuses too, and that surprised me even more.

"Don't you want to see how the garden is faring?" I'd cajoled him just last week. "I want to see the beautiful roses you had planted for me. And we could attend Easter Mass in our own church. The new stained-glass window is bound to be in place by now." All of us together at the altar, my daughter kneeling between us—and pray God, no betrothal for her yet. Not for *years,* if I got my way.

"You're the one who wanted to come to Rome," Orsino had pointed out.

"And you're the one who wanted it to be a short visit," I said in return. Why in the name of the Holy Virgin had my usually pliable husband changed his mind?

"My lady wife will be delighted to pay a call upon your sister," Orsino was telling Cesare in the rather grand tones he had been using lately. "Perhaps our Laura will someday be a countess like Madonna Lucrezia. His Holiness will have told you he is now considering a French *comte* for a betrothal?"

I hid my disquiet at that. It wasn't just the matter of returning home where Orsino seemed to have changed his mind. Lately he seemed more willing than ever to hear about these various suitors who had been sporadically proposed, one after the other, for Laura's hand. Perhaps because such gossip granted power at these small private gatherings between powerful men—my husband seemed to have discovered how much he liked moving elbow to elbow among such men, telling them so casually that he just might make his daughter a countess someday. "A countess like Madonna Lucrezia," he repeated importantly, and Cesare gave a bored blink.

"You forget that my sister is no longer a countess." The young Cardinal slid off without farewells, toward a dark-haired beauty laughing over a marble chessboard. This was one of the larger halls in the papal apartments; Rodrigo presided at one end in all dignity, but the dignity was somewhat marred by Caterina Gonzaga perching on the arm of his throne—a sight that still gave me a distinct, if small, pang of outrage. The rest of the company lounged merry and at ease about the room, trading soft jests and flirtations. Another of those easy intimate evenings I had once presided over; the ones that sent Burchard into spasms of indignation over the *impropriety* of having such company in the *papal apartments*, oh, *Gott im Himmel*!

But I had other things to worry me now than Burchard's proprieties.

"What's this about a French *comte* for Laura?" I said low-voiced to Orsino. "His Holiness didn't speak of it to me." His Holiness had been too preoccupied lately with possible alliances for Lucrezia to talk much about Laura's future—and I'd begun to breathe easier. "Where did this idea of a French *comte* come from?"

"He brought it up to *me*, Giulia. As is fitting." Orsino's worry that Rodrigo wanted me back had abated, the more he saw Caterina Gonzaga flaunting herself on the papal arm as though she were an empress and not a concubine. A concubine in too much jewelry, and tasteless two-tone velvet. "A French lord for Laura," Orsino went on. "We should consider it."

"Why? France is our enemy!"

"Politics have shifted now. A French alliance could be a great thing for our family." Orsino accepted a cup of wine from a page with a regal nod. "I've had time to consider the idea, and you should consider it too. Laura could get a far better match through the Holy Father than she could from us." I heard a hint of his mother's careful coin-counting in his tone. "Daughters are very expensive to marry off, you know. If His Holiness dowers Laura, well, we can save the expense for our own daughters someday."

"Orsino—" I heard my voice rising and brought it down with an effort. "My lord husband, if the Holy Father dowers her, there won't be a soul in Rome who doesn't assume she's his daughter, even if she has your name. I thought that to be the *last* thing you wanted."

"Every soul in Rome assumes she is his daughter, anyway." Orsino's voice was stiff. "A French marriage might be the best thing for her; get her away from all this scandal. Anne of Brittany has raised a great many noble wards at her court—the King of Naples sent his own true-born daughter there, Carlotta of Aragon. You know Cesare has an idea of laying aside his red hat and marrying her? Carlotta of Aragon, that is." Oh, the importance of trading such intimate gossip about the great and powerful of Rome! "Laura could join the French court there; be raised in the French fashion. By the time she grows old enough to marry, any malicious talk about her birth will be forgotten."

I stared at my husband. In my ears I heard the soft click of marble on marble across the room as Cesare moved a chess piece for his laughing girl; a ripple of laughter from Caterina Gonzaga as she allowed the Venetian envoy to kiss her hand; a page boy muttering an oath as he tripped over his own shoe and nearly dropped his decanter. "I am not sending my daughter away to France to be raised by strangers," I said at last, levelly.

"But it's how things are done among the great," Orsino assured me. "We must think of what's best for Laura. She won't be lonely in France, not among other girls of her own age. And we could send her pet goat with her, eh?"

My pet goat. *My* daughter. The things I'd brought from Rome when I came back to Carbognano, the things from my former life, the things my husband didn't really like to look at because they reminded him of painful times. Well, with Laura off in France he wouldn't have any such reminders left, would he? He could just keep on plowing me until I filled up his *castello* with little true-born Orsinis instead.

I shut my teeth on some very hot words indeed. *Softly*, I thought. *Soft and sweet, as a wife should speak to her husband.* I forced a smile, murmuring something dulcetly noncommittal, and he chucked me under the chin.

"That's my little rose!"

I did not feel very soft or sweet. And if he called me his little rose one more time . . .

"Giulia!" Rodrigo beckoned me, his rings glinting. "Where is Laura? We had particularly wished to see her."

"*My* daughter"—I didn't particularly feel like sharing Laura with either of her rumored fathers at the moment—"is abed. The hour is far too late for a child of four."

"Bah, she'll soon be five." Rodrigo chuckled, the jeweled crucifix about his neck glittering. "I'll give her a betrothed for a present. Did Orsino speak of it? 'Laura, Comtesse de Laval'—how does that sound?"

"It sounds like something that will never happen," I said. "Even if I have to fling myself across the road to prevent her taking one step in the direction of France."

Orsino stopped breathing, and Rodrigo's brows knitted together, but Caterina Gonzaga from her perch on the pontifical throne was clearly bored with all this talk that was not about her. "A game of cards, Giulia?" She fluttered an imperious hand at me to show off a clutch of emerald and sapphire rings. "Like those evenings we spent in dull little Pesaro when our dear Lucrezia was first married. Wasn't there a silly little contest of beauty that I won?"

"Lucrezia won," I returned. "But yes, it was very silly." And my brother Sandro was pulling up a stool beside mine, offering his own deck of cards with a breezy "Thirty-and-one, or *primiera*?" And Rodrigo gave a chuckle and said, "Giulia, how did you ever talk me into giving this good-for-nothing brother of yours a red hat? He's the most useless Cardinal in the lot!"

"But can any of the useful ones make you laugh the way I can, Your Holiness?" Sandro asked cheekily, and a game unfolded as the Venetian envoy joined us and Caterina Gonzaga made a spectacle of herself flashing her rings and her bosom, and Sandro leaned close to my ear as he filled my wine. "Careful, *sorellina*."

"If Orsino and the Holy Father think they can ship Laura off to France—"

"They won't." My big brother's eyes were unaccustomedly serious over his usual airy smile. "The Holy Father has his hands full arranging Lucrezia's marriage, not to mention that Cesare's angling now to get rid of his cardinal's hat. Wait it out, and the Pope will forget all about this French alliance."

I was not nearly so certain Orsino would. "Fight for Laura, Sandro," I breathed as the cards were dealt. "If the matter is brought up among the men when I'm not there to protest—"

"Who do you think pops up with a filthy joke to distract everyone as soon as any talk of Laura or her marriage comes up?"

"Spreading dirty jokes, and you a man of God?" I managed a little smile. "Don't you take anything seriously, Sandro?"

"My niece's future. I assure you I take that *very* seriously." Sandro gave my arm a squeeze. "I'll work on His Holiness, and you take on Orsino. Surely you can wind him around your little finger!"

Normally, I could. But when my husband's pride was hurt . . . and even if he enjoyed these intimate little gatherings of the powerful, he surely still heard the snickers that followed him. Orsino Orsini, the eternal cuckold with his soiled wife trailing her bastard Borgia daughter.

Give him a son, I thought. *Give him a son of his own, and he'll deny you nothing.*

But I didn't want to give him a son. I didn't *want* to, no matter how willingly I made myself lie under him whenever he wanted me. I kissed him and caressed him because it made him happy, because it was my duty, because I felt sorry for him—but that didn't stop my private little prayer every time he spilled inside me: *Please don't let him get me with child.* Every time I prayed it, and every time I stowed the sin away for my confessor because it was a wife's duty to want sons. When I was a virgin bride reciting my vows to Orsino, I'd assumed I'd bear him whole batches of sons, and I'd even looked forward to it because I was *supposed* to. But things had not turned out that way, and I had only the one golden daughter, and I had no intention of shipping her off to France so she wouldn't get in the way of some chinless little half brother who didn't even exist yet.

"Giulia?" At my other elbow, Orsino sounded anxious and showed me his cards. "Which should I play, my little rose? The deuce? Or—"

"The deuce," I whispered back, and tried not to sound irritated. Living in the Borgia household beside all those decisive men really had ruined me, hadn't it? Rodrigo, Cesare, Leonello—even Juan Borgia may have been an illiterate cat-killing despoiler of virgins, but at least he could decide what card he wanted to play. I ask you!

Orsino laid down the deuce with a flourish, looking about him with a pleased air, and my irritation changed to the more familiar pinch of guilt. "I'm a bad wife, Sandro," I whispered to my brother on my other side as the turn passed to him.

"Not anymore." Sandro tossed his own card out carelessly. "You're very well-behaved and boring these days, I assure you."

"But it doesn't come naturally to me anymore. All these wifely things our mother taught me, the things I used to take for granted—"

"Oh, *sorellina*." My brother looked a little sad. "None of our lives have turned out quite as we planned, have they?"

"No whispering!" Rodrigo called out. "I get enough of that in my formal audiences. Caterina *mia*, your draw—"

But a man's shriek broke through the companionable chatter of card-play.

Orsino started so violently he dropped his goblet. The wine spilled across Caterina Gonzaga's sleeve and she cried out, but the cry was lost in another shout from just outside the chamber. "*No, I beg you—*"

Sandro had already shot to his feet, thrusting me behind him, but over his protective arm I saw the handsome young man who staggered into the chamber leaving a trail of blood droplets across the patterned marble floor.

"Your Holiness," he gasped, staggering toward Rodrigo on his throne, and the papal guards moved but Cesare was there first, disappearing from his dark-haired beauty and her chessboard, and reappearing with sword drawn at the foot of his father's throne. "Perotto," he said in some exasperation, and I recognized the young man then. I'd seen him about the Vatican often enough these past months, when he hadn't been occupied running the Holy Father's messages to Lucrezia in her convent. One of Rodrigo's papal envoys, a young Spaniard who had endeared himself to the Holy Father with wit and swagger and charm. Handsome as well as charming, so I'd been careful never to look at him because Orsino saw all handsome men as rivals. Pedro Calderon, nicknamed Perotto, his charm all gone now, his mouth a dark agonized hole as he clutched at his shoulder. A shoulder with a knife hilt in it, I saw with glass-sharp clarity, and for the first time in my whole healthy life I thought I might faint. My knees buckled, because I knew that knife with its damascened hilt. I'd seen it quivering in the center of practice targets; I'd seen it core apples and crack nuts and whittle wood. Once I'd borrowed it to slash through a knotted lace on my sleeve. And I'd seen it snuff the life out of three brutal-faced French pike-men.

"Apologies, Your Eminence." I heard a familiar deep voice from the doors. "He was warier than anticipated, and I'm afraid a good deal too fleet for my short legs."

The whole chamber seemed deathly frozen, looking at the small man standing in the doorway. A small man in black, gently tapping another damascened knife against one thigh as he flicked a speck of blood off his collar. The Holy Father was agape. Only Perotto moved, gasping and trembling at the foot of the Holy Father's throne.

"Your Holiness," he began, and Cesare turned in one casual movement and ran him through.

Caterina Gonzaga gave a faint moan as the long blade went in and out again, unhurried as a serpent's tongue. Sandro tried to block my eyes, but too late. I saw the droplets of blood like a trail of rubies trickling from Perotto's doublet. I could hear one of the women behind me begin babbling a prayer, hear Perotto's small, astonished mew like a dying cat, but I couldn't take my eyes from that trail of red drops. I followed it back to Leonello, bare-headed and scarlet-handed in the door. Not really scarlet-handed, I suppose. His hands looked quite clean as he sheathed the knife at his waist. But his nimble, double-jointed fingers looked red to me, red, red, red. He glanced up and for a moment I met his eyes.

"A private matter, Your Holiness." Cesare sheathed his sword calmly, giving a nod to the papal guards. "A family matter. No need to concern yourself. Take him," he added, and two stone-faced guards seized a limp, gasping Perotto under his arms. He opened his mouth as though to scream as they hauled him up, but only a trickle of a moan came out, like the trickle of blood from the fists he'd clamped over his stomach. Not a very large wound, really, to turn a vigorous young man into this broken puppet.

"No need to concern yourself, Your Holiness," Cesare repeated as Perotto was dragged out. Rodrigo gave a nod; he no longer looked so gray about the mouth.

"Not so publicly next time, Cardinal Borgia," he chided, and held his cup out. A wide-eyed page boy had to be nudged twice before he scurried forward to pour the Holy Father's wine.

Cesare's eyes found Leonello, still standing quiet in the doorway with his boots apart. "You heard him, little lion man. More discretion in future."

Leonello bowed. "Apologies," he said again, and when he turned I saw the frisson of horror that rippled through the crowd of guests, how they flinched away from even looking him in the eye. They flinched like that for Michelotto, Cesare's human sword with the dead gaze. For Cesare himself.

I wasn't aware I was following Leonello until Sandro seized my arm. "No, *sorellina*," he hissed. I jerked my arm away, but Leonello was already gone. There was half a bloody boot print on the marble where he'd stood, and as Cesare curtly ordered the guests out I saw how superstitiously they skirted it. As though lightning would strike them if they trod on that bloody print.

"Giulia," the Holy Father called as Orsino took my arm and tried to lead me out. "Stay with Us a moment."

All I could do was nod mutely. "I should stay too . . ." Orsino ventured, but Rodrigo gave a little flick of his fingers and Orsino trudged out with a resentful glance but not another word. Sandro hesitated a moment longer, looking at me, but I nodded and he too departed with reluctance.

"Rodrigo," I began with a deep breath as the doors closed and left me alone with the Holy Father. But he was sweeping down from his throne with a fond beam.

"A moment," he said, taking me by the shoulders and dropping a kiss on my forehead. "I see you're cross with me, and you should be. Just as well you didn't bring Laura this evening, eh? That's nothing for a child to see."

"It was nothing for any of us to see! Rodrigo, what has *happened*?"

"A spot of tidying up. Hardly important." My former lover brushed that away. "I kept you behind so you could congratulate me, *mi perla*. Lucrezia has given me a grandchild."

All the breath left my lungs in a frozen rush. *"What?"*

He placed a finger to his lips, eyes twinkling. "Cesare will be very cross with me for telling you. He's gone to great lengths to protect our

Lucrezia's reputation, of course. But you're hardly an outsider, are you? You'll be pleased to know Lucrezia is in good health."

"But Perotto—" I said stupidly. I couldn't seem to think of anything else but that dying young man with his stunned eyes.

Rodrigo misunderstood me. "Did Perotto father Lucrezia's child, you mean? No, it seems not. That was Sforza. Lucrezia really was rather unwise there, but she is very young, after all, and her lapses can be forgiven."

"Of course," I echoed. The lapses of the Borgia children were always forgiven. A pregnant wife branding a decent man with the charge of impotence, under holy oath no less? Just a spot of tidying up; hardly important.

The Holy Father laughed. "I will say, I can appreciate the irony of it all."

Irony was not the word that occurred to me. I sat down, and luckily there was a cushioned chair behind me. "So why was Perotto attacked?" I managed to ask. "What has he done to deserve this?"

"It is Our plan to wed Lucrezia to Alfonso of Aragon." Rodrigo tossed off the rest of his wine, moving with all his old energy. "Sancha's younger brother, you know, so he's bound to be a handsome fellow. Lucrezia will like that, and their marriage will shore up my alliance with Naples very nicely. And since he'll expect a virgin bride, well, a virgin bride is what We shall give him." A small shrug. "Regrettable about Perotto, but he was Lucrezia's envoy. He knew."

My lips felt very dry. "And now I know."

"But for all your prattle, Giulia, you know how to keep secrets. Unlike envoys and maidservants, who trade in gossip." Rodrigo turned to look at me, hands clasped behind his back, and his face was very serious now. The candle flames danced merrily over the jewels in his robes, the pontifical throne with its gilding and carving, the cards and wine cups left behind by the frightened guests. "*Mi perla*, I know you don't like the idea of a French husband for Laura. No mother wants to see her daughter sent far away to a strange land. But marriage is a matter of state and must be considered without a mother's vapors. A French alliance would lay the foundation for Our future with France, and—"

"The French took me *captive*, Rodrigo!" I erupted onto my feet. "They took me captive and held me ransom and could easily have had me raped or murdered. You said you would have the French King's head if he'd touched even the hem of my dress—and now you want to give them *Laura*? Ship her off to be raised in the French court instead of by her mother—"

"Now, now, Giulia. I wouldn't leave you bereft like that." He clasped my shoulders again, and my heart eased a little. "There's another matter to consider, and that's my grandchild. The baby has been sent to the country with a wet nurse for the time being, but that will not do for much longer. The child needs a mother."

"The child has a mother," I couldn't help pointing out acidly. "And a father!" Foolish Lucrezia—

"Lucrezia cannot keep the baby, and she knows that. So *you* will raise my grandchild, Giulia. Raise it as your own."

My lips parted, but at first I could think of nothing to say. "Do you think anyone will believe Lucrezia's child is *mine*?" I scrambled after the old lie I had written. "I am carrying my husband's child even now!"

"I think you may have been fibbing about that." He pinched my chin in reproof, giving a glance to the voluminous skirts I'd been wearing for months to cover my flat belly. "I've seen you pregnant before, you know. If you were carrying his child, you'd be round as an apple by now! Still, the rumor will be useful for when you return home with a baby. I'll draw up a private papal bull for its parentage, dictate that the baby is yours and mine. My grandchild will have a mother, and you'll have another baby to raise if Laura goes off to the French court."

"What—I—" I wanted to put my hands to my temples to keep my head from splitting. Rage choked in my throat like a plug of hot molten wax. "What do you think I am, Rodrigo? A ewe? You think you can take one lamb away and just give me another to suckle because I'll never know the difference?"

"Bah, you'll love the new baby like your own, *mi perla*." Rodrigo cupped my face in his hands. "A fine healthy child, as rosy and noisy as Laura at that age." He gave me a fond little shake. "So, what do you say? A French *comte* for Laura, and another child for you?"

I saw all the old softness in his dark Spanish eyes. Caterina Gonzaga could strut and preen all she liked; if I wanted my old lover back I had only to say so.

But I took a deliberate step back, shaking his hands away. I had a moment's fleeting pity for Lucrezia's inconvenient child and its uncertain future, but I had my own child to protect. And I was done covering for Borgia sins and Borgia secrets.

"Your Holiness," I said, and my fury chiseled every word out sharp as new ice. "I am taking my daughter home, away from this murderous pit of vipers you call a family. If you attempt to take her away from me, or marry her off to some poxy Frenchman, or otherwise ruin her future the way you have ruined Lucrezia's, I shall scratch your eyes out. And if you think I will raise Lucrezia's bastard for her, you are dreaming."

But he was dreaming, of course. The Borgia dream, a family atop the world, united and perfect. Always perfect; never in any way wrong. Rodrigo looked like he'd been waked from that dream by a rude slap as he looked down at me.

His smile disappeared. "How dare you speak to Us in such a fashion, Giulia Farnese? You will not dictate to the Holy Father. As for Laura—"

"Laura is not your daughter," I hissed. "She is Orsino's, she has always been Orsino's, I have lied to you for *years*." Holy Virgin, help me lie now.

"Nonsense," my former lover said. "We see Our face in hers—"

"That's your own vanity staring back at you!" *Don't provoke him*, some little warning voice in my head cried. *Be careful, Giulia*—but what choice did I have? He wanted to take my daughter away, *my daughter*, and if my pleading and my sweet reason hadn't worked to dissuade him, maybe my lies would. I'd say anything, anything at all, if it would wrench Laura out of his clutches—and if I said it here, where just the two of us could hear the words, then at least my defiance and my lies would be a private matter and not a public slash against Rodrigo's pride.

So I threw my head back and gave the Holy Father the most vicious smile I could muster. "You think I was ever faithful to you?" I spat. "From the beginning, it was Orsino. We were together every chance I could find. My *true* husband, my *young* husband, whom I love more than life. Far more than I ever loved you, you foolish old man."

Something in Rodrigo's eyes died at that, but now that I'd started this flood of words they wouldn't stop coming. I hardened my heart.

"Laura. Is. Not. Yours." I enunciated each word and aimed it at him like a stone. "She is an Orsini. There is *nothing* Borgia about her. She's not a vicious brute like your precious Juan, or a coldhearted murderer like Cesare, or a vapid little twit like Joffre. And she's nothing like your darling Lucrezia, who is shallow as a cup and filled with nothing but fashion and spite."

I turned in a flare of skirts and stalked for the doors. The Holy Father did not stop me. "No French *comte* will want Laura for an alliance, Rodrigo Borgia," I called over my shoulder. "Because she is not your daughter. *And I am not your pearl.*"

CHAPTER FIFTEEN

There is no redemption from Hell.

—POPE PAUL III, FORMERLY ALESSANDRO FARNESE

Carmelina

I was very fortunate. Very fortunate indeed. Everyone told me so— Leonello, the prioress—and I had to agree they were correct. Cesare Borgia did not bother addressing one word to me, but he would have told me I was fortunate, too.

My hair had never been beautiful. Too thick and prone to tangle; too curly and always escaping its pins in frizzy tendrils. Not beautiful hair; not golden and silky and down to my feet. Madonna Giulia would have cried if she'd been the one kneeling on a stone floor as a sour-faced lay sister with a face like a withered plum sheared her bald. But I had been fortunate enough to have ugly hair, so I knelt dry-eyed as the shears went *snip snip snip* and all my unruly curls piled up on the flagstones.

"Please understand." Leonello's voice had sounded so deathly flat when we spoke in the frosty courtyard. "This is the best I could do for you."

I hadn't managed more than a dumb nod. He still had his knife in his hand, blade gleaming in the rising moon, and Michelotto waited with the reins of his horse and Pantisilea's stiffening body slumped before him in the saddle. He was playing idly with her limp fingers, twining them with his own as though they were fond lovers cuddling in the saddle, and it was not a sight that encouraged me to speak.

Leonello saw my gaze and followed it. "Pantisilea will go in the river," he said. "So will Perotto. For knowing that the Pope's daughter gave birth when she is supposed to be a virgin."

"Could we convince everyone it was a virgin birth?" My voice came out very high and thin.

Leonello had been far beyond jokes. I'd never thought I'd see that day, but it was here, and his face was so eerie-calm I just wanted him jesting and snapping again. I *knew* the old Leonello, even if he sometimes irked me to the point of madness. I didn't know this one at all. The one who had looked at me as Pantisilea still jerked in her death throes and said flatly to Cesare Borgia, "No need to kill the cook as well, Eminence. She's a renegade nun, run away from her convent in Venice. Lock her up here and leave her to God, and Madonna Lucrezia's secrets will stay inside these walls with her."

I suppose it was the only way Leonello could avoid putting a knife in me. "Hate me if you like," he'd said as he turned to go, not sounding as though he cared much. "Just don't think of stealing away from this convent as you did the last. Because you'll be found—Cesare Borgia can find anyone—and he won't send me after you, *Signorina Cuoca*. He'll send Michelotto, and you know how that will end."

Signorina Cuoca no longer, I could have reminded him. I was Suora Serafina again. But being Suora Serafina was infinitely better than being at the bottom of the Tiber with Pantisilea. More good fortune. I told myself that, as my chopped hair piled up around my knees on the floor. I was alive, and for that I could feel a dim, horror-stained gratitude toward the little dwarf who had done me one last favor as a friend. Or perhaps, a former friend. Men like Michelotto didn't have friends—and soon, Leonello wouldn't either.

Never mind Michelotto; I was too frightened of Leonello's death-haunted eyes to even think about running away again.

"Our newest sister," the prioress had greeted me brightly when I was ushered in to see her that evening, new-clothed and anonymous in my habit and veil. "His Eminence Cardinal Borgia has authorized that you are to resume your vows within our walls." A delicate pause. "He did not mention which order in Venice previously housed you."

I doubted Cesare Borgia knew or cared. Leonello had revealed I was a runaway nun, but he hadn't revealed anything else.

"The Cardinal's guardsman," the prioress went on. "The, ah, *small* one. He mentioned your name in religion was Suora Serafina, but he was very unforthcoming with further details . . ."

She looked at me hopefully, waiting for a morsel of gossip, but I wasn't about to bring altar desecration into this hellish mess if I didn't have to. Staying behind these walls was better than being shipped back to Venice to have my hands and nose chopped off. And if this sharp-eyed prioress learned I had my patron saint's hand in the pouch beneath my skirt, she'd take it away from me; put Santa Marta back in a reliquary to draw pilgrims and donations to her convent doors.

Maybe I should have given Santa Marta back—it was where she belonged, after all; in the bosom of the Church. Maybe undoing that old act of desecration would have . . . I don't know. Redeemed me? But I thought I felt the hand twitch in her pouch, and I didn't want to give her up.

I remained silent, and the prioress looked disappointed. "In any case," she went on, "you will resume your name of Suora Serafina, but without reference to your, ah, *prior* service in Venice. None of the other sisters within these walls will know that you are not simply a new lay sister who was moved to take vows after spending these months with us. No scandal at all, you see?"

"Very fortunate," I echoed.

"Yes, if I do say so. And we *are* delighted to have you. I understand you were once a cook for His Holiness's cousin?" My new prioress's face was alight. "Do you have any skill with marzipan?"

See, I could even go on being a cook. How lucky.

"Your new cell." The lay sister who escorted me and my small bundle of possessions from the guest quarters in the gatehouse to the quarters of the sisters themselves was entirely cheerful. "It's a good one, right on the east wall so you'll get a little dawn light through the window slit. Of course the choir nuns get *real* windows." She lowered her voice. "It doesn't do to annoy the choir nuns. They can make life miserable for us, so if I were you I'd squirrel away whatever coin you've got and save it for when you need a favor."

"Yes."

"Or since you've a skill you can trade, that works just as well. I've got clever fingers for braiding hair"—wriggling her plump hands—"and I trade that for a bite or two of meat during Lent. They do like their plaited hair, the choir nuns! They grow it out under their veils, you see. Us lay sisters, we'd be skinned if we tried that. But it's the way of things, so I don't see any use complaining."

"No."

"Now, you'll soon get used to the prayers, but for this first week you're to be allowed to sleep through Matins!" She beamed. "Isn't that fortunate?"

"Very," I agreed.

A week. And then another week, my body used to rising and falling with the bells as though I had never left them behind at all. And another week, my hands chapped from the cold that the sullen kitchen fires couldn't quite banish, the even more bitter cold in my cell. Four stone walls, a pallet and a prie-dieu of my own, a peg for my cloak and habit. I'd gotten used to the habit again too. Strange how much my hands remembered; how to adjust the veil and wimple over my poor cropped head. I didn't struggle with it, not the way novices were supposed to, and I suppose that drew comments, but the nuns were far more interested in the new gossip about the Pope's daughter.

"She's to marry Alfonso of Aragon, they say! A handsome prince from Naples—"

"Do you *really* suppose she broke her arm and that was all the screaming we heard on her last day? I saw that Perotto going in and out for months, he was so handsome. Do you suppose they . . ."

"*Ssshh!* Mother Prioress will have your head for talk like that!"

They asked me what I knew of the Pope's daughter and her secrets. "You served her, after all. She and that good-looking envoy, did they . . ." But I had nothing to say. Suora Serafina had no opinions. She faded into the crowd of black and white, just as anonymous as the others. Nothing to set her apart except maybe the small bulge in her sleeve.

And maybe on the nights Suora Serafina wasn't feeling so very fortunate, she opened the pouch in her sleeve and shook something out onto her bed. Something a little withered, a little dark and dried, but still boasting a filigreed gold ring on one small curled-in finger.

"*Move!*" she'd cry out in the dark. "Give me a sign! Give me *something*!"

But the dried-up old relic had no magic in it, not away from a kitchen. A proper kitchen, that is, not a convent kitchen with no spices to speak of and an oven that barely spat out any heat. It was a kitchen to make Suora Serafina weep, and that was where she did most of her weeping: tears sliding silently down her cheeks to land in the watery stews along with the turnips past their prime and the stringy cuts of meat. She didn't bother to wipe her face. *Those* stews couldn't be spoiled by a little salt water.

Weeping was for the kitchen. Screaming was for the cell, hunched into a ball with a pillow crammed over the face, screaming into it over and over because the walls were *not* moving in around her, they were *not*. Suora Serafina was used to stone walls; she belonged inside them, after all, and once her throat was hoarse and burning she could usually remember that.

At least you are not at the bottom of the Tiber, I reminded myself grimly. *There is no escaping the bottom of the Tiber.*

And at that thought, Suora Serafina would remove her pillow from her face and put her head down on it instead. Postponing, for just one more day, the thought of taking her belt from around her waist and hanging herself from the kitchen rafters.

Leonello

I have never enjoyed watching executions. I have no particular objection to hanging murderers or the rapers of virgins, but I've escaped the scaffold too many times myself to enjoy watching a man dangle from a noose with piss running down his jerking legs. Most of Rome would disagree with me; there is always a lively turnout for a hanging or a drawing-and-quartering or even just a branding.

Best of all, though, is a burning. And when the excommunicated Dominican Fra Savonarola was arrested in Florence and brought to Rome to burn for his heresy in condemning Pope Alexander VI, I went with the rest of Rome to watch him sizzle on the pyre. Why not? I didn't sleep very well these days anyway. Perhaps I'd see a mad monk stalking through my dreams tonight with his face burned off, and not Giovanni Sforza looking at me in such horror as I staked his hand. I didn't mind that part of the dream so much, but then he always turned into Anna looking at me in horror as I staked *her* hand, and then Perotto, asking if I would please just stake him through the hand and not kill him.

They did not build the great pyre in the Piazza San Pietro. The smoke would billow up into the windows of the Vatican, and Lucrezia Borgia—recovered now from the fever or the broken arm or whatever it was that had officially kept her to her bed, and looking rather slimmer too—had complained prettily that she could not bear such a stink of smoke and burning flesh. Her lightest word was law to the Pope; he was already showering her in gifts now that her new betrothal to Alfonso of Aragon had been sealed, so what was a relocated execution? The bonfire was built near the Ponte Sant'Angelo instead, where the bodies of common criminals hung on display. As I joined the eager press of the crowd, I passed under the crow-picked feet of a thief hanged a fortnight ago. The lad was mostly bones by now, though his hands, which had been chopped off and hung about his neck, still fared surprisingly intact.

What is there to say about an execution? I found a wall on which to sit, boots dangling over the cheerful chatter of the crowd, who had brought mugs of beer to drink and apples to gnaw as they waited, and children sitting on their fathers' shoulders. A great roar went up when Fra Savonarola himself appeared, flanked by two of his most fervent supporters who had also been sentenced to die, all of them shrinking inside in their vestments. I had seen the mad monk only once, from a distance, in Florence as he stood with arms spread over the roaring Bonfire of the Vanities, but I remembered him as taller. The great hooked nose seemed pathetic as a bird's beak now, not a fierce beacon to sniff out sin, and the curved red lips looked dry and gray as ash.

"I only saw him once," I heard a woman's voice say as the friar was led trembling toward his pyre. "But I remember him as taller."

I shouldn't have been able to pick her voice out in such a throng, but I could pick her voice out anywhere. Silently I slid down from my wall into the crowd, wending my way closer to the figure with the honey-gold cloak and honey-gold hair. I'd managed to avoid her for months in the festivals and ceremonies of the Vatican; just a glimpse of that gold hair and I disappeared into the nearest throng before she could lay eyes on me.

"It's no wonder he looks smaller." Giulia's companion shaded his eyes with his hand as the friar was hoisted up onto the pyre. Not her pretty young husband, but an older man with a Neapolitan drawl. I remembered him; a minor lord from Bozzuto. "They racked our good friar for days, you know. He recanted his confession twice, but the *strappado* has a way of proving persuasive."

"Would you confess, Signore Capece?"

"M'dear, they would not even have to hoist me up to the irons. One look at the rack, and I would thrust my hand out to sign whatever they wished."

The crowd let out a howl when it was announced that Fra Savonarola was to be hanged before burning. The writhing and screaming as the flames began to lick at the feet; that was the part everyone wanted to see. But they quieted again as he was noosed with a length of chain. Such a thick, eager silence. I saw the man tremble, the man who had been mad enough to burn a stack of Botticelli paintings and challenge a Borgia pope.

Giulia's voice was very quiet—she stood so close, I could have reached out and run a finger down the length of her sleeve. "I wonder if Fra Savonarola will speak."

"Wouldn't be allowed, m'dear. If I were His Holiness, I would have made a bargain with our good Dominican beforehand: he'll be spared the flames, but only if he refrains from stirring up the crowd with a gallows sermon. Who wouldn't prefer quick strangulation to slow roasting?"

For a hanging, it was a distinct anticlimax. The prayers, the condemnations read out in ringing voices. The ritual shaving of what remained of the victim's hair, so the flames could consume his face unobscured. Then the length of chain snapped taut, and Fra Savonarola's feet jerked once, and that was all.

Giulia had turned her face away. "I think I will go," she said to her escort as the crowd gave a satisfied murmur and the executioners began heaping brushwood about the friar's dangling feet for the fire. "I've no wish to smell burning flesh on such a beautiful day."

She half-turned, gathering her skirts, and I didn't slide away swiftly enough. *Fool to get so close, dwarf,* I cursed myself. But Giulia showed no surprise at seeing me. "Leonello," she said, as calmly as though we had planned to meet each other here. "What luck. Perhaps you will be good enough to escort me back to the *palazzo* of Vittorio Capece?" A light touch to her companion's shoulder. "I believe my host wishes to stay a while longer, and I do not."

Evasion was one thing, but not open flight. Not a second time. "*Madonna,*" I said, and bowed.

Vittorio Capece and I had played chess a few times, but he did not seem to notice my presence; merely sent a pair of his guards with Giulia in a distracted wave. The first flickers of flame were rising under Fra Savonarola's limp feet, and the crowd was cheering and laying wagers on when his robes would catch. Giulia's companion did not cheer or wager, only stood with folded arms and a hard face.

"Signore Capece is very grim," I couldn't help noting as the guards cleared a path for Giulia back through the crowd. "Why is he your escort to the most fashionable execution of the year, and not your pretty husband?"

"Orsino gets sick at the sight of blood."

"'My little rose,'" I mimicked. "What does he say when he pricks himself on your thorns?"

"He doesn't know I have any thorns."

But she couldn't help a faint smile at my mockery. And I mocked myself, silently, for how her smile still made my heart stop. "Evidently your host doesn't object to seeing a little blood," I said instead, waving a hand back at Vittorio Capece.

"Men like Fra Savonarola make life very difficult for men like Vittorio."

"You mean sodomites?"

"His Holiness doesn't bother persecuting such men here in Rome. He told me once that if he did, the College of Cardinals would be half empty. In Florence, Fra Savonarola did his best to put every such man to the rack."

"A sodomite escorting a whore," I mused. "Not such an unusual pairing, really. I have always suspected sodomites and whores find each other restful company."

"I am not a whore anymore, Leonello. Or hadn't you heard?"

Another roar went through the crowd as we reached the fringes of it. I looked back and saw the flames climbing hungrily over Fra Savonarola's robes, stretching greedy fingers toward his dangling head as the kindling under his feet spread into a nest of flames. Giulia did not look, merely drew her honey-colored cloak closer about her as though she found the bright spring day chilly. The guards beat a path for her through the outskirts of the crowd, toward the Ponte Sant'Angelo, and I followed.

"Why did you come to the execution?" Automatically I fell into my old spot: to her side and just slightly behind, the place where I could best keep an eye for attackers. "You don't like such things."

"Perhaps I have changed since you left me, Leonello."

"I don't believe so."

"I felt—" She hesitated. "Guilty."

I laughed. "Of all the sins on your shoulders, I doubt you can count Fra Savonarola among them!"

"He denounced the Pope and his family and his church as a nest of vipers. It was not true once, perhaps, but it is true enough now. Fra Savonarola speaks truth, and for that—" She twisted her head, looking back at the commotion around the pyre. The flames were rising high and bright now, visible even from here, sending a plume of black smoke into the air just as white smoke had been sent up when Rodrigo Borgia was elected Pope. Giulia crossed herself.

"If you hate this nest of vipers so much, why stay?" I couldn't help asking. "You were always singing the beauties of country life, and now you have Carbognano. Green hills, simple pastimes, and a handsome young husband to enjoy them all with. Eden before the fall; not a viper in sight. Why not go back to it?"

"Lucrezia has requested that I stay for her wedding." Giulia fiddled with a tie on her sleeve. "His Holiness would be just as happy to see the back of me now, but he won't deny Lucrezia anything. So, I've been ordered to remain in Rome."

"Why should that stop you? You've gone journeying before without the Holy Father's permission."

"Orsino wishes to stay too, for the moment."

I laughed. "Surely you can maneuver that weedy, chinless sprout wherever you want him to go!"

"My husband has become very stubborn." Her voice was careful, expressionless. "I must pick my battles these days, and I'm doing my best to discourage him from the notion of sending Laura to be fostered in France for a French marriage."

I thought of sunny little Laura being brought up in the stiff formality of the French court and kicked a loose stone out of my way.

"I think I may win on that front," Giulia went on. "I've quarreled very badly with the Holy Father, so he isn't so keen on giving Laura a dowry anymore. I don't see any French *comte* making an offer for her now." A faint smile. "And no son of Adriana da Mila will want to put up the coin for that kind of dowry, either. But Orsino is still hoping some grand match will present itself."

"What has any of that to do with not leaving Rome?" I still didn't like the thought of Laura being raised to speak French. That sweet, laughing child who had clung to my stubby fingers as she took her first steps . . .

"The Holy Father has made it clear he can't stand the sight of me—and Orsino likes that. He takes me to a great many parties now, so all the other men can watch the Pope snub me, and envy Orsino instead of pitying him as the cuckold." Exasperation colored Giulia's voice. "Though really, I don't think that particular plan is going as well as

Orsino hoped. He can introduce me all he likes as *the Rose of Carbognano*—I ask you!—but no one will ever think of me as anything but the Bride of Christ. Men don't honor him for having me for a wife; they just despise him for reclaiming soiled goods. They tell him he should have thrown me out like the whore I am, and then usually they come around and try to seduce me. Men!"

"Your husband is a fool," I said.

"And he is my husband, so of course I obey his wishes in all things." Giulia's voice went flat again. "We're to stay at least until Lucrezia's wedding. I pass my days sewing with Lucrezia, new gowns for her bridal chest. She chatters away like nothing ever happened, mostly about her new husband-to-be. Apparently he's young and handsome."

"Ah, yes, Alfonso of Aragon. I wonder if he'll last any longer than Lord Sforza."

"Poor man." Maybe Giulia meant Giovanni Sforza, or Alfonso of Aragon, but she was looking at me. "Why did *you* come to see Fra Savonarola's execution, Leonello? You don't have any reason to hate him."

I studied my former mistress. She had not guarded her skin in Carbognano; she'd come back to Rome with a faint golden tang to her face and bosom. Most ladies would never have gone out in public without covering themselves in white powder for the proper fashionable paleness, but she didn't bother, setting her golden skin off instead with a pale gold gown just a shade darker. She looked like one of her favorite golden roses, and now of course all the ladies of Rome would be leaving off their sun hats, hoping to look so ripe and beautiful. I remembered Savonarola's Angels attacking her for no other reason than that. They'd taken Botticelli's incipient portrait of her, they'd tried to take her hair, they'd even taken a kiss in all the struggling. I remembered the black pang of jealousy that had stabbed me when my mistress kissed that lout, even if it was only to push him over backward. No, I did not like Savonarola's Angels or the master they served. Perhaps that mad Dominican spoke truth of the Pope but his was an ugly truth, and I found him an ugly little man.

Perhaps it takes one such man to know another.

Giulia was still waiting for my answer.

"I came today because I like watching people die," I said at last. "Didn't you know that, *madonna*?"

"No. You don't like it at all."

"Well, I still do a great deal of it. Juan Borgia, Pantisilea—"

"Was that you?" Giulia's voice rose, and I saw grief flash through her eyes. "They pulled her body out of the river, and I thought—"

"No, she was Michelotto's. I don't like killing women, so when it came to parceling out the victims, I picked Perotto and he picked her."

"My poor Pantisilea . . ." Giulia's voice trailed away; she crossed herself and I saw tears in her eyes.

I still saw her face in my dreams, poor silly girl, but I couldn't say that. "She didn't suffer," I said instead, and kicked another stone out of my way. "I'll say that for Michelotto; no one suffers when he kills them. Better than me; I botched Perotto. He ran straight for the Pope as soon as he saw me coming. Am I perhaps getting a reputation?"

"Is it a reputation you deserve?"

"I am a killer, Giulia." I said it brutally. "I am small and amusing and you like me for that. But I am not your jester, or your bodyguard, or your poet."

"You are a man who understands Virgil and translates Homer and can hold a child spellbound with a story for hours," Giulia replied. "A man who once told me he dreamed of having enough time someday to translate the *Odyssey* into Italian, and study the verses of the Provençal troubadours."

"Spare me your sentimentality," I said. "My skills lie elsewhere. I am a killer of men, and now I do the work I am so good at."

"Spare me your brooding dramatics," Giulia shot back, and gestured to my knives. "There is much more to you than *this*!"

"Cesare Borgia knew what I was the moment he laid eyes on me."

"Cesare Borgia is empty inside." Giulia held my eyes in hers. "You are not."

"I tortured Juan Borgia and I enjoyed every instant of it." I spat the words at her, venomous and soft so the guards would not hear. "I staked Lord Sforza's hand to the letters of impotence until he signed them, and I enjoyed that too. Cesare Borgia told me to kill Perotto, and I never hesitated. I saw Michelotto sink a knife into your Pantisilea, a silly bawd of a girl who never did anyone any harm, and I didn't lift a finger to stop him." I swirled a hand about my face. "Do you see me now? Or will you bleat more idiotic questions at me?"

"Just one. Did you kill Carmelina too?"

The silence stretched.

"I didn't think so," said Giulia. "Tell me why."

I wound my hands through my belt.

"You didn't kill her because you *like* her. You always have. So when you got your orders, you saved her instead." I heard hope in Giulia's voice. "That makes me very glad, Leonello. For her sake, and for yours."

"Don't be sentimental." I began walking again, walking fast, but Giulia kept pace with me as we crossed the center of the Ponte Sant'Angelo. The guards tramped ahead, oblivious. "I didn't kill her, but she might as well be dead. I walled her up in that convent, and I assure you she would *rather* be dead."

"But you spared her life! Would Michelotto have done that? Or Cesare—"

An explosion rocked the city behind us. My hand dropped to my dagger, even though I knew what it was, and Giulia spun.

"The flames must have reached the gunpowder on the pyre." I let go of my dagger hilt, but my heart was still racing, and not just from the explosion. "They always salt the brushwood with gunpowder, just to give the crowd a bang. Though most people will still hang about for a few hours, making bets on how long it will take the good friar's arms and legs to roast and fall off."

"You never used to be callous."

"And I believe we have established that you do not know me as well as you think."

"But you know *me*." She hesitated. "Leonello—am I in danger?"

"From me?" My stomach twisted despite myself. "Didn't I say I dislike killing women?"

"And you said Michelotto doesn't mind." She shuddered. "Will he come for me, or for Laura?"

"Why would he? The Pope is done with you. It's that haughty bitch Caterina Gonzaga he's mounting now, and a stable of others besides. You don't matter."

Giulia brushed my barbs aside. "I angered him. When I saw Perotto die, I—" Her steps speeded, outracing the memory. "I just wanted Rodrigo away from Laura. I wanted *all* of them away from her, especially with all that talk about sending her somewhere far away—" A deep breath. "So I said Laura was Orsino's daughter. I threw it in the Pope's face and taunted him with it, as soon as we were alone."

Apparently it wasn't quite gone, my old habit of fearing for her safety. Maybe it never would be. "How could you be so reckless?" I demanded, and my heart kicked in my chest.

"I had no choice, Leonello! He wouldn't listen any other way, not to anything I said—it was lie to his face, or lose Laura."

She sounded very certain, but I was used to reading her expressions. "If you had no choice, then what troubles you? Why do you think you are in danger?"

"Rodrigo looked so *furious*." Very quietly. "Like he could throttle me on the spot. Many times he's lost his temper and shouted at me, but—" She gave a little shudder. "I've only seen him look like that once before. When he had that poor man at the menagerie masquerade hanged, just for calling Juan a bastard." She crossed herself. "I took one look at his face and fled the room."

I had another half-dozen barbs at my lips, but I didn't loose any of them.

"What will he do to me, Leonello?" Her eyes met mine square. "I never thought in all the world that he'd hurt me or Laura; not ever. He's no monster to wreak vengeance on a woman and a child, even if they offended him—"

"You aren't the only one he might decide to hurt," I pointed out. "What about your spineless little husband? You threw it in the Pope's face that your husband bedded you, after all, stole you back and fathered a child on you—"

"Orsino is Adriana's son and Adriana is Rodrigo's own cousin and ally. He's *family*, and we all know what Rodrigo thinks about family."

A bitter twist at that. "But I'm not family, and I've made it plain Laura isn't either. So will Michelotto come in the dark for one of us?"

I hesitated.

"Go ahead, Leonello," she said tiredly. "Tell me I was a fool to say such things to Rodrigo. Tell me I was reckless. Cut me up and down with that tongue of yours; I won't complain. Just tell me the truth."

"Truth?" I said, and shrugged. "The truth is that the Pope loves you. He may never hold you in his arms again, but part of him will love you till he dies. So no, he would not harm you or Laura. Men don't think that way, Madonna Giulia. Women and children are not fitting objects for vengeance. The Holy Father may find some way to punish you, but it will not come at the end of Michelotto's knife. Not in your heart, at least, or Laura's."

I saw the relief well in her eyes at once. Stupid woman, why would she place so much trust in anything I said? I was a killer of men, a stunted little monster with a dark soul and a list of crimes longer than my twisted body. She knew that, so why did she have such faith in my judgment?

"Stay for Lucrezia's wedding if you must," I said. "But after that, persuade your stupid, stubborn husband to take you away from Rome as soon as possible. Just get away."

She reached down and smoothed a lock of hair off my forehead. I recoiled as though she'd burned me, making a snap of my teeth at her fingers.

She snatched her hand back. "Leonello—"

"Don't touch vipers," I said. "We bite."

I turned and left her at the end of the Ponte Sant'Angelo, standing under the crow-picked bones.

Giulia

I was very late returning to Vittorio Capece's *palazzo*, so late I knew my host would return home before I did. Doubtless Orsino would be displeased with me for being so tardy; there was a masquerade he wished to attend tonight with me on his arm in one of my extravagant new gowns to be paraded and admired. But I felt too worn and shaky to go back just yet, so I went to the nearest church after Leonello left me. Holy Virgin knows how long I spent there on my knees, praying to Santo Giuliano the Hospitaller, who was patron saint of repentant murderers. I didn't know if he was patron saint of the unrepentant ones too, and it seemed like something worth begging for on my knees.

Leonello had looked so tired under all his bitter, spitting scorn. Exhausted and drained, as though his dreams were all black and his waking hours blacker, and any hopes he had of the future blackest of all.

I was so late returning, I thought I must have missed *cena* altogether. Hopefully Orsino and Vittorio hadn't quarreled over the dishes of spiced pears and wild duck. Without my bright chatter for a cushion, my husband could be a trifle uneasy in the presence of a rumored sodomite, and Vittorio could get a shade sarcastic with a houseguest of whom he had every right to be tired. I'd have been tired of us too. Orsino didn't see any reason why we should move ourselves elsewhere—"Doubtless he's honored to play host to visitors of our connections, my little rose." I'd whispered my private apologies to Vittorio for the length of our stay, and he'd patted my arm and said, "Bless you, m'dear, I'd be delighted to have *you* stay with me forever." Don't think I hadn't heard the faint emphasis on *you*.

Holy Virgin, why couldn't we just go home? Why did Orsino have to grow stubborn *now*, of all times?

But for once, I didn't dare press him. Even if the French match had blown away on the wind, well, Orsino would still be perfectly within his rights to send Laura for fostering elsewhere, "for her education." Somewhere she couldn't return too often to disturb his peace of mind with thoughts of the past. No, I had to keep my husband charmed and bedazzled and far too besotted to think of upsetting me by sending my daughter away. If he wanted to parade me on his arm tonight for everyone to admire, sparkling and beautiful and all his, then so be it.

I was trying to muster some sparkle when I came back to the *palazzo*, but everyone was in an uproar. I saw a cluster of maids sobbing in one corner of the long *sala*, and rough-shod workmen clumped up the stairs with tools in hand. "What—" I began, and Laura's nursemaid hurled herself wailing into my arms.

"Oh, Madonna Giulia!"

"What is it?" An icy finger of dread began wandering down my spine. "What's happened?"

She was sobbing too hard to answer. I looked over her heaving shoulder and saw Vittorio Capece running toward me, white as rice.

"Giulia, my dear," he said, and his words stumbled over each other. None of his usual elegant drawl. "I don't know how it happened. It was while we were all gone at the execution. Half the servants slipped out too to see—some strange man begged entrance, one of the maids said. Some excuse about visiting your Orsino, but Jesu knows the *palazzo* was half empty, he could have wandered about anywhere, he could have had something to do with it—"

"What man? Who?"

"—because I swear to you, the ceilings have always been perfectly sound!"

"What's happened?"

"The ceiling came down." There were tears in his eyes. "Only part of it, the arch over the doorway to your *sala*, but—Giulia, be brave."

I was already running up the stairs, screaming my daughter's name.

Carmelina

Your cousin is here to see you," Suora Teresa came to tell me, and I thought I was dead for certain. My skin crawled and for a moment I thought it was Marco waiting for me down in the convent parlor, Marco dead and stabbed through half a dozen times, staring at me accusingly in a cook's apron all stained with red, because he'd never have gone to work for Juan Borgia and thus met his death if I hadn't taken his post. It wasn't fair, but ghosts didn't care for fairness, and ghosts seemed much closer in a convent than they ever seemed in a busy kitchen. Maybe because the sisters all seemed like ghosts from a distance, gliding along the stone halls in their anonymous black and white. Who was to know if the veiled figure preceding me to Mass was really Suora Teresa or Suora Cherubina or Suora Paolina? Maybe it was some long-dead nun who was still tramping off to Mass every day because she didn't realize she was dead. Within these walls, I couldn't see much difference between being dead and being alive. Ghosts seemed entirely possible, especially at midnight prayers.

But it wasn't midnight now, it was bright afternoon and I was elbow deep in almond paste making little *biscotti* for the choir nuns who were ensconced in the visiting parlors with their noble mothers or sisters or aunts who came to visit, and who of course would expect sweetmeats to be passed through the grilles along with the gossip. Almond paste. I never wanted to see an almond again, and I blew a short curl of hair out of my face with a vicious muttered oath as Suora Teresa came bouncing into the kitchens and told me my cousin had arrived.

"*Cousin*, eh?" She winked as my skin crawled. "Come all the way from Venice, he says, and he's a handsome one. Doesn't look like you, not with that hair, but I won't tell if he's not really your cousin. Not if you sneak me some of those *biscotti* before you take the plate up—"

"As many as you want." The frightened squeeze of my heart as I thought of bloodied Marco coming to accuse me had eased, only to squeeze up again in an entirely different way. I stripped off my apron and crammed a few frizzy tendrils of hair back under my wimple, emptying half the plate of *biscotti* into Suora Teresa's greedy hands and flying up the worn stone steps into the parlor.

A convent parlor is something to make most men profoundly disappointed. Devout men want to see a convent's nuns praying through the grilles with worldly folk who have come to be enlightened by the balm of holy conversation. Perhaps kneeling in prayer with some courtesan in silk who has come to repent of her sinful life. Or the more worldly men have some vision of nuns meeting lovers through the grilles, passing love notes and locked in salacious embrace. Just how salacious anyone can get with a stout metal grille between them is something that particular fantasy never bothers to explain. In truth, a convent's parlor looks no different (bars aside) from any cozy gathering of women in an ordinary *sala*: nobly coiffed and silk-gowned wives with babies on their laps and little girls in tow, bending heads close to their daughters and sisters and aunts who took a holy husband instead of a mortal one, all of them gossiping their heads off. Convent parlors even see a few men: stern fathers like mine who come to make sure rebellious daughters are settling into their vows, young brothers come to tease a favored sister, or even a few of the swaggering *monachini*: those flashy and bored young gallants who think it great fun to pay court to a pretty nun through the grille. Not that such men ever get very far, at least not in the Convent of San Sisto, where the parlor was presided over by iron-eyed Suora Ursula. Named for a bear and had the temper of one too, and the Bear was casting a great many suspicious glances already at my tall cousin from Venice as he leaned against the grille with his corded arms folded across his chest and a lock of hair falling into his eyes.

"Cousin," I said, dry-mouthed as I approached the bars.

"Suora Serafina," Bartolomeo returned gravely, all formality, but his eyes raked me and I had a flush of humiliation. I had not seen him in almost a year. My shins showed below the too-short habit and my hands stuck out bony and chapped from the sleeves. I knew the stark black made me look ugly and sour, and my skin was sun-darkened and wind-hardened after all my hours this winter and spring spading at the stony convent gardens. I felt worn, tired, ill-used and repulsive, at least twice as old as my twenty-six years, and after all his letters I'd wanted him to come, but now I just wished he'd go away again.

"How did you know to ask for me?" I said instead, resisting the urge to tug at the wimple, which squeezed my chin.

"My last two letters addressed to you came back," he returned. "They said there was no one of your name inside these walls anymore. But if you'd left with Madonna Lucrezia, you'd have come to see me. So, I thought of asking here again, but for your nun's name."

"I only told you that name once."

"I remembered it."

"I'm not supposed to have any visitors—"

He laughed, drawing glances. "Do you have any idea what the sisters here will do for good food? I brought a hamper—"

I felt a smile tugging at my lips. "You and your hampers."

"Yes, me and my hampers. Cheese *tourtes*, apple *biscotti*, a *crostata* of fresh summer blackberries, candied walnuts—they fell on everything like wolves on a lamb. Nothing left but crumbs." He stretched his fingers through the grille toward me, but I withdrew, tucking my own hands into my sleeves.

"You're angry with me," he said, and blew out a breath as he pulled his hand back. "Well, you have a right to be. Your cousin, Marco Santini—"

"What? No, I'm not angry, Bartolomeo. I'm just being careful." I flicked my gaze at the wrinkle-faced choir nun staring daggers at us. "Suora Ursula," I whispered. "We don't want to catch her eye, and believe me, she's always got an eye fixed on any of the young men who come into this parlor."

"But I do want to explain about your cousin." Bartolomeo met my gaze squarely. "I wouldn't blame you if you still blamed *me*, Carmelina. I didn't mean him to die, but he did. And I had a role in that."

"My cousin was a greedy fool. That was what killed him, not you." I felt a knot in my stomach easing. Maybe I couldn't give my former apprentice much, but he'd at least have peace of mind in this one thing. "If Marco hadn't given me to Juan Borgia just to get a debt repaid, he'd still be alive today. So don't trouble your conscience on it any longer, Bartolomeo." I wished I could take his hand.

"Thank you." Bartolomeo curled his fingers around the grille bars instead. "I thought, maybe that was why you hadn't answered my letters."

"No. Not that, not at all." I could have laughed, or maybe wept.

"Then what's happened? Why are you here"—his eyes flickered over my wimple and veil again—"like that?"

I hesitated, because Cesare Borgia had killed everyone else who knew it. "I know something, about the Pope's daughter. This is how they silenced me."

"What do you know?"

"Better if *you* don't. Pantisilea did, and Perotto the papal envoy too, and they're both dead now." I crossed myself. "Cardinal Borgia's men flung them both into the river, God rest their souls."

"Then you're lucky," Bartolomeo said, low-voiced. "They could have killed you, too."

I hesitated before speaking. "I think I'm going mad here."

His fingers tightened a little around the bar of the grille, but his voice was still conversational. "You need *macaroni*."

"What?" My eyes stung.

"*Macaroni*," he said. "Layered in a dish with slabs of *provatura* cheese and lumps of butter, cooked slowly until it all melts together."

My mouth watered. "I didn't teach you that."

"Certainly not; it's my own recipe and its going into my compendium, too. It's just what you need right now. Pasta with a great deal of butter and cheese," he said seriously, "cures all."

I snorted laughter and stifled it behind my hand. Suora Ursula was still eyeing Bartolomeo, looking suspicious despite the crucifix about his neck and the pious little bow he aimed in her direction. A few of the visiting matrons in their rich gowns were eyeing him too, for different reasons.

He turned back to me, and his smile dropped away. "I will get you out of here."

"It's a great sin," I whispered. That meant very little to me, with my tattered conscience and list of offenses against God, but for a bright soul like my apprentice's . . . "Understand what it *means*, Bartolomeo. Stealing a nun from her convent? It's like stealing a man's wife away, only it's worse because it's a wife to God Himself. Adultery *and* desecration combined—"

And I couldn't help but remember my private, terrified thought after Marco died: *Is God so jealous of His brides that I'm a curse to any man who lays hands on me?*

"I don't care what kind of sin it is." Bartolomeo's voice was steady. "I'll think about that later. After I get you out."

"If I leave these walls, Cesare Borgia will see me dead. He's killed everyone else who knew—"

"I've an idea or two. Just be patient a little longer. I swear, I'll have you out soon."

A young cook against a Borgia prince? Those were odds too long for any gambler. But Bartolomeo's eyes burned into mine, that familiar bright cinnamon, and I felt warm for the first time in a year. Warm and safe and full, as though I'd eaten a whole platter of his buttered *macaroni*.

A young lay sister came flying in on noiseless feet and went straight to Suora Ursula. She looked at me as she began to whisper something.

"Maybe I'll get out of here," I whispered, fumbling in my pouch. "Maybe not. If I don't—"

"Carmelina—"

"If I don't, take this." I pushed the little bundle of Santa Marta's hand into his hand through the grille. "Careful, she's very brittle at her age. If you snap her fingers off, I shall lay a curse on you and you'll never cook *macaroni* again without burning it up!"

"I can't take her. She's *your* saint."

"She's yours too." I saw Suora Ursula clumping toward me on her great bearlike paws. "I'm no cook anymore, Bartolomeo. Not here. And she belongs with a cook."

One side of his mouth flicked down, wry. "I offer to marry you. I offer to commit desecration and adultery for you. I offer to make you *pasta*. And you offer me a dead severed hand?"

"You ass, it's all I have! So take it or leave it!"

He took it. "I'll give her back to you soon, I promise." He reached through the bars and gripped my hand hard and fierce, strong fingers lacing through mine, his thumb skimming along my knuckles. "When I take you home. Nothing's the same without you—even that old tomcat prowls around looking for you and moping—"

"That useless one-eared cat from the Palazzo Santa Maria?" I couldn't help asking.

"I took him with me when I left." Bartolomeo traced the livid mark left by Juan Borgia's knife, and the scar burned all over again. "I've got a soft spot for him. We both mope and sulk without you—"

"Suora Serafina!" Suora Ursula had a roar that would have made any bear proud. "I have checked with our prioress, and she informs me you are not to receive any visitors at all. Apologies to your *cousin*"—eyes sweeping Bartolomeo with mistrust—"but he will have to leave at once."

Bartolomeo didn't let my hand go. Not till Suora Ursula yanked me away from the grille and began marching me out of the parlor like a heifer being led off to the kitchens for slaughter. "Rest assured you have earned a suitable penance for this," she said in her vicious whisper. "And Suora Teresa as well, for allowing you into the parlor without first seeking permission!"

"Flay me bloody if you like, you hairy hag," I said loud and clear, loud enough for Bartolomeo to hear where he stood up against the grille. And I slid out from under her claws and stalked out with as much of my old swagger as I could muster, because I didn't think I'd ever see Bartolomeo again and he might as well see me leave his life as Carmelina. Not as scared Suora Serafina, who I was destined to remain for the rest of my days.

It wasn't until Bartolomeo was out of sight that I burst into tears. Not for my red-haired and handsome young man—not for Santa Marta's hand—not even for my own fate. Bartolomeo's last words were still ringing in my ears: *Even that old tomcat prowls around looking for you and moping . . . we both mope and sulk without you.* Suddenly I was crying, and I didn't know why. Everything that had happened within these walls, and I dissolved in tears over a useless, foul-tempered cat who should long ago have been made into a sausage.

CHAPTER SIXTEEN

*Love is when he gives you a piece of your soul, that you
never knew was missing.*

—TORQUATO TASSO

Giulia

"Well?" Lucrezia Borgia twirled before me, flaring her skirts. "How do I look?"

Her ladies squealed and burst into applause for the Pope's daughter, the former Countess of Pesaro arrayed in her bridal gown of gold French brocade worked all over with black silk embroidery and tucked scarlet velvet. Her waist circled by its girdle of grape-sized pearls might never have borne a child at all, and her sun-bleached hair flowed loose like any virgin bride's under a little jeweled cap, which she tilted at a rakish angle. A girl of eighteen with bright eyes and rouged cheeks and powdered bosom, and for a moment I remembered her as she'd looked at her wedding to Lord Sforza five years ago. A tremulous little swan in jeweled chains, with all the world before her.

"You are beautiful," I said, and managed a smile.

"I know," Lucrezia giggled, and her ladies descended on her for one last tweak of the sleeves or dab of scent. I just sat with my hands in my lap on the wall bench: my old chamber in the Palazzo Santa Maria where I'd tried on gown after gown before Lucrezia's first wedding, trying to find something that would make me pale and plain since no one should ever outshine the bride. But this was Lucrezia's chamber now, and Lucrezia's *palazzo* where she and her entire household of ladies and maids had come to wait for Alfonso of Aragon to arrive in Rome.

"I do wish you wouldn't wear black, Giulia," Lucrezia scolded me, peering into a hand mirror to arrange her little cap at a more dashing angle. "So gloomy! Even your complexion can't carry off all that unrelieved black, you know."

Caterina Gonzaga made sure to smile pityingly. She was piqued at me all over again because she had not been allowed to escort the Pope's daughter in her wedding vows as I had escorted Lucrezia to the Count of Pesaro. Lucrezia's vows with Alfonso of Aragon yesterday had been a mere formality, a private exchange of rings and a few words as confirmation to the proxy wedding that had already taken place in Naples. The real festivities would take place today with the wedding banquets, the feasts and gifts, and then the bedding of the bridal couple. But as the current papal mistress, Caterina clearly felt she had been slighted. It was the only highlight of my day so far.

"My pink silk," Lucrezia was enthusing at me. "I'm sure we can lace it to fit you in a trice, if you will lay off that dreary black velvet—"

"I am still in mourning," I said quietly. "It has been only three months, you know."

Lucrezia's little face creased in sympathy at once, and she dropped down beside me on the wall bench in a sigh of French brocade. "I'm sorry," she said remorsefully, and waved off her ladies. "I know you're still sad, poor Giulia. I shouldn't have insisted you come to my wedding banquet today—you haven't been out to so much as a masque in months—but I couldn't be married again without you. I just couldn't."

She flung her arms about me in a hug. I gave a brief squeeze and then eased her back. "Careful. You'll crush your embroideries."

"Straighten me, will you? I mustn't go to Alfonso all rumpled. It's his job to rumple me, but not until later." She giggled again. "*Such* a handsome man, Giulia, you can't imagine! My heart *stopped* when we exchanged rings; he has the biggest brown eyes, just like velvet—"

"My heart stopped too," I said. "When I exchanged the rings with Orsino."

"Of course you're thinking of him today." Lucrezia patted my cheek. "But you mustn't grieve! When my Alfonso and I set up a household of our own, you'll come as one of my ladies and I'll find you a new husband. These Neapolitan lords are very handsome, though of course none are as handsome as my Alfonso."

She looked pure, glowing, incandescent with love. Exactly as she'd looked as she gazed at Giovanni Sforza.

"Thank you," I said in the remote voice I couldn't seem to inflect with any feeling at all these past months. "But after the wedding I intend to return home to my daughter."

Laura. My sweet Laura, all I had left.

"Of course you miss her." Lucrezia lowered her voice, mindful of her ladies. "I miss my baby *so* much, you know. Such a dear little thing with those plump cheeks!"

I wondered how she even remembered the plump cheeks. To my knowledge Lucrezia had had only a day or two with her child before it was packed off to a discreet household in the country—a household staffed with servants and wet nurses well paid to keep quiet. The Pope's daughter had spent far more hours squealing over her own restored slimness than squealing over her child.

"Cesare says maybe I can have my baby back in a few years, when rumors die down. We can tell everyone it's Cesare's bastard, or maybe Father's." A vague wave of her hand, and I noted how careful she was not to mention whether her child was a boy or a girl. More Borgia secrets, and my privilege to hear them had been revoked. I didn't ask about the child's sex, lest my curiosity be taken for a sign that I might wish to raise it after all.

I'd left my own daughter in Carbognano with Adriana da Mila, after returning there with Orsino's crushed body for burial. "We must arrange the funeral rites together, Giulia." My mother-in-law had greeted me with a brave face, but her eyes were deep red wells and she peered out of them like a bewildered animal hiding in the underbrush.

"Of course." Orsino would have wanted me there: his little rose weeping behind black veils at his graveside. It was the last duty I owed him. But I let Adriana da Mila take chief place among the mourners, regardless of what her son would have wanted. He was dead, and his mother and I were alive, and of the two of us I knew who had loved him best. It was only after the last clod of earth had fallen that Adriana asked the question I dreaded. "Giulia, you never said—the accident . . ."

"A tragic accident." I cut her off firmly. "Rain had weakened the ceiling. Poor Vittorio Capece is beside himself with guilt over it all. Orsino was lingering beneath the archway when it fell—he would have known nothing."

Her eyes puddled with relief, and as I put my consoling arms around her, I bit down on the memory of Orsino's lean body crumpled among the fallen plasterwork. His blue eyes had been knocked clear out of his crushed skull—I'd seen that very clearly, before Vittorio led me away. Did a few falling stones from a collapsing archway really crush a skull like that? I thought not. His head had been beaten in by a sword hilt, I guessed, or a cudgel. Easy enough to smash loose the plasterwork above afterward, to make it all look an accident. Hadn't Leonello said something about that, a long time ago? Ways to murder without really murdering.

But I said nothing of my dark private convictions to Madonna Adriana, who had served Rodrigo Borgia with such long and faithful affection. My reckless words to Rodrigo had gotten her son killed—but she wouldn't know it. Let her have her grief and her peace of mind. I didn't deserve either.

My fault. My fault that my husband had died. Leonello had seen Rodrigo more clearly than I: *Women and children are not fitting objects for vengeance. The Holy Father may find some way to punish you, but it will not come at the end of Michelotto's knife.*

Wise Leonello. Maybe I hadn't been the one to end up crumpled beneath a collapsed doorway, but I'd still thrown it in Rodrigo's face that my husband had gone behind his back, had bedded me all along— and I'd been punished for it. My punishment had come all neatly tied up with vengeance against Orsino; there was a tidiness to that which I thought might have come from Cesare. I could see Rodrigo raging to his eldest son, and Cesare applying his cold and fearsome logic to the solution.

My fault. But my poor mother-in-law would never know what had truly happened to her son, nor would anyone else. That was my burden to bear. Mine alone.

"Would you look after Laura for a little while?" I had asked Adriana instead after drying her tears. "Lucrezia has required me to return to Rome for her wedding, but it's time Laura had the comforts of home. And she'll be such company for you." I wasn't taking Laura back to the Holy City ever again if I could help it. Not as long as the Holy City was under Borgia rule.

"Yes, of course I'll look after her." My former mother-in-law wiped her eyes. "Bless her, she's the image of Orsino already. Those beautiful curls—"

"His true daughter," I agreed. Cesare Borgia had once told me I could not lie, but this was a falsehood I'd gladly tell for the rest of my days.

I missed my Laura so dreadfully, but she was safe in Carbognano now. She was able to write me misspelled little letters under Adriana's tutelage, straggling words galloping up the page and back down again, all about her pony and the ripening nuts on the hazel trees and Fra Teseo who was teaching her French but it was *boring*. And when was I coming home?

Soon, I thought. *Soon, Laura.* One more thing to do. Just one more thing, I clung to that—when it was done, I would leave this snake pit and go home.

Oh, but I was so tired.

Lucrezia's first wedding had been a vast affair: hundreds of guests milling about the papal apartments, all the ladies going into raptures over Carmelina's sweets. I still remembered those little sugared strawberry cakelets shaped like roses . . . a formal occasion, that first wedding, at least until wine loosened inhibitions at dawn and squealing ladies had tossed all those cakelets out the windows to the watching crowds and Rodrigo had begun dropping candied cherries down my bodice. This wedding was no formal occasion at all, or perhaps it only seemed that way to me. There had been feasting and laughing and dancing much of the day, and the guests were already merry with wine as the bride made her way into the Sala dei Pontifici, where her papal father sat enthroned. Joffre lounged at his feet, trying to look languid and merely looking sulky, and Alfonso of Aragon stood at the ready in black brocade, with eyes only for his Borgia wife. He wore a black velvet cap with a brooch like a fat gold cherub that Lucrezia had given him, and I had to admit he was a handsome youth: dark and slender, with a narrow sensitive face.

They will eat you alive, I thought as we paced across the *sala*.

But young Alfonso had only smiles as he took Lucrezia's hand and bowed over it, and she smoldered at him through her darkened lashes. What a pretty pair they made as the viols struck up a lively tune and they danced for the Pope's smiles. Orsino and I had danced to viols at our wedding. A sedate tune, dipping and turning palm to palm as I prayed silently for him to love me, and he couldn't even summon the courage to look me in the eye. Regretting his devil's bargain already, perhaps. His whole blighted life had run aground after that dance like a cursed ship.

My eyes burned dry. I felt quick pressure on my hand as I watched the bridal couple pirouette through a lively turn, and knew my brother's touch without turning. Dear Sandro, he had been such a comfort since Orsino died. I'd retired to his modest household upon my return to Rome, and Sandro welcomed me with one of his enveloping hugs, but none of his usual chatter. He seemed to know that for once in my life I didn't want to *talk*, just sit quietly and perhaps lose a game of chess, or help his little mistress Silvia rock and croon over her babies, or listen to a chorus of pure-voiced boy singers who somehow had the power to bring tears to my eyes when the memory of my husband didn't. Sandro had just handed me a kerchief in silence, letting me have my tears, not asking any questions. Dear Sandro. I'd worried for a time that Rodrigo's anger at me might fall on my brother, but Rodrigo was far too practical to dispose of someone useful. Orsino had been a nothing to him, but my brother kept the peace in the College of Cardinals with his easy jests and droll capers. Rodrigo needed that, and thank the Holy Virgin he did. If he had ordered my brother murdered and not my husband . . .

Really, I was no better a wife than Lucrezia. We both placed our brothers above our husbands. Well, at least no one accused me of sleeping with my brother. However inadequate a wife Lucrezia had been to the Count of Pesaro in other ways, she didn't deserve *that* charge. Ugh, but people have such twisted imaginations.

The wedding banquet. Lucrezia and Alfonso presiding over the guests for the first time as husband and wife, the new Duke and Duchess of Bisceglie, holding hands under the cloth and dispatching dishes to their most favored friends. Sandro claimed my left side, some minor Neapolitan princeling my right. "Rumors of your beauty have not been false, Giulia Farnese! A true ornament to the papal court; Naples has nothing to match you! Excepting our radiant new duchess, of course. Perhaps I might call upon you . . ."

The Pope presided at his high table, watching with benevolent fondness. He was supposed to sit alone in his papal splendor, but Caterina Gonzaga perched on his knee playing with his hair and feeding him tidbits. I was surprised he didn't spit them out, because the food from the apathetic Vatican cooks was as terrible as ever—tough stringy capons and leathery oysters drying on their shells and oversugared *biscotti*—but Rodrigo seemed to enjoy licking the sugary crumbs off Caterina Gonzaga's neck as she tittered. His dark eyes found mine, dwelling for a moment's bitter satisfaction before he pulled Caterina into his lap and began fishing idly under her skirts with his ringed hand. Not my Pope anymore, not ever, and he hardly had a glance for me since I had been widowed. Why would he? I had insulted him; Orsino had cuckolded him; we had both been appropriately punished and were now dismissed from the Holy Father's notice. Borgia efficiency.

Lucrezia sent me a dish of sugared almonds with a queenly wave, a sign of the new Duchess's favor, but I waved them away.

"—a pleasure to see your radiant smile again, Madonna Giulia! You have been too long from our court!" A red beaming face bobbing before me at the table, one of the Colonna lordlings. I watched his mouth move, not listening to his words. "My deepest regrets for your lord husband, but so fair a woman cannot be allowed to molder in her grief. Perhaps you will allow me to call upon you soon—"

More dishes, more overbaked haunches of boar and sour greasy cheeses. Oh, but my head ached. "Madonna Giulia, perhaps you will allow me to meet that little daughter of yours? As beautiful as her mother, they say, and I have a young son of my own. Tell me, she is heiress to Bassanello as well as Carbognano, is she not?"

Cesare, ghosting about the tables like a black bat. Pulling all the strings for tonight's celebration, conjuring magic for his preening little sister, whom he watched with such fondness. Michelotto trailed behind, his usual colorless shadow, but I did not see Leonello. I had not seen my former bodyguard at all since the burning of Fra Savonarola. Cesare had sent Leonello away from Rome, some dark business in Romagna, where people whispered of deaths in the night among the Borgia enemies. "Cardinal Borgia's demon dwarf," people whispered, crossing themselves when they spoke Leonello's name. "They say he grows wings and slips through cracks in walls to do his master's bidding!" The demon dwarf had returned to Rome, or so rumor had it, but who knew for certain?

Gifts for Lucrezia—silver platters, *credenza* services of solid gold, frail blown glass, jewels. A necklace of rubies and wrought gold from her father, and Lucrezia squealed as Alfonso of Aragon hooked it about her neck for her. "You did not bring my daughter a gift, Giulia Farnese?" a supercilious voice sniffed behind me, and I smiled at Vannozza dei Cattanei because I knew it would annoy her.

"Lucrezia said my mere presence was a gift, since I am still in mourning and would not otherwise make an appearance in public."

"I don't suppose you had anything suitable to offer the Duchess of Bisceglie, anyway. Not from that little hole you live in now—Viterbo?"

"Carbognano."

"Yes, Carbognano. Dull little place. Your daughter's inheritance, I understand." Vannozza smiled, her feathered fan twitching like a cat's tail. "Well, not all our daughters can be duchesses."

"No," I agreed. "Not all our daughters are divorced, disgraced, and rumored to whore for their brothers, either. Whom do you count the luckier, Vannozza?"

Her smile disappeared, and since the guests were rising now to stream into the papal apartments, I found it a good note on which to leave her.

Cesare had worked his sorcery on his father's private papal apartments as well. Tableaux in every chamber: a *sala* turned into a garden with real apple blossoms scattered underfoot and vines twined over the walls and serving girls dressed as nymphs in transparent gauzes; another *sala* transformed into a forest with green boughs hanging from the ceiling and fresh leaves covering the carpets, a fountain taking up the whole of another chamber and splashing wine instead of water. The fountain writhed for a moment as I looked at it, and I saw it had been twined all over with vipers, empty scaly skins stretched and stuffed to look alive. All those jet-bead eyes and ivory fangs seemed to coil in my fevered eyes and I turned away, flinching.

Cesare stood beckoning the guests: master of revels in his black velvet. The servants were masked and costumed like mummers; nymphs and satyrs and beasts, and Cesare wore a mask with a single twisted black horn: a dark unicorn. I'd been the unicorn at the last masquerade, where Rodrigo had ordered a guest hanged for daring to insult Juan. Why had I not realized such a man would take revenge on Orsino, for the supposed crime of cuckolding him?

My fault. My fault.

"Snakes," a voice slurred, and Sancha of Aragon trailed forward with her reddened eyes fixated on the writhing fountain behind Cesare. "Snakes, snakes, you Borgia snake—" She hissed at Cesare, her little pointed tongue flickering, not unlike a snake herself, and she raised an unsteady hand to slap at him. She had been glaring at him all night, and she was drunker than a dockside slattern. "Borgia snake, you know what you've done to me—"

She fell on him, slapping and shouting, and his servants rushed forward in their masks and her servants too. A bishop staggered back with a bloody nose, Michelotto hit the Tart of Aragon so hard her neck wrenched, one of Sancha's guards drew his dagger, and for a moment I thought Lucrezia's wedding would see murder. Why not?

But the Pope's guards rushed around him with their own blades, Cesare's voice cracked like a whip, and Alfonso of Aragon came forward to put an arm about his sister and lead her off. "He gave me the French pox," I thought I heard Sancha snarl to her brother, but Cesare just shrugged as though he could not care less. He adjusted his horned mask, and I thought I saw the disease's livid marks spotting his sharp handsome face. The French pox would eventually rot your nose right off, or so they said, and then it drove you mad. But Cesare Borgia was already mad, wasn't he?

"Put up your sword, you fool," a deep voice snapped to the last of Sancha's Neapolitan guards, and I gazed at Leonello a long blank moment before recognizing him.

"You would not wear a costume for my masquerade," I said.

"Because people would laugh at me." His voice was muffled behind the huge lion mask; he wore a tawny doublet and absurd clawed gloves and an enormous furred ruff. "No one laughs at the demon dwarf now."

"You look—" I saw Caterina Gonzaga point at him and titter, and I wanted to claw her eyes out. "You look ridiculous."

"Indeed." His normally precise words had a blur about the edges I didn't recognize.

I lowered my voice. "I want very much to speak with you, Leonello. Privately."

"Do you?" He tossed down the cup of wine in his hand. "I don't."

He dipped his cup into the fountain for more. "Are you *drunk*?" I asked. I had never seen my abstemious, fastidious, dignified bodyguard drunk in his life.

"No, but I plan to be."

I had never seen him dance either, but he danced tonight. All the mummers in their masks danced for the Pope and the bridal pair and the laughing guests, and Leonello did a grave jig under his huge ruff that had everyone guffawing. I turned my eyes away, and promptly my hand was claimed by an eager-eyed lordling from the Piccolomini family. "Dear Giulia, your beauty dims even your black! Perhaps I can call upon you soon?"

Why did everyone want to call on me? Leonello in his lion mask was chasing after the mummer dressed as a stag now. Lucrezia giggled helplessly into her husband's shoulder.

"Madonna Giulia, surely you will open the dancing with me?" Another shiny-eyed man, taking my hand and giving it a squeeze. "I have so long admired your grace in the turns—"

Go away, I thought, *just go away, all of you*. But I had a cluster of men about me, and they didn't seem to care how little I spoke.

The farce with the mummers drew to a close, and applause rippled. The mummers descended in their masks into the ranks of guests, and the viols struck up a dance.

"Madonna Giulia—"

"Surely you will partner me—"

They were all vying to grasp my hand, and one fellow tipsier than the rest even gave my waist a moist squeeze. "May I rescue you?" Sandro murmured, and my little crowd of suitors looked on in disappointment as I gave my hand to my brother.

Lucrezia was whirling palm-to-palm with Alfonso of Aragon, one of her squealing ladies had seized Cesare's hand, and Caterina Gonzaga was dancing with the mummer masked as an elephant. I swept around to face Sandro and made the opening reverence. "Thank you," I managed to say. "They were pressing rather hard."

"They'll press until you marry one of them." Sandro's normally mischievous expression had gone quite serious as he made his bow to me. "You had better give some thought to a second husband, *sorellina*."

"I'm only three months widowed!"

"And a very tempting prospect to any unmarried man, as well as a good many of the married ones."

"As a soiled wife? It's been made very clear that's all I am."

"*Orsino's* soiled wife, Giulia. Now you're a wealthy widow free to marry another man, and you'll bring that lucky man a number of profitable little country properties *and* the loveliest face in Rome." Sandro raised his hand toward me with the first flutter of viols. "Most men will now find it quite possible to forgive you your reputation."

"What Orsino left me belongs to Laura." I put my hand against my brother's, gliding into the first pass. "Carbognano, the *castello*, it will all be Laura's dowry."

"And there is not a man in this room who does not hope to marry you, get sons on you, and take Carbognano and the rest for his own heirs." My brother made a turn about me with all his usual grace. "Be careful, Giulia. Choose your second husband wisely."

A little flame of resentment burned in my stomach. "I don't *want* a second husband!" Or sons either . . .

"You will need one whether you wish it or no, if you wish to safe-guard Laura's inheritance." Sandro's voice had a bleak matter-of-factness. "An older brother, even if he is a cardinal, isn't enough to protect a wealthy young widow in this wicked world."

I made a turn of my own, seeing my black skirts flare and seeing the eyes of men flare too as they looked on me. Of course. I was a prize now. Foolish of me not to have considered it sooner, in my frozen state after Orsino's death. I was a prize, and Laura was an even bigger one—and my brother looked at me with immense sympathy as he saw me realizing it. "When did you turn so cynical and wise, Alessandro Farnese?" I managed to ask.

"When I accepted a cardinalate from the Borgia Pope, Giulia. It's deep water I've learned to swim in, and there are serpents under every ripple."

I'd persuaded him to take the red hat, when Rodrigo offered it. I should have left well enough alone; should have let my big brother scamper on through life as a notary. Should have let him stay a scamp and a jokester, instead of this handsome, serious churchman who spoke so knowledgeably of serpents and dangerous waters.

"'Serpents under every ripple,'" Sandro mused, perhaps turning his voice back to its old airy amusement because he saw the look on my face. "Do you like that, *sorellina*? Perhaps I have a gift for rhyme. Everyone agrees I don't have any gift for church business."

"Oh, Sandro—"

"Now, Giulia, don't look so stricken." Sandro put his palm against mine again for a final turn. "I'll manage, and so will you. Just think about it, eh? What I said about marrying again."

"Yes," I answered, and a dozen men clamored for my hand before the dance's last notes finished. I looked over the sea of eager faces, and I took the hand of Vittorio Capece, my erstwhile host who had hardly been able to look me in the face after what had happened to Orsino in his *palazzo*. "You really must stop avoiding me, Vittorio. How often must I tell you nothing was your fault?"

"Good of you to say so." He gave me his kindly smile as we moved into the next dance. A livelier tune than the grave passes I'd trod with my brother, but Vittorio was as light on his feet as a young man, and he turned me capably about the waist. "You're looking very grave, m'dear. Thinking of Orsino?"

"In a way." I inspected the lord of Bozzuto as he spun me. "Tell me, Vittorio, have you ever thought of marriage?"

"Yes, dreadful prospect." Vittorio shuddered. "I've staved it off gallantly, but it may prove inevitable."

"Inevitable?" We checked, reversed, joined hands again.

"Our good Pope Alexander VI does not persecute . . . hmm, well, let's just say, men like me. But who knows about the next pope?" Vittorio arched an elegant brow at Rodrigo, reclining on a chair twined with vines as he tapped a jeweled finger in time to the music. "A wife would provide protection, shall we say, should the winds of change begin to blow. Because our Holy Father will not last forever."

It had always seemed impossible to me that Rodrigo would ever die. He had too much energy and vitality, too much *life* for that. But I saw now that his eyes were puffy and pouched, as though the late nights were beginning to tell upon that famous energy, and the food at his table was as terrible as ever but it was fattening him as it hadn't done even a year or two ago. He was an old man, old as he had never before seemed in my eyes, and I felt one last twinge of pity. Then his gaze passed over me with the same faint smile of malice he had bestowed on me after Orsino's death, when I had come before him with eyes full of accusation, and my heart hardened like hoarfrost.

The dance was done. Vittorio Capece bowed and released my hand, but I said, "Another dance?" and we trod three more tunes together, my other suitors falling back in disappointment. Vittorio made polite conversation, and I eyed him thoughtfully. Sandro watched us from across the room and raised his goblet to me with a silent, tilted smile.

Vittorio kissed my hand at the end of the music, gracefully begging my leave—"Allow a gray-haired man to regain his breath, m'dear?" He settled me courteously in a cushioned chair beside the fountain full of snakes, and I smiled thanks as he bustled off in pursuit of wine. Or perhaps a handsome page.

More suitors pressed, but I turned them all down, calculating just when I could make my exit. Lucrezia and Alfonso of Aragon were still dancing; they likely wouldn't be bedded down together until dawn. Sancha must have drunk enough wine to forget that Cesare had given her the French pox because she was dancing with him now, and the dress kept slipping off her shoulder. Caterina Gonzaga was dancing with the little masked lion in his huge furred ruff, and laughing when he stumbled. Surely it had to be long past midnight.

"The lion and the unicorn!" someone shouted, and Cesare broke from Sancha to lower his horn and go charging after Leonello with a cry of challenge. My former bodyguard gave a mock growl, waddling away, and in his chair the Pope convulsed with laughter. The mummer in the stag mask lowered his own horns and pricked Leonello in passing, and Leonello stumbled and fell. I saw his hazel eyes through the mask's eye holes, and they had a bitter shine.

"Another drink!" he cried, flopping on the floor. "The dwarf will need far more wine if he is going to endure all this!" And they were lifting him up, Cesare and the stag and even handsome Alfonso of Aragon joining in the fun, hoisting Leonello sky-high and carrying him over to the fountain, where they held him under one of the streams of wine and let it run over his face until he spluttered. "That's better!" Leonello shouted, not even struggling, and why was that? Why, when he had never allowed anyone to laugh at him in his life? They were laughing now, Lucrezia's eyes streaming as she doubled over, her ladies pink-faced and tittering like peahens.

They set Leonello on his feet and he reeled, trying to straighten his huge ridiculous ruff that made him look more like a mushroom than a lion, and only making it more crooked. "Make the lion dance!" someone called, and Cesare poked at my bodyguard with the sheath of his sword, and Leonello went into a crazy little caper, his eyes mocking himself as they laughed, and one of the ladies leaned down and smeared a kiss on his mouth. I saw him kiss her back, teeth catching at her lip, and she giggled. "The lion bites!"

"Such a funny little man," one of my new suitors snickered in my ear, and I smacked his hand as it tried to make its way under my bottom. The Tart of Aragon's dress had fallen off both shoulders now, and Caterina Gonzaga was sitting in the Pope's lap with her skirts bunched to her knees to show off her little ankles. Alfonso of Aragon had returned to his wife's side and they were lolling half reclined on the velvet cushions, Lucrezia's mouth loose and red as she nibbled at his ear. Blank-eyed Michelotto had grabbed one of the gauze-draped nymphs and yanked her behind the fountain of snakes. I could see the girl's head bobbing over his groin.

"Eden," Leonello said clearly, and slapped another of Lucrezia's giggling ladies across her rump. "This is Eden, fair people, but not for men. For beasts. Kiss me."

"Strip him!" Sancha called slurrily. "Show off your cock, little man—" And there was still no protest from Leonello as guffawing men held him spread-eagled, and laughing ladies fumbled at the ties of his hose. Caterina Gonzaga came wriggling down from the dais, her Pope choking with laughter as she tugged at the dwarf's doublet. Leonello just gave a howl of laughter at the ceiling like a baying dog, a howl of bitter self-loathing that ended in splutters when one of Alfonso of Aragon's laughing noblemen upended a cup of wine over his head, and I didn't realize I was moving until my fingers locked around Leonello's wrist. "Get away from him," I hissed at the crowd, and yanked my bodyguard to his feet.

"Do you want a look at his cock too, Giulia?" Caterina Gonzaga giggled, and I slapped the bitch so hard she sat down on her proud rump in the middle of the carpet. The Neapolitan nobleman who had emptied his wine over Leonello's head gave a hiccup and tried to kiss me, and I slapped him too. My hand stung, and so did my eyes. "Giulia, you're spoiling our fun," Lucrezia protested, but I ignored her. Leonello's wrist was boneless in my hand, and his head lolled on his shoulders, but he was not nearly as drunk as he was pretending to be. His eyes glittered at me, and his feet were perfectly steady as I hauled him behind me for the doors. Cesare Borgia blocked my path with arms folded across his chest. "Where are you taking my dwarf?" he drawled.

"Do you think any of them will be afraid of your pet assassin if they see him like this?" My teeth gritted on hatred as I clenched them together, but coming fast behind me I heard my brother's charming voice. "Cardinal Borgia, if I might question you a moment about some consistory business?" Cesare shrugged, willing to be distracted, and opened his hand to gesture me past. Behind him I saw Rodrigo tugging Caterina Gonzaga back onto his lap with a bull's roar, Lucrezia clapping her hands for the masked elephant and the masked stag who were now wrestling about the room in mock combat, Joffre and Sancha quarreling drunkenly. One last image of them all, and I dragged my little lion away on a stream of drunken laughter.

I never saw Rodrigo Borgia or any of his children again.

Leonello

Y ou're a meddling bitch," I told my former mistress as she hauled me through the private passage from the Vatican to the Palazzo Santa Maria, the passage the Pope had taken so often to visit her bed. "Go away and leave me in peace." But Giulia ignored me utterly, dragging me along like a sack of laundry to the chamber that she had been lent for the wedding festivities, and barking orders at the sleepy maids in such thunderous tones that they went fleeing before her like frightened birds.

"Get undressed," she ordered, rounding on me, and when I stood swaying and blinking mutinously, she stripped the doublet off me with her own hands as the maids brought water, towels, refreshments. In the past I might have conjured up a few idle daydreams in which she undressed me, but with tenderness rather than this brusque angry efficiency. Who would have guessed that the former Bride of Christ was such a bully? "Burn these," she ordered, dropping the lion mask and the huge furred ruff into the nearest maid's hands. "Burn them at once."

"I liked that mask," I said.

"Shut up!" She whipped around on me with a ferocious scowl as the maids hastily scampered out. "What in the name of the Holy Virgin were you *thinking*, Leonello? You've been hard sometimes, and you've been sharp-tongued, but you've never played the fool! Not for anyone!"

"I missed my calling. Don't I make a splendid fool?"

"You certainly do. Hold out your arms."

Her brow was stormy but her hands were gentle as she sponged away the wine that had soaked through my doublet to the skin. I should have been humiliated, standing half naked before my former mistress with a sheet clutched about my waist, but I was far beyond humiliation. My head rang from the sudden silence of the little chamber after all the raucous noise of the wedding festivities, and I closed my stinging eyes. For all my splashing about in the wine this evening, I was not drunk. I wished I were. *Fool. Buffoon. Demon dwarf.* The words rang nonsensical in my ears. *Show off your cock, little man.*

"I've been looking for you, these past few months." Giulia's voice was quieter now, though she tugged harder than she needed to as she dragged a wet comb through my wine-damp hair. "Where did you go?"

"My good master sent me to Romagna." I blinked hard. "The lords there are in disorder—when are they not in disorder? So he intends to wage war on them, and add their lands to the papal territories. I was sent to make quiet observation of the various fortifications."

"Better than sending you off to kill Borgia enemies, I suppose."

"Oh, there was some of that too."

"Sit." She gestured to the bed behind me, and I sat. She pushed a silver goblet into my hand, and I drank obediently. Lemon water, tart and chilled, cooling my fevered blood. Such a hot summer night; I could hear the insects calling through the shutters. Surely it would be dawn soon, and the wedding festivities broken up. Lucrezia Borgia would be bedding down with her new husband by now, and the Pope pumping and wheezing over his current mistress.

Giulia put away the basin of water, splashing a little on her own face. "I'm tired," she said.

"Then go to bed. I don't want you here."

She ignored me, massaging at her temples as though her head ached. "Do you know what I hate?" she asked me rhetorically as she began stripping the pins out of her coiled plaits. "My ridiculous hair. I've come to hate having floor-length hair. It sounds very romantic, but it takes hours to wash and even more hours to dress, and it's impossible to sleep on because it gets tangled around everything unless you bundle it into a net, and you can't do that because then you're sleeping in a hairnet and how romantic is *that*. I'd have cut my hair years ago, but Rodrigo loved showing me off in it, and then Orsino loved showing me off in it, because it was what I was known for: 'Giulia La Bella with her floor-length hair.' Perhaps now that I'm just a simple widow of Carbognano, I'll chop it all off."

"Go away," I said again, but she ignored me utterly, unraveling the last plait and shaking her hair down. It piled around her as she settled on the floor, cross-legged like a sewing maid, and drew my feet into her lap. "What are you doing?" I demanded.

"Your legs will be hurting you by now, after all that capering." Her fingers were already finding the aches that stabbed my calf muscles like knives. "Why did you let them humiliate you like that, Leonello?"

I closed my eyes again. "Because I deserve it."

"Do you?"

"You know what I do for Cesare Borgia."

"Did you know my husband was to be murdered?"

"No." Opening my eyes. "Cesare must have given that job to Michelotto. You need a tall man if you're going to pull off that trick with the ceiling, after all. Someone who won't need to drag a chair over to reach the archway."

"That's something, at least."

"Would you have forgiven me?" My knotted legs were loosening under her hands. "If I had been the one to smash Orsino's head in?"

"No." She paused to open a crock of some sweet-smelling balm, cool and astringent, and smooth it into my skin. "But I would have tried."

"If it's any consolation, I'd have warned you." I fumbled the words because I meant them—despite all my bitter self-loathing, I wanted her to believe me when I said there were still some things I would not do. "If I'd known Michelotto was coming for your Orsino, I'd have sent word." She looked at me, and I gave a shrug. "Even a little monster like me doesn't want a monster like Michelotto roaming about the same house with Laura."

"Still looking out for us, I see." There was the faintest softening of her mouth. "How many times have you saved me by now, Leonello?"

"Two?" I counted. "Savonarola's Angels. The French."

"And that fellow who tried to extract my rings from me on my way back from confession two years ago, remember him?"

"*Dio.* I'd forgotten." I took another cooling swallow of lemon water, letting the silence lapse. My skin tingled, but not from the balm she was rubbing into my legs—from her touch. Her touch could have undone a saint, much less one wretched, haunted dwarf.

"Now that the wedding is over, I'll be returning to Carbognano." Giulia moved from my calf muscles to my stunted feet. They looked like ugly misshapen roots in her small white hands. "Come with me, Leonello."

I found my tongue again. The rough side of it, anyway, and I let her have it, pulling my shredded pride around me. "You want a bodyguard again, my little rose? You're not the Pope's darling anymore, you know; no one will care about harming you. It's Caterina Gonzaga who needs guarding now, and with that nasty tongue of hers I'm sure someone will manage to kill her no matter how many bodyguards she has. The Pope may do it himself," I added. "She's *very* irritating."

"Laura has been asking after you." A curtain of hair swung forward, blocking Giulia's face as she kneaded at the arches of my feet. "Orsino wasn't very good with her—he didn't really like her, truth be told. He wanted to send her away to be fostered in France, or Milan, or Venice. Anywhere he wouldn't have to see her and be reminded of Rodrigo. And Rodrigo didn't want her either, once I said she wasn't his. You're the one Laura misses most."

"Then the little rosebud has no judgment," I mocked. "Just like her mother."

"Laura's cleverer than I am," Giulia said, undeterred. "Soon she'll start Latin studies. If you came to Carbognano, you could be the one to teach her."

"I hate the country."

"It would be far better for you than this snake pit, Leonello."

"And why didn't you flee this snake pit if you hate it so much?" I took another swallow of lemon water, turning the argument back on her. I didn't need knives; I could fend her off forever with nothing but words. "You could have stayed in Carbognano after your husband's burial. Why did you come back?"

"Because of you!" Her face lifted out of the curtain of hair, and I saw that her dark eyes were full of tears. "Holy Virgin, Leonello, are you blind? I was waiting for you to come back from Romagna or the ninth ring of hell or wherever it was Cesare Borgia sent you these past months. Lucrezia begged me to come back to Rome for the wedding, but I didn't come for her, I came for you. And God help me, but I am not going home without you."

I sat frozen, so small and absurd with my bare feet dangling off the edge of the bed and a sheet clutched about my waist.

"I have missed you every day since you left me." Giulia dashed angrily at her eyes. "There wasn't one hour I didn't look around for you and then feel so lonely when I realized you were gone. You've been at my side since I was eighteen, Leonello. I hear a joke and I run to tell you before anyone else, just so I can see you grin. I don't wear sandalwood scent because you hate the smell. I read silly poetry just so I can hear you making fun of it. You were with me when Laura was born and when she took her first steps; you taught her to read and you make her laugh and you're more her father than either of the men who were supposed to have sired her. You've been at my side for so long, and I don't know how to be without you. I did my best to be a good wife to Orsino these past months, but all the time I was thinking of you. I'd be with him yet if he were alive; he was my husband and I owed him that, and maybe in another year or two I could have persuaded myself that he was still what I wanted. But he's dead, and God forgive me, I can't even grieve for him. He was jealous of any man who looked at me, and he tried to send my daughter away, and every time he chucked me under the chin and called me his little rose, I missed you more." Her eyes met mine. "Orsino gave me a ring and Rodrigo shared my bed, but all this time—all this time, I think I was truly married to you."

My mouth was dry as tinder. Words; my last weapon; and she had utterly disarmed me. I averted my eyes from hers. *Dio*, but they burned. The cup in my hands shook, and I folded my fingers around the stem. "I won't take your pity," I said tightly.

"You think this is *pity*?" She looked at me a long moment, and then her face twisted and she averted her eyes. "Then let me tell you something," she said, and her voice was flat and bitter. "Something that happened when we were taken captive by the French. I saw you settled that first night, and you had so many wounds. So much blood, I could see the life leaking out of you with every heartbeat, but I couldn't stay with you. I had to go dine with the French general and his officers, and I put on every jewel I had and I flirted with them all. I *dazzled* them, Leonello, I dazzled them and I got everything I wanted. Extra guards to keep all those lustful soldiers away from the maids, and blankets and wine and a brazier to keep us all warm, and my carriage repaired and my stolen horses returned, and the messenger going to Rome that same night with a ransom demand. I got all of that. But the French general, that smooth bastard, he wouldn't give me a surgeon for your wounds. He wouldn't do it, even when I offered him my pearl necklace and all my jewels, and he had a thousand excuses, but what it all came to was that you'd humiliated him. You humiliated his whole army, a dwarf killing three of his precious pike-men without even trying. He wanted to let you die." She laughed, a tinny sound. "They'd been pawing me all night, all the French officers, kissing my hands, putting their arms about my waist, getting a nibble on my ears, but they didn't dare anything further. Even General d'Allegre. Until I got on my knees and told him no one would ever know, as long as he did what I wanted. And I did everything *he* wanted, and after that he gave me the best surgeon in the French camp, and you survived your wounds."

She lifted her head, and I thought I might see tears on her cheeks. But her eyes were proud and dry, and she met my gaze unflinching. "The one time in my life I've ever truly whored myself, Leonello. I didn't do it for the Pope, or for myself, or even for my daughter. I did it for you. And I'd do it again. I'd do anything to save you pain."

There was a roaring in my ears, and a vast rage. I could have climbed down and marched on France at that moment, to bury my knives to the hilt in that French general's eyes. I clutched the rage, welcomed it. Rage was better than the storm she'd lit in me with her words: shame and astonishment, agony and humiliation, and something else that wasn't possibly hope. It couldn't be hope; it was far too small and pitiful.

Like me.

"Come back to Carbognano with me," Giulia Farnese said. "Please, Leonello. Come back with me. Live with me. Love me."

I put my cup aside with great care, noticing that my hand shook. "I can't love anyone," I said, my voice coming from very far away, and I slid down from the bed to my feet.

"You idiot," Giulia said in a rough voice, and rose to her knees. On her knees she was shorter than I, and she reached her arms up around my neck as though I were the tallest of men, and kissed me.

She kissed me.

She—

Dio.

She kissed me.

Her soft mouth withdrew from mine. Her eyes were enormous, pleading. "Leonello?" she said, and she was still pressed so close against me, her lips brushed mine as they moved.

"I'm ugly," I whispered. "I'm so ugly." And as my eyes filled with tears, I wasn't just speaking of my looks.

She buried her face in my chest, her arms closing about me. My hand twined through her glorious hair, and she smelled of honeysuckle and gillyflowers and light.

"Orsino was handsome," she said. "Handsome as a dream. But he was gutless, and I've no use for a man who isn't brave. Not after knowing you. You are the bravest man I know."

"I'm a murderer." I said it harshly. "I've killed men in cold blood, I—"

"Rodrigo is a murderer." She cut me off. "He has no kindness at all, not anymore. And no desire to *be* kind, to *make* himself a better man. Not the way he once did. But you—Leonello, no matter how many sharp words you throw out around you, no matter how many enemies you've killed, you can still be the kindest of men. When you want to be." Her eyes were bright with pleading, terrible with hope. "Please tell me you want to be."

I closed my eyes and let the tears fall. I felt her cheek turn against my chest.

"You're not ugly, Leonello," she whispered. "And you're not cruel. You are a lion, and you are mine."

My arms closed around her. We rocked together, my cheek pressed against the top of her golden head, and I wept. I could not remember the last time I had cried, and I had never cried at all where another living soul could see me—but I wept now, my whole body heaving, and Giulia only held me tighter. I felt the dark core in me cracking in the cocoon of her scent, cracking to pieces and fleeing my soul like roaches fleeing the dawn.

By the time the tears passed we were coiled together on the embroidered bedcover, tangled up in her velvet skirts and her loops of silky hair. "See what I mean about the hair?" she whispered.

I gave a shaky laugh. "I don't care if you leave it, lop it short, or shave it off." She lay so close on the pillow that her lashes almost brushed my cheek, and she was so beautiful she filled me with despair. "What are we doing, Giulia? I can never marry you—the world would never accept it."

"No." Her voice was grave. "And I may need a husband. One who can protect my inheritance, and safeguard Laura's future."

"*Dio.*" I gave a bitter little laugh. "I can protect your body against harm, and Laura's too—against all the odds, I'm a man to fear when it comes to open attacks. I can lay my life down protecting you and Laura in the flesh, but I can't do one bloody thing about protecting your inheritance, can I?"

"Then I'll find a husband who can." She sat up, cupping my face on the pillow in both her hands, and her eyes were fierce. "No bitterness, Leonello, not now! I can find a husband who will give me his name's protection, who will keep the wolves away from Laura's dowry. But I'll make sure he's also a man who won't trouble me, won't be jealous of me, won't make me bear his children. I can find a husband like that."

"Where?" I gazed up at her, feeling my mouth twist. "Every man in Rome looks at you and wants you in his bed—"

"Not the man I have in mind. And I do have one in mind, Leonello. He will have me in public, and you will have me in private."

"Your stunted secret," I said, and my belly roiled. "Only in the shadows—"

"Maybe the world won't be able to know it, Leonello, but I am yours. I promise you that." She spoke quietly. "Will you accept me on those terms?"

She put up her hand and I matched my own to it, lacing my stubby fingers with hers. *My Aurora*, I thought, *my bringer of light*—and that bitterness that had been ready to gather was already leaving me. Orsino Orsini had been jealous, and so had Rodrigo Borgia. They had lost her.

Not me.

Maybe the world won't be able to know it, Leonello, but I am yours.

I let the last of that dark taste in my mouth trickle away on a seeping breath. "I do not care if the world ever knows, Giulia." I slid my other hand down the smooth silk of her throat, down the slope of her naked shoulder where her sleeve had slipped down. "As long as you *are* mine."

I took my beautiful lady in my arms, and I felt as tall as a mountain.

CHAPTER SEVENTEEN

Remember tomorrow, for it is the beginning of always.

—DANTE

Leonello

Y ou look ferocious." Cesare Borgia surveyed me briefly. "What
ails you?"

I gave an even blacker scowl. "Nothing." In truth, I frowned because
otherwise I would be grinning like a loon. A grinning dwarf is such a
comic sight. Even more comic is a dwarf who capers, dances, and carols
love songs, and I felt like doing all three this morning, but I did none
of them. I forced myself to scowl, planted my boots firmly, and locked
my hands behind my back. "A private word, Your Eminence?"

"I am very busy this morning, as you well know." Cesare frowned
into a glass held up by one of his manservants, giving a twitch to his
sword belt about his hips. The wedding festivities for the new Duke and
Duchess of Bisceglie had run past dawn, and it was not yet anywhere
near noon, but the Pope's eldest son looked as bright-eyed as if he had
slept the night through. His private chambers adjacent to the Holy
Father's were all a-bustle: pages running to fetch wine and sweetmeats,
servants holding up doublets and pairs of hose for the young Cardinal's
inspection, squires hovering with basins and towels for shaving, and of

course Michelotto blearily cleaning under his nails with a dagger. Cesare glanced at me as he dunked his hands in a basin of rosewater. "What is so important, little lion man?"

Giulia, I thought. *Giulia is important. The only thing important on this earth.* The warm fragrance of her, the golden ripple of her voice, her velvet mouth as she whispered my name in the darkness. I had been glad of the darkness last night, hardly wanting her to look on me no matter how much I ached for her—and I had felt the heat of her cheeks between my hands and realized she was blushing too. She was one of the most notorious names in Rome and I was one of the most feared, yet the pair of us came together shy as children. The dawn had brought her maids knocking on the chamber door, and me flying up from a sound sleep ready to scuttle under the bed. But Giulia had called through the door for the maids to go away for another hour, and then tossed a loop of her hair about me like a rope and tugged me back down to the pillow. Where we'd lain quietly, braiding our fingers together and unbraiding them again, as the light crept across the bed. By the time the sun reached my pillow I no longer wanted the dark, no longer wanted it anywhere around me or within me, and *that* was important.

But to Cesare Borgia none of that mattered, or ever would, and I pitied him.

"What hour will the ceremony be held?" I asked instead.

"Noon." My master's scarlet cloak and red hat lay across the wall bench, ready to be put on for the last time. After noon today, Cesare Borgia would be cardinal of the Church no longer.

"How is it done?" I couldn't help wondering. "If no cardinal has ever resigned his red hat before, then what is the proper procedure? Poor Burchard must have had fits."

"He did. It was decided I would give a brief speech before the College of Cardinals, announcing my unfitness for a religious vocation, after which the Holy Father will release me from my vows."

"And then?"

"I meet with the French King's chamberlain immediately afterward." Cesare tied the laces of his shirt at the cuff. "He is to make me Duc de Valentinois. He may offer me a French marriage as well, but an alliance with Naples will be more useful once I launch my campaign against Romagna. I'll take a Neapolitan bride."

"Sancha of Aragon, perhaps?" There had been rumors that Cesare's cardinalate would simply be traded to pouting little Joffre, an even exchange of red hat for Neapolitan wife.

"Sancha of Aragon is a bastard-born slattern with the French pox," Cesare said casually. "I will have a legitimate princess of Naples."

You want Naples itself, I thought. *Romagna first, then Naples—and after that, the world.* But I would not be there to help him get it.

"With Your Eminence's permission," I said, "I will be leaving your service."

His hands stilled a moment on his shirt ties. "Interesting."

"Not very. I would merely rather go to Carbognano than Naples."

Cesare tilted his head at his servants, his bustling squires, even Michelotto. "Leave us."

They filed out mutely. Any other servants would have whispered, but Cesare Borgia required perfect silence and perfect obedience from his menials. And they were all far too terrified of their master not to give him exactly what he wanted.

"Leave my service," he said as the doors closed and left us in the stifling richness, "and you leave by way of the river. Face down."

"I have done good work for you, Your Eminence." I saw that the laces of his other cuff still dangled, and crossed the room to do them up for him. He allowed me to make the knots at his wrist. "Not to mention the fact that you rather like me. I would request that you allow me to retire, rather than drown me."

"Why should I do that? You'd be nothing but a loose thread, Leonello, and I dislike loose threads. They need to be tidily cut off."

"Who knows how to keep his mouth shut better than a dwarf?" I brought him his cardinal's robes over the fold of my arm as he gestured for them. "You have nothing to fear from me, I assure you."

It was the wrong thing to say. His face darkened as though the sun had come down over it. "I fear nothing."

"Certainly not me," I agreed swiftly, and took a slow breath as I played the only card I had. "But you do *owe* me, Your Eminence."

"Owe you?" He laughed. "For what?"

"For killing your brother for you."

A small silence fell at that. We looked at each other for a while, and then he shrugged into his scarlet robes.

"I always wondered if you knew," I said.

"Of course I knew!" He looked offended. "I could have made life difficult for you, little lion man, had I wanted you caught. I could have pointed out to the Holy Father that it was your 'mishap' with the guards that saw Juan off to the Piazza degli Ebrei without his usual squires. You never made such a mistake before, and you only did it that night to get my brother alone."

"I did you a favor," I said. "The Duke of Gandia was a mad dog. I saved you the trouble of putting him down yourself."

"Yes, that business with the whores really was getting out of hand," Cesare agreed. "That girl who was killed with my dagger—who but Juan would steal it to smear my name? The whole scene had his clumsy paw-marks all over it."

"And you still allowed him to get away with it?"

"I did more than *allow* him. I covered for him." Cesare smiled. "The girl who was killed while Juan was away in Spain? You must have wondered about her. Michelotto killed her, on my orders."

I gave a slow swallow, easing down the lump in my throat. The last piece of the puzzle left unsolved. "Why?"

"You were asking too many questions. You had your eye on me, but if the drought of dead girls had gone on much longer, you'd have started thinking about Juan, off in Spain. I had Michelotto execute a girl, in roughly the same style, when both my brother and I could be accounted for."

"Why?" I asked again. "A dwarf asking questions; what could that possibly mean to you?"

"I protect my family. Even the ones I hate."

"So why didn't you have me killed, when you knew I'd done away with your brother?"

Cesare declined to answer, tilting his head at me. "Tell me something, little lion man. Will you try to kill me for the girl I ordered executed, as you killed my brother for all the others?"

"No." The word came from me before I could even consider it. "I'm done with vengeance."

But I would have Masses said for the girl's soul. Killed not for Juan Borgia's dark lusts, but because a dwarf had asked questions—and for that, I would always grieve.

I forced the thought from my head and returned Cesare's dark stare. "See?" I managed to say. "I am no threat at all, not when you have Juan's death as a sword over my head any time you wish it. If a single rumor leaks from me about any of the things I saw in your service, you have only to loose the Holy Father on me for his son's murder. Believe me, Eminence," I added with utter sincerity, "that is more than enough to keep me silent all the rest of my days."

"Perhaps." Cesare smoothed his hair over the dent of his tonsure, which had already begun growing in. "But why do you wish to leave my service, little lion man? What is it you wish for?"

The question he had asked when we first met. *Books*, I had answered at the time, silently. *To be tall. To matter.*

Well, I had books, books I would soon be teaching a little girl who was almost my daughter to read. And in Giulia's eyes, I was tall as a giant. Oh yes, I mattered. I mattered to them, the family that by the grace of God or Fortune had become mine, and I'd already vowed that I would spend the rest of my days proving myself worthy of them both. I'd leave my teeming city of Rome for good and make my home in sleepy little Carbognano; I'd roll up my sleeves and help Giulia organize the harvest; I'd keep my lady's accounts for her, and comb her hair at night, and write out her letters when her eyes were tired. I'd read her poetry in bed and make her laugh by poking fun at it; I'd write her more poetry of my own and maybe not tear every other sonnet to bits. I'd draw up a plan of lessons for Laura, something to get the Latin declensions and the French verbs into a child's head without deadening her love for books. I was already thinking I'd teach Laura in the mornings, and then in the afternoons when she went off to her dancing master or her music tutor, I'd retire to the cool quietness of the little study I was already planning for myself, a study with a stone bust of Cicero and a desk fitted to my height, and work on translating *The Odyssey* into Italian. I'd always fancied translation work, but it would take years; it was the sort of job a scholarly nobleman took on for the sheer pleasure of it, and I'd always been too busy surviving to afford such leisurely pleasures. But now I could afford such things; I could work on Homer while Laura shrieked and giggled on the shore of the lake outside my window, and Giulia rolled through the *castello* laughing and chattering with her maids. And when dusk fell, we would sit at *cena* around the same table and tell each other of our day, and my account of the hours I'd spent would never again include women staked through the hand, or men dead under my knife, or any spilling of blood at all. That was what *mattered*.

Cesare Borgia would not care about any of that, either. And he was waiting for my answer.

"I have recently discovered happiness," I said at last, flippantly. "Or perhaps God."

He wrinkled his nose. "How commonplace."

"Is it? I think it rather rare." It had been enough to take me this morning from the woman I loved more than anything on this wide earth, away from her to come here. "Don't go, Leonello," Giulia had warned as I hopped on one foot, tugging up my boots. "Who knows what will happen if you face him? Let's just climb into a carriage and *leave*."

"Not without finishing things here first," I'd said, and Giulia said, "*Men.* I ask you!" and stalked off muttering some very uncomplimentary things about the lot of us. Possibly to cover up how white her face was at the thought of me confronting Cesare Borgia.

"You really wish to leave?" Cesare said at last, clapping his red hat onto his head. "Pity. I could have used you in Romagna."

I took a deep breath, feeling oddly serene. If Cesare twitched a finger and Michelotto came through the door to cut my throat, well, at least I had won Giulia Farnese's love first. Poets had died for less, and my lady had succeeded in making a poet of me.

Just hopefully not a dead poet.

"Will I still be leaving Rome by way of the river?" I asked Cesare Borgia. "Face down?"

"You were right about one thing, Leonello." Cesare turned to face me: a cardinal one last time in all his scarlet finery. "I do rather like you. How do I look?"

"About as clerical as a bull in a red hat, Your Eminence."

With a great sweep of his arms Cesare shed the cloak and the hat all at once. The scarlet cloth billowed away in a flutter like a dying bird's wings. He wore stark black velvet beneath, and the long sword of the future Gonfalonier of the papal forces at his lean hip. "My new sword," he said, and unsheathed it for my eyes. I read the motto inscribed along the gleaming blade.

"Aut Caesar, aut nihil."

"Either Caesar"—he grinned—"or nothing."

"You be Caesar, then." I took out my Toledo blades for the last time, the ones he had given me years ago when he first offered to make me his family's hired killer, and laid them out before him one by one. "And I'll be nothing." Of the two of us, I thought I'd be the happier. Even if no one remembered my name in a century, as they probably would Cesare Borgia's.

Cesare tilted his head at my array of blades, all ten of them. "You don't wish to keep them? The world is a dangerous place for dwarves, little lion man."

I shook my head. "No, thank you." I'd always have knives—I'd protect Giulia and Laura till their lives ended, or mine did—but I'd have new blades; ones that weren't marked by torture or vengeance or the stain of Juan Borgia's tainted blood. And maybe I didn't need *ten* anymore. The most threatening I anticipated having to do in the future would be when it came time for Laura to marry; when I would take her suitors aside one by one and gently, benignly explain their duties as a prospective husband as I did a little target practice with my blades into the wall behind their heads. Yes, just two or three knives would do for that.

Cesare's servants flooded back in then, the squires and pages and little Burchard wringing his hands over his usual pile of lists. "Your Eminence, *Gott im Himmel*, you will be *late*—" I slipped away, and no one gave me a second glance in all the storm of activity. I saw Cesare

Borgia half concealed behind a cluster of pages as he conferred with Burchard, swamped in the bustle, and I never saw him again. But the last view I really had was of a pope's son like a worm wrapped in a scarlet cocoon, tossing away the tangling folds of silk to emerge with sword drawn: a dark moth unleashed upon the world.

The image blotted my eyes as I made my last, swift retreat from the Vatican, back to my Giulia, who had gone to pack her belongings, and who surely had the whole household in an uproar by now. The woman couldn't go to Mass without packing for an army. I was already smiling, lining up jokes to tease her with, when I ran into a tall figure in the *palazzo*'s anteroom.

"Messer Leonello," Bartolomeo said, raking at his red hair. "I need your help."

Carmelina

"Three eggs, whisked together with a mixture three parts sugar to two parts strawberry honey," I recited aloud as I swept the convent courtyard. "Add two cheeses; a soft sheep's milk cheese and a very fresh pecorino cheese from Pienza, and then a double handful finely chopped walnuts . . ."

The lay sisters were supposed to recite their prayers as they went about their work—a rosary, or perhaps an Act of Contrition if one were feeling guilty about anything. I recited recipes. Curiously I couldn't seem to remember many of my father's recipes, the ones I'd had at my fingertips for so many years. The convent's walls had a way of leaching memories away, at least the memories that came from your life before the grilles closed behind you with a *clang*. Part of that soft, relentless process that turned girls of all shapes and sizes, all tempers and dispositions, into faceless identical sisters in their identical black and white. I didn't have my father's recipe book anymore, so I couldn't always remind myself how his recipes went—but I still had Bartolomeo's letters hidden away in the pouch that no longer held my patron saint's hand, and he'd written me so many recipes over the months before the letters had been stopped. I knew every one of his new dishes by heart, and it comforted me to recite them out loud. Some nuns told the decades of the rosary as they worked. I told the ingredients of a toasted walnut and pecorino cheese *tourte*.

"*Beat with twelve egg whites and turn out into buttered* tourte *pan . . .*" The broom in my hands went *swish swish swish*. A warm purple twilight, and soon we'd be called in for Vespers. Hardly anyone would bother praying of course—all the younger nuns could speak of was Madonna Lucrezia Borgia's wedding a few days ago. They were whispering away even now, three of them as we swept the convent courtyard together.

"They say she has forty thousand ducats for a dowry this time, and the jewels on her gown cost at *least* that much!"

"They say Alfonso of Aragon is as handsome as a dream . . ."

"They say the Count of Pesaro has taken his own life out of grief, to see his wife wed another . . ."

"No, it was Perotto who took his life, out of love for Madonna Lucrezia . . ."

"I don't believe she really did break her arm when she was here. Did you hear her scream? I had six brothers born after me, and *I* know what a birth sounds like!"

"You served Madonna Lucrezia, Suora Serafina. Did she really . . ."

"Serve *tourte* warm with soft sugar and whole shelled walnuts," I told them, and they didn't bother talking to me after that. Most of the lay sisters thought I was slightly mad, and I couldn't say they were wrong. Who knew? Maybe in a year or two I would be completely mad, fit for nothing except stirring the kitchen pot. At least I'd do it more contentedly than I did now. Even now, when I was starting to float through most of my days in that fog of bemused detachment that Old Bear Ursula liked to call *a state of grace*, the smell of convent gruel without garlic or cinnamon or even, Santa Marta forbid, *pepper*, had the power to rouse me to rage.

The rumble of carriage wheels halted at the gates outside, but I paid no attention. Wedding guests had been making their way out of Rome for days now, and every night we'd had at least one illustrious noble lady beg shelter in the gatehouse accommodations because her carriage horses had gone lame, or because she didn't feel like continuing on for the night. More fodder for gossip, the lay sisters already clustering by the gate for any look at the visitor and what she might be wearing. "A fresh *crostata* of Tiber eels," I recited instead, sweeping absently over the same patch of ground and smiling. *Be proud of me*, Bartolomeo had written me after that particular recipe. *You know how I hate eels. I've finally managed to skin one without pinching my nose shut. Remember that summer in Capodimonte with Madonna Giulia, when I screamed like a weasel just because I saw a water snake?*

I did remember that. I remembered it very well, the way the summer light made his freckles glow gold, the way he'd leaped to the top of the trestle table with all the hair on his head nearly standing on end. I dwelled on it, every detail, because you have to work very hard at remembering things behind convent walls. Or else you wake up for Matins one day and everything else besides the prayers is gone.

"Her gown," one of the lay sisters was squealing. "And that *pearl*—"

"It's the Bride of Christ! Don't let Mother Prioress hear you call her that, but everyone knows the Pope's mistress—"

"Former mistress, I heard . . ."

"Well, former or current, it's certainly La Bella. Just look at the hair—"

My head jerked up and I saw her striding through the gates into the courtyard: Madonna Giulia Farnese in a sweeping sable-lined traveling cloak thrown back to show her high-piled hair and the great pearl at her throat. She was tugging off her embroidered leather gloves finger by finger, frowning, and she snapped over her shoulder to the small figure in black trotting behind. "See my horses stabled at once. We shall leave in the morning as soon as I've rested."

"Yes, *madonna*," Leonello said with a bow, doubling back, and my heart caught in my throat. The broom clattered out of my hand, and before I knew what I was doing I gathered my habit skirts up and raced toward them. "Leonello," I called, suddenly feeling the breeze in the warm summer twilight, the hovering drone of the flies, the flap of my veil against my back—feeling *something* again, rather than the drugged bemusement of that old bitch Suora Ursula's *state of grace*. "Leonello," I called again, pulse hammering in my throat. "Madonna Giulia!"

Giulia Farnese looked at me with a faint frown. "Yes?" she said without much interest, and moved on without waiting for an answer. "Have a foot-bath drawn for me at once, Leonello, my feet ache so *abominably*—"

"Yes, *madonna*," he said, and scuttled past me without a second glance.

I stared after them. Was I invisible? Had I died and become a ghost, and never noticed? Perhaps I had already gone mad.

Or perhaps the memories of Carmelina Mangano had faded away outside these walls as fast as they were fading inside. Maybe there really was only Suora Serafina left in this world.

N uns aren't supposed to go roaming about at night, but they do. There are no bolts on any nun's private cell; the authorities are far too afraid of what will happen inside those cells if we can lock ourselves inside with utter privacy. We were required to sleep with a candle burning and the door ajar, so the appointed night sister could check throughout the night that we were all safely tucked up in godly sleep. But no night sister ever gave more than a cursory yawning glance before going back to her own bed, and most of the time they didn't even do that. As soon as the night bells rang, there was always quite a busy creaking of cell doors opening and shutting as the younger nuns visited each other to gossip and braid hair, the older nuns visited each other to gossip and drink wine from someone's private stores, and the occasional pious nun actually felt moved to go to the chapel in the dead of night and pray. And yes, a few daring sisters did manage to visit a lover in some remote part of the convent, bribing the portress to allow a man inside for an hour or supply him with a rope to scale the walls. It happened, though it didn't happen as often as men liked to think it did.

As for me, I went to the kitchens. It was warmer there than in my cell, and in the face of Leonello's rejection I felt particularly cold tonight.

Madonna Giulia—well, she had always been kind to me but she was a woman of noble birth, a respectable one now, even, and she couldn't be gossiping with cooks the way she used to when she had no one else to talk to. Leonello, though . . . after the whole black business of Juan

Borgia, I'd begun to think that Leonello and I were friends, funny sharp-tongued little man that he was. And he hadn't even had a glance for me.

The kitchens were usually dark, the fires thriftily banked, and I was already thinking of making myself a little stewed nettle tea, nasty stuff. But I saw lights flickering as I pushed the door open, and I looked around to see candles lit everywhere. "That's a week's supply of tapers," I said indignantly as I pushed my way in, fully expecting to find Suora Crestina raiding the sugar supply again, the greedy bitch. But behind me I heard an odd sound like a whoop of joy quickly stifled, and felt a man's arms seize me about the waist instead.

"Told you I'd come for you," Bartolomeo whispered in my ear. And then he kissed me.

Of course I smacked him. With my hand, not the ladle, because he grabbed the ladle away the moment I seized it up from the table, and he held it up far over my head with an infuriating grin.

"Wretch!" I pummeled his shoulder instead. "Not one *word* to me for weeks and weeks—"

"You think I was going to spoil all my plans by putting them into a message?" He was still grinning. "A message that could be intercepted?"

I stopped hitting him long enough to drag a trestle table in front of the kitchen doors. All we needed was Suora Crestina coming along now to raid my sugar, or some other sharp-eyed choir nun with her high-bred nose sniffing out scandal. "So Madonna Giulia—and Leonello—"

"Leonello owed me a favor—owed me *quite* a favor, in fact—and he recruited Madonna Giulia. D'you think he's in love with her? I've always wondered." Bartolomeo put the ladle up on the tallest shelf where I wouldn't be able to reach it without dragging a stool over. "Officially speaking, I've left Signore Capece's household for Madonna Giulia's. She's busy setting the stage for us now, throwing tantrums and keeping everyone busy. For someone so obliging, she's terribly good at being a nuisance, isn't she? Do you thinks she models it more on Madonna Lucrezia or the Tart of Aragon?"

"Bartolomeo!" Even staring right at him, I could hardly believe he was here. He was a vision I hadn't dared allow myself to dream of because

it hurt too much: tall, ruddy-haired, taking up half the kitchen as he strode up and down gesturing and waving his hands, and I couldn't stop drinking in the sight of him. His eyes sparkled as he looked back at me, and my mouth still felt bruised from his kiss. "Will you get to the point?" I demanded, a trifle unsteadily.

"So, I'm supposed to be fixing Madonna Giulia some warm honeyed wine right now—"

"Keep your voice down!"

"—she made a huge fuss and refused to sleep without it. Wouldn't let anyone but me prepare it either. Your poor portress, the one who's supposed to be looking after honored guests, well, she wasn't supposed to let a *man* into the kitchens under any circumstances, but she's so worn out running Madonna Giulia's errands by now, she'd do anything for a little sleep. So, with the solemn promise that I wouldn't venture outside the kitchens, not to mention the bribe of a flagon of good wine . . ." Bartolomeo made an elaborate bow. "Here I am."

My heart thudded. "Do we escape now? Over the wall, or—"

"No, no. You'll see. Better if you look surprised tomorrow." He took me around the waist again. "Trust me."

Guilt stabbed through me like a kitchen spit. "Do you realize the trouble you'll make for yourself? If anyone discovers you helped a nun escape her vows—"

"I find that doesn't trouble my conscience in the slightest." Bartolomeo looked very serious. "Maybe Leonello's rubbed off on me. Tragic, isn't it? A black-hearted assassin corrupting a pure young lad like me—"

I saw the hilarity dancing in his eyes, and I smacked him again. "How did you know I'd be here? Here in the kitchen, I mean."

"Don't know," he shrugged. "I just had a notion I'd find you here. Leonello said you looked so stricken when Madonna Giulia stalked by. And when you're stricken, you always go to the kitchens."

"Well, don't you know everything." Self-consciousness made my voice waspish. I felt ugly all over again—a wimple was bad enough, but without it my short curls were undoubtedly springing out in all directions like a nest of bracken, and I had a flea bite on my chin from the old straw in my pallet, and—and Bartolomeo looked so . . .

"What?" He looked at me.

"I hate my hair," I burst out, running a hand over my cap of frizz.

"I'll wager it smells the same, even if it's shorter." He leaned close, burying his nose in the hair by my cheek. "Cinnamon," he confirmed. "Still cinnamon."

"You smell like marjoram." I let my own nose rest in the dent of his collarbone. "And mint." I remembered that very clearly, from the time we'd spent on his lumpy apprentice's pallet.

"Nutmeg," he continued, inhaling his way down the side of my throat. One hand stroked the length of my back, and the roughness of his jaw brushed my skin. "And pepper. Plenty of pepper—so that's where you get the temper . . ."

"Wild thyme," I said, putting my nose against the center of his wide chest this time. "No wonder you're so insolent."

He set his lips in the base of my throat, tasting me. "Salt."

"Salt," I agreed, tasting the outer edge of his ear. Even his earlobes were freckled. "All cooks taste like salt."

He laced a hand through my hair and bent his mouth to mine. The first time he'd kissed me had been all eager boyish hunger, but some woman must have taught him patience as well as passion. Perhaps it had been me, whacking him on the shoulder and telling him to *wait*, that *zuppa* wasn't ready yet, don't be so impatient, Bartolomeo! He kissed now without haste, not impatient at all, taking the time to taste me. "Honey," he said, murmuring against my lips. "Salty without, sweet within."

"Flatterer," I told him, and dragged his head back down. But he stopped suddenly, looking at me with a scowl.

"This is all wrong," he said.

"Why?" I pulled away, hand flying to my head. "You do hate the hair, don't you?"

"I was supposed to cook for you," he complained. "I had it all planned! I'd find you in the kitchens somehow—I wasn't sure how I'd manage that part, but I thought it could be done. And then I'd finally get to cook for you. I even knew what I was going to cook: *tortellini* with a basil and parsley filling, and a sauce of French wine and cream—"

"You're not supposed to serve *tortellini* in a sauce," I started to say.

"I know, and that was the point. You'd eat my recipe, *mine*, and you'd tell me it was good, and maybe we'd finally get over this whole apprentice business." He glowered, but with a hint of a smile. "And now I'm here, and I did find you, so that part went according to plan, but this pathetic excuse for a kitchen doesn't have any of the ingredients I was counting on. Not one! I brought my own olive oil—" Helpfully he produced a little vial. "Because a good cook always supplies his own good-quality oil, you taught me that. Actually, I brought a hamper—"

I burst out laughing.

"—olive oil and French wine and some good cheese and so forth. Corinthian raisins, very tasty, you'll like them. But I need at least a few extra ingredients to work with, and this kitchen doesn't even have *basil*. Whoever heard of a kitchen that doesn't have *basil*?" His voice rose. "I can't cook you *tortellini*. I can't cook you anything!"

I put my finger across his lips, stilling the flow of words. "Bartolomeo Scappi," I said firmly, trotting out his rarely used second name for this most sacred of occasions. "You are no longer in any way my apprentice."

"I wanted to prove it," he grumbled.

"You proved it in my bed, didn't you?" I said just a bit saucily. "After the fried tubers . . ."

That made him grin. "But you really would have liked my *tortellini*."

"Stop talking about food," I said for the first time in my life, and stood on tiptoe to kiss him again, and he bent and picked me up so my legs circled his waist. The vial of olive oil went *smash* all over the floor, and so did the little dish of raisins. So much for his hamper.

"Do you have a chamber somewhere?" he murmured. "A cell? Something with a bed?"

"Here, the storeroom—"

He backed into it, kicking the door shut without lifting his mouth off mine. "Does *that* have a bed?"

"Better. It has a lock." I dragged the shirt over his head as he pulled me down to the floor between the flour barrels. "Mouth shut, Bartolomeo. Hands moving!"

His lips against my ear made my skin prickle all the way down to my toes. His hands were already following the prickles, down my back, down my hip, tugging my thigh up around him. "Yes, *signorina*."

Giulia

Considering that I never wanted anything to do with *la famiglia Borgia* ever again, I really do think my final performance as the Borgia mistress was remarkable. I quite enjoyed myself. Perhaps I missed my true vocation in life: I was never a very good wife, or a very good whore either, and I was certainly never going to be a nun—but Carmelina had always said there were shadowy spaces between that stark trinity of futures, and she was right. Perhaps I should have been an actress of pantomimes and miracle plays!

"There's no need to involve you, Giulia," Leonello pointed out the previous night when he was brushing my hair for me, as had become his nightly habit. Even after so short a time, we had our traditions! All the hovering maids and nuns had finally been dismissed, but I'd complained of a headache and demanded that my dwarf stay behind to read to me. If he'd been a tall handsome man there would have been talk, but when was there ever talk when a lady was alone with a dwarf? I thought we could manage our lives very handily around that blithe assumption.

"Truly." My lion frowned at me in the glass, stroking a comb through my hair with those clever hands of his. "You think I cannot intimidate a prioress all on my own? I have Bartolomeo to lurk and loom for me, after all. There's no need to drag you into it as well."

"It will all look more convincing if you have me pouting in attendance," I promised, putting down the glass. "Don't you want to see me pout?"

"You do have an enchanting pout," he admitted with that grin that looked far better without its usual cynical tilt. He pressed a wave of my hair back behind my ear, adding, "You also have enchanting earlobes."

"That's absurd. How can anybody have enchanting earlobes?"

"I've no idea, but you manage it. When we get to Carbognano, I shall write a sonnet about them." His thumb traced the outer edge of my ear in the way that gave me such happy shivers. "You're wasted on me, you know."

"What do you mean?" I turned away from my glass, taking the comb from him.

"The most beautiful woman in Rome, bestowed first on a coward, then on a corrupt old man, and finally on a dwarf?" Leonello's eyes crinkled. "Hardly fair."

"Tell me something, Leonello." I put chin in hand, looking up at him from my stool. "Did you love me from first sight, the way Orsino and Rodrigo told me they did?"

"No." He was very certain. "At first sight, I thought you a giddy girl who was very pleasant to look at, and probably even more pleasant to look at unclothed."

"So it wasn't all this"—I made a gesture at the hair, the breasts, all the things men usually stared at—"that made you love me."

"I didn't notice any of it"—making the same gesture—"after the first few months. A pretty face is like a fresco on a wall: you admire it for a time, and then you don't even see it anymore because it's always there."

"How very ungallant!" But I beamed. "What changed? When did you start to love me?"

He put a hand on the crown of my head and smoothed it slowly down the fall of my hair. "When I saw you were kind. When I saw you were brave. When you had special reinforced boots made for me because you understood how my legs ached, even though I'd never told you . . ." He pulled one lock of hair gently through his fingers, all the way to the very end. "Who knows?"

I took his hand and put it to my own cheek. "I have been a *prize* all my life, Leonello. Prizes exist to be paraded; to inspire envy. Maybe lust." I turned my lips against his palm. "Not love."

"You are still wasted on an ugly thing like me."

And I had not seen his looks in a very long time, either. If he was small, well, I was not tall either, and I was tired anyway of being carried about by the whims of large, peremptory men. But I rather thought

Leonello would need time before he truly believed that I didn't find him ugly.

Time we had. "To bed?" I suggested.

He gave that smile of his that made him so handsome. "To bed." Only a few days and I was already used to his quiet warmth beside me, the way his hand held mine through the night as we slept. I was not used to having a man beside me as I slept. Rodrigo had always been too busy to stay the night; he had to rush back to the papal apartments to resume his work, and Orsino didn't think it seemly for husband and wife to share a chamber. Perhaps it wasn't, but I'd long since given up on being seemly, and I didn't intend to go any longer without a shoulder to sleep on. It would be more difficult to manage in Carbognano than it was here in the solitary splendor of the convent's gatehouse quarters, but I already had plans. If I was bringing a certain devoted former bodyguard of mine back to Carbognano, a man who would now take up official position as tutor to my daughter, then wouldn't he need a chamber of his own to teach her in? Wouldn't I need to hire a woodworker, someone skilled enough to make bookshelves and writing tables all fitted to a small man's height, and after that a stonemason to carve scenes on the walls from Leonello's beloved Homer? Behind that frieze of Trojan ships and Greek warriors, I was already planning the construction of a discreet passage leading to *my* chamber. If the Pope used to visit me unseen through a private passage, why couldn't Leonello?

And if I married again, well, my next husband wouldn't expect to sleep by my side either. Because Sandro had been right; I would need a second husband someday if I meant to protect Laura's inheritance. And I already had my eye on a proper candidate: Vittorio Capece of Bozzuto, who would not want sons from me, or my presence in his bed, or anything at all except my occasional promenade on his arm to keep the gossip away. An ideal second husband, and Leonello agreed with me when I shared the name. Vittorio could live in Rome or in Naples with his handsome young pages, and I could reside in Carbognano with my lion. I had it all perfectly planned.

"And what happens if I put a child in you?" Leonello had asked me that the very first night, grim-faced, holding himself back so fiercely. "That would break your plans into pieces, wouldn't it? You could never pass a dwarf child off as Vittorio Capece's."

"I'm not very fertile," I'd pointed out. "One daughter in all the years with Rodrigo, and he *tried* to get me with child—he always hoped I'd give him a son. And Orsino tried too, tried every night for months and months, and nothing happened then either. I think it might have been Laura's birth. She came so hard, and the midwives say it can damage the womb." That should have marked me a great failure, my inadequacy as a breeder of sons, but not for the life I had chosen now. "Besides, there are ways to be careful, if you're worried. Let me tell you just what can be done with a lime . . ."

It was already part of my evening disrobing: a night shift, a little rosewater for the face, and a halved lime. Of course it was a sin, but I was racking up such a number of sins these days, a lime didn't add much to the tally. Fornication; lust; the taking of a lover outside the laws of marriage. Not to mention the fact that this lover and I had cooked up a plan between us to steal a nun out of her convent. No, a lime wasn't much compared to all that.

And I must say, the plan we had cooked up for Carmelina worked beautifully. My little lion and I really did make the most marvelous team. That poor prioress never stood a chance against us!

"I would speak to you, Mother Prioress," I said in bored tones after deigning to take Mass the next morning with the sisters. I hadn't seen Carmelina in the ranks of black and white, but finding her was Leonello's task. I rustled off after the prioress, who showed me to her private *sala* with great alacrity—a *sala* any *palazzo* could have boasted, with its fine woven carpets and inlaid table and carved chairs. Mother Prioress offered a velvet cushion for my back and a very unmonastic wine to sip, and I rustled my skirts and flashed my pearls and made offhand mention of a donation I had been planning to make for the sisters of San Sisto. "Or shall I say, a donation the Holy Father urged me to make? After the great care you have taken of his daughter the Duchess of Bisceglie, he is most interested in furthering the prosperity of your establishment."

"His Holiness is too kind," the prioress purred in her carved chair, patting her own skirts with their rustle of silk beneath and no doubt seeing new stained-glass windows for the altar and even better wine for her private stores.

"There is just one *small* matter he has entrusted to me first . . ."

Leonello burst in on cue, and I felt like cheering. What a picture he made! Back in his black livery I had designed with its handsome touches of white, he strode like an only *slightly* small colossus toward the prioress, who recoiled visibly from his steely gaze. Cesare Borgia's notorious demon dwarf, with whispers of blood and murder and poison whispering around his footsteps . . . and right behind him, a hulking red-haired guard in Borgia livery, dragging a tall and terrified young nun.

"That's the one," Leonello told me, hardly bothering to glance at the prioress. "Suora Serafina, she was calling herself."

The red-haired guard jerked to a halt, pushing Carmelina before him. Her eyes bulged over the big freckled hand that covered her mouth, and her wimple and veil had been yanked away. Holy Virgin, what had they done to her *hair*?

"I don't understand," the prioress gasped. "This is Suora Serafina, yes—a holy sister, fled from her orders in Venice. His Eminence Cardinal Borgia ordered that she resume her vows here."

"*His Eminence* no longer." Leonello took up the narrative now, as I yawned down at my nails. "Did you not hear? Cardinal Borgia renounced his red hat two days ago. He is a prince of the world now, not a prince of the church. And now that he is no longer bound by the church's laws, he has different plans for Suora Serafina. She is no longer to remain here as nun."

"A nun cannot be released from her vows," the prioress began.

"But she can be released from these walls," Leonello cut in effortlessly. "Suora Serafina served the Pope's daughter here, as you know. The Duke—you are aware Cardinal Borgia is now Duc de Valentinois, or Duke Valentino? He wishes his sister's reputation, and those who might wish to damage it . . . more closely guarded. We are to take Suora Serafina with us."

The prioress looked from Leonello to Carmelina and back with something like horror. "For what purpose?"

I flicked my eyes at Bartolomeo. He really was holding her entirely too gently to be credible here. I'd coached him last night in his role as brutal henchman—"More swagger, Bartolomeo, and do try to leer occasionally. Is a little brutality too much to ask?" But Carmelina's former apprentice, I'm afraid, had no talent for mime. He stood there holding Carmelina between his hands like a bouquet of roses, and what we really needed here was a good snarl and a cruel yank on her arms. Fortunately, my clever cook produced a stifled little cry as though he *had* yanked cruelly on her arms.

"Where will you be taking her?" the prioress repeated, horrified.

My turn in the drama, and I leaned forward earnestly. "It's been decided that I will find her suitable work in the countryside. She'll come to no harm, I assure you." At that, Leonello smirked behind me in amused contempt. *Naïve females.* "No harm at all!" I continued with a dim-witted little trill. "But it was thought better if she took up another name there, and Suora Serafina was pronounced dead and buried behind these walls."

Leonello drew one of his little knives and began to clean under his nails with it, giving the prioress a silky smile. *She'll be dead and buried soon enough*, that smile whispered, and the prioress stared mesmerized at the knife.

"And for your trouble, naturally you shall be compensated." I produced a purse and dropped it to the table beside me with a negligent *clink*. I'd sold my diamond rose brooch for a purse that heavy. I liked the idea that Rodrigo Borgia, Pope Alexander VI, was so kindly funding a nun's escape from her vows.

Carmelina managed another little cry. Leonello cleaned his nails some more, looking sinister. Bartolomeo lurked, looking not very sinister, but the prioress had no eyes for him as her gaze flicked from the knife to the purse.

"You know the reason Suora Serafina ran from her convent in Venice?" I added, careless. "It's a shocking story." Leonello had told me all about Carmelina's grisly little piece of dead saint, and I'd had an idea how to use the information.

"Cardinal Borgia gave no details." The prioress sounded cautiously interested. "I assumed Suora Serafina ran away to join a lover. It's usually the reason, with these feckless young nuns."

"No, it's far worse than that!" I leaned close, lowering my voice to a horrified whisper. "A charge of *altar desecration!* She absconded with a most holy relic—"

"Surely not!" The prioress crossed herself.

"It's a wicked world," I sighed, and kept my eyes away from Leonello who was giving me a long stare. This line of conversation had not been part of our little playlet, but I'd thought all along that this avaricious smooth-faced prioress with her love of good wine and silk shifts might need more grease for her palm than mere gold.

And yes, she was looking very interested indeed. "This stolen relic . . ."

"As you can imagine, Suora Serafina could hardly sell it at the market!" I reached under my cloak. "My guard found it hidden in her cell."

Everyone caught their breath as I tossed it to the table: a long braid of golden hair as thick as a man's wrist, coiled like a lustrous blond snake.

"The hair of Mary Magdalene," I said, crossing myself. "The hair that tumbled over the feet of Christ Himself. Can anyone doubt it? Look how it gleams after so many centuries!"

I heard a sudden explosion from Carmelina. Fortunately, with Bartolomeo's hand clapped over her mouth, it sounded like a sob.

"A worthy relic indeed," the prioress breathed. She took a glance at my own hair, but I'd picked a pearled velvet headdress this morning that covered my head completely.

"A worthy relic in need of a worthy resting place," I agreed. "Caretakers more cautious than the sisters of Santa Marta in Venice. Even if they heard of it resurfacing in Rome, they could hardly look to reclaim it when they allowed it to be stolen in the first place."

The prioress crossed herself. She was seeing lines of pilgrims, I thought: pilgrims dipping eagerly into their purses to see the braid of (my) hair all locked away in a rock crystal reliquary, bringing fame and wealth to the Convent of San Sisto.

A far better bribe than a mere bag of coins. She already had no eyes at all for Carmelina, standing pinioned in the not-really-very-brutal grip of Leonello's red-haired henchman.

"I am sure Cardinal Borgia—that is, Duke Valentino—has the wisest possible plans for Suora Serafina." The prioress gave a glittering smile, and the golden braid of hair disappeared into her sleeve faster than I could blink. "I shall send him word myself that she has died of a fever and has been buried upon these resting grounds, God rest her soul."

"God rest her soul," I echoed piously, and it really was a miracle that we all got into the coach before exploding in laughter.

Carmelina

I brought a hamper," Bartolomeo announced, and then my red-haired lover looked puzzled when everyone burst out laughing all over again. "What? I thought we might want a bit of a nibble on the road—"

"Of course you did," I choked against his shoulder. The Convent of San Sisto was already behind us, and so was Rome. The coach was a hired vehicle, and it racketed along the dry summer road with none of the cushioned comfort of the conveyances La Bella had enjoyed as Pope's mistress, but I had never been so happy in my life to be jolted about like an apple rattling around in an empty basket.

"What did you put in that hamper, Bartolomeo?" Leonello poked at the woven basket at our feet. "It's moving."

"I almost forgot." Bartolomeo untied the lid. "That's not for eating. Though Carmelina always threatened to put him in a *crostata*—"

My old notch-eared kitchen cat put his head over the basket with his rusty *mrow*.

"He should go into a *crostata*," I said. "I've no use for cats who won't catch mice!" But I lifted the cat up out of the basket and settled him on my lap.

"She wasn't so happy to see *me*," Bartolomeo complained.

"Thank you," I whispered, and kissed the cat on the nose and then Bartolomeo on his.

"There are other ways to thank me." My former apprentice looked meditative. "Do you still have that giraffe costume?"

"I take all credit for that," Giulia said. "Now, let's see this hamper you keep talking about. I'm starving!"

Bartolomeo dragged another basket out from under the seats, and my former mistress dove right in. "Sicilian olives, oh, I adore Sicilian olives—almond *biscotti*, they're a little crumbly, so we might as well eat them right now—grapes, sugared violet blossoms, candied orange peel, oh, and marzipan *tourtes*! Bartolomeo, you're marvelous." Giulia popped a little *tourte* whole into her mouth. "I always eat when I defraud convents."

"For myself, I feel the need of a drink," Leonello announced, and managed to decant the flask of French wine into the four cups Bartolomeo had also packed into the hamper. The four of us grinned at each other over the jolting rims: Bartolomeo with his lean-muscled legs hopelessly too long for the cramped space; me curled up against his shoulder while the cat purred against mine, Leonello with his boots swinging above the floor and his hazel eyes sparkling, and Giulia as beautiful and glowing as ever with her velvet skirts filling half the coach. I felt a pang, looking at her. "Madonna Giulia, your hair—"

"Wasn't that clever of me?" She stripped off her pearled headdress, showing us a still-considerable coil of plaits. "I've been wanting to cut it for ever so long, so I just lopped off the bottom arm's length this morning. Can I tell you what absolute heaven it is to have short hair? Only down to my hips! And speaking of hair—" She pressed a little vial firmly into my palm. "Use daily."

"Thank you," I said, and not for the vial of hair rinse. It was a beautiful summer morning, blue and gold and cloudless overhead, and the dusty outlying villages around Rome were beginning to give way to dry yellow plains dotted with grazing sheep. There was color and warmth and noise in the world again, not bells and grilles and cold. I wanted to stretch, I wanted to dance, I wanted to sing, and I wanted to cry.

Suora Serafina was dead and buried. Most officially.

"It was all Leonello's plan." Giulia dropped a kiss on her bodyguard's brow, looking so very wifely that I had to wonder one or two things. "But thank me if you like, Carmelina. I hope you feel grateful enough to come be my cook in Carbognano forever?"

Bartolomeo and I looked at each other. He'd been buttering bread and laying out little slices of marbled *prosciutto* and whisking napkins into impromptu baskets for the grapes; he had a smear of butter in his hair already and he had been muttering under his breath about the lack of a proper *credenza*. We grinned at each other, and looked back to our former mistress.

"We'll stay in Carbognano for a little while, Madonna Giulia," I agreed. "But we want to move on soon to Milan."

"The court of Il Moro," Bartolomeo said, nudging the cat's curious nose away from the *prosciutto*. "What do those Milanese know about proper food? We'll take it by storm."

"We?" Leonello looked between us, and sharp-eyed Giulia clapped her hands and squealed.

"A *ring*!" Seizing my left hand to look at the band of delicate filigreed gold. "Let me see—"

"*Dio*," Leonello said. "Women!"

It wasn't a true ring, not the kind passed between husbands and wives when they recited their vows. "I still can't marry you," I'd said to Bartolomeo last night in the convent storeroom, pressed so tight between barrels of bad flour that my only option was to lie along the hard freckled length of him with my nose up against his. It was exquisitely uncomfortable, and I wouldn't have moved for the world. "Even if we manage to get me pronounced dead, I've still given vows. Any vows we said afterward would be invalid."

"In a new city where no one knows you, who's to know about the vows?" Bartolomeo pointed out. "Either the ones you took to God, or the ones we didn't say to each other?"

"God will know." I couldn't help crossing myself. "Don't pretend that doesn't trouble you."

"I think God looks a little more kindly on oath-breakers than we like to believe. Cesare Borgia got released from his vows as a holy cardinal, after all, and the Heavenly Father didn't smite him for it. And Cesare Borgia does more evil in a day than you have in a lifetime!" Bartolomeo laughed. "God smiles on you every time you so much as break an egg into a bowl, Carmelina."

"What do you mean?"

"If you didn't have some kind of divine approval, then how do you keep getting away with everything?" Bartolomeo's eyes were merry and serene. "How did you end up guardian of your patron saint's hand? How did you escape unscathed from not one but two convents? How did you not get caught by *anyone*, over all these years?" Another laugh. "Haven't you heard our Pope say it to Madonna Giulia? 'God means as much by his inactions as his actions. If He doesn't act, He approves.'"

"You've turned cynic," I said accusingly.

"On the contrary." Bartolomeo kissed my knuckles. "Maybe it's not the usual way of things, but in every way that counts, you're my wife."

My throat felt thick. "I'm also a bride of Christ. After Marco died, well, I kept thinking it was because of me. That any man who beds me is doomed—"

"Ah, but you're wrong. We have as much heavenly blessing as anyone could want. Here's proof." Bartolomeo's hard chest moved against mine very pleasurably as he squirmed to get hold of something from the tangle of clothes at our feet. "A blessing from our very own patron saint."

"That's Santa Marta's ring!" I looked at the little band of gold, horrified. I knew it as well as I knew my own nose, as long as my patron saint and I had been together. "You can't steal a ring from a saint!"

"We already stole her whole hand," Bartolomeo pointed out. "Besides, she wants you to have it. She's spent the last few weeks dropping it on me every time I opened the pouch."

I must say, it fit me very well. I put my hand into the sunlight outside the coach's open window, admiring the gleam of old, old gold, and I thought I felt Santa Marta twitch her approval back in her usual place beneath my skirt. Madonna Giulia had emerald and pearl and sapphire rings, enough of them to sink a ship, but I preferred something plain like this. Something I wouldn't have to take off to knead bread dough.

"That nun's habit is absolutely ghastly," Giulia was saying, looking critically at my convent wool. She had eaten all the marzipan by now and was starting in on the almond *biscotti*. "We'll have to be sure you get some new gowns before you go out to Milan—"

"Do you even have the money to support yourselves in Milan?"

Leonello was asking Bartolomeo. "Of course Giulia never thinks of money—"

"We're the best cooks in Rome," my Bartolomeo said with the arrogance I was glad I hadn't managed to smack out of him as an apprentice. "We won't lack work for long."

"Then here's something to fund a new career," Giulia said, and unhooked her huge teardrop pearl from around her neck.

My mouth dropped open like a fish. "Madonna Giulia, I can't possibly—"

She was already shaking her head, brushing *biscotti* crumbs off her skirts. "I don't want it. The rest of my jewels I'm saving for Laura, but that—" She looped it carelessly about the cat's furry neck when I refused to let her put it into my hand. "That was the Holy Father's first gift to me. It feels like a noose, now."

We all looked at each other for a moment. I had half an impulse to put my head out the window of the coach and look back on Rome. The Holy City had been a haven to me once, an escape from all my troubles, and now it seemed more cesspool than salvation: a blood-drenched pit with the Borgia dream of power swelling black and hungry overhead, like some great ravenous snake. Their emblem *should* have been a serpent. Something poisonous and devious. Not a blunt and straightforward bull.

But it didn't matter. I wasn't ever going to lay eyes on a Borgia again, and I didn't think anyone else in this coach would either.

"You all look like masks of tragedy." Giulia looked around at our momentarily grave faces. "Especially you," she said to Leonello, and I very definitely saw her fingers stroke against his for a moment behind the spread of her skirts. He smiled, which I hardly thought I'd ever seen on his cynical face, and Giulia twinkled back at him before looking to me where I sat with my head leaned against Bartolomeo's shoulder and the cat purring on my lap in his pearl necklace. "Of course, there is one thing to be sad about," she added. "Very sad, in fact."

"What's that, Madonna Giulia?"

She leaned forward, looking at me very seriously. "We've eaten all the marzipan *tourtes*."

Rodrigo Borgia, Pope Alexander VI, died five years later without realizing his dream of founding a lasting Borgia dynasty. Despite his lurid reputation, he was in many ways an effective pontiff: energetic, intelligent, hardworking, with great toleration for free speech, homosexuality, and Judaism. But his Achilles heel was his adoration of his children, who in his eyes could do no wrong. In their defense he committed his most shocking acts, such as the impromptu hanging of a party guest who dared offer his favorite son a mild insult.

The murder of **Juan Borgia**, the handsome, vicious, and incompetent Duke of Gandia, was never solved. Whoever killed Juan, Pope Alexander was truly devastated and resolved to reform both the church and his own life. If he had stuck to that resolve, history might well remember Alexander VI as a visionary. Many modern scholars attribute Juan's murder to Cesare, who was certainly ruthless enough to kill his much-hated brother for a chance at the military career Juan had squandered.

Cesare Borgia would go on to a military career of such brilliance and ruthlessness that he would inspire Machiavelli's political treatise *The Prince*. The violence lurking under his surface self-control was legendary; he kept a personal assassin on retainer in the form of the much-feared Michelotto, but Cesare was always willing to do his own dirty work, such as the time when he stabbed the papal envoy Perotto literally at his father's feet in the Vatican. Cesare's career and power ended with his father's death; he died at age thirty-two fighting a minor battle in Spain.

Lucrezia Borgia endured a sinister reputation but seems to have been largely a pawn among the powerful men of her family. During her third marriage to the Duke of Ferrara, she outlived her youthful reputation for frivolity and became known for piety and good works. She died at age thirty-eight, the mother of at least seven children, having survived all her brothers.

Joffre Borgia eventually separated from his wife, **Sancha of Aragon**. She died in her twenties with a lurid reputation, and he went on to an undistinguished adulthood as Prince of Squillace.

The Roman Infante was the title given to an illegitimate Borgia child born in 1498. He was formally claimed by papal bull as Cesare's son, and by a contradictory papal bull as Pope Alexander's son. Rumor of the day claimed the baby had been born to Lucrezia during her convent stay, but she always maintained that the Roman Infante was her half brother.

Giovanni Sforza, Count of Pesaro, went on to marry again after the annulment of his marriage to Lucrezia. He fathered a son with his next wife, disproving the farce of the impotence charge leveled by the Borgias. He retaliated for the loss of his reputation by accusing the Borgias of incest, a charge that dogs their reputation to this day.

Alfonso of Aragon, Lucrezia's second husband, was murdered two years later by Cesare Borgia once the Neapolitan alliance was deemed unnecessary.

Adriana da Mila remained a Borgia intimate even after the death of her son, acting as escort to Lucrezia when she went to Ferrara to join her third husband.

Johann Burchard managed not to crumple under the difficulties of serving as Rodrigo Borgia's master of papal ceremonies. He kept a meticulous diary throughout his life, and his writings give us firsthand glimpses of the Renaissance's most notorious family: the French invasion, the details of Lucrezia's various riotous weddings, and the sequence of events surrounding Juan's murder.

Laura Orsini may or may not have been the daughter of Pope Alexander VI, but her life lacked the turbulence and tragedy of Lucrezia's. Laura married a nephew of Pope Julius II and bore him three sons.

Bartolomeo Scappi would become one of the greatest cooks of the Renaissance. He worked as Vatican chef to two popes, and he penned a massive compendium of recipes and career advice to cooks that is still in print today. Most of the recipes from this book have come directly from Scappi's own words. The details of his personal life are extremely vague: there is no surviving birth date for him (though he was probably born somewhat later than in this story), and it is not known if he ever married or had children. But he enjoyed a long life and a brilliant career, and he must have traveled a great deal since his recipes show familiarity with the regional cuisine and markets of Rome, Venice, and Milan. It is not known who taught Bartolomeo Scappi to cook—Renaissance cooks were trained without the oversight of a formal guild—but whoever trained the young Bartolomeo instilled him with iron discipline, a great love of his craft, and an unshakable belief that preparing and serving good food was honorable work.

Sandro Farnese would later go on to take the Throne of Saint Peter as Pope Paul III. Among his achievements he laid the foundation for the Counter-Reformation, supported Katherine of Aragon in her tumultuous divorce appeals, and excommunicated Henry VIII.

Vittorio Capece of Bozzuto married Giulia Farnese some time after the death of her first husband, Orsino Orsini. Little is known of Giulia's second husband, who was historically named Giovanni (I renamed him since this story already had too many Giovannis and Juans). He died some years after their marriage without giving Giulia any further children.

Giulia Farnese survived all the Borgias, going on to a long, wealthy, and apparently happy life. It is not known exactly when Giulia's affair with her Pope ended, or whether the break came from her or from Rodrigo Borgia. However it happened, Giulia returned to the country and devoted herself to her daughter. After her second widowhood, she took over governorship of the town of Carbognano, where she is recorded as a lively and capable administrator.

Leonello is a fictional character. Many Renaissance lords kept dwarves as entertainers, jugglers, and companions. They were generally treated like pets: they might be pampered or they might be abused, but they were always looked down upon as lower beings.

Carmelina Mangano is also a fictional character, though many women suffered similar plights in being stuffed into convents against their will. The Renaissance was an era of dowry inflation; even wealthy families found it very expensive to marry off more than one daughter. Spare daughters were usually sent to convents, and the result was a great many unwilling nuns leading very secular lives within convent walls. There are records of nuns who managed to smuggle lovers into their unlocked-at-night cells, and other nuns who donned men's clothes and escaped over the convent wall in desperate attempts to forge a new life. There is record of a convent in Venice that boasted a religious relic of the hand of Santa Marta, patron saint of cooks, but there is no record of the relic ever being stolen.

I have taken some liberties with the facts in order to serve the story. Orsino Orsini's exact death date is not known, but records indicate that it happened a year or two later than in this story. There is no indication that his death was murder, but it seems like a convenient mishap, and other notorious assassinations of the Renaissance were covered up by just such rigged "accidents." And Juan Borgia was not recorded as a serial killer of low-born women, though his wild evenings of drinking, whoring, fighting, and killing stray dogs are well documented.

My supposition that Lucrezia Borgia gave birth to a child while waiting for her marriage to be annulled is based on the widespread rumors of the time. The young papal envoy Perotto is frequently named as the father of Lucrezia's supposed child; not only is his death at Cesare's hands suspicious, but he was one of the few men with access to the Pope's daughter during her convent stay, However, there is no proof that Perotto's relations with Lucrezia were anything other than formal; her pregnancy could well have been legitimate. Lord Sforza officially parted from his wife the Easter before her convent stay, but not all his travelings during that year have been recorded, and a private visit from the Count of Pesaro to his wife is not impossible: he fought hard to keep her, indicating that their marriage had its happy moments even if it ended sourly. If Lucrezia had borne a legitimate child to her husband, their union could not have been annulled and the Borgias would have lost their chance for the longed-for alliance with Naples—a reasonable explanation for the ruthless secrecy with which Cesare Borgia removed both Perotto and Lucrezia's maid Pantisilea, who would have been the only other people besides the enclosed convent nuns to know about the pregnancy. If Lucrezia did give birth, we have no way of knowing if her child was a boy or a girl, whether it lived or died, or whether it was in fact the mysterious Roman Infante who was born at about the same time.

Rodrigo Borgia's enemy Fra Savonarola was excommunicated and executed as described, but in Florence rather than in Rome. Savonarola's famous Bonfire of the Vanities was not attended by Giulia Farnese, nor to our knowledge was she painted by the great artist Botticelli, who is rumored to have tossed a number of his own works onto Savonarola's bonfire. And while the poetic romances of Dante and his Beatrice and Petrarch and his Laura are well known, there are no sonnets written by an Avernus to his Aurora.

One final bit of fancy on my part is Bartolomeo Scappi's experimentation with "tubers." Potatoes were just beginning to make their way into Italian cuisine, but Scappi apparently had few dealings with them. He was in many ways the greatest cook of the Renaissance, but alas, he cannot be credited with the invention of the French fry.

The Borgias were certainly the high—or low—point when it came to scandal in the Vatican. There can be no doubt that the flow of papal power did its damage in corrupting this intelligent and energetic family. Unlimited power turned their virtues into vices: Rodrigo's affection for his children became blind nepotism, Cesare's ambition became hubris, Juan's arrogance became violence, Lucrezia's love for her brothers became an eagerness to excuse them every crime. Perhaps Giulia Farnese was glad to get away from the Borgia family, before they tainted either her future or her daughter's.

But all the conflicting facts, contradictory rumors, and hidden secrets are gold for novelists, readers, and historians, who will forever continue trying to unravel the Borgia myth.

CHARACTERS

*denotes historical figures

THE BORGIA FAMILY

*Rodrigo Borgia, Pope Alexander VI

    *Cesare Borgia, his eldest son, Cardinal Borgia

    *Juan Borgia, his second son, Duke of Gandia

    *Lucrezia Borgia, his daughter, Countess of Pesaro

    *Joffre Borgia, his youngest son, Prince of Squillace

*Vannozza dei Cattanei, Rodrigo's former mistress, mother of his children

*Giovanni Sforza, Count of Pesaro, husband to Lucrezia Borgia

*Sancha of Aragon, Princess of Squillace, wife to Joffre Borgia

*Maria Enriques of Spain, Duchess of Gandia, wife to Juan Borgia

*Adriana da Mila, a cousin to Rodrigo Borgia, former *duenna* to Lucrezia Borgia

    *Orsino Orsini, her son, husband to Giulia Farnese

THE FARNESE FAMILY

*GIULIA FARNESE, mistress to Pope Alexander, called Giulia La Bella, the Bride of Christ

    *LAURA, her daughter

*CARDINAL ALESSANDRO FARNESE, called Sandro, Giulia's older brother

*GEROLAMA FARNESE, Giulia's sister

*PUCCIO PUCCI, Gerolama's husband

IN ROME:

MARCO SANTINI, *maestro di cucina* for Adriana da Mila

CARMELINA MANGANO, his cousin from Venice

PIA, *PANTISILEA, TADDEA: household maidservants

LEONELLO, cardsharp and bodyguard

*MICHELOTTO CORELLA, Cesare Borgia's private assassin

*BARTOLOMEO SCAPPI, kitchen apprentice

MATTEO, ALFONSO, OTTAVIANO, GIULIANO, UGO: other kitchen apprentices

*JOHANN BURCHARD, papal master of ceremonies

*MAESTRO PINTURICCHIO, an artist

*CATERINA GONZAGA, Countess of Montevegio

ANNA, a tavern maid, Leonello's friend, killed by a masked murderer

*PEDRO CALDERON, called Perotto, papal envoy

SUORA SERAFINA, a lay sister at the Convent of San Sisto

AVERNUS, a poet

SANTA MARTA, a holy relic

IN ITALY:

PAOLO MANGANO, Carmelina's father, *maestro di cucina* in Venice

MADDALENA, Carmelina's sister, married in Venice

*FRA SAVONAROLA, Dominican friar in Florence

*SANDRO BOTTICELLI, artist in Florence

IN FRANCE:

*CHARLES VIII OF FRANCE, claimant to the throne of Naples

*GENERAL YVES D'ALLEGRE, leader of the French armies

READERS GUIDE

The

LION
and the ROSE

DISCUSSION QUESTIONS

⁂

1. The novel opens in the middle of the action, as the Pope's mistress and her friends are held hostage by the French army. Did you come to their story fresh, or did you read *The Serpent and the Pearl*, which came before it? How did this affect your enjoyment of *The Lion and the Rose*? Did you have any other preconceptions about the Borgia family from legends, rumors, television, or other books?

2. The dwarf Leonello and the cook Carmelina are quickly introduced as enemies. How do their feelings toward each other change over the course of the novel? Did their relationship change in the ways that you expected, or did it end up surprising you?

3. Sancha (the Tart of Aragon) is roundly denounced for being a harlot, whereas Juan and Cesare, who behave in the same way, are not. Do you think this is fair? Why is Giulia not despised as Sancha is, though she is equally notorious?

4. Leonello's pursuit of a mysterious killer leads him to a dangerous game of cat and mouse with Cesare Borgia, and Giulia observes that both Cesare and Leonello enjoy "needling people just to see their reactions." What are other similarities and differences between the Pope's son and the dwarf bodyguard? What about Leonello and Cesare's other bodyguard, Michelotto?

5. Giulia's affair with her Pope is filled with genuine affection at the beginning of the novel. When do you see her feelings begin to change? Did the change come from inside Giulia, or from Rodrigo's actions, or both?

6. Kitchen apprentice Bartolomeo is the only character who can match Carmelina's love of food and skill at cooking. How does the delicious food they make alter the course of events at various points in the novel?

7. The murderer sought by Leonello meets a vicious end. Did he deserve that end, or was there another way to stop him? What about the man acting as his squire, who was killed accidentally?

8. Did you hope that Rodrigo Borgia would reform the Church and the city of Rome after his breakdown and epiphany? Were you pleased or disappointed by the outcome?

9. Reread the conversation in which Leonello leaves Giulia's household. Did you expect their exchange to play out as it did? Were you as surprised as Giulia was?

10. Carmelina speaks bitterly of the life that nuns lead. In your opinion, did nuns or married women lead more restrictive lives in the Renaissance?

11. Each of the three narrators has a relic or a symbol of power that defines them: Carmelina has a true relic in the withered hand of her patron saint Santa Marta; Giulia has her floor-length hair; Leonello has his knives. What power do these relics really hold for their owners? How do they feel about their respective relics by the end of the novel?

12. All the Borgias change radically over the course of the novel. Did you find their descent believable? Who do you think changed the most radically, and why? What do you think the future holds for them, beyond the end of the novel?

PRESENTING A SPECIAL EXCERPT
OF KATE QUINN'S

LADY *of the* ETERNAL CITY

An Empress of Rome Novel

AVAILABLE NOVEMBER 2014
FROM BERKLEY BOOKS

Vindolanda. Home—or was it? I hadn't set foot in northern Britannia since I was eighteen, after all, when I'd left my family for golden dreams of glory in Rome. Was Vindolanda my home just because my parents had settled there in their happy exile? Or was Rome my home because it was the place I'd chosen for myself?

"Who would settle any place so cold and misty?" Mirah shivered in the red wool cloak that brought out the brightness in her cheeks and kept off the summer rains that greeted our arrival. "It's summer, and it feels like autumn!"

"My parents are utterly mad, that's why they settled here."

"And you haven't seen them since you were eighteen." Mirah poked my side, hunting for the gap between my breastplate and backplate where she could tickle me. "You're nervous, aren't you?"

"I charged a Parthian army at Ctesiphon. You think I'm nervous to see my own mother and father?"

She gave me one of those looks of wifely amusement again. Maybe I *was* nervous, just a little. Would I find them unbearably changed? Worse yet, would they find *me* unbearably changed? Maybe they wouldn't like what they saw. I didn't altogether like what I saw in the mirror anymore, after all. Why should they?

So when I first arrived in Vindolanda, I didn't go to my old home. I dawdled. I had to survey the troops who kept order in these bleak windswept moors. Then there was the *praetorium*, which I had to see enlarged into a place where the Emperor could house his entourage once he arrived, a place with proper shuttered windows, plastered and painted walls, a tiled floor. "I have to make special preparations," I insisted when Mirah raised her eyebrows. "If Hadrian's bringing Empress Sabina, I've got to see the *praetorium* made fit for an emperor's wife."

"Who, according to you, is quite accustomed to odd adventures, and probably wouldn't care if her floor was tiled or not," Mirah said. "You're stalling, Vix."

"You know, I am beginning to regret taking you along." I glared. "Women don't belong on long journeys."

"The Emperor doesn't agree. Not if he's bringing Empress Sabina this time."

"Never mind her."

"Why do you get twitchy whenever you hear her name?"

I suppressed the urge to twitch. "Maybe I should send you and the girls back to Rome if you're going to be this meddling!"

Mirah smiled at me. "Vix? Go see your mother and father."

It was a gray, blustery morning when I turned off the muddy road and slid down from my horse. I knew this road. It hadn't changed much since I'd gone charging down it at eighteen, all afire with dreams of glory. I hadn't owned a horse then; I hadn't owned anything except my pack of clothes and the amulet of Mars which was the very first of my good-luck tokens. Now that I was going back up the muddy slope, a man grown with more baggage visible and invisible than a pack of clothes, I wanted to be on foot again. Mirah slid down from the saddle where she'd ridden behind me, winding her fingers through mine, but the girls squealed at the mud and so they stayed on their mule. "That's girls for you," Antinous groaned, but he led their mule along behind me good-naturedly enough, his long legs swinging through the mud.

I saw the crowning roof of a snug little villa. Stone, not wood; better built than most of the huts in this windswept place. Wooden buildings behind—cow byres; those were new. Things were prosperous, then, since I'd left. I swallowed, and felt the quick pressure of Mirah's fingers. Rich grass ran up the slope toward the house on either side of the road, grass thick and soft with dew, and hedges flowered against the villa's walls. My feet took me unthinkingly around the east wall to where the morning sun came strongest, where I remembered there had been a meager excuse for a garden.

There still was one. Someone had put in a fruit tree of some sort, but it looked pinched and leafless, and the herbs in their pots weren't much more than a collection of twigs. I smiled at that. He still wasn't any good at gardening, then, the broad-shouldered man in a blue tunic who squatted among the herbs with a spade and a trowel.

My feet were soundless on the grass, but the man whipped about before I got a step farther, one gnarled hand dropping his trowel and drawing the dagger at his waist instead. He was up in a crouch and ready to face me in an eyeblink, and his shoulders were bent and his hair entirely gray, but that crisp *secutor* stance could have graced any arena in Rome. And had.

"You haven't gotten slow with age," I told my father. "But you still can't garden worth a tribune's arse."

He dropped his dagger and I dropped Mirah's hand. We'd neither of us ever admit it, my father and I, but when we came together in a thunderclap of an embrace, we were both crying.

I t was downright frightening they way my mother and Mirah took to each other. It didn't start quite smoothly—Mirah was unaccustomedly shy meeting my mother's dark eyes (anyone who knew my mother's history would be), and there was a certain awkwardness when Mirah introduced the children. My mother took one look at Antinous and smiled warmly. "How did a lummox like Vix ever sire such a handsome son?"

Mirah looked just a little stiff at that. She stood between Dinah and Chaya, one arm about each, and I could see her arms tighten protectively.

Our girls were pretty things, dark-haired and pink-cheeked and dimpled, but it was Antinous everyone noticed first: his carved Bithynian face that broke into such a radiant grin, his lean-muscled height, his curling hair the color of dark honey . . . And Mirah gave a little sigh, month after month, when she saw the evidence that her own belly hadn't decided yet to produce a boy just as beautiful.

I'd told her it didn't matter; I wasn't one of those arses who divorced their wives if they couldn't pump out heirs. But Mirah wanted to give me a son of my own blood, and she prayed daily to her God asking Him to put a miracle in her belly. I was starting to think it might take a miracle—she'd conceived our two girls easily, one after the other, but Chaya's birth had come very hard indeed, and my wife hadn't quickened since.

My mother must have seen the little flicker of disappointment on Mirah's face, because she turned with all her quiet warmth to the girls and clasped them against her. They were shy with strangers, but she addressed them in fluid Aramaic, and Mirah smiled and in the same language offered the traditional greeting of a daughter to a mother-in-law. My mother had a low, melodious voice that could charm shy children and savage emperors in any language, and soon my daughters forgot their fear and my wife her diffidence, and all four of them were chattering away.

"More than thirty years with your mother," my father mused. "And I still don't speak a word of that odd tongue of hers."

"I'm not so quick at it myself," I admitted, and we traded quick grins and looked immediately away because we were damned if we were going to cry again.

"Vix!" Mirah exclaimed, switching out of Aramaic. "No wonder our girls both turned out dark. They look like their grandmother!"

"I am now officially old, if my firstborn has given me grandchildren," my mother announced with a smile. She was really only fifty or so, and barely looked it: a tall woman with threads of silver through dark hair, and in her red linen gown and tooled sandals she had the same serene elegance I remembered from the days she'd worn silks and pearls. She *had* worn silks and pearls, my mother, and yet she'd ended up here in this cozy villa on a hilltop in Britannia. Never mind how; I'll tell that story another time.

The conversation had changed to Aramaic again, and Antinous was chiming in now, warming cups of wine for Mirah and my mother so they wouldn't have to get up. "I see you've raised this boy well, Mirah." My mother approved as Antinous served her. "Even though you're clearly far too young to have borne him! Tell me . . . "

"Our women want to chatter," my father announced. "Let them."

We went wandering, my father and I. Past the garden and up the slope, to another wooded hill thick with flowers. "Apple trees," he said, ducking under a branch. "Blooming very late this year—we had a long winter. The fruit isn't much, not this far north, but I still walk here every morning with the dogs."

"When did you finally lose that old three-legged bitch of yours?"

"God love her, she lasted a long time. These are all her descendants. Grandpups, I suppose." Three dogs frisked at his heels: two curly-haired, one sleek and black. "Maybe your boy would like a puppy? We've got a new litter."

"He'd love that. He's always collecting animals. Mirah keeps telling him she's not keeping a menagerie, but it doesn't stop him."

We walked in silence a little ways, trading glances now and then, and we both grinned when we noticed I was walking just like him: hands clasped behind me at the small of my back. He was as gnarled as a badger now, my father, his shoulders bent but still burly. He'd never been sure of his age, but he had to be sixty at least, and unlike my mother, he looked older than his years. Well, he'd lived hard. The last few decades might have been easy, but the ones before hadn't been. The ones in Rome, full of arena fights and blood, chains and whips and sand.

I showed him my campaign tokens; told a few stories of my campaigns in Dacia and Parthia. He told me of my younger brother and my three sisters; all grown now, living with families of their own in Vindolanda. "Your brother's a stonemason. Never wanted the sword, not the way you did." Another flick of a grin. "They none of them gave me trouble the way you did."

"I turned out all right, didn't I?"

"That you did." He turned and walked backward, appraising me. "Praetorian Prefect, eh?"

I shrugged. "It's a pisser of a job."

"It's still high for a boy like you to climb." There was pride in his voice, but a certain wry sharpness too. "Son of a gladiator and a slave. I killed Romans, and now you serve them."

"I order them around! In fact, I'd have had a legion of my own to command if not for the Emperor."

"And that's an improvement? Romans made me fight, and now you're fighting for them?" But his grin had more pride in it this time. "Legionary commander; how did you manage that?"

"The Tenth Fidelis was supposed to be mine." My old legion. Emperor Trajan had promised it to me at the end of the Parthian wars, said he'd find me a spineless legate with the right bloodlines who would look official if I'd just do the real work and step on a Chatti rebellion for him. I'd gotten drunk in celebration, and had a victorious X tattooed on my shoulder, for "Tenth." Then Trajan's collapse in Selinus, and then Hadrian, and you know the whole blasted rest of *that*. I told my father, briefly.

"Hadrian's a bastard," I concluded.

"Most emperors are." My father ducked around a sapling without looking.

"You'd have liked Trajan." I had loved him dearly, that grizzled, grinning, swearing giant of a man—I'd wept like a baby at his death, and not because I was losing my legion. I'd wept for him, for the best man I'd ever known outside my father and maybe Titus Aurelius. "Even you would have liked Trajan."

My father gave a slanted smile at that, but didn't contradict me.

"Emperor Hadrian, though . . . " I hesitated. "He's different. He's my enemy."

"You've had emperors for enemies before."

"Not like this."

We'd reached the top of the hill, coming out from the flowering trees. There was half a crumbling stone wall at the top, marking the border of the land, perhaps. The view behind it was more thick trees, more hills, the glitter of water somewhere from a stream, but my father turned his back on the view, leaning against the wall, his dogs settling themselves panting about his feet, and he folded his broad arms across his chest and looked at me. "Tell me then."

I told him. Hadrian, making me his bodyguard and his desk-man. Hadrian, making me butcher his enemies. Hadrian, for whom I'd cast off most of my friends and lived separate from my wife. "I hate him," I concluded. "But sometimes . . . sometimes I forget that I hate him. When I'm riding along behind him on the Rhine as he's surveying the legions, or when he tells me to do what I like with training the Praetorians because he knows I'll make a fine job of it—that's when I forget." It was worse since we'd begun traveling—in Rome I could keep the hatred stoked, during those long idle watches where I did nothing but watch the bastard's back as he worked at his desk. Nothing like idleness for hatred. But on the road, so many new things to see, so much to do, his energy subsumed by movement instead of idle viciousness—that's when I forgot.

It wasn't just for the sake of seeing Mirah more often that I pressed to travel ahead of Hadrian's court, out of his company, to make his preparations as he journeyed while Boil held the bodyguard watches. I was more comfortable out of range of the man, where I could keep what he was clearly in mind. Because I was a dim, rock-headed bastard who apparently couldn't keep his grudges straight, and it made my eyes prick with shame. "He once threatened to have Mirah and the children killed if I didn't do his bidding," I said, "and yet sometimes I forget that I hate him."

My father said nothing.

"Did he *break* me," I managed to say, "and I'm only now noticing?"

"No one could break my son," my father said calmly. "Not the Young Barbarian."

My old gladiator name. How foolish it sounded—so foolish I almost laughed. "Not so young anymore."

"And grown more stubborn, not less." My father looked at me. "Nobody's broken you, boy. Not the Emperor, not anyone."

I wasn't altogether sure he was right, but I still felt a violent relief pierce me like a spear. Fathers do that to you—here I was, thirty-eight years old, the Emperor's protector, commander of hundreds, and I still felt relief because my father had told me things weren't so bad.

Or maybe it was just relief at admitting my secret guilts and shames at all; my fears of what I had become. How long had it been since I'd been able to speak like this? At one point my confidante had been Titus, but I'd buggered that up to Hades and gone. My eyes pricked, and I dashed a fist across them angrily. "Dust," I growled, but my father wasn't fooled.

"Don't you talk to that wife of yours about any of this, boy?"

I was taller than he, but I'd always be "boy." I didn't mind that. "Of course I don't talk to her, not like this. Who talks to wives about this sort of thing?"

"I do."

"You're still a barbarian, you know that? You have no idea how things are done."

My father just waited, arms folded across his chest, scarred as an old oak, though not as yielding.

I shrugged. "Mirah thinks I'm a bloody hero. I don't want her knowing the things I've done."

"I've done worse," my father said calmly. "You know how many I killed in the arena? Men, unarmed prisoners, boys young enough to still count as children. Women—there was one dressed like an Amazon. I still think about her. I've killed more than you, I'll wager; they called me The Barbarian, and I earned it." Arius the Barbarian—the city had resounded to that name once. "Your mother knows all my stories. Even the bad ones."

"That's different. You were a slave; you didn't have any choice. I did." I rested my fists on the wall, looking down at the wooded hills. "I let the Emperor make me his dog. And Hell's gates, he's even *tamed* me."

"You could kill him," my father said. "But I don't advise it. It's a lot of trouble, killing emperors, and you don't need more trouble."

My father *did* kill an emperor, long ago. Never mind why. "Mirah wants us to leave Rome. I reckon I could, get far enough away from Hadrian to make it not worth the chase, but . . ."

"But you've never liked running."

"Still don't."

"So what's your plan? Keep taking everything he dishes out; smile and say 'Thank you, Caesar'? I know you, boy. You're no tame dog. You'll slip your leash someday, and then you'll crack him open like an egg, and that'll be the end of you."

I had no answer, not for him and not for me.

"My Roman son," he said, shaking his head, and we trailed down the flowered hill in silence, the dogs loping between our feet.